Black Arrow

Third book from the tales of the Black Powder Wars

J P Ashman

I0586571

Black Arrow
Third book from the tales of the Black Powder Wars
J P Ashman

Published by J P Ashman through
Ingram Spark's POD Service.

Date of Publication
September 2018

Cover art by Pen Astridge

Series map illustrated by Charles Richardson

Edited by Jeff Gardiner

Author's Note

I want to give my readers the heads-up on Black Arrow as I did on Black Guild, because neither are your usual sequels.

Black Guild and Black Arrow were originally one book, as I mentioned in the author's notes of Black Guild. The original Black Guild/Black Arrow was bigger than Black Cross, which proved only just viable to print without pricing it out of the market. Second to that, the original Black Guild/Black Arrow had so many twisting and turning and crossing storylines, my editor and beta readers suggested I split it in two.

Unlike the usual split into halves of such a tome, Black Guild and Black Arrow run side by side in the Black Powder Wars timeline. I know, it's unusual, but it's how I felt the split worked best. When reading Black Guild, you experienced events through characters such as Cheung and the Caravaneers, Longoss and his friends, the goblin war galley crew and so on. Within Black Arrow, you get so see events elsewhere in Brisance, that were happening at the same time. Fal and the pathfinders, Sears and Biviano etc. And, you get to read what actually happened to King Barrison!

And now, I'll let you crack on, because I'm sure you're eager to find out what's been happening whilst the caravan was rolling and the Black Guild was falling. Enjoy!

J P Ashman

Map of Brisance

Dramatis Personae

Pathfinders

Correia Burr, King Barrison's Spymaster & daughter
Falchion, sergeant-at-arms
Errolas, Broadleaf ranger **Sav**, scout **Gleave**, sergeant-at-arms
Starks, crossbowman

Altolnan Nobility & Households

Barrison 'The Benevolent', King of Altoln
Edward 'The Black Prince', Prince of Northfolk
Rell Beresford, Duke of Adlestrop, Earl Marshall; son of Earl
Beresford, nephew to Barrison
Grannit, sergeant-at-arms to King Barrison

Will Morton, Duke of Yewdale, Lord High Constable of Alton;
brother-in-law to Barrison

Hugh Torquill, Earl of Royce, Lord High Treasurer, Lord Keeper
of the Privy Seal
Temn, Baron of Landon Hill, Baronial Marcher Lord of Altoln
Hudd, Captain of 'Royce's Reds'

Bagnall,
Earl of Stowold, Constable of Wesson, Watcher of the Deep
The Lady Elsane Stowold, Bagnall Stowold's wife
Sir Bryant & **Sir Mechel**, Captains to Earl Stowold
Sir Bollingham, knight to Earl Stowold, former City Guard
Sears, **Biviano**, **Jay Strawn**, **Dom** & **Pelse**
men-at-arms to Earl Stowold, former City Guard

Ward Strickland, Master of the Wizards & Sorcery Guild, Lord
High Chancellor of Altoln

Giles, Earl of Bratby, Marquess of Suttel, Marcher Lord of Altoln
Sir Allon Bratby, Giles' son, commander of the Suttel army
Mits, man-at-arms to the Earl of Bratby

Sirreta

Velenn, Queen of Sirreta
Eudes de Geelan, Marquis d'Easson, Marcher Lord of Sirreta
Croal de Geelan, Seneschal d'Easson, nephew to Eudes
Guiscard, Sieur de Steedon
Flavell de Steedon, daughter to Guiscard
Amis de Valmont, chevalier & chaperone to Flavell
Jehan, chevalier to Croal de Geelan
Rasoir, gaoler **Salliss de Pizan**, witchblade **Cateline**, maid

Sessio

Captain Mannino
Hitchmogh, first mate   **Charl Spendley**, officer
Parry, blade master
Lefey, Kareem, Joncausks, Boxall & Tahir, sailors

Goblin War Galley

Charlzberg, Admiral of the goblin fleet

Tri-Isles

Antreas, Achiad & Andarna, The Three
Rina, concubine to Antreas   **Emms**, waitress
Quinnell Pallister, apprentice shipwright
Badham, Hillside gang master
Stone, Croxon & Pester, Hillside gangers

Others about Brisance

Crackador, the legendary great-dragon
Dignaaln, emissary   **Molurus**, Naga warlord
The Red Goblin, Chieftain of the goblin clans
Core, necromancer & commander of goblin-held Beresford
Stubley, inn-keeper of the Twin Inns, Sirretan holding
Cook, Twin Inns cook, Sirretan holding

Prologue

Sudden intakes of breath spread through Guiscard's line of militia as a small boy staggered into the clearing, his skin pale and his features gaunt. He wore nothing but dirty linen braes and his bruised skin clung to bones like a corpse. Tears streaked down his cheeks as a trickle of blood followed them down from his nose.

The boy didn't attempt to wipe the crimson line from his face. His bony fingers stretched out towards the line of serfs, cottagers and the like, their heads shaking in disbelief as they looked from the boy to their companions and back.

Guiscard swallowed hard as his bay destrier stepped to the side, pawing at the ground with iron-shod hooves. He held the snorting beast firm, head spinning as he attempted to formulate a strategy in what seemed like an impossible situation. Only days before he'd sent away a good number of his men-at-arms and all of his crossbowmen, as requested by the Duc du Sud. He'd heard nothing since, of his men nor of the Duc's army they'd been summoned to fight alongside. And now he faced Orismaran raiders on the borders of his own estate. He needed those men.

Looking down his meagre line, Guiscard cursed as one of his men threw down his scythe and ran to the child whose wracking sobs were audible across the otherwise tranquil meadow.

Several men called to their companions as another man followed the first, breaking free of grasping hands despite Guiscard's orders to hold.

There were noises from the tree-line as the men ran, but no enemy came forth.

The handful of archers with the militia, woodsmen all, fixed broadhead arrows to the strings of their bows and awaited anything that might make a move towards the two men closing on the crying boy.

Rising in his high-backed saddle, Guiscard watched as the first of the men, a thatcher by trade, reached out to grab the dishevelled child. The boy's dry lips cracked to reveal bright flesh beneath, spreading into a horrific grin. Sharpened teeth parted as clawed fingers snapped forward and plunged into Thatcher's thighs.

Guiscard swore as Thatcher cried out in pain and terror. The boy's head jerked back revealing a gaping maw that clamped onto, and came away with, the man's left hand.

Blood arced up and across the second militiaman as Thatcher turned, chunks from his thighs tearing free in the boy's hooked claws.

Thatcher's companion pulled him away, attempting to flee back to the line of men who screamed out, incredulous at the horror they witnessed.

Several backed away from the scene, before experienced reeves, their brows wet with sweat under the glaring sun, pulled and pushed them back into line, shouting orders to make ready their weapons after Guiscard shouted for them to do the very same.

High on his horse, Guiscard moved forward a few paces and raised his lance, unsure what else to do but to steady his men by giving them focus.

The men of Steedon pointed their crude weapons towards the tree-line whilst the two men ran back towards them, colour vacant from their faces, one man's hand clamped on the bloody wrist-stump of the other.

The *boy* gave chase.

'Take the thing down!' Guiscard pointed his lance towards the boy, who ran on all fours, gaining on the two retreating men. There was a pause. 'Take him down, for White's sake!'

An arrow arced through the air, followed by two more. All three missed as the boy leapt left then right, fast then slow. Three more bounding manoeuvres allowed him to avoid the two arrows following the first three. The sudden speed he released allowed him to catch Thatcher and his friend.

Both men went down hard.

More arrows crossed the gap between horrified line and screaming duo.

The boy was struck twice as he tore into the wailing men, their screams cut short as arrows struck them too, finishing all three simultaneously.

Breathing heavily, and with the heat of the day and the cloying padding, maille and plate he wore agitating him more than ever, Guiscard called the line to hold and, thankfully, it did, but for a moment. From the darkness of the forested Kaja Strip came a bass thud of vocalisation which trailed off before another followed, then another.

There must be hundreds in there, Guiscard thought. 'I said hold, damn you,' he shouted, riding along his line, bulbous visor raised and lance held high. He reached the centre and turned his mount to face the trees, to face the children who were sallying forth.

White be with us...

Men shouted and men wept. They wept at a sight more horrific than anything their minds could conjure; scores of boys and girls emerged from the darkness. Some staggered, some limped and some fell and crawled; all looked like victims of torture, all looked like the boy who had torn two men to pieces.

Guiscard didn't know what to do. He looked left and right along his line, finishing on those few with good weapons, armour and plenty of grim experience. They looked back, lost for answers, eyes pleading for a life-saving order.

Some of the children called out, untainted, their cries pulling at the hearts of fathers most of all. The children looked about them, terrified, hoping and wishing and praying for a father or mother, or any adult, to come and whisk them away from all they endured. They feared each other as much as they feared what hid in the trees behind them; that much was clear to Guiscard, who watched on, pained and helpless, his daughters at the forefront of his thoughts.

A few of the children ran forward as if by some silent command. They ran with a strange gait, twisted in their ongoing transformations whilst others dropped to all fours and accelerated like a hound on a hare.

Arrows flew and children fell. Men fled.

Guiscard's call to hold was ignored.

The meadow was mottled with flattened grass, red stains and bodies clumped and separated. Men and children. And the tree-line remained dark, remained empty of a conventional enemy. Three more bass thuds filled the space between the remaining militia and the Kaja Strip; thuds issued forth from the throats of men.

'Why do they hide?' a shaking, wisp of a lad asked, face spattered with blood for the first time in his life and linen braes damp with piss. No one answered.

The near rout saw men leave the field, but many more rallied to the shouts of their liege and his too few retainers. Some braved the meadow, bringing in the children crying for their help rather than tearing into their fellows. Several of those men returned cut and torn, girls and boys in arms, their relief at rescue not yet understood as their weary, confused little faces stared at everyone and nothing at once, sobs silent, breathless. Others fell to or hacked down those changed; those small people who launched for throats or ripped at bellies. The impossible mix stayed archers' hands after the first few volleys took the charging, altered children. All those remaining in the open meadow lay dead or dying and no one dared venture forth to check on those who moaned and cried, wept and pleaded for it all to stop; for the White Light to take them beyond.

Guiscard walked his horse up the line once more, grinding his teeth in an attempt to focus his mind away from what he'd witnessed, what he continued to witness out in the meadow. He'd faced Orismaran raids before; faced other creatures before, but this was like nothing seen or heard in a lifetime, and he'd survived four decades. What he would give for a coven of Queen Velenn's Witchblades by his side, to counter the child-altering arcane with more of the same.

Another three vocal thuds caused many of his men to step back, some to turn, if only briefly, away from the trees and the gory scene laid out before them. The reeves shouted to hold, so Guiscard didn't have to.

'Movement!'

Guiscard looked left to the axeman who'd shouted. The long-hafted weapon was held out, horizontally, and Guiscard followed its lead-weighted wedge of a head to the tree-line.

Half a dozen, a dozen, more. Orismaran warriors walked from the trees, square shields painted, heavy bladed weapons and spears held high. Their faces a picture of colour, a myriad of spiral and angular tattoos. Some carried totems, carved wooden poles with crude idols held aloft; living not so long ago. Sirretan children, or parts of them, decorated the totems and square shield-fronts.

The Steedon militia shouted their curses, anger swelling like a flash-flood of sickening rage given focus. Guiscard took a deep breath through his nose, filling his lungs. Jaw set, he lowered his visor, the view becoming little more than a bright strip filled by tree framed savages. It was all he needed to see. His closest men saw the action and cheered, before hammering weapons on shields or stamping their feet; the sacrificial children – their children – enough to harden their resolve. The repetitive clatter and clunks they emitted was met with three vocalised bass booms – the loudest yet.

The similar sized line of Orismaran warriors dropped to a half crouch as one. Tongues out on many, cheeks filled on others; they held their poses with weapons offered offensively, shields out to the sides to reveal tattooed chests. Few wore armour worth mentioning.

The militia quietened despite their attempted resolve.

A large tribesman emerged from his hissing and panting line, led by two black-furred creatures pulling on thick ropes. The newcomer was clearly the Orismaran commander. Several of the closest tribesmen shuffled forward, around him, maintaining their crouched stance, maintaining their twisted and contorted expressions as the black-furred beasts pulled at the ropes barely held by their muscle-bound master.

'What are they?' a man asked, voice but a whisper.

The nearest reeve turned to him, face grim. 'They call them gorillas.'

The great apes stood, as if hearing their mention. Mighty fists pummelled black chests as the silverbacks revealed bright canines and roared their anger.

Many men took a step back. It was becoming a habit.

'Hold, damn you all!' Guiscard shouted through his visor. 'They're savages, the likes we've faced along our borders time and time again.'

'I ain't never seen 'em like this before, messire.'

Guiscard turned back, towards the speaker. 'No, not like this, but posturing and pets do not make a man.' He stowed his lance and drew his sword, holding it high, before clanking it on the side of his polished bascinet. 'Good Sirretan steel and good tactics make a man!' he shouted, for all to hear. The latter was overlapped by the calling of the enemy commander, pulled forward several steps by his great apes.

The Orismaran line shuffled forward with him. Weapons bobbed and faces were pulled. Their tattooed chests heaved as they sucked in air, blew it out, bared teeth and extended tongues.

The grating, foreign words coming hoarse from the commander was lost on the Sirretan militia, but after one strange word bellowed loud and clear, the hundreds strong reply from the men behind the beastly Orismaran knocked the men of Steedon back.

Tribesmen changed position as one, an aggressive ripple across the line. They shifted a half circle one way, looking sidelong at the Sirretans whilst their commander issued forth new words in his guttural tongue. Hundreds of men turned back in a mass of

11

shifting feet, proceeding to clatter weapons on shields which outdid the previous clattering of Sirretan weapons, makeshift or otherwise. Totems hammered the ground, keeping beat as tattooed warriors stamped feet and shuffled forward, following their commander's slow progress towards their enemy. They chanted as one, the thuds progressing and amplifying with well-rehearsed verses, punctuated here and there by roars from gorillas and defiant shrieks from the warriors of the Orismaran line.

'Fear not,' Guiscard shouted, turning his horse a full circle before riding the line. He kept his visored bascinet pointing to his own men, calling them to focus on him, focus on the horror those opposite had inflicted on the children scattered across the meadow between.

The aggressive chant continued. As the tribesmen stamped and clattered weapons, as they lifted hairs on the backs of their enemy's necks with voice alone, they advanced; slowly they came forward, making room for all those in the forest behind.

Guiscard turned as the noise grew and neared. He stared as hundreds more of the painted warriors shuffled from the tree line, feet stamping, fists thumping thighs and chests, and weapons ruining the already grizzly trophies adorning the square shields they held out or aloft. Hundreds of deep voices in a fearsome harmony that entranced even him.

'The dance before war,' he whispered to himself, voice trapped behind steel, matched only by the heavy breaths coming quicker and quicker as he witnessed; as he realised... 'They aren't raiding—'

'The fuckers are going to war,' the closest reeve said from behind Guiscard.

And here was me wanting my men-at-arms and crossbowmen back from the Duc, Guiscard thought, a half-laugh escaping his lips but not his visor. *The Duc du Sud's army should be here... they should all be here; all of Sirreta's chevaliers.*

A final roar emitted from every Orismaran mouth, accompanied by a leap into the air.

When they landed, they charged.

The pace was incredible. The tattooed warriors sprinted forward, shields held before them and weapons ready. The gorillas launched from the grip of their master, thumping forward on all fours in an ironic mimicry of the beastly children that came before, fists pounding the meadow as they ran.

Too few arrows flew; many of the archers having fled, carried surviving children away to assumed safety with other militiamen or died during the altered children's assault; more now ran for their lives despite the calls to turn and face from the reeves.

'Close ranks and set spears!' Guiscard shouted through his visor. His heart thumped within the plate-lined brigandine protecting it. His palms were wet with sweat within his fingered gauntlets, as was his brow, covered as it was with padded cap, maille and Sirretan steel.

Those with spears set the shafts to the ground and braced, but it wasn't many. They were flanked by a few men-at-arms brandishing polearms, swords and shields, hammers and axes, and the remaining militia, trade implements gripped by trembling hands. It was a wonder any of those men stood to face the charge at all; fathers all, Guiscard mused.

'Think of those children!' he roared, thinking again of his own three girls. 'Think of those Sirretan sons and daughters!' He faced front again, suddenly aware he was the only mounted man on the field. 'Our numbers are few, but our weapons strong.' *We're done for,* he thought honestly, eyeing the rapidly closing mass of brutal warriors. *We're all done for.* He heard his reeves calling again for men to hold. 'If we flee they will cut us down!' Guiscard shouted without turning. 'If we stand, we can take them down!' *We have no chance... White be with me.* 'White be with us all!' he roared.

Bodkin tipped spurs slashed into bay flanks and the lone destrier snorted before launching forward, its rider leaning into the sudden surge.

'He charges them!' a swordsman shouted. The line cheered.

Iron-shod hooves pounded the soft meadow's earth and a yellow lance lowered. The pure bulk of Guiscard's target enforced doubt upon him that the lance's tip would even puncture the approaching beast's black hide. A handful of arrows overtook him, dropping tribesmen to either side of the hulking ape, their accuracy the best yet.

Lance point neared its mark. Sirretan nobleman braced, prayed. Gorilla leapt.

A collective intake of breath, of fear, took the Sirretans as Guiscard was smashed from his high-backed saddle. His armoured body crunched to the ground behind his rearing destrier, the wind escaping his lungs as he lay unmoving, stunned.

The horse went berserk, bucking and kicking, lashing out at any and all who came close. The crazed animal took down several warriors until spears brought it low.

The militiamen fled.

Before Guiscard could lament the loss of his horse or men, huge fists pummelled him within his harness of steel, breaking bones and winding him further. And before he could make a move, before he could even make sense of what was happening to him, one of those fists struck and forced his visor back into his helmed head in a pressure-releasing explosion that ended it all.

Chapter 1 – An arresting development

One skip, two, three and a wide grin between red bristles.

A loud splash was followed by a colourful curse.

'Get low when ye throw,' Sears said, demonstrating his technique. 'Throw the stone, a flat stone, across like ye would bounce it from a table-top.'

Biviano grunted and scratched under his kettle-helm. 'I've never bounced a stone, a flat stone...' He dodged Sears' meaty fist. '...across a table-top,' he finished with glee.

'Watch me, ye shit.' The flat stone glided with little hops across the Park District pond. One of those hops was atop a lily pad.

Biviano's breath was long and ragged. 'I don't want to come here anymore, Sears.' Biviano walked away, or began to; frowning, he turned to Sears, who stared at nothing in particular. 'Mate, ye alright?' Biviano asked.

No response.

'Sears, ye prick, what is it?'

Sears took a beat and turned to his friend, smiling as he did, albeit weakly.

'I don't like where this is going, big guy.'

'I don't suppose ye will. Nor where I'm going.'

Biviano closed his eyes for a moment, accompanying his heavy sigh. 'Ye know what length we went to, getting ye out of Dockside, and ye want to go back in? And for what, Sears? A former assassin and his—'

'Don't!' Sears warned.

'I was going to say lass, ye goon, not whore.'

Sears conceded and nodded. 'Fair enough. Go on with yer mothering.'

'It's more than mothering, Sears. It's—'

'Shit!'

'It is shit, aye, but it's also—'

'Not that, Biv.' Sears reached out and grabbed a flinching Biviano by his maille-clad shoulders and turned him to the park gate. 'That! Or should I say them.'

''Morl's wrinkled scrotum, Sears. What've ye done now, eh?'

All Sears could do was frown and shake his red head. *I have no idea,* he thought, as a dozen burgundy clad magistrates' guardsmen approached, hands on sheathed and belted weapons, not cudgels.

'I take it yer here for more'n a chat and a skim of stones, eh lads?' Sears said.

The sergeant stepped forward as the armed group fanned out before the two city guardsmen.

'You can leave,' the sergeant said to Biviano, before locking eyes once more on Sears.

'Like dog shit I can, ye fat bastard. The man asked ye a question and ye'll bloody well answer it.'

'As you wish.' The sergeant's eyes remained on Sears, although one twitched at Biviano's insult. Sears and Biviano noticed the battle mage at the back of the group, also wearing the burgundy of Wesson's magistrates.

Sears filled his bearded cheeks before letting the breath out slowly. 'I'm under arrest, aren't I?'

The sergeant nodded.

Biviano half-drew his short-sword, but Sears stopped him with an iron grip. They looked to one another and Sears shook his head. 'Don't, Biv. They're just doing their duty, like we do.'

Biviano swallowed hard and slammed his sword back into its scabbard, turning to the sergeant as he did so.

Sears stepped forward, arms away from his sides. 'Can I ask—?'

'Do you know who this man is?' Biviano interrupted Sears and took a step toward the sergeant. Several men half-drew their weapons.

'Of course they bloody well know who I am, Biviano,' Sears said. 'That's why they're here. Can't imagine it's a case of mistaken identity with this.' He ran fingers through his red beard.

'Will you come along calmly and relinquish your sword, Master Sears?'

Sears nodded to the sergeant. 'If I must, aye.' He walked forward, but not before drawing and turning his sword so the well-worn hilt faced the magistrates' men.

The sergeant nodded his thanks and took the offered blade. He raised a hand and placed it on Sears' broad back as he guided him through the burgundy men and away from the pond; away from Biviano.

'And what of me?'

'I'll see you in the magistrates' court, ye prick,' Sears shouted, without turning.

16

'Aye, but for what, eh? For what? Ye bunch of shites!'
No one answered Biviano as his friend was led from the park.

Chapter 2 – Evening encounters

It was like the warmth of the first true day of spring. Sun kisses your face, illuminates the shadows and chases them away. Tendrils of relaxation move in and around your muscles, your skin warming as you take that long, sweet breath. It was like that, but so much more.

Quin moved his hands around Emms, letting his fingertips and palms glide over her pale skin. Once round her front, he pulled her closer to him, her back meeting his chest. He squeezed gently as he brought his knees up behind hers, mirroring her position in the bed. Quin didn't care that she smelt of stale ale and sweat, nor did he care about the noise coming from the tavern below; a rowdy chorus of deep voices chanting what sounded like a galley rowing song. He smiled.

Never did I think she'd look at me twice, let alone take me to be her own; to be her love.

She shifted in his arms, against him, the movement arousing him. His grin turned wolfish.

'Emms, you awake?' he whispered.

'I am now,' she whispered back.

Quin tickled her ribs, causing her to squirm and giggle. Oh how he loved that sound. He laughed as she spun on him, jabbing fingers into his side. Their playfulness soon turned into something more and before long they both lay on their backs, faces and chests red as they stared at the mottled ceiling above.

'I'll never tire of that,' Emms said, glancing sidelong at Quin.

'Nor will I, my love.'

Curling into him once more, Emms stole a kiss before pushing him away and rising.

'You're getting up?' Quin sat, covers about him like a poorly attempted nest.

'I must. I've work.'

He watched as she dressed, and smiled when she pulled on the patterned wool dress he'd bought her, the burgundy of it suiting her fair hair. Although Quin thought anything would suit her well; she already stood out from the crowd with eyes of blue, so different to the dark eyes and olive skin more common to the Tri Isles. She caught his eye and smiled.

'I love it,' she said, patting down the creases from the garment's night on the floor. 'I should have hung it last night.'

'There wasn't time, the way we got to it.'

Emms frowned. 'You romantic you. Perhaps you should leave your apprenticeship and become a poet. A jongleur of song and tale.'

Quin's laugh turned her frown, his mirth bringing more of the same from her.

'Ah, Emms, I know not how I'd ever live without you now, you know? You have me sure as if I was a selkie and you had my skin.'

She pounced on the bed and onto Quin. 'Again with the romantic turns of phrase, Quin. You certainly know how to woo a lass.'

'I don't want to woo anyone bar you,' came his muffled reply from between her clothed breasts. 'I want to stay here for the day.' He shook his head vigorously, drawing another laugh from Emms.

'Well you can't. I'm needed downstairs.' She rolled off him and back to her feet. 'And you're needed, to be taught shipwright stuff.'

'You're right, of course.' Quin climbed to his feet and searched the floor for his pantaloons.

'Of course.' Emms shoved Quin to the floor, laughed and moved to the door. 'Until later!'

'Until later, my love,' Quin said, gazing at her and forgetting his half-drawn pantaloons for a moment. 'When do you want me to come by? As soon as I finish? I don't mind waiting at the bar until you're done with your work. I could help you, if you like?'

The questions came like the bolts from a repeater ballistae and knocked Emms back a step.

'Or not,' Quin said. 'I don't mind coming later, if you'd prefer that? Whatever you want. I'll wait on you, you know.'

Emms smiled and nodded. 'Come later. Give me chance to bathe and change.'

Quin's face dropped. 'I knew you didn't like the dress.' Shoulders slumping, he dropped to the bed and continued to dress himself.

'Quinnell Pallister, you know that's not true!'

Looking back to her, Quin offered a weak smile. 'I'm sorry,' he said. 'I can't quite believe you're mine. It's been three months already and, well…'

'I know,' Emms interrupted, 'but there's no rush, is there? We've our lives before us—'

'Our lives together, yes,' Quin said, grinning once more. 'Now off with you, girly. There's patrons need serving.'

With a wink, Emms left the room and closed the door behind her.

After a good long look at the peeling wood where she'd stood, Quin took a deep breath and let it out slowly.

'Oh Emms,' he said aloud, 'how I never want a day to pass where we're not together.'

Turning back to his scattered clothes, a garment of which moved across the floor seemingly of its own accord, Quin smiled at the memories of the night before and jumped up, invigorated and ready for the day ahead.

***

'It burns when I breathe,' Starks said, rubbing at his red nose.

'Here he goes again.'

Correia flashed Gleave a dangerous look as the young crossbowman continued.

'I can't help it, Gleave. For days now my eyes have stung and my nose has run.' He rubbed again at his nose with the back of his hand. 'And now… now my throat feels dry whether I swallow or not. Whether I bloody drink or not.' Starks slumped back in the saddle.

'I'm not going to lie,' Gleave said, looking back to the sniffing lad behind, 'with the plague fresh in my mind, your coughing and sneezing isn't making me feel all that convinced that the elves and mages cured it.'

Starks' eyes widened. 'Oh great, thanks Gleave, now I feel worse.' He pulled up his green tunic and checked for buboes.

'Gleave, shut up,' Correia said, her weariness of the subject clear. 'And Starks, don't listen to him, he's prodding you is all.' She held her hand up as Gleave made to reply. 'Now, Fal will be back soon with Sav and Errolas, so let's stop here and make camp before we lose light.'

Voicing their acknowledgement, followed by three sneezes from Starks, they stopped their horses and dismounted. With practised efficiency, they untied, unloaded and made use of their saddle bags' contents to set about making camp. Gleave found a suitable tree to set a lean-to against and Starks cleared a space before it and struck flint against steel, dozens of times. Soon after, a small fire glowed and a moss-covered shelter was well under way. Correia kept watch whilst her men worked. She looked for the others, and hoped that's all she would see.

Another bout of coughing alerted Correia to Starks' approach.

'Looks like rain,' he said, pointing up the road. Correia nodded.

The thickening gloom approached the camp, bringing with it a wall of water that flattened the grass as it approached.

Sniffing some more, Starks gathered as much dry kindling as he could. He took his armful to the shelter and slid it under.

'They should be back by now,' Starks said. Before Gleave could reply, the rain fell, its cold touch bringing a shudder to both men as it struck. Hoods were pulled up, but not before Gleave cursed the unseasonably cold drops running down the back of his gambeson.

'No sign,' Correia said. She crossed to the fire, her cloak and hood already wrapped about her as rivulets ran off the waxed canvas. The horses whinnied and threw their heads as the rain continued to fall, despite being tethered under a large oak.

'The lads know our path.' Gleave crouched beside Correia. Starks followed suit and all three huddled about the hissing flames. 'They'll see the fire and be with us soon.'

Starks groaned and rubbed his nose. 'They've been gone a long while though.'

Gleave nodded. 'Aye, but they've the elf with them. Errolas will see them right.'

Rain dampened everything, including sound; owls refused to fly in it; hunters struggled to hear their prey, although the prey also struggled to hear the hunters. It was *that* fact that set people's nerves on edge. Despite camping by a main road, the companions knew brigands operated in the area, and without their ears to help them, they knew they were vulnerable.

'Can't see much,' Starks said, looking about, 'and it ain't fully dark yet. Not right for summer, this. Not right at all.'

'Keep your weapons close.' Correia's eyes were darting about as much as Starks'.

'You have a funny feeling, don't you?' Gleave asked.

Correia nodded. 'They should be back.'

'Towton wasn't far ahead.'

'No, Starks,' Correia shook her head, 'it wasn't far at all.'

Starks coughed and looked to the woman beside him. 'Why not ride on?'

'We'd be approaching Towton at night. Risky and not worth it if it can be avoided,' Gleave said, before Correia could. 'You know, twitchy guardsmen and all.'

Nodding his understanding, Starks scanned the gloom.

The sound of the rain was constant as it fell in sheets. The wind blew it at them more than they would have liked, but into it they looked, willing their friends to appear.

'I'm hungry,' Starks said.

Gleave grunted. 'We all are.'

'Is it all gone?'

Gleave nodded, but as the darkness fell about them, it wasn't seen.

'Is it?'

'Yes, Starks, the food has gone,' Correia said, before Gleave could snap. 'Tomorrow we teach you to hunt and trap before we move on.'

'By we, she means me.' Gleave held his hands over the pitiful fire, hoping to cover it from the rain more than anything else. It hissed and crackled some more, and spat at the trio, but the small amount of light and heat it gave off was appreciated.

Gleave laughed, although it sounded more like a growl. 'They'll be shacked up in a brothel.'

Starks sniggered and Correia scoffed.

'Good-boy Falchion? Proud Errolas?' she said. 'I think not.'

'Sav?'

Correia didn't answer Gleave, not with words anyway.

'Aye,' Starks said, eventually. 'Sav would be, given half the—'

'Hush!' Correia pointed forward. 'There.'

They strained to see through the darkness and shifting rain, but they knew what approached.

'Riders,' Starks whispered.

Gleave nodded. 'Aye lad, but there's more than three of 'em.'

Memories of ear thudding retorts and flashing lights passed before Gleave's eyes. Screams, curses and shouts in the night. He saw the riders draw near and a familiar voice spoke to him. *All is well*, Mearson said. *All is safe.*

'I think we're alright with these.' Gleave lowered his sword and axe.

Correia turned to Gleave as Starks kept his crossbow levelled, cursing the rain and dark.

'How could you know?' she asked, looking back to the approaching riders.

'I just do. These aren't brigands,' he said, walking forward. 'They're Towton's men, I'd wager on it. Anyhow, what brigands around here could afford a dozen horses?'

Starks filled his cheeks and let out a long breath. 'I hope he's right.'

A hand went up as the silhouettes approached.

'Greetings,' Gleave called.

'Stay sharp, Starks,' Correia said, following Gleave forward, swords drawn. 'If they charge us now, Gleave…'

One of the riders pulled away from the others. 'Your friends sent us!' he shouted as a gust brought more rain with it.

'Nice and vague,' Correia said, preparing her and the other two for the worst.

'Who'd they be?' Gleave asked as the rider reached them.

Correia moved to the other side of the horse, giving the man separate targets should he act against them.

'Errlus… or some such, the elf and his companions: a tattooed fellow and a tall, gobby bastard.'

Gleave grinned. The other riders held back.

'And you are?' Correia asked, remaining defensive.

'A simple messenger of Towton is all, my name unimportant. Your men, however…' his eyebrows rose, just visible under his dripping kettle-helm.

Correia sighed. 'Come,' she offered, 'warm yourself by our fire and tell all.'

The messenger smiled at that, and nodded. He half-turned in his saddle and waved an arm. Correia watched, warily, until the other riders rode back the way they came.

'So, Messenger,' Gleave said, smiling up at the man, hand held up to protect his face from the rain, 'what shit have the lads got themselves into this time, eh?'

'Gleave.'

'Ma'm?'

'Go scout the perimeter, will you?' Correia smiled, Gleave scowled, and Messenger laughed.

As Gleave disappeared into the darkness, mumbling to himself, Starks lowered and unloaded his crossbow – after a nod from Correia.

'You do right to be on your guard,' Messenger said. He dropped down from his horse and handed the reins to Starks, who took them after a moment's pause; he walked the horse over to the others, leaving Correia alone with Messenger.

'The lad's trusting, leaving us be like this,' he said, winking at Correia.

'He is,' she agreed, smiling. 'Although he knows me well by now does Starks; knows I don't cut people without good reason.'

Messenger laughed and held his empty hands out wide. 'I deserved that.' He crouched by the pitiful fire. Correia moved around the hissing flames and mirrored him.

'Tell me,' she said, voice low, for his ears only, 'are they well, my friends?'

The man nodded. 'Aye, well enough.'

Starks returned, only to be waved away by Correia.

'They're held up in the town, drinking and making merry.' He picked up a stick and prodded the fire until he was sure Starks was out of earshot. Throwing the damp stick in to crackle, Messenger looked up to his King's Spymaster. 'They nearly missed me, Correia.'

'Go on.'

'I was to ride out with the baron's company. There's been activity about—'

'Goblins?' Correia interrupted, leaning in for confirmation.

Messenger looked surprised at the question, but shook his head. 'Nope, not goblins. Brigands are growing bolder, witchunters are refusing to disarm. Strange goings on are… well, going on, in Knipewood and the surrounds.'

'Like what?'

A shrug. 'Folk talk of murders. They talk of sacrifices and dismembered bodies left hanging in trees and scattered over briar patches, the eyes of which track passers-by. They talk of demons in the sky and…' Taking a deep breath, he looked away.

'And?'

'Other things. Larger things.'

'Dragons?'

Messenger winced at the word and pulled his wet cloak about him, but he nodded all the same, the light glinting orange off the rim of his rain-tinkling helm.

'You should know better than to listen to such rot,' Correia said, catching his eye once more.

'Aye, I should, but when it's on many lips?'

'Tell me what you know, not what people think they may have seen after one too many ales,' she ordered, bringing another nod from him. *Damn but his neck should be thick as a trunk the amount of nodding he does.*

'No one's come north to us for weeks. No one passes The Marches. We hear nothing from the marcher lords, ours or theirs. Or that's how milord Towton tells it, between banquet and joust and games and such.'

Correia pursed her lips and paused a moment, before going on. 'I hear Towton tilts well?' she said of the young baron, a statement more than a question. 'Nevertheless, games or not, I'm surprised he doesn't send riders to find out what's afoot in The Marches? Bratby would answer him.'

Another shake of the head. 'Milord says it's not safe for such things. Without proper word from The Marches, he says he must look to his own lands, although I'm not convinced he hasn't had word. A bird flew in yesterday, but he's said nowt about it to anyone. Alas, he says he must tend to his own flock and his neighbours be damned.'

Correia rolled her eyes. 'Your baron's pious nature is why the bloody witchunters don't disarm, and his love of the Samorlian faith is why he struggles to control his own lands.' Correia cut off whatever protest Messenger was about to make. 'He needs to make decisions based on fact, not fiction. Whether tilting lances or dancing at court is what is needed right now or not, he must send messengers to Earls Bratby and Royce, be them heralds or knights. He *must* look to his neighbours. We all must.'

Wind, rain and the whinny of horses filled the gap that followed. Correia held her hands over the fire and thought hard on what she'd heard. Messenger waited patiently.

Eventually, Correia spoke. 'In the morning, we ride into town with you, collect my men and ride on to the keep and your baron. I may have need of him before I move on.'

'On to where?'

'On to The Marches, of course, and maybe into Sirreta itself.'

Messenger balked as Correia winked.

By morning, the wind had dropped and the rain ceased. The air smelt fresh or 'green', as Sav would call it. A chiffchaff sang its repetitive song, grinding on Gleave as he rode along. Starks smirked at the irritation on Gleave's face, a smirk that dropped when Gleave looked back.

'Are we eating there?' Starks said, turning back to face Correia and Messenger.

'Yes, Starks,' Correia said. 'Your hunting will have to wait another day I'm afraid.'

'At least we'll eat well,' Gleave muttered, replacing his irritation with amusement.

'I'll do fine, Gleave. Just you wait.'

'We'll see, lad. We'll see.'

Starks' reply consisted of three sneezes in a row.

'You bring that plague with you, lad?' Messenger's tone revealed the jest.

'You wouldn't find it funny if you'd seen it,' Gleave said, without turning. Starks smiled to himself and rubbed his nose.

'Tough crowd.' Messenger nodded towards Gleave and Starks. Correia said nothing.

'Up ahead,' Starks said. 'I see rooftops peeking over the ridge.'

'Aye, that's Towton. That's home.' Messenger beamed.

All four fell silent for a few heartbeats, a sickening sound reaching them.

'And if I'm not mistaken,' Gleave said, kicking his horse into motion, 'that sounds like a fucking scrap.'

The other three dug heels in and raced down the road, after the big man.

Chapter 3 – More than just a game

Men roared and women screamed, children joining in, vocalising their support or fear; dogs barked and a crowd cheered.

Gleave rode into the town, following the sounds of shouts and curses from many lips. 'There's no smoke,' he said, 'but it sounds bad all the same.'

'That way,' Starks shouted from behind, overtaking Gleave to guide his horse down a wide street. The others followed, weapons drawn, except for Messenger's.

Entering a large square, they pulled up quickly to save riding into a mob of chanting townsfolk.

'Woah!' Starks commanded, trying to regain control of his spooked horse. Messenger came alongside, taking the reins and holding the animal still with practised skill.

'Hush now,' Messenger said to Starks' mount, leaning over so the words could be heard over the din.

'What in The Three is going on here?' Correia demanded.

Messenger turned to her and grinned. Correia noticed his sheathed sword.

Another cheer arose, this time from the far end of the square.

A group of men stood around two tall posts. Perhaps three dozen strong, the men were jumping, hugging one another and cheering to the crowd about them. They wore Towton's colours to a man, as well as bloody injuries. Walking away from them, towards the riders stood in their stirrups, were a larger group wearing different colours. They looked as battered as the others, although these men wore anger and defeat on their faces, rather than mirth and hubris.

'One more chance for you lot to beat us?' a brute shouted from Towton's grinning faces.

'You're on!' came the reply.

'Oh shit,' Correia said, recognising the voice.

'Was that Sav?' Starks asked. Gleave laughed out his answer.

'I wanted it to be a surprise.' Messenger's grin was wider than ever.

The crowd erupted as a stuffed pig's bladder was tossed into the middle of the square.

'Oh, the football might be a surprise,' Correia said, dropping back into her saddle, 'but that dumb bastard's involvement isn't.'

Sav's voice was clear above all others, as was his head as he scooped the bladder up and ran for an opening in the Towton defensive line.

'Is that Fal?' Gleave said, standing taller whilst trying to hold his mount still.

No one answered as a tattooed face burst from the defensive line and made for Sav. The crunch, thump and grunt that followed lifted pigeons from tile and thatch as the broad-shouldered bladder carrier hit the dirt hard. The bladder rolled free, to be scooped up by a short man with fast feet. The Towton man ducked left, right and side-stepped a swinging fist to dart through three sets of grabbing hands.

'He's gonna make it!' Messenger shouted, forgetting Starks' reins in the process.

A collective 'oof' sent a whinnying horse bucking back along the street as the bladder carrier was tackled to the floor by a man of similar size. Both fell hard, leaving the bladder free for Fal to pick up.

'Gleave,' Correia said, eyes failing to pull away from a charging Fal, who'd turned to make for the game's single goal, 'go get Starks before he breaks his neck.'

Colourful curses followed as Gleave pulled back. Another collective 'oof' followed, as Fal's ankles were kicked from under him by a bloody-nosed Sav.

'What happened?' Gleave called from somewhere behind the crowd. A horse whinnied and Starks screeched.

Sav grabbed the bladder and threw it across the square, long and far, his bow arm put to good use. It was a shame the receiver couldn't catch.

A mix of hisses, boos and laughs spread through the crowd.

'What's happening?' Gleave shouted again.

'Where's Star—'

'I've got him,' Gleave shouted.

A huge cheer set more dogs to barking.

'And Fal's lot have won a point,' Correia replied as Gleave came alongside, a shaken Starks beside him on a snorting beast.

Fal danced about, pointing at Sav whilst two men were dragged from the square, unconscious or worse.

'I see what you mean about your baron and his bloody games,' Correia said.

Messenger kept his eyes on the continuing game whilst answering. 'This ain't a game, Correia. It's much more serious than

28

any melee or tilt.' She turned to him, eyebrows high.

'Please, enlighten me.'

He swallowed hard, cleared his throat.

'It's a matter of pride,' Gleave interjected, back to standing in his stirrups for a better look as the bladder flew high and wide.

'Male pride.' Correia sighed. 'Why am I not—'

'No,' Gleave interrupted, again without turning. 'Town pride. The town I grew up in played football against our neighbouring town. Each year there was a game. Each year we won.' He turned to face the others, teeth showing.

'He's right,' Messenger said.

Another collective 'oof' and shouts of anger mixed with laughter.

'Go on.'

'Well,' Messenger continued, 'whichever town wins, gets three whole days off the following year, to travel to the other town for the celebration and game.'

Gleave spun on Messenger. 'Really? We used to get a dozen free barrels of Minston Mead supplied to the summer fête.'

Messenger's eyes widened and he whistled appreciatively.

'I've heard enough,' Correia said, moving her horse around the crowd and towards the stables. Gleave and Starks sighed, followed by Messenger.

'She means for us to follow, doesn't she?' Messenger asked. Gleave and Starks nodded.

The crowd cheered and cursed in equal measures; Sav cursed louder than most.

***

The scent of her golden hair, of the rose petal water she used to soak it in the previous night. The smell was... perfection. Quin opened his eyes slowly, as he always did, wanting to allow his beloved's form to materialise in his vision slowly; softly.

And there she was, lying next to him. Would he ever get over the amazement he felt at that?

A gentle chuckle and she stirred. He hadn't meant to wake her, but struggled to contain his continuous adoration for the girl besides him.

She rolled, met his eyes and smiled back, blue eyes sparkling.

'You are the manifestation of the perfect dream,' Quin said, voice catching through emotion or a night's sleep, he had no idea, but he suspected it to be the former.

'And you're soft in the head.'

They both laughed, hers sounding to him like the tinkling of delicate wind chimes.

'I need to leave,' she said, rolling away, up and off the bed.

'So soon?'

'Yes.'

He watched her back now, bared by the falling of her night dress.

'You're not making it easy for me to accept your leaving.'

A laugh, short this time, no chimes present.

'I'm to work, Quin, nothing more,' she said whilst pulling on her layers. 'You have the same to do most days. I can't help having to do it at different times. We can't all be apprentice shipwrights you know.'

He watched her bend and retrieve, watched her lift and watched her pull on her final layer, the tightly-woven green wool dress she wore most days; not the burgundy dress he'd bought her.

'When I'm a journeyman, I'll buy you the most fabulous dress,' he promised, sure now that she hated his gift.

Emms spun on him. 'A tavern maid in a silk gown?' She laughed, mocking him. 'Not likely.'

Quin sat up. 'I'll make it so, and you'll need not serve ale and food any longer.'

She paused at that. 'But I enjoy what I do. And anyway, a silk gown, any gown, wouldn't hide the marks on my face.'

He never saw the marks from the illness she'd had as a child. He knew they were there, but he saw past them every time.

'A lady wouldn't pass for much with these,' Emms went on, prodding her pitted cheeks with both index fingers.

'*My* lady would!'

Fingers fell away and blue eyes narrowed in all seriousness. 'Stop it,' Emms said. 'You're either making fun of me or building me up to something I'm not. At least in the tavern I'm somebody—'

'Because men pinch your bottom and coo at your golden hair?'

Emms' face reddened. Without another word, she stomped from the bed chamber, Quin's bed chamber, and slammed his door behind her.

Quin sighed and his stomach twisted. 'Why does it always come back to this of late?' he whispered, head resting back on the pillow as he slid down the bed. 'When will she learn that I can offer her so much more?'

The only response to Quin's question was a dual, throaty hiss from under the bed.

***

Smoke sensitive eyes tracked two men as they walked into the low-ceilinged tavern. One had to bend over so as not to bump his head on the oak beams, the other gingerly prodded at the swelling around his right eye, which distorted the tattoos surrounding it.

'Pleased you could join us, lads,' Gleave said from a table, winking at the two men and holding a pot of ale up high. Sav and Fal smiled, although their smiles slipped when Correia sat forward, from the shadows.

'Fuck,' Sav said, smile fading completely.

'Fuck indeed, Sav,' Correia said, 'because that's what you two are: fucked.' Both men sat on the bench opposite Correia and Gleave, shifting Starks along in the process.

'Aw...' Sav's smile returned, 'were you worried about me?'

The table allowed enough room for a boot to connect with Sav's shin.

Fal grinned at the following grunt.

'I don't know what you're grinning at, sergeant?' Correia chided.

'Sorry.'

'You two were sent forward to scout, with Errolas. Not piss about... Where's Errolas?' Correia frowned and looked about the dingy tavern.

Sav shrugged and waved for one of the tavern girls, wincing as he did so.

'He's about,' Fal said. 'Somewhere.'

'That's accurate,' Starks said, after taking a swig of small-beer. All eyes turned to him. 'Oh, these jokers can say whatever they like, but if I—'

'Leave it, lad,' Gleave said. 'She's not in the mood.'

Starks slumped and scowled, but said no more.

Correia looked back to Fal, head tilted, nostrils flared.

Fal held his hands out wide and rolled his bottom lip.

'You're bloody useless, the lot of you.' She sat back into darkness.

31

Gleave and Starks made to argue, mouths opening and then closing, thinking better of it.

'We're to ride to the keep, to see Baron Towton,' Correia said, 'but not without the elf. So, I need him with us by morning. Do you think that will be doable, gentlemen?'

All four nodded.

'Good, now go find him.'

Gleave and Starks moved to finish their drinks, but two curved swords emerged from the shadows. They forgot their drinks, stood and left, Fal and Sav in tow.

Correia took a deep breath, sheathed her swords and caught the attention of one of the tavern girls – the one who'd ignored Sav.

'Yes, milady?'

'Bring me a recipe.'

'Eh?'

'Tell your cook that Lady Burr requests his finest recipe, then bring it to me.'

The girl looked confused, but offered an awkward curtsey all the same, before rushing off.

At least I'll get one decent report out of all of this. Correia reached for and downed the forgotten ales.

***

'Where is she?' Quin asked at the bar, after having to push his way to it.

'Working,' the woman said, spittle flecking Quin's face. He wiped it away and frowned.

'I know that, Mag,' he looked about, 'but where?'

'Here and there, on errands,' Mag said, shaking a clay jug in Quin's face. 'You drinking ale or your own drool for that girl?'

Unable to stifle a laugh, Quin smiled and nodded. 'Go on, one won't hurt.'

'Ooh, how about some mead, if it's just the one?'

A coin rapped on the counter and Quin grinned.

'Someone's got paid today, have they?'

'Someone has, yes.' Quin beamed and reached into another pouch on his belt. 'And someone…' he went on, as Mag filled clay pot from barrel and placed it in front of Quin whilst snatching up his coin, '…has bought someone else this…' He held up a silver ring, its dull shine illuminated by the tallow candles behind the

32

taproom's bar.

Mag's eyes widened for a second, before narrowing.

'No, no!' Quin said, hands out in defence. 'I'm not going to, you know...'

'Well see that you don't, Quin. Despite bards' tales, girls don't want to be battened down as soon as sailed, if you get my meaning.' Before Quin could respond, Mag erupted into a coughing mess of a laugh, before turning and making for a young but large lad who'd approached the bar further down, two more flanking him.

Following Mag's movements, Quin looked away when he saw who she now served.

'Badham, my boy!' Quin heard Mag shout, but he managed not to look. Whisking the ring away, into his pouch, he did his best to slink through the throng of patrons to a small table in a shadowed corner, away from the taproom's central fire pit, which gave off most of the tavern's light, as well as the cloying smoke the patrons were used to.

'Quinnell!'

The sound sunk into Quin like a teratorn's talons. He groaned before quaffing the pot of mead in one. *Woah, that's strong,* he thought, eyes widening a moment before he placed the empty vessel on the table and stood.

'Quin!' the shout came again, as did the lad voicing it; as did his two companions, faces as grim as the Adjunct's Guard.

'Badham,' Quin greeted, managing to keep the shakes from his voice. 'Good to see you.'

'Is it?' Badham's eyebrows raised, forehead creasing up to the smoothness of his shaved scalp.

'Of course, Badham,' Quin said, holding his hand out to placate the big lad, 'it always is.'

Eyebrows down but lips now pursed, Badham came forward quickly, suddenly, and took Quin's offered hand, his own dwarfing Quin's. The crushing shake brought tears to Quin's eyes, but he bit the inside of his cheek and continued the shake until Badham released him.

'Take a seat,' the brute said, nodding to the stool Quin had risen from.

Nodding, Quin did as he was told, for there was no denying Badham anything. Those who did, well, it didn't bare thinking about.

33

'Take a walk, see what you can see,' Badham said over his broad shoulder. His two friends, if they could be called that, disappeared into the nervous crowd.

'So, what's new with you?' Badham asked, attention back to Quin. 'No floor sharks with you tonight?' Badham scanned under the table and about their feet before looking back up.

'Erm—' Quin started, glad he hadn't brought his polecats.

'Great stuff,' Badham interrupted, eyes flicking about rather than settling on Quin's eyes.

Quin sat there, not daring to speak or move or think, whilst the known thug and killer looked him over. The silence between them grew tense and Quin's stomach turned circles. He wished he hadn't drunk the mead; his head already felt thicker than it should.

Badham lunged across the table and Quin rocked back, would have fallen if his head hadn't connected with the tavern wall.

'Calm yourself, Quin,' Badham said, his lunged retrieval of Quin's empty pot bringing a smile to the big lad's face. 'You scare too easily.' Badham sniffed the empty container.

Quin said nothing.

Turning the cup over several times, Badham eventually put it down and looked up. 'Pay day?' he asked, the corner of his mouth twitching.

'What makes you think—?'

'The mead, Quin. Expensive stuff is that.'

Quin felt hot all of a sudden. Hot and bothered. Before he could think of what to say next, Badham smiled and winked.

'You scare too easily. I don't want your money, Quin. We're old chums, aren't we, lad?'

Lad? We're the same age. 'Of course—'

'Great, you won't mind sharing something with me then.'

I'd rather chew my own arm off. 'Sure thing, Badham.' *Or not, as it seems.*

Badham looked about, eyes narrowing. 'Where's Emms? Where's that sweetheart of yours?'

Quin's stomach dropped through the sticky floor. He managed to bunch his jaw muscles three times before losing the courage to keep Badham waiting any longer. As he made to answer, Badham brought a large knife from beneath the table and proceeded to pick his filthy nails with its hooked tip.

'I scare too easily?' Quin offered, pleased with himself as he cottoned on to Badham's string of jokes at his expense.

'Aye, you do,' Badham agreed, looking up from his nail picking, 'but sometimes it's wise to be scared.' He stood. Quin hit his head on the wall again. 'Not tonight though, friend.' Badham winked. 'Tonight's your pay night and you should enjoy it with your girl. Say hi from me though, eh? To Emms.' Another wink and a flash of white teeth and Badham was gone, his bulk lost to the press of bodies in the tavern.

Breaths coming faster than they had the night before, or that morning, Quin balled his fists and struck the rickety table, sending his empty pot clattering across its top.

'Quin?'

All fear, all anger and all frustration rushed to the floor and washed away as Quin looked up to see Emms' face appear before him.

'Thank the gods,' he said, smiling once more.

'You alright?' She rushed to his side and sat on his lap, arms about his neck. 'You look flushed, like you've had a fright.'

Letting his head drop to Emms' shoulder, Quin took in her scent with a deep breath and let it out in a satisfied sigh. 'I am now, my love. I'm alright now and no, there's nothing to worry about. A hard day is all. A good one, but a hard one in ways.'

'Well you're with me now, Quin, so how about we sneak off upstairs and see if we can't make something else hard, eh?'

Looking up, Quin felt a stir before his mind could even catch up to what she'd said.

'How about I show you what I got you first, and we'll head up after.'

Beautiful eyes widening in intrigue, Emms nodded for him to go on.

'Oh,' she said, as Quin rummaged in his pouch with the tips of his fingers.

'Yes?' he said, eyes meeting hers as he found what he was looking for.

'I saw Badham as I came in.' Her smile widened. 'He said he'd seen you. Pointed you out, in fact.'

'Oh, that's good of him.' Quin's fingers turned the ring over once, twice, before letting it drop back into the pouch. His stomach turned more than the ring had done; more than his stomach had done when Badham sat before him.

'You know,' she said, trying to look at what he was doing by his belt, 'I swear that lad's got bigger since the last time I saw him in here.'

'You think?' Quin said, closing his pouch again and bringing his empty hand up to the table.

'Yeah, I reckon,' she said, frowning at Quin's empty hand. 'Now where's this surprise?'

'I think I'll get another drink first, my love, before showing you. If that's alright by you?'

'Oh, yes, if you like.' She climbed off his lap. 'I'll get them in—'

'No, I will. It's my pay day, you see.'

'No, it's fine, Quin. If you want to drink, I'll fetch them. It's what I do, and you don't have to ask my permission every time you want to do something. In fact, I'd rather you didn't.'

Before Quin could say a word, probably 'sorry', Emms was off into the crowd, dodging the groping hands and verbally batting away the lude comments she was used to.

Quin, you prick, you have to go and ruin everything.

He wasn't sure if it was the mead or what had happened with Badham, but a little sick reached his mouth. Swallowing down the burn, Quin leaned back and banged his head against the wall for the third time, this time on purpose.

***

Night had taken the town of Towton, children and women in bed. Most, anyway; those who weren't soon would be, for a coin or two.

Sav whistled as he walked past a couple of painted ladies. The one with gapped teeth whistled back tenfold.

'Ha, she likes me.'

'She likes pennies more'n she likes you, Sav,' Gleave said, guiding the bruised footballer down a dark alley.

'Where we off to?' Sav asked. 'And why didn't the other two come along?'

'They're off to find Errolas.'

'And we're not?'

'Nope.'

'Helpful,' Sav said, pulling his arm free of Gleave's grip.

An awful din reverberated through the wall Sav leant against, broad arms folded. 'I want answers, Gleave. This all seems very cloak and dagger to me, and Correia sent us to find Errolas, nothing more.'

Gleave sighed. 'I wanted a little bet is all. I rarely get the chance

36

these days.'

Sav frowned, although the action was lost on Gleave in the dark alley.

'Cock fighting,' Gleave said, matter-of-factly. 'This town's renowned for its prize cocks. Stop smirking.'

'You can't see my face?' Sav protested.

'I don't need to, now follow me.'

The two men continued on down the alley. A little further down and Gleave rapped on a door. A hatch opened and eyes peered out, along with a roar of men's hoarse voices.

'Two for the cocks,' Gleave said. 'Stop it,' he added.

Sav's laugh halted before it got going.

The eyes betrayed a nod of the head. A bolt slid and the door opened.

Noise and warm, stale air struck them.

'Sounds like the game, today,' Sav said, following Gleave inside. The space was cavernous, which wasn't at all obvious from the outside. Sunken stalls were set here and there. Around them stood men, all of whom were stamping, shaking fists or holding heads in hands.

Cockerels crowed and others shrieked.

'I didn't know they made such sounds…' Sav thought aloud.

'Eh?'

'Nothing, Gleave. Just lead on, but make it quick, I'm not sure this is for me.' Sav eyed the torn remains of a small, long-legged cockerel dangling from a man's hand.

Dogs barked across the crowd of men.

'Pit dogs over that way,' Gleave said, pointing to the right. 'But I'm here for the cocks. It's what I'm best at judging.'

Sav frowned, but followed Gleave to the nearest, quietest stall.

'Here we go. This one's yet to start.'

Grand, Sav thought, not sure what he would make of it. A slap on the back rocked him forward, and he looked across to the brazier-lit features of Gleave, who was studying two caged fighting cocks. Their legs had small blades tied to them. Sav cringed.

One bird was farmyard size, with half its wattle missing. Black feathers with white flecks. The cockerel looked mean, if that was possible. The other looked…

'That's not on!' Gleave shouted, pointing at a much larger bird.

Oh shit, here we go. Sav moved his hand to his short-sword, before realising he wasn't armed.

'What's with ye?' a bald man said, pushing through the crowd and poking Gleave in the chest, repeatedly. Several men turned.

Oh shit, oh shit, oh shit, Sav continued, in his head.

'That ain't no fighting cock,' Gleave accused, removing Baldy's hand from his gambeson.

'Ye think ye know cocks, do ye?' Baldy stepped closer to Gleave.

'Oh, I bet he does,' said another, to a chorus of laughter.

Gleave sneered. 'I do, aye, and even if I did that too, it'd be nowt to do with you lot. Now own up! Who's running that over fed hen as a fighter? Who's for taking good folks' money when it's a given that it'll lose?'

Nothing.

'Which two of you are in league for stealing?' Gleave went on. It was his turn to point the finger.

Several men agreed with Gleave, much to Sav's surprise and relief. Baldy reddened in the cheeks as more gamblers came over to see what was amiss.

'Tell 'em!' Gleave shouted, prodding Baldy back. 'Tell 'em how you and that other bird's owner are for cheating good hard pennies from them, by offering up a duff cock!'

Despite the want – need – to comment on those words, Sav froze. He could have called it. His years on the City Guard in Wesson was enough to know a fist would come after those words... Why it hit him, though, he would never know?

Sav went down hard.

Gleave went berserk.

Cockerels crowed and pit dogs barked.

Men gasped, others laughed.

Sav rolled as feet came in, bruising ribs and adding to what he'd received during the football game. He tried to stand but failed as a body fell across him, face bloody. He heard Gleave roaring, heard bones break – heard them! – and pottery smash. Stalls and cages cracked, splintered and the latter opened. The razor bound feet of a black cockerel lashed out, slicing shins and calves alike.

In the commotion that followed, all Sav remembered was being grabbed by the scruff of the neck and hauled to his feet. A familiar voice sang into his ear, and before he knew it, he, Errolas, Gleave and an overfed hen were charging from the building, angry voices following.

I'm never going to another cock fight again. Sav followed his friends through the door. It never even entered his head, until later, that Errolas had been there all along.

Chapter 4 – A flash in an alley

Two men, an elf and a big brown hen moved through dark streets and darker alleys, determined to leave the ensuing gamblers brawl behind and work their way back to Correia at the tavern.

'The thing's following us,' Sav said, turning a corner and glancing back.

'Keep moving.' Gleave looked back to see that Sav was right.

'He's thankful to you,' Sav said, wincing as he ran, fresh pains flaring with each step.

Gleave grunted. 'She, and don't be stupid, Sav, she's a hen.'

Errolas moved ahead of the other two. Reaching the end of a particularly long alley, which nestled between tall homes with crooked overhangs, the elf stopped and backtracked, quickly.

'That's not a good sign.' Gleave halted, hen by his side.

Errolas motioned for them to turn and head back, but before they could, and before the elf reached them, two figures turned into the tight space and gave chase.

'Who the fuck are they?' Gleave asked. Sav shrugged.

'I don't know, but since we're unarmed, I suggest we do as Errolas wants and run.'

Gleave grabbed Sav, turned him and set off the way they'd come, hen and elf close behind.

Reaching the other end of the alley, another figure stepped out, silhouette topped by a wide brimmed hat.

'Shit!' Gleave dived left and Sav right, leaving Errolas and the hen to face the twin flashes that preceded two lead balls and a loud snap and cracking thud that echoed from the walls and left white smoke hanging between.

Had he not been an elf ranger, the balls might have hit. As it was, Errolas leapt high as soon as his eyes saw the striking hammers' spark. Lead sped beneath elf feet and above shrieking chicken, to slam into the pursuing thugs. The Samorlian witchunter cursed as thugs' ribs turned to shrapnel. One cried out in pain, one didn't. Both hit the ground.

Gleave roared. Sav cursed. Hen ran in circles and elf charged.

Gleave pushed himself up and followed the elf in, the sulphurous smell of black powder strong, reminding them all of their last encounter with witchunters. And the loss of Mearson.

Rapier and dagger were drawn by the witchunter, an unfair match compared to the knife Errolas held and the fists Gleave clenched.

Sav cursed some more as recently healed cuts from the game reopened and bruises throbbed. He got up in time to see the hen follow Gleave into a furious show of fists and blades.

'Shit!' Sav took a moment to think, knowing there was no room for his assistance. He turned to the dead and dying men on the ground, and grinned.

Errolas twisted and turned, narrowly avoiding the steel reaching for him. A fist came across his vision, connecting with the boiled leather the witchunter wore and doing little good.

Gleave cursed and roared some more, until dagger found his thigh, sending him low with gritted teeth and an intake of cold air.

Errolas launched a rapid assault of knife and palm, intent on taking his enemy quickly, before the rapier could be used to effect in the greater space of the street they spilled into, leaving the smoke and stink of sulphur behind.

A chicken clucked and Gleave shook his head in disbelief as the bird looked at him, head cocked to one side, then the other.

'Out the way, out the way,' Sav shouted, leaping over man and bird.

Wings flapped, feathers flew and Gleave covered his head. He smiled when he looked up and saw a hatchet in Sav's hand.

The witchunter said nothing, mouth busy with a snarl as he lunged in at Errolas. The snarl increased when the blade narrowly missed its mark.

'I lost one witchunter, back in Wesson,' Errolas said, a snarl of his own twisting his words. 'I won't fail this time.' Errolas stepped past a lunge and slapped palm down, knocking the brim of the witchunter's hat in front of his eyes. 'Ridiculous thing to wear—'

A sharp pain took Errolas' words – intended to force anger and mistake from the witchunter – as the same dagger that'd sliced Gleave struck Errolas in the same place.

Errolas fell to the side, leg giving way.

The witchunter's snarl turned to a smile as the point of the rapier came down.

Smile turned to gape as rapier and hand fell atop the prone elf.

The witchunter hardly had time to react to the severing of his hand before the offending hatchet took him in the face.

The witchunter collapsed, dead.

Errolas was pulled to his feet and a man and a hen appeared from the dark alley.

'I'm keeping this hatchet, at least for the night,' Sav said, nodding to his friends. They nodded back, hands pressed to wounded legs.

The hen clucked merrily and climbed a small hill. Once atop the blood-stained mess of cuir bouilli, flesh and bone, the bird let out its own version of a victorious crow.

'And I'm keeping the bird,' Gleave said. The others agreed.

Correia moved into the dark alley and closed the door behind her. She looked upon her three pathfinders, eyes narrow.

'That's not a good look,' Sav said. He ran a finger up and down the shaft of a bloody hatchet.

'What happened?'

'She's straight to the—'

'Not now, Sav,' Errolas said, bent double, hand pressed against his bleeding leg. Gleave was doing the same. 'Witchunters,' Errolas explained, not shying away from Correia's gaze like the other two.

Sav turned to Errolas. 'Was that plural?' He squinted into the darkness of the alley.

Errolas sat down, tore cloth and bound his leg. Gleave did the same, with Correia's help. 'Yes,' Errolas confirmed. 'I've been hunted since I got here, trying to evade them until I could make it to you.' He directed the latter to Correia.

'Why did you leave Fal and this idiot in the first place?' Correia held a hand up to stop Sav's protest. Gleave grinned despite the pain, but said nothing.

'I needed to meet with a fellow ranger who I knew to be in town,' Errolas said, whilst Sav crouched to help him bind his wound.

'And what did you find?' Correia asked.

'They got to him first,' Errolas said. Gleave's fading grin fell from his face completely. Correia and Sav both cursed. 'That's where the witchunters *met* me.'

'I'm sorry, Errolas,' Correia said. 'Why were you meeting? You're lucky the bastard only glanced you,' she added to Gleave, who nodded and clenched his teeth as Correia pulled the binding tight. Standing again, she looked back to the elf, motioning for him to continue.

'No reason,' Errolas said. 'I knew he would be here and wanted to know if he had heard anything from The Marches, or home.'

Correia took a deep breath. 'Baron Towton sits tight in his keep.

He lets witchunters and inquisitors roam free to dispense their justice without question. His magistrates have fled, and apparently...' She rubbed at her face and looked both ways, into the darkness.

'What is it?' Errolas said, his concern mirroring Correia's.

She looked to him and continued. 'It's happening all over Altoln. Witchunters and their like flee the cities where the high lords demand their disarmament, and imprison them or worse if they refuse, and flee to towns and baronies where they know they are favoured and safe.'

Sav weighed the hatchet in his hand. 'King Barrison meant well with his action, but—'

'He's driven the problem underground, so to speak,' Gleave said.

They all nodded at that. A hen clucked. Correia jumped.

'Lords above, what—'

'Ah, here's the thing...' Gleave held his hands up in an attempt to calm the dark look in Correia's eyes.

'You know what, Gleave?' she said, glancing at the large hen. 'I don't even want to know.'

'Probably best,' Sav added. The hen clucked some more and began scratching at the floor.

'What does this mean for us?' Gleave was quick to return to the main subject.

'It means I'll find it harder to travel,' Errolas said. 'As will my kin, or any other non-human for that matter.'

'He's right,' Correia said. 'Whilst under king's law, the Samorlian church at least adhered to it. Overtly, anyway, and on the main. Now though...' She looked up to the starless sky and shook her head.

'Now they do what they like.' Sav spat on the floor. The hen darted for it. 'Now they know they're outlawed, there's nothing barred to them. They'll choose their targets as they want, knowing that anything they do is illegal anyway, and so they may as well do as they like.'

'You mean kill as they like?'

'Yes, Errolas, I do.' Sav turned to Correia. 'We need our weapons and we need to move on.'

Gleave pulled on Sav so he could stand.

'And can you?' Correia pointed a sword they hadn't seen her draw to Gleave and Errolas. 'Either of you? Can you move on with

43

those wounds?'

Man and elf nodded.

'We'll be pained to ride,' Errolas admitted, 'but it will be better than walking. We need time to heal, and if that wasn't the case I would want to stay. I would want to see this baron and clear his lands of the Samorlian threat.'

'And I'd agree,' Correia said, 'but we have more pressing matters. We need to ride for The Marches. The Samorlians plague us within, but it's what lies beyond our borders that scares me more. Towton can wait.'

They all nodded at that, including the hen as she walked back to Gleave after her scavenging.

'Alright,' Correia said, sheathing her sword and turning for the door. 'I don't care what the militia say, we're to arm ourselves as I have, find Fal and Starks and ride out at first light.'

'Agreed,' Errolas said.

'I think Pecker will be able to sit in my lap, once in the saddle,' Gleave said in all seriousness.

Correia sighed and moved back through the tavern's rear door.

'You're making it too easy for me,' Sav said, before following her.

'What's wrong with holding Pecker in my lap?'

Even Errolas smirked as he limped after the other two, another limper close behind, Pecker at their feet.

Chapter 5 – Overcooked

Starks shuffled forward on his stomach, screwing his face up as a cobweb stretched across it. With great resolve, he pushed the tickling, dew decorated web from his mind and continued to focus on his target. The faintest of rustles alerted him to his two companions. He glanced one way then the other, taking in Fal and Sav. They nodded to him and Sav motioned down into the meadow. With a deep breath, Starks nodded back and reached to his belt quiver. Careful not to make a noise, he drew forth the first bolt he came across and laid it onto the crossbow's groove without looking. It was second nature to him, allowing his eyes to focus on his target.

The target stopped and looked their way.

We're spotted, Starks thought, heart pounding. He licked dry lips and otherwise held still. The target continued about its business, as it had been for quite some time.

Scanning the rest of the meadow and the tree line surrounding it, Starks ensured the surrounds were clear before releasing a long, slow breath. Halfway through his exhale, he depressed the trigger. He felt rather than saw the releasing of the cord. He heard and felt also the seemingly underpowered snap of the elf-rune augmented bow and the lazy drop and whoosh of the bolt.

'Fuck!' he shouted as the bolt sped towards his startled prey.

The deer's head rose, Starks' voice alerting it to danger a heartbeat too late.

Starks, Sav and Fal pressed their heads to the damp ground, hands covering ears.

The deer exploded in a rush of intense flames and chunks of meat, the latter raining down on the men after a few thudding heartbeats.

'Sorry sorry sorry,' Starks said, the other two cursing from their head covered positions, pieces of deer slapping and thwacking down, on and around them. The overwhelming smell of charred meat moistened mouths and churned hungry stomachs.

'Next time,' Sav managed, voice muffled, 'check which bloody bolt it is you've drawn.'

Looking up at the mixed levels of cooked meat all about, it wasn't long until laughter filled the morning. Starks' wasn't present.

***

It was perfection, how she moved; Quin couldn't help but think it every time he saw her stretch. Every time he saw Emms do anything, in fact.

'You're staring, again, Quin.'

'Sorry.'

She turned and glared at him.

'Sorry,' he said again, and winced.

'You're sorry for saying sorry, are you?'

'No,' he said.

Emms grunted.

'Well that's an improvement.' She offered him the flash of a smile and the flash of a breast. He grinned. 'Thought you'd like that. I have to reward you, you see?'

'For not being sorry?'

'Men are dumb.' She pulled on the burgundy dress Quin had bought her.

Quin frowned as his eyes traced her, toes to fingers. 'Where's your ring?'

'The Three with you, Quin. Can I not get dressed without an Adjunct's inquisition?'

'Sorr—'

A glare that could level an army cut him off.

'No sex for you tonight,' she said, tying her hair up within a silk scarf, a scarf Quin had bought her.

'That's alright,' he said, smiling. 'I'm happy to sit or lie together. Perhaps we can go to the jetty and see if we can see the Scales move?'

'Pfft,' was all Emms said to that.

Quin frowned. 'Or not,' he said, looking for any clue as to what he should be saying. 'We can do whatever—'

'No! Don't say it, Quin.' She pulled the silver ring from a pouch under her skirts and placed it on her right middle finger.

Sitting up in the bed, Quin leaned forward, arms wide as he looked up to Emms.

'Well what do you want me to say, love?'

'I thought you might have fought a little harder, or at all, to sleep with me tonight… I mean, sex! Sex and you shrug it off like it means nought to you. Three take me, Quin.'

'Don't say such things.' Quin reached out and pulled her to him. He wrapped his arms about her and squeezed tight. Emms

46

squirmed and broke free, stepping away from the bed and holding his gaze with a glare of her own.

'Don't say what? It's a blasted curse, Quin. You're quick to scare, that's your problem, and too slow to fight… even for sex with me! Gods.'

Before Quin could protest, and whilst his heart thumped and the sickness he'd been feeling of late rose in his throat once more, Emms screamed and jumped back, releasing a string of the most imaginative curses.

'Sorry, sorry,' Quin repeated, jumping to his feet and hissing at the underside of the bed. The darkness hissed back. A throaty, prolonged hiss that built before ending suddenly.

'Those two shouldn't be in here,' Emms scolded. She shuddered before kicking out at the darkness under the bed.

Before her foot returned, a ball of sable fur, teeth and claws bounded out, mouth wide, tail fluffed like a brush and legs rigid. The hissing returned and the creature was matched by another ball of fur, which hopped in circles, clattering about randomly.

Emms stamped and shouted, the polecat at her feet pouncing on said foot, teeth squeezing tender flesh and holding it fast.

'Don't move!' Quin warned her, before diving on top of his polecat and scruffing its neck.

Emms shrieked and the second polecat, hopping around near Quin's piled clothes, dived into his pantaloons before poking its black masked face out, pink nose twitching.

'Get it off, get it off.'

A low hiss was Quin's response, right in the small ear of his pet, which hissed back, its over-sized teeth gripping Emms' reddening foot, its claws holding her firm.

When the scruffing and hissing did no good, Quin rushed for a cup of small-beer on the side and threw it over the animal's head, and Emms' foot.

Another hiss, a re-puffing of its tail and back-fur, and the polecat shot off under the bed, its companion rushing across the open floor to join it.

'I'm so—'

'Don't you dare, Quinnell,' Emms said, crouching to wipe her foot with the sheet she'd pulled from the bed.

'But—'

'I said don't!' she yelled, throwing the sheet at Quin before storming from the room, slamming the door behind her.

Shoulders sagging, Quin dropped onto the bed. He refused to move even as pinpricks reached up his leg, revealing two masked snouts, one on each knee. Quin looked at his polecats and snarled. One stood up on its hind legs, front paws held together as the other hopped off Quin's knee and proceeded to nose around the bedding, unconcerned about Quin's anguish and more concerned with what it could smell.

Dropping back onto all fours, the other polecat waddled up Quin's body to curl in a circle on his chest, one eye looking up at Quin, who'd risen to his elbows.

Quin expelled air through his nose in a huff, before allowing a half-hearted smile.

'That was poor timing, Arrik. Trust you to barge out, teeth first, as soon as her foot presented itself.' The polecat merely closed its eye and fell asleep, its little flanks rising and falling.

'And as for you,' Quin said, turning to the other, which was teetering on the edge of the bed trying to work out whether it could jump across to the side unit or not, 'you should know better, Guse. You're supposed to be the sensible one and keep this one in check.' Arrik opened one eye, but shut it when Quin looked at him.

Head dropping back to the straw mattress as a loud clatter came from Guse's direction, Emms' angry face came back to Quin, and the sick rose in his throat once more.

Well done, Quinnell, you've managed to upset her once again.

***

Warming his hands on the fire, Gleave looked into the yellow flames. The flickering light accompanied the warmth flowing through his palms and fingers, taking him back to a night he couldn't forget.

Mearson's burnt, motionless face stared back at him from those flames. Horses whinnied and people talked; elves. Dirt covered Mearson now, shovelled there by the elves who came to rescue them. Gleave last saw his friend, his brother-in-arms, disappearing into the earth, face and body mangled, bloody and crisp from the gnomish grenado that took him. A grenado thrown by a Samorlian witchunter, the Witchunter General himself for all Gleave knew.

Jaw bunched and teeth ground as the heat built, as the pain grew in Gleave's fingertips. What must it have been like for Mearson? Did he have time to know the pain? Did he have time to know the end was upon him?

'Gleave!'

Gleave jumped as Correia shouted. Pulling his hands back and rounding on the woman stood over him, his own pain became real. A white pain that shot through his fingers in time with his pulse.

'What in Brisance were you doing?' Correia said, crouching besides the man.

'I...' Gleave looked down to his fingers. They looked fine. A little red, but fine; they felt destroyed, the pain building, the throbbing pounding on. He winced and started to flex them, wave them through the air, attempting unsuccessfully to cool them. They were taken, his hands, his burning fingers, by Correia. Taken and the tips placed in her mouth. He looked to her as if in a dream, the image hazy. She returned his look and the sharpness there cut through the haze. She shook her head ever so slightly, but it was enough for Gleave to look away. The saliva helped, a little, but helped all the same. That was clear, for when Correia removed Gleave's fingers from her mouth, the throbbing pounded once more.

'There was nothing you could've done, Gleave,' she said. 'I've been through it enough times in my own head. Mearson was a tough soldier, one of the best. He didn't need us looking after him. What happened was... well—'

'I know,' Gleave said, cutting over her words. He took a slow, deep breath as Correia placed his tender fingers back in her mouth, leaning against him as she did.

'Perfect,' Sav said as he walked up and dropped a blood-stained sack on the floor. 'Bloody perfect.' He walked out of camp as quickly as he'd arrived.

Correia pulled away from Gleave and the two of them shared a look of confusion, a look that changed to realisation. Correia closed her eyes and sighed across Gleave's fingers. When she opened them again, Gleave grinned.

'Well, that twat made me feel a whole lot better.' Grinning all the more, Gleave removed his fingers from Correia's mouth, thanked her with a nod and limped towards the nearby stream.

'Where's Sav going?' Fal asked, as he and Starks approached.

Correia stood. 'Never mind that,' she looked to the sack Sav had dropped. 'Where's Starks' deer, and what's in that sack?'

'Fal can explain,' Starks said, rushing after Gleave, away towards the stream.

Correia looked to Fal, who shrugged.

'Where do I start,' Fal said, looking down to the sack.

'You can start, Fal, with why I can already smell cooked meat?'

Fal chuckled. 'Oh no, that's the end of the story. Needless to say, we won't be doing any cooking for a while.'

'Gleave?' Starks said, as he approached. Gleave was holding his hands in the stream, enjoying the numbing sensation the fast-flowing waters allowed.

'Starks m'boy.'

Starks crouched down next to Gleave. Filling his water-skin, he looked to the weathered man besides him. 'What happened to your hands? They look red.'

'Correia burnt them with one of her stares.'

Starks smiled and stoppered his full skin.

'That damned bird is driving me mad.'

Looking about, Starks cocked his head. He heard the repetitive call. 'It's a chiffchaff,' he said. 'Errolas pointed one out on the way to Broadleaf Forest. After the fight with the goblins in Beresford. Pretty sure I've told you that—'

'I don't give two shits what it's called, Starks. It's a pain in my arse.'

There was silence between them for a while, interrupted only by rushing water and the chiffchaff, which caused Gleave's right eye to twitch whenever he heard it. Which was a lot.

'So, slotted your first deer, did you?' Gleave asked, breaking the silence. 'I hope so, since you three are back. I ain't for going hungry, lad, and I ain't in any fit state to hunt, what with this leg and these fingers. It's been rough going since Towton, and no mistake.'

'You're in the wars alright,' Starks said, sitting back out of Gleave's periphery. 'Perhaps Errolas will bring something back, anyway.'

Gleave half-turned, so he could see Starks, who was looking upstream.

'Why would he need to, Starks, if you stuck you a deer? A deer would feed us for days.'

'Didn't say I didn't hit it.'

'Ha! Good lad.'

'Didn't say I did though, either.'

''Morl's sweaty arse, Starks, out with it.'

Starks swallowed hard. 'I chose the wrong bolt.'

Gleave screwed his face up. 'Eh? A bolt's a bolt.'

'Some bolts are more than others, Gleave.'

Gleave spun on Starks. 'Oh shit.'

Starks nodded.

Filling cheeks with air, Gleave held the breath a moment before letting it out. Images of explosions in the dark filled his head again. He sat back, pulling his numb hands from the stream.

'Gleave?' Nothing. 'I did hit it, at least.'

Gleave nodded slowly, a nod that became an equally slow shake of the head. 'You need to improve, lad.'

Starks looked down a moment, then back up to Gleave. 'I'm trying.'

'Oh aye, you're trying alright.' Gleave bunched his jaw, like he'd been doing earlier when first thinking about Mearson's death. 'Being a pathfinder's tough, Starks. You can't walk in and pretend to be one.' Gleave's eyes were locked on his red fingers, whilst Starks' dropped to his own. 'Takes a certain man, with certain skills. Hunting is the basics to survive outside a city. It isn't a pathfinder's skill, Starks, just a basic one, you hear?'

Starks nodded.

'I don't know what we're to do with you, lad.' Gleave groaned as he rose to his feet, his leg – despite his fingers – the worst of a myriad of aches and pains. 'We're having to waste time training you on the basics…' Hard eyes settled on Starks, who didn't look back. 'We went from a strong unit, strong men like Tom and Mearson, to… well, you.' A heavy sigh, a shake of the head and Gleave limped back to camp, leaving Starks to stare at his hands.

Starks' eyes moistened and he cursed himself for it, wiping at them aggressively with his padded sleeve.

After a few moments listening to water rushing over stones, through roots and past his own feet, Starks surged up and set off across the stream, splashing as he went. He balled his fists and clenched his teeth, nose wrinkling as anger churned in his stomach, in his chest.

'Starks?'

The melodic voice made Starks jump. He turned to see Errolas leaning against a nearby tree. Now he saw the elf, it was obvious he was there, but before that, Starks would have walked straight past him.

'I heard all of that,' Errolas said, nodding back towards the stream.

'Course you did, you hear everything,' Starks said, his tone harsher than he'd intended. He relaxed a little. 'I'm sorry—' A hand cut his apology short.

'No need, Starks. You have nothing to apologise for.'

'The deer? Gleave?'

'Nothing,' Errolas asserted. He came forward and pulled Starks into a casual hold, walking him besides him, as Fal usually did, although Errolas carried a limp not too dissimilar to Gleave's.

'Gleave has a troubled mind and he takes it out on you, because you are the easiest for him to do that to.'

Starks made to talk, but Errolas continued.

'That is in no way a criticism of you, but of Gleave.' They followed the stream up its winding path, through the undergrowth. They stepped over fallen branches, pushed through bushes and avoided brier patches. 'We all have issues,' Errolas went on, squeezing Starks' shoulder. 'Some of us more than others, but we all have them. We all deal with them differently, too. I believe you would call Gleave a bully, but he struggles with his friend's death.'

'Mearson?'

'Yes. He feels responsible, I believe, and so takes it out on others when he can.'

'On me.'

'Yes. However,' Errolas looked to Starks, who turned to him upon hearing that word, 'I believe part of Gleave's heavy handed tactics with you is because he likes you—'

'I highly doubt that,' Starks said, looking away again.

'Do you? Truly?' Errolas stopped and turned Starks to face him. He held Starks at arms-length, a hand on each shoulder, gentle, yet a solid presence. 'Does he not banter with you? Does he not talk to you at other times, as an equal?'

'Not as an equal, no,' Starks said, angry at the thought. 'He talks to me like a child, like a—'

'An apprentice?' Errolas smiled. Starks frowned. 'He has taken you under his wing, whether you realise it or not. I'm not even sure he realises it, but he hounds you about hunting and other things because he worries for you and he wants you to improve, to succeed. He doesn't want to see another friend die, when he could do something about it.'

52

Starks swallowed and tried to turn away, tears threatening him again. Errolas held him firm.

'I think you are clever enough to know the truth in what I say, Starks. Aren't you?'

'I don't know.'

'Well, we can never know such things for sure, but I have a few centuries on you, on all of you, and I've seen such things countless times.'

'Amongst the elves?' Starks asked, eyes widening a fraction. His mind raced to Leiina, the red-haired elf dancer who'd made him feel more a man than any other being he'd ever met.

Errolas laughed. 'Yes, Starks. We are not infallible you know, us elves.' He laughed again, a short, sharp, musical skip of a laugh. 'Far from it, in fact. If you humans only knew half the truth about us… Well, perhaps one day I'll elaborate more, for such a friend as you.'

Would that I could go back there and live with Errolas and his kin, with Leiina. Be with her and leave all this behind. Shaking the melancholy away as Leiina's face and hair and the memorable feel and taste of her lips lingered in his mind, Starks smiled and Errolas offered the same in return.

'Now come, Starks, let us return to the camp and partake in some crisped meat.' Errolas laughed all the more at Starks' crestfallen face, and pulled Starks alongside him, drawing laughter to match his own as they made their way slowly through the wood.

Chapter 6 – All too much

Couples twirled, swayed, danced to the melodic tunes that flowed through the grand hall of Eudes de Geelan, the Marquis d'Easson, Marcher Lord of Sirreta.

Spectacular tapestries lined the château's stone walls, candle-topped chandeliers hung from the oak-beamed ceiling and a large hearth acted as a focal point for all in attendance. Until *they* strode into the room, that was, through oak doors studded with iron.

A slender, elegant woman practically glided alongside an impressive young man in black hose and a tight fitting, yellow coat, arming sword dressed to his left like every other man present. The beautiful young woman wore rich burgundy, from subtle headdress to floor skimming open surcoat, her full-lipped, down-turned mouth spreading into a wondrous smile that disarmed the regal air of the gentlemen who looked upon her; as her companion's subtle smile melted the hearts of the ladies who looked upon him.

Eudes de Geelan rose from his chair at the side of the room, his lady wife and daughters three doing the same as the new arrivals crossed stone slabs, parting the crowd to be announced by Eudes' herald. The herald smiled and bowed low to the stunning duo, before turning to his liege. He cleared his throat before announcing the new arrivals in the finest Sirretan.

'Messires and mesdames, may I humbly announce Mademoiselle Flavell de Steedon, daughter of Guiscard de Steedon, and her trusted companion and protector, Amis de Valmont, chevalier.'

Flavell curtsied, burgundy skirts bunching about her as Amis bowed low. The marquis and marquise of the hall, their three daughters in tow, mirrored the formal greeting.

Flavell smiled wonderfully and glanced sidelong at Amis, waiting for him to compliment the noble family.

'Good evening to you, messire,' Amis said, with such a soothing tone that the hard-faced marquis smiled back. 'And to you, madame,' Amis continued, bowing again. 'And, of course,' he said, smile broad yet soft, 'your most beautiful daughters.' Amis presented his largest bow yet.

Flavell stopped herself rolling her eyes as the children giggled.

'We thank you for your attendance, mademoiselle,' Eudes said, eyes locked on Flavell's unusually high and wide cheekbones and green eyes, features commented on often during her journey north. 'It is a pleasure to have you accept our invitation to my ball,' Eudes went on, eyes lingering on Flavell, who blushed under the intrusive gaze, especially when it dropped to her tight bodice and partially visible bosom.

'Not at all, messire,' Amis said, drawing Eudes' attention. 'It was a pleasure for Messire Guiscard, the Sieur de Steedon, to receive an invitation to such a prestigious event. He sends his apologies that he could not attend in person, for he has heard much about your wonderful balls…' Amis left a brief but obvious pause before continuing, causing a flash of anger to show on Eudes' face. '…and thus decided, with ease, to send his most beloved daughter in his stead. May I ask, messire, how you came to hear of the Sieur de Steedon? It is a far-off land he holds for our Queen; close to the Kaja Strip. Not a place I thought you would have heard of this far north?'

Gods below, Amis, bate the beast why don't you, Flavell thought, her disarming smile carefully maintained. Eudes' eyes flicked back to Flavell, his anger fading away. *Men have swords to clank together, we have smiles.* Flavell's smile almost slipped as she noticed the stern gaze of Eudes' wife upon her. Almost.

'I know much, young man,' Eudes said, eyes remaining on Flavell whilst he plucked at his greying moustache 'Enjoy your time here, Amis de Valmont, and I shall look forward to seeing you tilt at the joust four days from now. Perhaps you can ride against my nephew, the Seneschal d'Easson?' It was only at the end that Eudes' eyes moved back Amis.

Amis guided Flavell away, without answering the question, their bow and curtsy rushed as they moved across the hall, dozens of eyes following them.

'Must you antagonise him so, de Valmont?' Flavell said through her maintained smile. 'We are his guests, are we not?'

'Apologies, mademoiselle.' Amis flashed her a sidelong glance that pulled at her mouth, hinting at the mirth she hid. She allowed him that much.

'You didn't like the way he was looking at me, did you?'

A group of women meandered past, trying to hide their lust for Amis.

'I doubt your *father* would be impressed is all; the ageing marquis isn't whom you are intended to meet and wed.'

Flavell scoffed, her slip of a nose wrinkling as she did so. She glanced about the hall, from gaudily dressed women to stiff-backed men of all ages, some of whom openly leered at her.

Amis looked about the room, eyes searching as much as Flavell's. 'Do you see the seneschal at all?'

'No, de Valmont, I do not. Nor was he what I was looking for.'

Amis frowned. 'Food?'

'Food. It's been a long road.' Her stomach churned and her mouth watered at the thought of sating her hunger and thirst.

Amis took Flavell's arm once more. 'Come, let us wine and dine.'

Her smile continuous, Flavell allowed Amis to guide her around the hall. 'If you keep this up, the seneschal will think me spoken for, by you.'

It was Amis' turn to scoff. 'A mere chevalier such as me? I doubt it. I'm here to escort and guide you, mademoiselle. I'm quite sure no one will think otherwise, what with your breeding and all.'

Flavell's smile slipped from her wide eyes, but not her mouth. 'You overstep the mark sometimes, de Valmont. You know that, don't you? You're lucky I allow it.'

'I am indeed very lucky.' Amis scooped up two glasses of ruby wine and offered one to Flavell whilst sipping the other. The fruity scent and rich taste brought satisfied sighs from them both.

'I'm not as lucky as some,' he dared say, nodding past Flavell to a handsome man who entered the hall.

'Nephew!' Eudes bellowed, surging to his feet. 'Come, join your favourite uncle.'

Croal de Geelan made his way through the crowd to stand by Eudes' side, smiling and nodding greetings to people as he went. He wore white hose tied to a richly embroidered blue doublet, nothing covering it. Looking around the room, Flavell realised the uncovered doublet was some sort of summer fashion for many of the men present, all of which wore colour-matching stalked caps, unlike Amis. She frowned at that.

Amis guided Flavell closer to their hosts, so they could hear Eudes speak to his nephew.

'Croal is a handsome man,' Amis said, although it sounded bitter to Flavell.

'Indeed, he is,' she said, smirking when she saw a flash of anger play across Amis' face, even if it were for half a heartbeat.

Eudes slapped his nephew on the back, before pulling him into a tight embrace. At arm's length now, Eudes spun Croal to face a barrel-chested man off to the side, who stepped forward and offered the young seneschal a curt nod in greeting.

'You know my guest, nephew?'

Croal smiled and clasped the stranger's hand. 'I do indeed. I remember the last time you visited us, my lord Earl,' Croal said, the latter in Altolnan.

'But of course,' the Earl said, breaking the grasp, 'how could any of us forget my last visit. Even if it were years passed.' Although the Earl spoke Sirretan well, his accent butchered the language. Flavell hid a smirk. She liked the big man. She didn't know why, but she did. She watched the exchange intently, as did Amis at her side.

Croal smiled. 'When you said we'd meet again, I had no idea it would be like this?'

'Fine attire,' Croal added before the Earl could respond. He nodded to the well-fitting tunic and hose of green and black the Earl wore.

The burly man nodded his thanks. 'Your uncle was kind enough to have me measured and fitted. I can only compliment the tailor and seamstresses who made the garment. It wouldn't have done to attend in the attire I arrived in, would it, my lord Seneschal?'

Croal smiled and bowed his capped head to the man without saying another word. He turned back to his uncle, who led him away to the food tables, Eudes' daughters pulling at their cousin's doublet as they giggled and skipped alongside.

'Who's the Earl?' Flavell asked, tipping her wine glass towards the sour faced man Croal had spoken to.

Amis shrugged. 'I'm not sure, but judging by his accent and his current expression, I wouldn't be surprised if he's an Altolnan prisoner through chivalric code.'

Flavell actually rolled her eyes this time. She pulled from Amis' hold and made her way back to the wine servants. 'Men,' she cursed, whilst dodging attempted offers to dance from more of the same, Amis de Valmont close on her heels.

***

'My love is as an inferno, Emms. It burns in my heart—'

Emms huffed. 'Well, I'm sorry to be such a pain, Quin.'

'That's not what I meant, my love.'

A deep sigh and a sudden tear came from Emms. 'I know,' she said, unable to meet Quin's eyes. 'I know… but it's not enough anymore. Not now, at least; not as I am now.'

Quin frowned. 'What do you mean?' His voice shook, hands trembling to match. He dropped to his knees and took Emms' cold hands – they were forever cold, he mused – in his own.

'I need action, Quin. Not words,' she said, looking down at him. 'They say they speak louder, don't they? They say actions speak louder than words, and all you can offer me is words it seems, and the love that comes with them of course…'

Quin made to speak, to protest, but was cut off.

'And that's fine,' Emms said hurriedly. 'Just not right now. It's all too much for me right now.'

Quin's eyes searched for Emms' own, but no meeting was made.

'You've spent so much time talking about us,' Emms went on, after an uncomfortable silence, 'about our future together, that you've missed out on the now, on the couple we are *now* and on the moments we had.' She looked down at him. 'I can't do that anymore: miss out. I'm not for marrying off,' she went on, her bottom lip quivering, 'like some lord's daughter. I have no dowry—'

'And I expect none, nor want one.' Quin's voice broke, caught on the last, his insides twisting.

'I know. Again, I know…' her eyes drifted, welling as they were. 'I know you so well, Quinnell,' she whispered. 'Too well.'

Quin's face wrinkled, creased, and he squeezed her hands. She looked back to him.

'There's nothing left for me to discover about you. No wonder to be had. Nothing to skip my slowing heart.

'Quin, I'm sorry, truly I am.'

Breaking down fully, Quin failed to hold onto Emms as she pulled away from him, a silver ring left in his grasping hands, a folded, gifted dress on the bed. He failed to speak, failed to use the words she claimed were all he had.

'I hope you can forgive me,' Emms said, without turning, as she walked to the room's door.

'All I want to do is love you…' was Quin's only reply, once he managed to choke back the tears. When she didn't turn, he slumped to the floor, his world spinning away from him.

He barely heard the door close as Emms left the room.

Chapter 7 – A different light

After circling a hillock topped by a copse of trees, the pathfinders halted below a shallow dip in the ground, the edges of which were thick with gorse. Beginning to dismount, they turned to the sound of hooves as Sav rode in.

'I take it we won't be stopping in the hamlet I scouted to the west?' Sav reined in alongside Fal.

'Doesn't look like it,' Fal said, removing his mount's harness. 'Correia said we're camping here.'

'We haven't set up yet, we can move on,' Sav said, leaning down from the saddle.

Fal continued what he was doing. 'Go ask her.'

Sav swung down off his horse. 'Never mind.'

'Ask me what?' Correia said from the dip where she'd taken her horse.

'He's scouted a hamlet,' Fal said, loud enough for Correia to hear as she went about clearing the ground, Errolas helping her do so.

'We need to avoid populated areas for now, in case of witchhunters,' she said, Gleave now joining in with the clearing. 'You know that, Sav.'

Sav huffed and handed the reins to Fal. 'See to the horses, mate,' he said, before stomping off.

'Sav?' Fal looked to his friend, who didn't reply.

'What's with him?' Gleave said, walking over to Fal with an armful of stones. He dumped them at Fal's feet.

'Thanks.' Fal kicked the larger stones aside.

'You're welcome.' Gleave stood and watched Sav descend the hill. 'Well?' he said, when Fal offered no more. 'Was it my fingers in Correia's mouth the other day? He's been a moody dick ever since.'

Fal turned and Gleave was grinning. Before he could say anything, Correia appeared.

'Button it, Gleave. Now head out with Starks and hunt, we need to replenish our stock, that deer didn't last as long as I'd hoped.'

'Great,' Gleave said, hands on hips, looking to Starks who glared back. 'I'm to go hunting with the deer stalker, eh? Fair enough. Starks!' he shouted.

'I can hear you. I'm stood right here.'

'Grab your crossbow and follow me, I'm not waiting all night.'

Fal and Correia shared a withering look before going about their business.

'Errolas,' Correia said, as the two hunters walked off, picking at each other all the while.

'Correia?'

'Grab the pot from my saddlebag and let's get a fire going, a tripod and some water on the boil, eh?'

Errolas smiled, nodded and got to it. Correia pulled Fal to one side.

'What's wrong?' Fal asked, looking into Correia's eyes, eyes heavy with a burden.

'Sav.'

'Sav?'

'Yes, Sav, and you know it, Fal.'

Taking a deep breath, Fal nodded. 'Aye, I do.'

'Go on,' she said, lifting her chin for him to explain.

Fal grunted a laugh. 'Can you not see what's eating at him?' Correia frowned so Fal went on. 'It's you, Correia. He's sore because of you.' She rocked back, genuinely shocked. 'Surely you know he likes you?'

'Well yes,' Correia admitted, eyes leaving Fal's to follow the path Sav took. 'Of course I know, but like doesn't do this to someone.'

'It might when they think the person they like is with another.'

She looked back to Fal. 'Who? Who would I be with, here?'

'Gleave?' Fal raised his eyebrows in anticipation, but again Correia looked shocked. Fal leaned in. 'The fingers?'

'Eh?'

'In the mouth...'

Correia's laugh drew the attention of Errolas, although both knew he could probably hear every word they said anyway.

'The fool burnt his fingers. I was cooling them is all.'

Fal's laugh matched Correia's. 'I know that, but does Sav? And even if he does, would it matter? When you feel...' Fal paused, fidgeted.

'Go on.'

'When you like someone like he does you, you don't often rationalise things. You over react to them, no?'

Correia took a deep breath and released a heavy sigh, rubbing at her face as she did so. 'I didn't ask for this,' she said through her hands.

'And you think Sav did?'

60

'No.' Again, muffled through rubbing hands. She lowered them to look at Fal. They both heard flint on steel as Errolas made fire.

'What do I do?' she asked.

Another laugh. 'You think I know?' Fal shook his head.

'Well you're his friend.'

'We're all friends, Correia. Or so I'd like to think.'

'You know what I mean. You've known him years.'

'I have, and I've seen him swoon over many a lass, but not like this.'

'Oh don't say it like that.' Correia walked away a little, turned a circle and looked up to the empty sky.

'Talk to him.'

'Not likely.'

'Then this'll continue,' Fal said, moving to and putting his hands on Correia's shoulders. 'We can't let this continue though, can we? We need our wits about us, every one, and we need to work together, not fight or avoid each other.'

'That goes for Gleave and Starks too,' Correia said, looking back into Fal's kind eyes. He smiled.

'Don't change the subject. We'll cross that one in time. Talk to Sav, I'm sure it'll help. Explain what happened with Gleave—'

'I shouldn't have to.'

'No, Correia, maybe not, but it might help. Talk to him.'

'And say what? I can't change how he feels about me, can I?'

'Tell him how you feel about him.'

Correia snorted and pulled away, turning her back on Fal. 'Please,' she said. 'There's nothing there.'

'If you say so,' Fal said, smiling, 'but talk to him all the same. The mission can't be put at risk because of such things; tell him that. He's professional if nothing else, when it comes down to scouting and fighting and such. Gods, tell him it's something that will have to wait, to see if anything will happen between you two.'

'No!' Correia said, incredulous. 'I'm not giving him false hope where there might not be any.'

'Might not?' Fal grinned.

'See to the horses, Sergeant.'

Smile remaining, Fal bowed his head and moved away, Correia hesitating before moving in the opposite direction.

'Who'd you think will bring food back first?' Correia asked Sav, who was sat on a smooth outcrop of limestone. His shoulders rose then fell.

'Oh please, Sav,' Correia said, sitting next to the scout. 'Don't be so melodramatic, it doesn't suit you. Took me a while to find you.'

'That's what you want of your pathfinders isn't it? Hard to find. Sneaky.'

Lips pursed, Correia nodded. 'Sneaky, yes, that's a preferable skill set for a pathfinder. Mardy arse isn't, though.'

'You're one to talk.' Sav's head lifted from his knees at that, turning to take in the woman by his side.

'And you're treading thin ice.'

Sav looked forward again and dropped his head to his knees. 'Ice. Cold like you, eh?'

'You think I'm cold, Sav? Well that cuts to the quick.'

'Pfft. Not likely.'

'You think I lack feelings? You think because I have to be hard all the time that I enjoy it? Eh?' Nothing. 'Sav?' Another shrug.

Correia stood and held out a hand. 'Walk with me.'

Sav didn't answer, didn't even look to the offered hand.

'Treat that as an order if you prefer, scout.'

Sav stood and hesitated a moment when he saw her outstretched hand.

Correia moved forward and took Sav's, since he failed to offer it. She pulled him along, back up towards the camp. 'We need move,' she said, 'before one of Starks' bolts blows us to bits.' She caught a smirk on Sav's face at that.

'He's doing well,' Sav managed, as they walked along hand in hand.

'He is,' Correia said. 'I know it, you know it and *Gleave* knows it.' Sav's hand tightened around hers.

'Burnt fingers,' Correia said, when Sav remained quiet.

'Sorry?'

'Gleave burnt his fingers and I was cooling them, nothing more, Sav.'

On they walked for a time, nothing being said.

'I know.'

Correia's eyes widened. 'You know?' She looked at him as they continued to walk.

Sav nodded. 'What I don't know, is whether you'd do the same for me. You and Gleave have been together a long time.'

'Yes, Sav, we have. A long time and yet nothing more than

soothing burnt fingers has ever happened between Gleave and me.'

Sav swallowed hard, before licking dry lips.

Correia stopped and pulled Sav's hand, turning him to face her. *I don't know what to tell you, Sav,* she thought. *I don't even know how to deal with how I feel, let alone how you feel.*

Sav offered her a tight smile as he swallowed once more.

'You're normally full of confidence, on the verge of hubris I'd say. Especially when it comes to talking about women.'

Looking away, Sav took a deep breath. A pull on his hand brought him back round to Correia, who smiled.

'I don't know what to say to you.'

Sav smiled weakly. 'You don't have to say anything, Correia.'

'Maybe not, but I want to. I want you to be... you! I want you to be set for the mission, not distracted—'

'For the mission,' Sav said, laughing suddenly, bitterly. He pulled his hand free and continued on towards the camp.

'Sav!'

On he walked.

'Sav! Stop walking. Now!'

Correia's tone of voice stopped him dead. He turned and she was there, before him. Reaching up on her toes, Correia pulled Sav's head down by his chin, until they were close.

'Honestly, Sav... If you want that; if you want honesty?' He nodded. 'I don't know how I feel right now, about you or any of what is happening to the south, within the kingdom. I need my head straight and I need constants around me so I can operate properly. So I can do the best for my King. Can you understand that?'

Sav took a deep breath but nodded.

'I can't explore feelings right now. I can't go there, Sav. I'm asking you not to make me, not to push me. Is that so bad?' He shook his head, although she noticed his breaths were ragged. He chewed at his bottom lip and several muscles in his face twitched. It was all Correia could do not to cry, and that scared her more than anything else. *Oh Sav, what are you doing to yourself,* she thought. *What are you doing to me?*

Sav raised both hands and placed them on Correia's face, leaned down and kissed Correia on the forehead. 'Thank you,' he whispered, and offered the sincerest smile she'd seen for days.

'I can't promise there'd be anything from me in the future—'

'I know.'

'But I wanted you to know there's no games, Sav. I do what I need to do and I come last to all of it. If, once all this is figured out, all this is resolved and the kingdom finds itself in some semblance of normality again, perhaps I can explore what might be. Does that make sense?'

Sav was nodding before she'd finished. He smiled again, turned away and wiped at his eyes, although he made it seem as though there was something in one of them. Correia was no fool.

'Come on,' he said eventually. 'We need to be back to stop Gleave rubbing Starks' face in the fact he failed to bring food in first, if at all.'

Nodding, Correia agreed, before following the man she was now thinking of in a different light.

By the time they reached the dip in the hillock, the light was failing and there was laughter and the flicker of firelight illuminating the camp, followed by the smell of roasting venison.

'Well? Sav said, walking up to the firelight, Correia close behind. Fal looked to Sav, eyebrows raised. Sav shook his head, almost imperceptibly, but smiled all the same. Fal nodded, looked to Correia and received the same from her.

Starks was sat back against his saddle, positively beaming. Gleave, on the other hand - Pecker nestled in his lap - looked thoroughly pissed off. That was, until Correia caught his eyes and he offered a wink.

Chapter 8 – Shore leave

'How'd ye feel, lad?' The voice was rough, as was the face looking down on the young officer. Charl Spendley groaned. Hitchmogh grinned, spittle stringing between crooked teeth.

'What happened?'

Hitchmogh barked a laugh and moved away. 'He's fine, Cap'n,' Hitchmogh said, leaving the darkened room.

'You, young man,' Captain Mannino leaned in where Hitchmogh had been, 'are very lucky to be alive. As are we all, after what befell us.'

Spendley looked about, the movement sending rocks tumbling within his skull and neck. He saw a familiar smile.

'Nearly had us they did.' Lefey winked.

'I owe you a debt,' Spendley said, locking eyes with the woman, who scoffed.

'Hardly that, mate.' She smiled before leaving the room, Spendley's bloodshot eyes following her out.

'Yes, you do, man,' Mannino said, sitting on the edge of Spendley's bunk. 'As you do the rest of *Sessio's* crew, for almost losing the ship, and our lives.'

Spendley swallowed hard, but managed to meet his captain's unreadable eyes.

'But,' Mannino said, before Spendley could reply, 'I doubt I would have fared any better, nor would any of the other men aboard.' He stood again, leaving Spendley to wonder why he'd sat down in the first place. 'However,' Mannino continued, moving to the wall of the room and pressing both hands against the wood, 'I hope next time *Sessio* is in your hands, Master Spendley, that you use what you have available to you, which would have been Lefey in this case, and not try and take on the impossible yourself.' He looked over his richly adorned shoulder, half his face lit by lamplight, the other lost to shadow. The eye that was visible creased in what might have been mistaken for a smile, if Spendley didn't know any better, before Mannino spun dramatically and crossed to a clay jug full of rum. 'Anyway,' the captain said, pouring a small cup and offering it to a now sitting rather than laying Spendley, 'It's time for you to get off your backside and get on deck, we're about to make port.'

Taking the offered cup, Spendley frowned.

'Tri Isles,' Mannino explained, taking a deep breath afterwards, whilst fingering the ornate basket hilt of his sheathed cutlass. He caught Spendley's prolonged look of horror and nodded. 'I know, Master Spendley, but needs must and oh do they ever. It seems Squall wasn't looking favourably upon us at all this trip, for we took damage shortly after the sirens were dispatched by Lefey and her sister-mates, and these damned and cursed islands were the closest port available to us.' Offering what Spendley thought was a tight smile, Mannino pursed his lips and made for the door.

'The boy, Captain?' Spendley asked, leaving his formulating thoughts and fears about the port behind as the boy in the crow's nest sprang to mind.

'Is well...' Mannino looked back once before exiting the room '...thanks to you!'

Spendley slumped with relief as the door closed behind the captain. 'Well at least there's that,' he said aloud, before necking the rum in one and climbing to his feet. 'At least there's that.'

Squall's salty bones, Spendley thought heavily, whilst placing the empty cup on the side. *Of all the places to make port, the bloody Tri Isles... and after all that's happened to this crew there.*

'Squall and 'morl save us,' he said finally, pulling on the clothes laid out for him. 'We'd have been better with the bloody sirens.' His face flushed at the recent yet vague memory.

'Remember, lads and lasses,' Hitchmogh said to the gathered crowd on board *Sessio's* main deck, 'ye're to lay low, to keep flapping lips battened down and for Squall and 'morl's sake, ye're not to attract the attention of the Adjunct's Guard, do I make meself clear?'

A chorus of 'aye's' followed.

'Grand,' Hitchmogh said, before looking to Mannino, who nodded back to him from the front rail of the aft-castle.

'Feck off then, the lot of ye,' Hitchmogh shouted. A cheer followed and a surge for the port ramps. Hitchmogh grabbed two passing sailors, who leaned in to hear him over the din of the rest.

I said lay low and they cheer, Hitchmogh thought, shaking his grizzled head before speaking to the two he held onto.

'Make sure those with duties on land carry them out, will ye?' Both of the women nodded. 'And make sure everyone's back before sunset, too. I'm holding you two accountable if owt happens.' Two groans followed that, but two acknowledgements thereafter. 'Now crack on with it,' Hitchmogh said, whining as he pressed a small pouch of coins into the closest hand of each sailor.

Beaming, Lefey and her friend rushed from the deck and off into the milling crowd that accompanied any busy wharf.

Reaching the top of the aft-castle's steps with a huff and an over exaggerated puff, to be heard over the countless gulls above, Hitchmogh moved beside his captain and leaned on the rail, the two of them watching the majority of their crew disappear into the crowd and surrounding blue tiled, white buildings.

'You think we should have limped on to a Sirretan port?' Mannino said, eyes on the crowds as he drew on an empty pipe. Hitchmogh stood straight and packed tobacco into his own ivory pipe.

'No, Cap'n.'

Mannino looked to Hitchmogh, who glanced back.

'I don't,' Hitchmogh reasserted, lighting and drawing the smoke into his lungs before letting it out in a vivid ring that dissipated on the salty breeze.

'You surprise me, Master Hitchmogh,' Mannino said, running his hands back and forth on the wood of the rail.

'I surprise myself sometimes.'

Both men smiled, which was followed by a companionable silence, bar the cry of gulls, the clanging of rigging on masts and the hundreds of voices that assaulted them.

After some time, Hitchmogh turned about and took in the great Scales in the distance, and the two suspended land masses those Scales supported. A shudder ran through him. He turned back, removed his pipe from his mouth and spat over the side. 'Have that, Squall,' he said, before descending the aft-castle steps once more.

'Master Hitchmogh,' Mannino said from above.

Hitchmogh looked up, the sun offering a halo behind Mannino's head.

'We don't know the state of the Sirretan ports, man.' Mannino was nought but a silhouette now, his expression unknown. 'I can't risk *Sessio* to unknowns, not when we're damaged; not when we're slow and vulnerable. Otherwise—'

'I know,' Hitchmogh said, nodding all the while. 'I know.' He offered a smile to Mannino and made for the main mast. 'I'll check on the boy,' he said, largely to himself. *Common sense tells me I'll serve* Sessio *better up there with him whilst we're docked here.*

Putting out and packing away his pipe, Hitchmogh started the painful climb to the fortified crow's nest above and the lad who'd spent his life living in it.

'This must be a bloody record, Lefey,' Hitchmogh said, hanging over the side of *Sessio's* crow's nest and staring at the wincing face below him, mere hours after he'd sent her and the rest of the crew forth.

Lefey swayed on the rigging she clung to. 'I think it could be,' she offered, wincing once more at Hitchmogh's colourful string of curses. She looked about, to the azure waters below, the milling crowds, off to the cloud cutting Scales in the bay.

'Lefey?'

'Aye? Apologies,' she said, realising that his curses had flowed seamlessly into a question.

'I said, do you know who has them?'

Lefey shook her head.

'This gets worse.' Hitchmogh chewed his bottom lip a while, before looking back to the woman. 'Does the captain know yet?'

'Not by my mouth.'

'Well, he needs to. Anywhere else, you, Spendley and me would sort it, but here...' he looked at the hovel clad land rising up to the mountain that matched the great Scales for height. 'Here we need the captain involved.'

Lefey closed her eyes, took a deep breath and sighed long and hard.

'That sigh be about right, lass, to describe the shit we're in. Mannino told me to tell ye all to lay low. Ye think anyone were actually listening when I said that?'

'Course,' Lefey said, nodding several times, 'but it's... well... it's the Tri Isles, ain't it? If owt's to go wrong off the ship, it's to be here.'

It was Hitchmogh's time to nod. 'Aye, but we had no choice and you lot've been cooped up below for far too long, never mind how big *Sessio* gets below the waves at times.'

'What're we to do, Master Hitchmogh?'

After a pause Lefey didn't dare interrupt, Hitchmogh hawked and sent a gob full of phlegm far and wide. They both watched it arc, twitch in the wind and land in the waters below.

'Right you are,' he said finally, locking eyes with Lefey. 'Ye're to go see Spendley and bring him to the aft-castle, and I'll do the same with Mannino.'

The relief on Lefey's face was clear. 'Thank you,' she said, before descending.

'Yer welcome, lass. Ye're a good'n and I wouldn't be askin' ye to tell the captain this news, not here, not now. Not before we've even bloody effected repairs on his girl.'

Patting the side of the crow's nest and calling a quick explanation into the depths of said nest, for the boy, Hitchmogh hauled himself over the edge, swallowed down the vertigo that threatened his senses, and began his slow descent to the main deck.

'I hope ye're in a good mood,' Hitchmogh said into the wind. 'For it ain't gonna last, Cap'n. It ain't gonna last.'

Chapter 9 – And so it begins

'Decided to re-join me have you, Master Hitchmogh?' Mannino's eyes remained forward, his back to a narrow alley.

A crooked toothed smile was the only reply Mannino received from his first mate.

'Well, I can't very well blame you, man,' Mannino said, fingering the empty pipe in his hands. 'That goblin sends shudders through me every time I see him.'

'Aye, he does me too.'

'*Admiral* Charlzberg, Hitchmogh. Can you believe him?' Mannino scoffed. 'Admiral!'

Hitchmogh hawked and spat.

Mannino shot Hitchmogh a sidelong glance and pointed across the street their alley adjoined, changing subject. 'Is that the place?'

Hitchmogh nodded, right hand wringing the hilt of his cutlass.

Mannino rubbed at the back of his neck, beneath his high collar.

A few moments passed with neither saying a word, eyes locked on the door of the tavern opposite them. They watched the patrons come and go. They watched the street urchins come and go too, although none got too close to the tavern door.

'Were they gambling, Master Hitchmogh?'

After a deep breath, Hitchmogh answered. 'Gambling, aye, Cap'n, but mores to the point, they were gambling with the wrong sorts, see. They were gambling with Hillside gangers.'

Mannino closed his eyes before watching the door once more. 'Is the rest of the crew aware?'

'Most,' Hitchmogh said. 'Lefey and Master Spendley have rounded up those they can. Spendley will watch *Sessio* for you, with a good crew to hold her if needs be—'

'And Lefey?'

'Is in position,' Hitchmogh said through his fingers, whilst chewing his nails. 'Or will be,' he added, 'if we give her a little while longer.'

Nodding, Mannino strode towards the tavern. Hitchmogh jerked before following suit.

'I'm thirsty,' was all Mannino said as his long strides took him across the road.

'And I don't believe you,' Hitchmogh muttered.

'Eh?'

'Nothing, Cap'n. Nothing,' Hitchmogh said, hot on Mannino's

heels.

Laughing rippled out from a corner of the taproom as a man picked himself from the floor, his cheeks reddened.

'Reckon' he'll hit back?'

'No, Master Hitchmogh, I don't,' Mannino said, only half looking at the commotion on the far side of the fire pit.

Hitchmogh wrinkled his nose and sniffed, drawing Mannino's attention.

'*You* do?' Mannino asked, frowning. He turned to look at the blushing man who'd been knocked to the floor. Hitchmogh grinned.

A collective and prolonged 'Ooh' was the next sound to ripple through the patrons of the tavern, as the blusher slotted the rather rotund man who'd originally knocked him to the ground.

Mannino and Hitchmogh winced as several fists, feet and foreheads started flying, making connections here and there. Everyone was watching now, everyone except Mannino that was. He turned his gaze back to a table of gamblers in the opposite corner to the continuing brawl. The men sat there returned to their game. Mannino, ignoring the sound of shouts, curses and threats, watched one man in particular. He was poorly dressed yet he won hand after hand. He certainly wasn't the sort Mannino would have pinned as a professional player. Brow furrowed, Mannino watched on, quickly catching the scam for what it was. He sighed as he imagined his sailors cottoning on to the very same, mid game.

'Oh lads.' Mannino sighed.

The rotund man who'd started the fight was dragged passed Mannino, unconscious. Pulling in his stool a little, Mannino looked to Hitchmogh who looked back, eyebrows raised.

'The big lad, Master Hitchmogh, at the gambling table...' Hitchmogh glanced over, then back, '...he's in league with two of the others, who, I suspect, are making him look better than he is.'

'Which would have been happening whilst our lot were at the table, too.'

Mannino nodded, eyes on the gamblers.

Hitchmogh took a deep breath and released it as a sigh, before finishing the pot of ale before him. 'They wouldn't have taken that.'

'No, Master Hitchmogh, they wouldn't. Alas, I would think that here, in the numbers they were in, they were very much the smallest fish in the pond. They certainly shouldn't have challenged what they suspected.'

'Walk away? Our lot?' Hitchmogh grunted a laugh.

'When the situation dictates it, man, yes. Coin and pride isn't everything. You know that.'

Hitchmogh conceded the point with a nod. 'We both know that.'

'Well drown me, man, if I didn't think we'd taught our crew that too.' Mannino reached for his glass of port, before realising he'd finished it already.

'Another, Cap'n?'

'No, man, no. I think it's time, now we suspect who has our men, to make enquiries.'

Hitchmogh leaned across the small table, voice hushed now the trouble in the corner had abated. 'I could go over there, plonk myself down and, well... ask?'

Mannino's tailored coat raised at the shoulders as he snorted a laugh. His first mate sat back like he'd been mocked, so Mannino held up his hand placatingly as he explained.

'You go over there and do the sort of thing I think you'll do, and the Adjunct's Guard will be in here and on us faster than you can say 'morl's balls.'

A quiet curse came before Hitchmogh's reply. 'There is that, I guess.'

'Guess? Oof, what! You *know*, Master Hitchmogh. You don't need to guess.' Mannino shook his head at his first mate, before reaching again for his empty glass and holding it aloft. After a few moments, a bar girl came over and refilled it with port. Mannino saw the big gambler's eyes stray from his cards; the shaved headed lad's eyes strayed Mannino's way, or to be specific, the girl's way. Mannino caught the girl's blue eyes before she smiled and moved on.

'Pretty,' Mannino whispered, drawing a further frown from Hitchmogh.

'Aye,' Hitchmogh said, 'but in a plain way and not enough to be a distraction to ye, Cap'n?' Hitchmogh said, knowingly.

'No, my good man.' Mannino offered a wolfish grin that didn't become him. 'Not a distraction, but an opportunity; an opportunity has presented itself that we cannot pass up, not if we're to move soon, and without turning the streets into a bloody battleground.'

Eyes wide, Hitchmogh glanced back at the gamblers, all of

72

which were again engrossed in their game of not so chance, and across to the unusually fair haired girl now behind the bar. His following smile matched that of Mannino's, and before anything else happened, Hitchmogh flashed a combination of finger movements to a table across the way, before watching Lefey and another girl rise and move to the bar.

'And so it begins,' Hitchmogh said, looking back to his captain.

'And so it begins,' Mannino replied, knocking his port back in one.

Chapter 10 – Cornered

'I told you, I don't know… I can't tell you anything about it,'
Emms said, her eyes red from the tears she'd shed, through fear of
those who'd cornered her, and another.

A long sigh escaped the one called Lefey. 'Can't or won't?
That's what I'm not sure about here. Can't,' she said slowly, 'or
won't?'

Swallowing hard and looking about for help she knew wouldn't
come, Emms shook her head and shrugged. 'I'm sorry,' she said,
breaking down into tears once more. Would they beat her? And
even if she knew and told them, would her man, her Badham, be
forced to beat her again, so as not to lose face in front of his
soldiers. The latter scared her more than the former, although she
found it hard to admit it to herself. The fear of her new love was
exhilarating, or had been. Right now it was just fear, plain and
simple.

'For Squall's sake, lass, I've not even laid a finger on…

'It's them, isn't it?' Lefey said, leaning close and catching Emms'
eye. 'You're scared of them, not us two?'

Emms' eyes flicked past Lefey to the second woman, who was
looking up the street, hands on the knives at her belt. Emms
nodded whilst looking back to Lefey.

Lefey offered a tight smile and leaned back. 'Fair enough, lass, I
get that. These ganger types can be exciting, draw you in and…'
Lefey sighed again. 'You've got caught up with one and now you
can't get away, am I right?'

Emms shook her head, felt a surge of anger and resolve. She
straightened her back and lowered her hands as she replied. 'I don't
want to get away from him,' she said. 'Why is it everyone thinks
they know what I want more…?' Emms stopped as she saw a smile
play across the flat features opposite her.

'Well thank you,' Lefey said, hands now on hips. 'You've finally
told me something I believe.'

'It doesn't mean I know anything about your sailors,' Emms
said quickly, too quickly she realised when Lefey smiled all the
more.

'Go on, off with you,' Lefey said, shocking Emms, and her
partner it seemed, for the other sailor rounded on Lefey.

'What're ye doing?' the woman said, reaching out and pulling on
Lefey's shoulder so she'd look at her. 'Ye heard Master

Hitchmogh, we're to drag her to the captain if needs be.'

Emms' stomach lurched and her eyes widened. Instinct kicked in and she tried to flee. A vice-like grip stopped her, pulling her forcefully round. It was all she could do not to fall to the ground, hands covering her head in anticipation of a thumping pain that never came.

'I said you could go and I meant it,' Lefey said, shrugging off her shipmate. 'There's no need to run off like a bloody child. Now get out of here, I'm done with you.' Lefey released Emms, and the other sailor cursed and turned back to look up the street once more, hands playing with the hilts of her knives.

Emms didn't need telling twice. She turned and walked as quickly as her tired legs would carry her, off down the road and around the first corner, a million thoughts and fears filling her head.

'Well?' Mannino asked Lefey as she entered the rented room.

'She's being followed.' Lefey's eyes flicked to Hitchmogh, who stood in the shadows, pipe glowing now and then.

'Very good, very good.' Mannino nodded, eyes drifting off to the side. They flicked back, piercing as ever. 'Get back to it, Lefey, and keep us posted.'

'Captain,' Lefey said, rocking back at the abruptness of her captain before leaving the room.

'I told her to drag the wench back here,' Hitchmogh said around his pipe's mouthpiece.

'And luckily for you, man, the girl had the sense to use her initiative.'

Hitchmogh grunted.

'Lefey knows what she is doing, you said as much yourself. She is from the Tri Isles, after all.'

'Aye, so am I, remember.' The words were bitter in Hitchmogh's mouth.

'Neither of us could forget.' Mannino leaned back and closed his eyes. 'And if it weren't for that terrible fact, we'd likely have our men back already, using none other than your own heavy handed tactics. No?'

Another grunt from the corner.

Mannino smiled. 'I thought as much. Now leave me be, will you, Master Hitchmogh?'

'If ye wish, Cap'n,' Hitchmogh said, repairing to his own rented room.

'Emms!' The word caught in Quin's throat and his heart thumped. His gut spun and twisted and lurched this way and that. She was more beautiful than his most recent memories allowed.

'Hello, Quinnell,' Emms said, offering a weak smile. 'I've not seen you in the tavern for a couple of days…' She trailed off, her hands working around themselves as she struggled to maintain eye contact.

'Well…' Quin offered a smile of his own, his lips pulled in; sad.

'Well…' Emms returned, along with another, similar smile. Her eyes never stopped scanning the dark streets. They stood before one another, an awkward silence filling the void between, broken only by a dog barking in the distance, then another.

'Are you well?' Quin searched eyes he knew; eyes that strayed left when she answered yes.

Quin frowned. 'I know a lie when I see one, especially on a face I know so well.'

'Don't,' Emms said, trying to move past him. He caught her arm, firm but gentle.

'Tell me?' Quin pleaded, forcing a returned look.

'I can't, not now.'

'Emms.' He turned her towards him. 'You can still trust me, with anything.'

'I know,' she whispered, the sincerest smile yet showing through.

'So tell me. Maybe I can help? That's all I want to be able to do.'

Her eyes flicked about the empty street once more.

'Are you in trouble?' Quin asked, concerned, grip tightening.

'I'm not, no,' she said flatly.

'But someone else is?'

A nod.

'Who? Your brother?'

'No, Quin. Listen, it's nice to see—'

'Oh no you don't, Emms. Not that easily.' He held on to her, stopped her walking away. 'Let me help. Please.'

She looked to him. 'He's gone too far, Quin. I don't know what's happening fully, but it's too much. It won't end well, I know it.' It all came flooding out, her concern, no, her *fear*.

'Who?' Quin asked, confused.

'Badham.'

The name thudded into Quin like an arrow strike. His gut churned in a different way and his face flushed, he could feel it. Emms did too.

'No,' Quin said, in denial, although it was barely more than a whisper, accompanied by tears and slow nodding from Emms.

'I'm sorry,' she said, hands now holding his.

Quin turned to pull away, but she held on tight.

'I didn't plan it. You have to believe that—'

It was Quin's turn to say 'don't', head shaking, eyes filling with tears to match Emms' own. 'Don't.' He pulled harder but she held on with a firmness Quin hadn't felt from her before.

'I'm scared, Quin.' It was genuine and that sobered him a little. 'Scared of what he's done,' she went on, 'scared of what he'll do next, or what they'll do, to him.'

'He's a bloody ganger, Emms,' Quin said, doing his best not to shout. He wiped his wet cheeks with his sleeve. 'What did you expect?'

'Three take me,' he said when she didn't reply. He looked away from her, unable to stomach the sad look she was giving him. 'The Scales can have me,' he muttered.

'Don't say such things!'

'Words, and that's all I ever have, isn't it?' He started as he caught her eyes and the fear behind them. There was a pause. Emms' grip softened and Quin's heartbeat slowed, calmed as she held his gaze.

'What's he done?' he asked quietly.

She offered a slight smile. 'Thank you.'

'What's he done, Emms?'

She took a deep breath before explaining all.

Quin cursed and his eyes closed as he took it all in.

'Oh Emms,' he said, her hands held within his own.

'Perhaps it will pass. Perhaps it'll all blow over, as they say.'

Quin, despite the situation, laughed, and when he opened his eyes, he saw by Emms' expression that she believed what she'd said about as much as he did.

Chapter 11 – Threats

'I'm not jousting,' Amis de Valmont said, head in hands as he sat in the deep-set window seat nestled in the nine-foot thick walls of the chateau. He was looking out over the colourful bell tents and pennants hanging around the arena, erected outside the curtain wall, on the opposite side from the town. 'I don't even have any retainers to assist me. Nor lance or jousting plate.'

'You're no fun, de Valmont.' Flavell lay across her four-poster bed, twirling the curls of her fair hair around her fingers.

'And you're in trouble if I'm found in your room. People will talk.'

'Let them. I don't care. Nothing has happened between us, despite you wanting it to.'

Amis spun on her, eyes wide.

'Come now, de Valmont,' she giggled, 'do you not think they know your desires, from the way you watch me?'

'It's my job to watch you,' he said, eyes back on the goings on outside.

'It is. It's also your job to ensure I have an audience with Croal de Geelan. I haven't seen him since the ball, three days ago.'

'I hear he's busy.'

'I don't need someone with your skills to tell me that, de Valmont.'

'Stop addressing me so. We've travelled for weeks with you calling me Amis. I think that will suffice, *mademoiselle*.'

'We're not on the road now, de Valmont.' Flavell smirked at the huffed sound that came from the window. 'I don't think these people will find it proper, a lady of my standing calling her chaperone by his given name, do you? We're to make a good impression you and I, and I intend that to be the case. You should be glad I don't make you walk several paces behind me.'

'There he is.'

Flavell frowned. 'There's who?'

The Queen's seneschal, Croal de Geelan, of course. Your intended husband, whether he knows it or not.'

Flavell rushed from bed to window. She leaned heavily on Amis' shoulders to peer over him and down into the outer bailey. 'He's even more handsome in his armour.'

The shoulders sagged. Flavell laughed.

After they watched the armoured seneschal mount a blue and

white caparisoned destrier and ride for the colourful camp beyond the curtain walls, Flavell moved away from the window. 'Are you coming?' she asked, without looking back.

'Where?'

'To enter you into tomorrow's tourney before it's too late. I think it's the best way for me to meet him.'

Amis cursed and turned, head shaking. 'You can't be serious?'

'Go easy on him, when you get to him, won't you?'

'Go easy on *him*? I've never tilted in my life!'

'Still,' Flavell said, full lips pursed and green eyes as wide as ever, 'I don't want him injured before I've had a chance to capture his heart.'

Amis sat back against the stone of the window and tapped the back of his head against it. 'You're in a fairy tale, mademoiselle. You truly are.'

Flavell beamed and hopped up and down. 'And the Seneschal d'Easson is my knight in shining armour!'

'And me?'

Flavell laughed. 'You're the evil beast he's to rescue me from.' She left the room before Amis could respond.

'Very clever,' Amis said before rising and dutifully following Flavell from the room.

***

A long shadow cast across Quin in the alley he walked down, followed by another. His polecats dived into the nearest cranny, peeking back out a moment later. Unsure what to do next, Quin froze. All he wanted to do was run, but his legs refused to co-operate. He'd expected something like this since talking to Emms the night before. Since finding out she was... his stomach turned.

'Who is it? What do you want?'

'Well, which is it?' a woman said, from behind.

Arrik hissed from his hiding place and Quin tensed all the more.

'What do you want?' Quin repeated.

'So, me name ain't important, as long as ye know what it is I want?'

Licking dry lips, Quin merely nodded.

'Fair one,' the woman said, stepping closer.

Quin failed to turn, despite wanting to. 'Did Badham send you?'

'Badham?'

79

'Yes.'

'Maybe he did.'

'We talked, Emms and I. There was nothing in it… not anymore.' There was a pause after the words, no reply, and Quin felt a warm breath on the back of his neck, which sent a shudder down to his toes.

'She's a pretty lass is Emms. So, I guess I couldn't blame ye if there were something still going on, Quin.'

Heart thumping in his chest, breaths coming quicker, Quin heard Arrik hiss again, long and throatily this time. Swallowing down bile, he finally managed to find the resolve to turn and face the woman talking to him.

'Ah, nice of you to join us,' she said, smiling.

Quin took an involuntary step back when he saw the stocky woman was flanked by two hard looking men.

'I don't recognise any of you,' Quin managed, frowning.

'And should you? Know everyone on the isles, do you?'

'Well no,' Quin admitted, 'but I know most of those under Badham's command.'

It was the woman's turn to frown. She looked to her companions then back to Quin. 'Command?'

Quin's frown deepened further, brow creasing with it. 'Yes, his soldiers.'

'Soldiers?' One of the flanking men laughed. 'What soldiers?'

Head pulling to the left, Quin now looked side on at the trio, his fear abating but a little. 'Badham's gangers call themselves soldiers. But if you…

'You're not here by his command, are you?'

The woman smiled and shook her head. 'I'm here by another's.'

Quin let his shoulders relax a little, along with the rest of his tense body. 'Whose?' he asked, the relief that they weren't Hillside gangers flooding him to the point where he didn't care who else they could be.

'Captain Mannino's.'

Quin took another step back, eyes wide and mouth open.

'I'm Lefey,' the woman said, holding out her hand, 'and our dear captain needs your help.'

Mouth snapping shut, Quin failed to take the hand, but managed to find the courage to turn and run.

Arrik and Guse hopped about with their mouths open, teeth bared and tails puffed up as their 'dad' was tackled to the ground by Lefey.

'That wasn't a request,' she said into Quin's ear, her weight pressing on him. 'We've been waiting since last night to corner you, and the captain's sick of waiting, so I'd do as I say, Quin. And if you want to see Emms safe from those fuckers she's knocking about with like a doe-eyed girl, you'll bloody well grow a set of 'morl's usuals and help us. Now, do we have an accord, Master Pallister?'

Cheek pressed against the hard-packed earth of the street, Quin offered his best attempt at a nod. And when Lefey climbed off him and pulled him to his feet, polecats bouncing about, hissing as they went, Quin voiced his accord. After all, the thought of freeing Emms from that bastard, Badham, was all they'd needed to say, although a very real fear made up the rest.

***

A floorboard creaked. The sound was slight, ever so slight, but Mannino heard it. There was no point in opening his eyes, for he knew full well there was no light. The wooden shutters on the windows blocked out any that might come from the street lamps outside, and he'd snuffed out the beeswax candles in his room hours ago. Of course, the creak could have been the building settling, as buildings do, but...

Mannino surged up and threw himself off the bed. He struck the floor hard and grunted, before rolling away from the mahogany legs of the grand bed.

I should have stayed somewhere less ostentatious, he managed to think, before his roll crashed him into two more legs, albeit human ones.

A man cursed and those legs moved, stumbled. A grunt followed the stumble. Mannino picked up on it and lashed out with his fist. He grunted himself when his punch connected with something hard.

Heart racing, Mannino scrambled across the floor, clattering into some piece of furniture and sending it crashing over. Panic took him. It was rare, but not impossible. Was it the gangers? Were they on to him and his men? He didn't have time to think any more as his ears picked up the scuffing of someone crawling towards him at speed.

A louder curse this time – Altolnan in nature – as Mannino's kicking feet met his unknown assailant.

81

Before anything else happened, a shout erupted from the room outside his. A heartbeat later and a strip of feint light stretched out from beneath the door, enough to allow Mannino's eyes to use it for reference, to use the sudden ambient light to realise where it was he was lying, and kicking. He grinned.

The large, shadowy figure fell back as Mannino grabbed and hurled the chamber pot at whoever it was. Cursing, the man rushed for the shuttered window as more voices came from the room beyond.

'Hurry!' Mannino shouted, surging to his feet and giving chase.

The door burst open and light flooded the room as the cloaked intruder literally threw himself through the wooden shutters and out of the first story opening.

Hitchmogh, two sailors at his back, and Mannino, looked out of the splintered opening and down to the street below. All four gaped as they saw the intruder, who'd landed amongst the remnants of the wooden shutters, climb to his feet and make off down the road, towards the docks, seemingly unhurt.

'Tough bastard that,' one of the sailors said, the other nodding.

'You hurt?' Hitchmogh asked Mannino, whilst motioning for the other two to leave. They swiftly obeyed.

'No, man. No.' Mannino moved back to and sat on the edge of his bed, heart racing, hands shaking in the shadows. 'It was luck though, Master Hitchmogh. Luck and nothing more.'

'What happened?' Hitchmogh retrieved his pipe from his pouch, packed and lit it.

'A floorboard happened, and if it hadn't, I'd likely be lying on this bed, soaked through with my own blood.'

Hitchmogh glanced at the window again. 'He moved quick, and quiet, for a big man.'

'I thought him one of the Hillside gangers at first,' Mannino said, but Hitchmogh was shaking his head as his captain spoke.

'Whereas I'd say assassin.'

Mannino looked to Hitchmogh and nodded, face ashen. 'It shook me up,' Mannino admitted, 'and I don't mind saying it, man.'

'Well, it bloody would.' Hitchmogh took a long draw on his pipe and began to pace, leaving a white cloud in his wake. 'Who'd want you dead?'

Mannino laughed, the sound bitter. 'The shorter list would be of those who don't want me dead, and you know it.'

'Aye, I do, but it sounds shit when people say such things.' Hitchmogh grinned, despite Mannino's scowl. 'And anyway, it'd likely be a list of who wants *us* dead, not just you.'

Mannino merely nodded at that.

Hitchmogh stopped pacing. He looked to Mannino, face falling. 'What if they know we're here? What if I've not done enough to hide myself?'

Looking to his old friend, Mannino offered another laugh, albeit a single shoulder-bobbing, breathy one. 'If that was so, Master Hitchmogh, it wouldn't be assassins in the night we'd have to worry about, but the Adjunct's Guard... the whole bloody lot of them.'

All Hitchmogh could do to that was nod his head and draw on his pipe.

'The whole bloody lot of them,' Mannino repeated, glancing at the broken shutters and breezy hole in the wall.

Chapter 12 – Tilt and Parry

Dawn silhouetted the great Scales in the bay as gulls cried and hawkers did the same. Ignoring it all, Mannino took a deep breath and watched an approaching sailor, whilst more dotted the street, looking out for their captain's safety after the previous night's events.

'Quin's in,' Lefey said, walking up to the two men in the doorway.

'Did you give him a choice?' Mannino asked, a single eyebrow raised.

Lefey shrugged. 'I wasn't aware he had one, Captain.'

Hitchmogh grinned.

'Are you well, Captain?' Lefey asked, her eyes searching the man for signs of injury. 'I heard what—'

'He's fine, Lefey. Now crack on will ye, lass.'

'Of course, Master Hitchmogh,' she said, turning and hurrying up the steep street.

Turning to Hitchmogh, Mannino raised both eyebrows. 'I can answer for myself, man.'

'Of course, Cap'n, but we don't have time, see? We need to move and move tonight. Our lads have been holed up long enough as it is. Two days already, or near as damn it and I feel bad that we came up with nothing yesterday.'

Lips pursed, Mannino looked back up the alley in time to see Lefey disappear around a corner. 'Oh, I wouldn't say nothing, man, but moving on…

'Did Master Spendley get my message?'

'Yes, Cap'n,' Hitchmogh said, stepping out from the doorway and looking left then right. 'He sent Parry to meet the others.'

'Did I do right there?'

Hitchmogh made a humming sound before answering. 'It's been a good while since Parry's set foot off *Sessio*, Cap'n, but I think the man can handle it.'

'I know he can handle it, Master Hitchmogh, it's whether he knows when to stop handling it is what worries me. We can't step in entirely here, you and I. Not here.'

'I know,' Hitchmogh said, biting his lip afterwards. Without another word, he walked off to the left and through a narrow gap in the white buildings. Taking a look around, Mannino did the same.

***

Clods of earth flicked into the warm summer air as two powerful destriers charged one another. Each beast thumped along on its own side of a colourful wooden barrier stretching across the arena. Their riders leaned into the charge, lances lowering and straining jolted muscles as they closed on one another; one caparisoned in the blue and white chevrons of Easson, the other in nought but yellow. Shields held close, and tight, the moment of impact came. Croal de Geelan lifted his modern frog-mouthed helm a little to avoid splinters from the shattering lance striking his shield, whilst his opponent remained still, eyes on Croal through the slits of an ageing sugarloaf helm.

The clattering explosion of wood on wood and wood on steel was drowned out by the cheer from both sides of the tourney ground. Women gasped as others shrieked in excitement and glee. Men roared and cursed and, some, wept as their bets were made or lost. The loved Seneschal d'Easson hung from the side of his high-backed saddle as his men ran out to catch hold of and calm the snorting beast he rode. His opponent, the rider who'd almost unhorsed him, slowed his mount to a proud trot, bringing the bay stallion around to prance in front of Eudes de Geelan's box. Lowering his gifted lance to the marquis' herald, the yellow knight received a blue and white striped victory ring, which slid down the remainder of his shattered lance to sit above his steel-clad fist. Amis de Valmont punched the air to a renewed vocal frenzy of the crowd. Horns blew, drums pounded and the distinctive whine of a hurdy-gurdy played along with the chants. And Amis buzzed from it all, his breath loud against the borrowed steel before his face. He turned his mount and scanned the marquis' box for Flavell. When he found her, he cursed within his facial enclosure, the single harsh word louder than the cacophony of his heavy breaths. Flavell wasn't in the stand. She was rushing to Croal's squire- and page-swarmed side.

'Well, my lady,' Amis said for no one but himself, his mount sidestepping beneath him through excitement, 'you have what you and my master wanted, it seems. I doubt the good seneschal will escape you now.' Grunting a laugh at that, resigned as he was to his position in the whole affair, Amis punched the air once more with his broken lance and relished the cheers of the crowd.

Dozens of white campaign tents scattered the vale like breakwater atop a choppy sea. Closer to the centre, white canvas gave way to a large pavilion striped in the Marquess of Suttel's green and black, white harts emblazoned on pennants of the same. Surrounding the pavilion stood bell tents of various sizes and colours, as well as the staked and rotting bodies of half a dozen men in the marquess' own colours.

'This isn't good,' Sav said, coming into view of the camped army, eyes flitting between tents and men, alive and dead.

'Oh, I don't know,' Gleave pulled up beside him, Pecker clucking away in his lap, 'there's usually money to be made at such places.' Gleave patted his dice belt and grinned. A prod from his other side stole that grin.

'Follow me in,' Correia said, encouraging her mount forward.

Gleave did as he was told, as did the others.

As the group walked their horses down the gentle slope to the edge of the camp, a picket of archers fanned out, arrows casually knocked on the strings of their tall war bows. Correia held her empty hands out wide. The others did the same.

'Spymaster Burr,' she announced. 'I'm here to speak with Bratby. Move aside.'

'I love it when she talks like that,' Sav said, louder than everyone thought necessary, his confidence once again high after the words he and Correia had shared at their hillock camp. One of Correia's hands lowered all but one finger. Sav laughed, others smiled, including most of the archers facing them.

Before those archers could make a decision on whether to let the group through or not, despite their smiles and grunts of mirth at Correia and Sav, a sergeant-at-arms in Suttel colours strode from between two tents, shield on back, hand on sheathed sword. He waved his free hand to shoo the archers away and beckoned for Correia to move forward.

'Greetings, milady,' he said, southern accent strong. 'The Earl of Bratby isn't available, but his son will see you, if you have time to wait on him?'

Correia stopped her horse before the sergeant and scanned the camp, saying nothing, nostrils flaring. The pause was awkward, with everyone bar Correia chewing lips or looking anywhere but the now nervous sergeant.

With a simple nod, Correia rode forward, allowing her horse's reins to be taken by the man.

'Where is the marquess?' Correia asked.

The sergeant shrugged. 'Not for me to say, milady. None of us are sure, bar his son and his officers, of course.'

'And the army's purpose?' she asked, noticing carpenters sawing, nailing and fixing together wood in the ominous shapes of siege engine components.

Another shrug.

'Not your place, eh?' she said, unamused.

'That's right, milady.'

The rest of the walk through camp passed in silence, apart from the usual camp noises; dogs barked, men shouted and others laughed. Metal clanged as field forges were worked by smithy teams whilst horses whinnied and pack animals lowed and bleated. A cockerel crowed and Pecker attempted a reply. Sav laughed. Gleave glared.

On top of the sounds were the smells. The group pulled various faces as they passed butchered animals, open latrines and the general sweat and stink of hundreds of men and camp followers.

'Here we go, milady,' the sergeant said, leading the group to a bell tent striped red and black.

'Whose tent is this?' Correia asked, brow furrowed.

'Sir Thomas Gaskin's, milady. He's a day or so away, so won't be needing it yet. I knew it to be free, so thought you might want it whilst you wait on Sir Allon, the Earl's son.' He grinned at Correia as she dropped from her saddle. The others copied her movement.

'And I'm expected to wait here for how long, that I need a tent?'

Fal and Sav winced, expecting the sergeant's shrug to be followed by a clout, or at least a sharp word, but Correia sighed and nodded.

'Very well, Sergeant. Have me brought to Sir Allon as soon as he's willing, I have pressing news for him since his father is absent.' The sergeant inclined his head and made off at a quickened pace.

'Nice tent,' Gleave said, checking the seams after placing Pecker down in a corner, the bird sleeping soundly.

'Yes, it is,' Correia agreed, pulling Gleave round to face her. 'And I want no trouble from you. Do you understand me this time?' Gleave's smile faded. He swallowed hard and nodded once.

'I mean it,' Correia went on. 'Nothing like last time we were in someone else's camp. I know what Mearson, Tom and you did.'

Gleave sucked in a breath and rubbed his mangled ear whilst his narrowed eyes looked anywhere but Correia's. She let him go with a shove and he almost stumbled, what with his injured leg. 'Go see what you can find out before settling and changing your dressings. You too, Errolas.' She pointed into the camp and the two disappeared.

'What did they do?' Sav asked. The look he received may not have answered the question, but it was enough to silence him.

'Shall we make a fire?' Starks said, turning away from Correia and Sav.

'Aye, let's,' Fal agreed, rushing off with Starks to source firewood.

'Think I'll tie up and tend the horses,' Sav said, since he'd been handed everyone's reins bar Correia's. She handed him hers and he moved away.

Taking a deep breath, Correia took one more look about, at the tents and the curious faces looking back, and ducked into the dark, striped tent to find space to think.

***

Flavell laughed and leaned in to Croal, the formal bench they sat upon doing little to deter their closeness.

'I think I threw up a little in my mouth,' Amis said, watching from his standing position by the window, always by a window.

'I might have done the same,' the Earl of Bratby said.

Amis glanced sidelong at the Altolnan Earl, a smile creeping across his face. 'It's a pleasure to meet you properly, Messire Bratby.'

'Please, Amis, call me Giles. I insist. We're both prisoners here, although yours is of a different internment to mine.'

Amis chuckled and nodded. 'I can't argue that, messire.'

Giles rolled his eyes. 'You chevaliers struggle to drop formalities, don't you?'

Amis shrugged. 'I can't speak for all chevaliers, Giles,' he glanced sideways again and smiled, Giles doing the same, 'but I have to agree that I do indeed find it hard. I'm no hedge knight, but grow up with your betters reminding you that they're your betters, day in, day out, despite my family having a certain standing

88

of their own, and you start to believe it.'

'I never said I wasn't your better, lad.'

There was an awkward pause until Giles laughed and Amis followed suit.

'Look at her,' Amis said a moment later, nodding for Giles to do just that. 'My master sends her here to attempt a coupling with this powerful family and she takes to it like a—'

'Pig to shit?'

Amis laughed. 'Yes, although I was going to say a duck to water.'

'You care for her?'

The question struck Amis, but he recovered well. 'In a way, messire. In a way.'

'You'd bed her if you could? She *is* beautiful; does something to the loins, like a kick, but a pleasant one if there is such a thing.'

Amis' eyes were wide as he turned to the powerful man next to him.

Giles held up both hands. 'I meant no offence. Man-talk is all.'

Nodding, Amis turned back to the now kissing couple. *I* like *these Altolnans*, Amis admitted.

'Didn't take them long, did it?'

Amis shook his head. 'No.'

'And all because you slotted Croal in the tourney.'

'My first.'

Giles' barked laugh drew looks from the canoodling couple, as well as from the normally unseen servants dotted about the room. 'Truly?' Giles said, turning on Amis.

'She wanted me to tilt, so I did. I had to borrow men to assist, and lances. I borrowed them from the very man I beat. I had to borrow some armour too, since mine is for guarding her on the road, not charging in for an intended lance strike.'

Giles nodded. 'Nasty business, jousting, at times. The armour thickens each year, but so too do the lances.' He grunted a laugh. 'Lost my youngest son to it two years past.' Giles flinched at the hand which appeared on his arm.

'I'm sorry for your loss, messire.'

'Don't be,' Giles said, taking a deep breath and releasing it slowly, before smiling at Amis, who removed his hand and offered a sympathetic smile in return.

'He loved it,' Giles went on. 'He died doing what he loved. People say that, have always said that and I never quite understood.

Imagine this though, Amis. Imagine never being able to do as you please, with anything. Then imagine dying. You wouldn't know about it of course, you'd be dead and buried, unless you believe in better places and all that, as most do. But, how dull, no? My lad, he did everything he wanted. I wasn't a pushover, mind, and nor is my wife, but we allowed him to pursue all sorts, from archery – despite being of noble birth – to falconry, and finally tourney fighting and jousting. He was wicked with a longsword.' Giles took Amis' shoulder and squeezed it tight, a light in his eyes. 'You should have seen how he handled such a weapon, Amis. Using every part of it to score points and win!' Giles' enthusiasm fell away. 'Jousting, however…' He turned back to the room, eyes set on nothing in particular. Amis listened, intently. 'Well, jousting wasn't his thing. You won your first tilt, Amis, and my son lost his, along with his life. Oh, how he loved it though. The training and preparation, the wearing of the Suttel colours on his shield and surcoat and mount's trapper. The cheering and the excitement. He was as happy as I'd ever seen him, before I placed that helm, very similar to the sugarloaf you wore, upon his head.' Giles smiled. 'My last look upon my son was a happy one, Amis.' There was a long pause, with nought but the sound of giggling and whispers coming from Flavell and Croal in the centre of the room. Amis said nothing, awaiting Giles' continued tale. Eventually the man went on. 'I didn't allow his helmet to be removed after his death.'

'I can understand that, messire,' Amis said, after a while.

Giles nodded and smiled. 'I reckon you could, lad. I reckon you could.' With another deep breath, Giles turned and slapped Amis on the arm. 'Come, let us leave these love birds to their lips and tongues and find some mead to quaff, instead of this Samorl forsaken wine they keep thrusting upon us, eh?'

Amis hesitated as Giles took off.

'Come, de Valmont,' Giles said without turning. 'That's an order from one of your betters. The lass is fine with Croal, he's a bloody pussycat compared to most around here.' With a barked laugh, Giles left the room. After a few moments, eyes locked on Flavell, who was locked on Croal, Amis followed.

Chapter 13 – Spaulders

The tent flap opened, letting in a burst of camp noise; dogs, horses and hundreds of people talking and shouting, all accompanied by a strong smell of wood smoke.

Sav looked up, back down and back up as Gleave limped into the tent.

'King's teeth, Gleave,' Sav said, 'where'd you get plate spaulders?'

Gleave's armoured shoulders scraped together as he shrugged.

'They're expensive,' Starks said, looking up in awe at the polished strips of steel.

'Found 'em. No big deal.' Gleave took a seat on the cot opposite the others, groaning as he lowered himself.

Correia, who was crouched nearest to Gleave and threading a leather thong through her left boot, was clearly unimpressed. 'Found them where, Gleave?' she asked, without looking up from her work.

'Lying about they were.'

'Lying about,' Correia repeated. 'Plate spaulders, lying about.' She closed her eyes and drew in a long, steady breath. 'Lying about, where?'

'In a posh looking tent…'

Sav and Starks laughed. Correia pushed her tongue into her left cheek and glared at Gleave.

'Not a campaign tent,' he went on, with no apparent care for self-preservation. 'I mean a real posh, colourful thing. Even nicer than this one,' he added, looking about the canvas walls. 'Was even darker inside. Funny that, ain't it? Brightly coloured on the outside, dark on the inside. Worked in my favour though.'

Fal spoke for the first time, rolling over to look across the tent at Gleave and the spaulders.

'What were you doing in a tent like that?'

Gleave shook his head as he picked at his dirt-filled nails. 'Wrong question, Fal.'

Fal screwed up his face, as did Starks. Correia continued to glare at Gleave whilst Sav laughed.

'Fal,' Sav said, 'you need to ask 'who' was he doing in a tent like that, not 'what'. Right, Gleave?'

Gleave grinned and Correia stood, having tied her boot's thong into a knot. She cringed and left the tent, calling behind her, 'I'd rather not know anymore.'

Starks looked even more impressed now. 'Who was she, Gleave?'

'Damned if I know.' Gleave brushed his spaulders off carefully as he spoke. 'But I got more out of it than I was hoping for.' He grinned again then stood with a wince. 'Better go and green these.' He tapped his new armour. 'As nice and shiny as they are, they ain't gonna do us any good if they draw attention to us in Sirreta—'

'Or in this camp,' Fal interrupted. 'Should the owner see them.'

Gleave grinned again before checking on his sleeping hen. Satisfied all was well with her, he turned and left the tent. Starks stood to follow.

'No you don't, lad.' Fal shook his head. 'You'll end up on a knight's sword, along with Gleave, if he's seen prancing about in those.'

'Typical,' Starks said under his breath.

'Not quiet enough, that.' Fal smiled as he lay back down. 'Now get some rest, we've no idea when we're moving on. Might be sooner rather than later.'

Starks scowled. 'Gleave's in the best mood since we left Wesson, what with Pecker and his new armour. All I wanted was to make the most of it and build bridges with him.'

'The bridges are fine and can wait if they're not,' Fal said, nodding towards the empty bunk.

'Yes, Sergeant.' Starks dropped onto it and folded his arms, eyes locked on the spindles branching out from the centre pole of the tent.

Sav laughed as he crossed his feet over one way, then the other. 'You'll find some plate of your own one day, Starks. I bet. Only don't be too eager, as it'll most likely be after an ugly fight and you'll have to scrape the previous owner out of it before you can put it on.'

'Wouldn't bother me none.' Starks continued to stare at the conical, canvas ceiling.

Fal and Sav glanced at one another knowingly.

Correia walked through the camp as darkness took its hold. She'd worked her way up and now circled the command tents, trying to catch a glimpse of an officer or better yet, the marquess' son and heir, Sir Allon. Cloak tight about her, the hood of her woollen mantle pulled up, she skirted an occupied camp fire and passed through shadows, deftly avoiding guy ropes and camp rubbish scattered here and there. She passed several bell tents striped in the colours of Suttel, and others worked in the house colours of other minor lords and knights.

This young lord has pulled in an impressive number without his father present, Correia thought, looking down the hill, past the colourful, if not dulled by night, tents and on to the shanty-town-looking spread of white campaign tents beyond. The latter looked like ghosts rising from the darkness, creeping up to her position as if assaulting the staunch, colourfully striped defenders stood tall about her.

Taking in the scent of wood smoke, animals and sweaty bodies, Correia turned and continued up, weaving in and out of closely pitched canvas and avoiding the true walkways of the camp. She changed direction when she heard raised voices. A bellowing baritone of a man was trying to shout someone down. She made for the source of the sound.

'It is folly,' the hidden man said, 'as I have said all along. Your father—'

'Isn't here, my lord. Now please, I want your council on what's to come, not on decisions I have already made.'

Correia found the back of the large tent the voices came from. Its black and green panelled walls illuminated from within, but not enough to silhouette those inside. The second voice sounded young, but firm.

Giles Bratby's son, surely? Correia thought, leaning in to the sloping side of the large double-belled tent as much as she dared without touching it.

A deep grunt preceded a voiced, yet reluctant Correia noticed, apology from the baritone within, before another, third man spoke.

'I believe we have a visitor, my lords.'

Correia froze. All within the tent went quiet.

Turning to move away, Correia became aware of the moving of armoured men. Multiple boots on the ground, maille links against plate, and weapons being drawn. She ran.

Straining her eyes in the dark and attempting to listen to her surrounds over the blood rushing in her ears, Correia leapt over ropes and sleeping men alike, drawing shouts of alarm. She knew she had power, as King's Spymaster, but it gave her little defence when spying on a noble, especially on his own land.

'Watchya!' a soldier shouted, cock in hand. Correia cursed as her leg became wet whilst pushing past him. He shouted at her some more as she disappeared into the darkness between camp fires.

A hue and cry went up.

'Intruder in camp!'

'Intruder!'

'To arms to arms!'

Shit! Correia sped up as much as she dared, skidding round one corner as her hobnailed boots failed on the flattened grass. Managing to stay on her feet somehow, she sprinted down an open path, towards half-dressed men climbing out of tents, weapons in the hands of some, jugs and pots in others, their weary faces not expecting the passing, hooded figure.

'Down the hill!' Correia shouted with confidence, pointing as she ran. 'He's making off down the fucking hill, for 'morl's sake!'

Men looked from her to the campaign tents spread out below them. She wasn't surprised when more than one climbed back into their tents. The rest took off down the hill, swords, axes and jugs held aloft, shouting for others to take up the chase.

Gods below, I hope Gleave's not down there, up to no good… Correia changed tack and turned across the hill rather than down, employing the same trick wherever she encountered armed men or scared camp women and children. Before long, torch wielding riders were thumping past, searching for a man who didn't exist and calling for the pickets to turn inward.

Some poor bastard's going to get mistaken for a spy at this rate, Correia thought as she slowed her pace, closing in on the tent she'd been given for the night.

A horn sounded from down the hill, followed by another. A mage somewhere launched a bright light into the sky, followed shortly after by another, and Correia mused that the mage was likely the one that'd known she was outside Sir Allon's command tent. The mage's lights descended slowly into the surrounding vale, illuminating tents, trees, men and horses alike. What Correia witnessed was like the chaos that ensues when one disturbed an ant nest.

Heaving in the cool night air, Correia stopped outside her tent, before ducking inside. She never thought why her pathfinders weren't outside watching the madness; the unasked question was answered once she entered the tent.

'Ah, Spymaster Burr,' the sergeant who had led them through camp said. The following grin was wide. Correia did her best to calm her breathing, but it was clear to all she'd been running. Her pathfinders looked on with a mix of intrigue and amusement, their expressions dancing between the two.

'Sir Allon would like to see you now, it seems,' the sergeant said, inclining his head as he moved past her, exiting the tent. 'If you would follow me,' he added from outside, once it was apparent Correia hadn't followed.

She took a deep breath and released a long sigh, all eyes on her, including Gleave's, who it seemed had managed to green his new plate and return in the time it'd taken Correia to unintentionally rouse the camp.

'*Now* who's the naughty one?' Gleave said, grinning uncontrollably.

Running her tongue over dry teeth, Correia couldn't muster a response. Instead, she pointed to Fal and Sav and beckoned them to follow, before moving back outside.

'Great,' Sav cursed, trying to pick up the coins on the bunk he sat beside.

'Ah ah,' Gleave said, moving to scoop them up first, 'you forfeit if you leave a dice game.'

'Second thoughts,' came Correia's voice from beyond the red and black, 'Gleave, you're with me. Sav, you stay here.'

Gleave cursed, Sav laughed and so did Starks. Fal failed to hide his smirk as he and a reluctant Gleave pushed through the tent flap, the latter cursing his healing leg, despite all he'd been up to since their arrival in camp.

Chapter 14 – Soldier, soldier

The night was chilly, despite the heat of the day before. The thin linen shirt Lefey wore did little to keep out the cold, but it was all she wore up top, bar the under-binding. It was all she was used to wearing. Looking back, she saw the group of men at her back and smiled inwardly. When her shipmates were with her, it was all she needed, to keep a warmth inside, and that was why it was so damned important to rescue the three idiots who'd got themselves taken. She reached into her pouch and brought forth the ransom note she'd originally been given. Unfolding it, she took in the local scrawl. It wasn't as if she could read, but she didn't need to be able to read to understand the scribbled drawings that made up the unofficial scripture that was Hillside slang.

'We're lucky those they took didn't fight back,' Lefey said, to no one in particular.

'I would've,' Kareem said.

'You'd be pit roasted,' Lefey replied, eyes on the pictures before her.

'What's that mean?'

'It's pretty self-explanatory, ye fool. The Hillside gangers are known for it.'

'Go on.' Kareem again, his boarding axes held loosely, confidently.

Sighing, Lefey stowed the note away and turned on the big sailor, making cutting gestures with her hands. 'They chop off your arms and legs and throw you in a shallow grave, before dousing you with whatever flammable substance they can find, usually fish-oil, and torching you there and then. Men, women… kids.'

Screwing his nose up, Kareem merely shrugged. 'Seen worse.'

Shaking her head, Lefey turned back to the building they were watching. 'Well let's hope we don't tonight, eh?'

'Oh, I don't know,' Kareem went on, 'depends on whether—'

Kareem dropped dead, a crossbow bolt jutting from his throat, arterial blood arcing over Lefey's back as he and his axes thumped and clattered to the cobbles.

'Shit!' one of the other sailors shouted, bursting into motion a heartbeat later, scimitar in hand. He sprinted past Lefey, towards the building opposite, his ebony skin and matching attire making him hard to see as he sprinted from shadow to shadow. Lefey wasted no time in following him, and heard the feet of the others following behind. There was no time to spare a thought for Kareem. His hot blood on her back and neck, she ran on, hoping the second group fared better. She didn't even know how they'd been spotted, although giving it what little thought she could, she wasn't surprised.

This is Hillside, Lefey thought, whilst running. *This is the ganger's territory and we're slap bang in the middle of it...*

A bolt clattered off the wall beside her as she reached the building they were targeting. 'That bloody Quin better not have lied to us,' Lefey managed, whilst gulping in the night air.

'Fuckers strut around like they're soldiers,' she continued, putting her booted foot through the door they'd reached, before jumping aside in case anything came out to meet her.

'They won't think that after this,' one of the other sailors said as he passed her, ducking in through the door as another crossbow bolt cracked off the wall besides them. The shot was followed by a blood curdling cry. The cry was followed by a body falling from a nearby roof. Lefey looked round at the noise to see two more sailors dropping lithely from said roof, both of them her sister mates. They made for her position.

With the flash of a smile, Lefey followed the ebony-skinned blade master through the door. 'Leave some for me, Parry,' she said, as the sounds of grunts, curses and metal on metal came from within.

The scene was pure chaos. Tables turned, stools and benches scattered; men lay slumped over both whilst others grappled and more slashed and hacked at the too few sailors storming their lair. There was no sign of any hostages, no sign of the crewmen that had been taken.

'Where are ye, lads?' Lefey said through gritted teeth whilst kicking out the knee of a ganger who ran at her from another room. Someone screamed from off to the side as Lefey stabbed at the dropped man, her rapier cutting into the man's bare chest with a meaty squelch, pulling skin, flesh and blood free as she twisted and withdrew the weapon. Not stopping to see if the man was dead, Lefey moved on, close on the heels of Parry and her other shipmate ahead, who was now barrelling through into the far room.

A clatter behind marked the arrival of her sister mates. Lefey pushed on, through into the next room, where three gangers were brandishing falchions and axes. They jeered and held their arms out wide, taunting and egging her and her shipmates on. Their hubris was palpable.

'You fucking dare come here?' one of them shouted, an axe in each hand, much like Kareem had held. 'You fucking come to my house, to my hill. I kill and burn you bitches. I cut and roast you fucking pigs! And I enjoy it whilst you scream.'

'Well, come and try it,' Parry offered. 'But not before you tell us where our boys are.' His deep voice was calm, very calm. That seemed to cause the gangers to falter a little. 'You so-called soldiers tell us that and I'll kill you quick, not slow—'

'Parry!' Lefey snapped. *Squall take me, that's not the way to get answers...* Before her thoughts moved on, a gobbet of spit struck Parry's face. Lefey and her companions closed their eyes and sighed as one. Before anything else happened, fresh shouting from the front of the building drew the sailors' attentions. Lefey motioned for everyone to go back through, which they did, weapons leading whilst she stayed to watch Parry's back.

The bolstering sound of more gangers had caused the three in the room to smile, but for a heartbeat. After that, *Sessio's* blade master was amongst them... as was his scimitar.

Lefey grimaced as she saw limbs fall. She pulled yet more faces and choked back a mouthful of sick, despite all she'd seen and done in her life, as the back of a ganger's skull came away with a sodden thwack, dropping the lifeless man to the floor where his brain eased out of his half-skull.

The sound of Parry finishing the axe-wielding man was enough for Lefey to want to be done with it all, for her to want to return to *Sessio* and be under way once again.

They're bullies all, she told herself. *Not soldiers, but bullies with bulk and weapons and numbers. Think of the roasting pits and what they do to folk around here.* It hardly helped as she heard Parry's final wet slap of blade through flesh.

The first room they'd entered, that Lefey now walked back into, wasn't much better than the one she'd left. Her ship brothers and sisters stood there, checking bodies, blood spatter covering most of them, and the room. One of the women proceeded to smash the teeth from a dead ganger, surprised, she was muttering, at how white they were.

'This was a damned waste,' Lefey said, looking about the place.

'It sends a message,' Parry said from behind, startling Lefey.

'Saying what?' one of the other men said. 'That we want a

bloody war? Any more of this and the Adjunct's Guard will be marching in, then we're all for the scales.'

Two of the others nodded, before leaving the building.

'He's right,' Lefey said over her shoulder to Parry.

'I don't rightly care,' the gore spattered, black clad man said, picking his way across the destroyed room and making his way outside to join the others.

'This wasn't worth losing Kareem over,' Lefey said to the two remaining sailors, both of whom nodded their agreement.

'Nope,' the one with a handful of bloody teeth said, 'but saving the three idiots who got themselves caught is, and you know it, Lefey. And Kareem knew it too.'

Nodding, Lefey ushered the two women out. 'I do,' she said to their backs, 'because it's the fact we'd come for each other no matter what that keeps us all going.'

She followed the two nodding heads out into the dark street.

'What now?' Parry said, from the shadows by Lefey's side.

'Now, Parry, we go see that Quin lad again. We go see him blooded up as we are and we let him know it's his last chance to do right by us.'

'The captain won't let me kill him, even if we don't.'

'Squall's shit, Parry,' one of the female sailors said, 'you do know you creep even us out when you talk like that, don't you?'

A white smile was the only response Parry gave, before he skulked off into the night, the rest of them attempting to keep up, Kareem's body slung over Lefey's shoulder.

***

Badham strode into the room, picked up a clay jug and threw it against the wall, shards scattering every which way.

Emms jumped at the outburst, to which Badham merely grunted before dropping down onto the pile of furs she was sat on.

'What is it?' Emms managed, eyes trying to find her lover's own.

Lying back against the piles of fur, Badham grunted again, but said nothing.

'Sweets?' Emms dared, but Badham's raised hand quietened her. She knew better than to push him, despite their relatively short time together, and so let him be. He would turn to her when he was ready, and tell her what troubled him; like she didn't already know, or suspect.

That's when he's himself, when he releases... That's when I'm with the true Badham, the man no one else sees.

After what seemed like an age, with Emms closing on her love, hands caressing his bared chest, arms and shoulders, his eyes met hers.

Badham smiled and Emms smiled back.

'You with me now, sweets?'

His smile broadened and he rolled over and on to her, pinning her to the furs by her wrists. Emms giggled, despite the pain. *He doesn't know how strong he is,* she told herself, the thought of his power taking her breath away. He kissed her. Fully, passionately... forcefully.

'Ouch!' Emms pulled her head away, the tang of blood in her mouth.

Releasing a sigh, Badham let go of her wrists and rolled away. Sitting up, he rested his thick arms on his knees.

'I'm sorry, sweets,' Emms said, sitting up behind him and gripping his shoulders. 'You're a little too rough sometimes.'

He grunted, before turning and winking at her. 'You like it, I know that much.'

'Sometimes,' Emms said, winking back. 'You're so tense though,' she went on, pressing her fingers into his knotted neck.

'There's a lot on. I lost soldiers tonight.'

She swallowed hard, her mind's eye flicking back to the sailor called Lefey.

'How?'

Silence, bar a dog that had started to bark a way off. *There's always a bloody dog barking somewhere,* she thought, kneading Badham's shoulders.

'Sweets?' she said, when he didn't reply.

'The bastard sailors I took. The ones that drew blades on me and tried to take my money in the tavern.'

'Oh yes,' Emms said, feigning vague recognition. *The ones you were scamming.*

'Well...' He grunted and rubbed at his face, before letting Emms push his arms back down into a relaxed position again.

'You don't have to tell me.'

A few moments passed whilst she continued to massage his shoulders. Eventually, Badham went on.

'Someone's talked, Emms.' She froze inside, hesitated but for a moment, before continuing to work his muscles.

'How do you know that?'

'It's my job to know that. My troops do my bidding because I know what's what. I start to slip up there and I'm as likely to be roasted in the pit as the next little bastard who puts a foot wrong on Hillside. Life's a war, Emms. If you don't keep your soldiers on their toes and keep your ear to the ground, you'll lose. I'm not one to lose.'

Swallowing hard, Emms did her best to maintain the motion her hands and fingers were making, despite her mind flashing images of the sailor, Lefey, and Quin and his pleading attempts for her to leave Badham after she told him all about it; the fact that she'd told her ex-lover everything now scared her half to death, both for her sake and his.

'Oh, that wouldn't happen now, would it, sweets? You're practically king here.' She kissed the side of his neck. 'And I'm your queen,' she said, wanting now to change the subject.

'Have you seen Quinnell lately, Emms?'

Her kissing stopped.

'He might have been in the tavern,' she said. 'I don't recall.'

'I see.' He slowly nodded his shaved head.

'Why'd you ask, sweets?'

'No reason,' Badham said, before changing tack. 'You know I couldn't let them three sailors be, that night, in the tavern. You now that, don't you?'

'Of course,' Emms said, back to kissing his neck and shoulders.

'Good. I wouldn't want you to think bad of me—'

'Course I don't!' She turned his head to face hers. 'How could I?'

With a smile and another wink, Badham held her gaze a moment, a moment that dragged out into an uncomfortable one.

'That's good to know,' he said, pecking her on the lips before pushing her away and climbing to his feet. 'I needed to know you're with me,' he said, without looking at her. Emms stared at his broad back as he went on. 'I know it wouldn't have come from you, but I think someone told Quin about those sailors and I think he told their crew.'

Fear gripped Emms. A fear that tore at her insides. Memories of her and Quin spun through her mind and it was all she could do not to physically shake at the thought of what Badham would do should he truly believe what he was saying.

'Quin and I are in the past, sweets. You know that. We have

history, yes, but that don't mean he knows your secrets, certainly not through me, if that's what you're implying?' She didn't know where the courage came from, but it showed through in those words. She stood and spun Badham to face her.

'Look at me. Look at me and tell me you think otherwise.' She held his gaze. After another tense moment, Badham smiled.

'Course not, lass. How could I, eh?'

She smiled back, reached up onto her toes and kissed him long and hard.

'You always know how to make me feel better,' Badham said, reaching round, squeezing her backside and kissing her once more.

'Now,' he said, stepping back, 'I've places to go and people to see.' With a look that drained all her confidence that had appeared mere moments before, Badham turned and left the room.

Oh Quin... It was all Emms could do not to cry.

Chapter 15 – Pax

'Will it work?' Parry asked, holding Lefey's stare.

'We'll see, won't we.'

'How do we know he'll come, himself?' Parry seemed unconvinced.

'Oh, he'll come,' Quin said, wringing his hands together without realising it. His nerves were shredded, especially when the ebony skinned killer turned on him.

'What is your profession again, boy?'

'Shipwright's apprentice,' Quin said, straightening his back.

Rolling his bottom lip, Parry nodded at that. 'Not bad,' he admitted. 'Perhaps you could have a place on *Sessio* should the captain agree to it. It'd be wise for us to have a shipwright on board, even an apprentice like yourself.'

'On board?' Quin frowned.

Lefey released a short, sharp laugh and turned back to the dark street in front of them.

'Well,' Parry went on, 'if you're right and he does come, this Badham, it'll be because he thinks you ratted on him, to us, remember? How did you think you'd continue with your little life, eh? You'd be no better off than those on the scales, methinks.'

Eyes wide, Quin's chest felt tight as he thought it through.

Parry smiled and nodded. 'Think on that some more, whilst we wait on this Badham fellow.' He turned back to the street.

Quin glanced behind and received a nod and a wink from one of the two sailors there, both of whom held large windlass crossbows in their arms. Quin looked back front, in time to hear, rather than see, a commotion coming up the street.

'How'd you know where he lives?' a deep voice said. 'Your tart tell you?'

Quin grimaced, recognising the voice and knowing of whom the man spoke.

'That's Croxon,' Quin whispered between Lefey and Parry. 'He's one of Badham's officers, so to speak.'

'…not,' someone else said.

'And that's Stone, another officer,' Quin added, as Stone continued.

'The lass is still sweet on Quin, ain't that right Badham?'

A grunt and a laugh followed as the gangers' footsteps grew louder.

There was a loud curse.

'What were that for, ye prick? It were a joke.'

'Well I didn't find it funny. Anymore and you'll be for the roasting pit, same as that little kid with the big mouth we turned over last week.'

Lefey turned on Quin. 'Badham?' she mouthed.

A cold grip reached in and took Quin's heart, but he nodded all the same, and watched as Lefey motioned to the two sailors behind. He heard feint footsteps move away from him.

'What we gonna do?' Croxon again.

'Drag the shite out,' Badham said, 'after showing him around his own gaff, if you get me?'

Several men laughed and Parry and Lefey shared a worried look. They turned to Quin again, but he shrugged to the unasked question of how many.

'This it?' Croxon asked.

'Yep,' Badham replied.

'Who's knocking?'

'Since you asked, Pester, ye skinny shit,' Badham said, 'you can.'

'There ain't no way I'm busting through that door on my own.'

'Pester has a point,' Croxon said, followed by a grunted laugh. 'He's likely to break bones trying.'

'I'll fucking do it,' Badham said. 'This shit's personal anyway.'

Quin heard a growl and the splintering of wood.

'Wakey wakey, Quinnell!' Stone shouted, to the vocal amusement of Croxon and Pester. There was no other sound from Badham as the man stormed inside, his officers following.

'We wait for them to come out,' Parry said. Quin merely nodded, shuffling from foot to foot. These sailors were an unknown to him, but the reputation of their captain wasn't. He both feared what would happen to Badham, a lad he'd known his whole life, and feared what would happen to himself if such things didn't happen to Badham. He'd thought he would feel pleased when such a moment came, but now, looking at the wicked scimitar *Sessio's* blade master gripped, and the blood on the man's face and clothes, he wasn't so sure.

More voices came up the street. Lefey looked to Quin, who shrugged.

'Passers-by?'

'At this hour?' Lefey said. 'And rowdy as they are?'

Again, Quin shrugged as the voices neared.

'They're already in,' they heard one say. 'Hurry up lads, it's time for some fun.'

Parry's shoulders bobbed in amusement. 'Soldiers my black arse,' he said, running a finger across the front curve of his blade. 'They're armed and mob handed bullies with nowt better to do that terrorise honest folk.'

'Hit 'em now?' Lefey whispered to Parry, ignoring his mutterings. Quin only just heard her. 'Before the others come back out?'

Parry sucked his teeth and nodded. 'Now!' he said, kicking a small crate out into the street.

'Wha—' a voice was cut short, followed by a grunt and shouts of anger and panic both. The crossbowmen would already be winding back their weapon's cords on the roof, spanning-mechanisms clicking as they ratcheted the powerful draw weights back, ready for another long bolt.

Lefey and Parry rushed from the darkness into the lamplight beyond, as a man reached the crate, eyes caught by it but for a heartbeat; the short distraction, combined with the loss of two of his companions to crossbow bolts, was enough to transform the ganger into easy prey for Parry, whose scimitar bit into the man's side so deep the blade master had to forcefully work it side to side to pull it back out the dropping, screaming man, torso all but cleaved in two, guts and more spilling to the floor.

Quin turned in the alleyway and threw up. He failed to see what happened next, but it sounded quick as more men cried out, cursed and grunted, before all fell silent in the street.

Wiping at his mouth, Quin stood straight and heard shouting coming from the house.

'Here they come,' Lefey said, from around the corner. 'Be ready.'

'Always am,' Parry said casually, before whistling long and loud.

Quin jumped and nearly wet himself as several boots pounded the ground behind him. He spun in time to be knocked to the side, colliding painfully with the white wall as half a dozen sailors ran past, weapons drawn and faces grim.

Heart thumping and breaths coming quick, Quin found the courage to move to the alley mouth and peer around the corner, in time to see Badham's officers pile out of his home and into the waiting sailors. He knew Captain Mannino wanted Badham alive, but failed to see how that would be possible as the two sides clashed. His ears took in the clanging of metal on metal, the thud of hits and the wet slaps of blades biting into unprotected flesh.

Another crossbow bolt flew in, although to see it required luck, the speed it travelled. Alas, it missed its target, breaking on the white wall with an echoing crack that followed.

Two sailors fell quickly, injured but not dead, as far as Quin could make out. He saw Stone knock one of them down, a small mace in one hand and a buckler in the other, which he used to parry several blows from Lefey, who came at him fast and hard after seeing her shipmates fall.

Quin was reluctantly impressed as he saw Pester, a lad he'd quite liked a few years ago, before he was recruited by Badham, fending off a rapid assault of arcing slashes by Parry. The defence didn't hold for long and the bile returned to Quin's throat as he saw Parry's wide blade split the lad's skull from crown to neck. The pieces fell towards each shoulder as the skinny body dropped. Parry moved on, careless for the horror he caused.

Croxon and Stone fought well together, Stone's buckler clanging again and again as he used it to thwart incoming blows from cutlasses and falchions, although the defensive aid was starting to look battered, dents appearing with each blow. As Quin looked on, the large man cursed and threw the plate sized shield to the side. Stone's hand looked like someone had taken a hammer to it, all blood and pulp. Despite the painful wound, the man fought on, taking down another sailor, this time for good.

Parry stepped in, around a feint from Lefey. He dropped low as he did so and took Croxon's leading leg off, a clean cut through the man's shin. A shrill scream that didn't match Croxon's size followed and he crumpled to the floor, dropping his daggers to paw at his bleeding stub of a lower leg.

'Pax!' Badham shouted, appearing in the doorway. 'I'm here. Pax!'

Quin looked on, incredulous as the sailors stopped their attack, the lot of them backing off a pace or two, their fallen comrades pulled back to safety in the middle of the street, whilst Badham and Stone dragged a roaring Croxon into Quin's house.

'What're you doing?' Quin ran out into the lamplight of the street, all eyes, bar those badly injured, now on him.

'Bastard!' Badham shouted from the doorway, coming for Quin before sense checked his move.

'I'm sorry, lad,' Lefey said, lowering her cutlass, 'but the man

106

called pax. He's the captain's to deal with now.'

Quin's eyes widened. 'You're taking him to Captain Mannino?'

Lefey shook her head. 'No, the captain's coming here.'

Quin felt sick once more and ran into the alley, succumbing to the feeling.

He's in there, Captain,' Lefey said a short while later, eyes on Quin's damaged door. She'd been assured by Quin that there was no other way out for Badham, or his remaining officers.

Lips pursed, the impeccably dressed Mannino nodded.

'What ye thinking, Cap'n?' Hitchmogh said, cutlass in one hand, an ornate, dwarven flintlock pistol in the other. Mannino said nothing. There was a long, awkward pause before Parry walked up and spoke.

'The lads are carrying the injured back to *Sessio*, Captain.'

'Thank you, Master Parry,' Mannino said, without turning. 'That'll be all for now.'

Eyes wide, Lefey looked to Hitchmogh as Parry disappeared down the alleyway, following the other sailors. Hitchmogh shrugged, before looking back to the white building.

'Sun'll be up soon,' Hitchmogh said, craning his neck to look past the roof to the lightening sky above. Stars flickered here and there, but most were fading into the hazy blue that was taking over the sky.

'And?' Mannino rubbed his chin with his free hand – cutlass held as it were in the other.

'Just sayin', Cap'n. There may be more gangers on the street now folk be waking. Won't be soon until they swarm down here, like rats from that fat cat of ours.'

'You have a point there, man,' Mannino said, 'so let's get on with business, shall we?' Eyes locked on the building, Mannino strode towards the splintered door, which managed to cling on to the top hinge. Those remaining few in the street moved with him. Free hand held high, all but Hitchmogh halted as he and Mannino pushed through the door and into the darkness beyond.

Eyes and mouth dry from a night without sleep or a drink, Quin made to say something, but Lefey raised her blooded hand to stop him.

'He knows what he's doing.' She didn't turn from the building.

'I bloody well hope so,' Quin said.

'As do I,' one of the crossbowmen said from across the way,

'for the majority of us already headed back to the bloody ship.'

'Like I said,' Lefey said, voice stern, 'the captain knows what he's doing. They both do.'

'And as I'm saying now,' the crossbowman replied, hefting his crossbow, 'for the sake of Joncausks, Boxall and Tahir, I hope he does too.'

Chapter 16 – Maps, plans and dogs

Sir Allon Bratby's tent was finer than most houses in Wesson, Fal mused, as he and Gleave followed Correia into the grand space. He looked to the thick fur-covered oak bed. Bed. Not cot. He looked to the lavishly decorated camp chairs and the large table, covered as it were in bowls of food, goblets of wine and a small map to one side.

Always pictured giant maps in such a tent, with wooden pieces to be strategically positioned, Fal thought, disappointed.

'Lady Burr.' A young man dressed in a velvet tunic and matching green stalked cap inclined his head. He came forward and offered his hand. Correia took it and he raised hers to his lips. Fal noted the bastard-sword at the man's side, the scabbard inlaid with silver, or so it seemed; despite several clay oil lamps and candles in glass lanterns, such detail was hard to make out. The weapon reminded Fal of Will Morton, the Duke of Yewdale, and Fal's audience with King Barrison regarding Wesson's plague, all of which seemed like a lifetime ago.

'Lord…?' Correia retrieved her hand politely and awaited an answer.

'This is the marquess' son, Sir Allon Bratby,' a baritone voice said from the shadows; the man stepped forth, grey beard leading as he jutted his chin towards the young Bratby.

Fal saw a flash of anger pass across Sir Allon's face, before taking in the brute of a man who'd spoken last. A bastard-sword dressed this man's side too, although it looked small against the thick legs of the noble. He wasn't so much tall as wide. Fal mused that the man could probably wrestle a horse to the ground without breaking a sweat. He was as well dressed as Sir Allon, although he seemed incapable of eating without spilling half of it down his beard and tunic.

'And you are?' Correia asked, turning to the man.

He barked a laugh. 'You don't remember, lass? King's Spymaster and you don't remember the likes of me?'

Gleave grunted something under his breath and Fal struggled not to smile, despite missing the remark.

'It seems I don't.' Correia offered her hand to the man, who wiped his on his tunic before taking Correia's and pressing his thick lips to it, eyes never leaving hers. She grinned and they both laughed. Fal looked to Gleave, but his eyes were locked on the

109

man.

'I should have recognised your voice when...' Correia trailed off. An awkward pause followed.

'When you were listening in, from back there,' Sir Allon said, jerking his thumb to the tent wall. The sound of the wild goose chase outside continued.

Fal noticed Gleave tighten his grip on both sword and axe, so he did the same on his falchion.

'My lords,' Correia started, but Sir Allon smiled and held up a hand to stop her. 'No apologies or explanations, please. It is I who should apologise for leaving you in that poor tent, waiting for so long. It was not my idea. And please, Sir Allon is good enough.'

Correia smiled and nodded her thanks, before nodding to the man beside her. 'The tent was the baron's idea?' she asked Sir Allon. The baron released a rumbling laugh that trailed off to a throaty growl.

'You know him well, it seems.' Allon smiled.

'Oh, I don't know about that, Sir Allon.' The baron nudged Correia. 'She could know me far better if she wanted.' He laughed again. Correia smiled, but was the only one.

Good job Sav's not here after all, Fal thought.

'It's a long story for another time, Sir Allon,' Correia said, the man beside her nodding.

'Very well,' Allon allowed, 'there are matters we should discuss anyway, you and I.'

Correia bowed her head and moved to the table.

'Like why you have an Orismaran dog to heal?'

Fal gritted his teeth and stole a glance Gleave's way. Gleave's cheek rose, hinting at a smile, which calmed Fal's ire.

'Orismaran dogs are savage things, Sir Allon. If I had one of those in here, we'd all know about it. Mind you, I have seen Fal angered before...'

The baritone baron laughed and took a seat.

'Actually, Sir Allon, Sergeant Falchion received honours from the King himself, not so long ago,' Correia added, when Allon's eyes remained on Fal, who stared ahead dutifully.

'Did he now? Well, what pleases King Barrison pleases me. I would have thought,' Allon said, eyes moving down to Fal's side, 'someone of such standing would carry a sword to match.'

'Well there's the thing,' Correia said, stepping in to break Allon's line of sight and so stealing his gaze, 'I've witnessed my

Orismaran dog in combat with that common blade and, after seeing what I saw, I wouldn't wish any other sword in his capable hands; defending my back, as he so often does.'

Sir Allon sniffed and looked away, the conversation seemingly surpassing his interest.

'Wine?' he offered, looking back to Correia after an awkward pause punctuated by the heavy breathing of the baron, and the ceaseless noise of the roused camp.

'Yes, thank you,' she said, taking a goblet offered to her by a servant neither Fal nor Gleave had noticed enter. It seemed there was more than one opening into the large tent.

'A toast?' Baron Baritone said, snatching up a freshly filled goblet and sloshing a good portion of it on the floor; more on his hand and sleeve.

'Already, Harold? We haven't discussed anything yet.' Allon frowned.

'We'll toast to discussions to come,' the baron, or Harold it seemed, roared, before quaffing the remaining wine in one and slamming the goblet down. 'Fill it, damn you,' he shouted into a dark corner. The same servant as before rushed forth and did as told.

This is going to be a long night, Fal thought.

As Correia spoke to Allon Bratby and Baron Baritone, Fal and Gleave had to stand, watch and listen. Formalities were followed by questions, which were followed by answers that didn't satisfy Correia who asked more questions. Answers led to disagreements and near full-on arguments at times, one of which started when Correia learnt that the staked men out front were Giles Bratby's own men, the ones who'd been with him when he was captured by his Sirretan counterpart, Eudes de Geelan. The matter was not resolved, nor were several others, much to Correia's obvious annoyance. Food was consumed by the three, again whilst Fal and Gleave watched on, mouths watering and lips being licked. Wine was consumed, although not as much by Correia, who Fal noticed was sipping rather than gulping or quaffing like Baron Baritone. Fal mused that, despite the baron's name being mentioned throughout the night, he couldn't think of the crass man as anything else.

'So, you'll wait here? For my word?' Correia said, elbows on the pretty but 'inaccurate' map the Cartographers Guild had apparently sold Sir Allon for a small fortune.

111

A heavy sigh was drowned out by the sudden grating snore of the baron, who'd slumped back on his precariously balancing chair.

'Is that an agreement, Sir Allon?' Correia asked again, eyebrows and goblet raised.

The young man nodded, took his stalked cap off and threw it down on the table from where he stood, and wavered. He raised his own goblet and drained it.

'I'll take that as a yes,' Correia said, doing the same for the first time that night, or wee hours of the morning, as was now the case.

Setting the empty goblet down with a dull thud, the marquess' son wiped his red lips before leaning heavily on the table.

'The army will remain here,' he confirmed, eyes locked on Correia's, 'although it'll cost, in coin and morale.'

Correia nodded at that. 'And...' she prompted, circling her hand for him to go on.

Oh, how she plays him. Fal fought the smile that attempted to push through his exhaustion.

'I remain unsure.'

'You don't have to be sure, Sir Allon,' Correia said, standing so she was level with Allon's stare. '*I'm* sure and that should be enough for you, because if I'm sure, your King is sure. As I've said countless times tonight, there's something pushing at us, something silencing Sirreta and pushing on *us*. I don't know what it is, so no one does. That means we could have that push break through—'

'I know, I know,' Allon said, exasperated. He dropped into the closest chair before looking back at the woman.

'Send the scouts.'

'I will,' he said, defeated. 'They'll ride tomorrow, for Stonebridge and...'

'And?'

'And Royce's border with Sirreta.' He dropped his head into his hands.

'Very good,' Correia said, moving to stand by Fal and Gleave.

'If Royce retaliates,' Allon said, looking back up. 'If he misreads my father's men scouting his earldom?'

'He won't,' Correia insisted, and Fal marvelled at the re-assuring tone that eased the tension from the powerful young man. 'Hugh Torquill may well be aware of the happenings on his border by now, but I am not.' Correia moved over to the man, crouched before him. 'You sit an army here, Sir Allon. A large army. It's best that Royce sees and knows your scouts, and therefore your goodly intentions. If his own men scout your father's lands, your lands, Sir Allon, and see a camped army with no known reason as to why?' She let the question hang.

Allon nodded and sighed once more. 'It is settled,' he said, with a flat smile. 'I will have the borders scouted east to west and the army ready to move on either, with messengers sent to Royce, too. But should you fail to negotiate my father's release, Lady Burr. Should you fail to return by the agreed date—'

'Then you best come and get me and your father out, eh?' She smiled at that, as did he.

'Agreed.'

'Don't underestimate anything your scouts discover or Royce tells you via messenger. For me to receive no news from my Sirretan contacts, for my network to have gone dark...' She looked worried, or rather let it show, for the first time since Wesson. Fal's stomach turned at that.

'I know,' Allon said, his understanding clear.

'Whatever might be coming, I fear it has bested, or is besting, Sirreta and her armies. And if that is the case...'

A chill ran through the tent, standing hairs on hands and necks, and shudders throughout. A servant had entered through the main opening, but the feeling it brought was not lost on those present.

'I'll hold, my lady.' Allon stood. 'Whatever comes, I'll hold.'

'You do that, my lord Bratby. You send riders and you do that. If to the west, Royce will come, if to the north, the central barons if not Adlestrop, Yewdale or Rowberry, you have my word and you have my mark on those orders.' She pointed to wax sealed papers she'd written, signed and sealed earlier that night, the marks of the young lord and baron upon them also. 'Send riders with these and I promise you those who can will come to your aid.'

'Go,' Allon said. 'Go and ride the forest trail for my father. Warn the Twin Inns and tell them to send word should they need aid. I can't hold the line there, if this threat comes, but I can assist them with a fighting retreat back here where we can and will hold.'

Correia frowned. 'You wouldn't fall back to Bratby Castle? Who would defend her should forces skirt this army?'

Allon grinned. 'My mother commands the garrison.'

Correia's smile was uncontrollable and she inclined her head before replying. 'I shall say no more on that matter, for I dare say the castle is in better hands than were your father home.' Both shared a laugh. Fal and Gleave shared a curious look.

'Off with you, Lady Burr, and your two dogs. I'm for my bed before the cock calls.'

Charmed, Fal thought. Gleave grunted.

'And Harold?' Correia asked, looking to the gaping, groaning mouth of the sleeping baron.

'Bah, leave him.' Allon waved a hand. 'He'll crawl out of his own accord when he wakes. Now be gone.' Another wave of the hand before the young lord clicked fingers for his servants, who rushed forth to undress him.

'Away we go,' Correia said, turning and pushing through Fal and Gleave. 'Heel, boys.'

A grunt from Fal this time, a smirk from Gleave and a laugh from the already half naked Sir Allon Bratby, who turned to watch the three leave, the remainder of his clothes falling to the floor as he swayed on the spot.

Chapter 17 – Me, thee and The Three

'Are we in agreement?' Mannino asked, reclined as he was in the large chair he'd insisted on sitting in.

With a snarl followed by a gobbet of spit that landed off to the side, near a dying Croxon, Badham nodded. 'Yep, we have a deal.'

Lips pursed, Mannino nodded. 'Splendid, man.' He looked to Hitchmogh, whose vacant stare seemed to hold Stone in check. The big ganger stood swaying like a tree in a gale, as he'd been since he'd tried to make a move on Mannino soon after the captain had entered the room.

Looking back to Badham, Mannino stood, stepped forward and offered the gang master his hand. Snarling once more, Badham stood and shook the offered hand, albeit briefly.

'You'll help him now?' Badham nodded to Croxon, who looked pale and close to death, bloody wrappings around his severed leg.

'Of course,' Mannino said, slapping Hitchmogh on the back. The grizzled old sailor jerked and blinked several times. At the same time, Stone gasped and looked around as if he'd appeared in a strange place. Upon seeing Mannino and Hitchmogh, he reached for his weapon, only to be held back by one of Badham's thick arms.

'Not now, Stone,' Badham said, with a single shake of his head. Stone made to speak, but Badham cut him off with a short sharp hiss. The man scowled but held his tongue.

'I'd like you to help the man on the ground, Master Hitchmogh,' Mannino said, eyes remaining on Badham, who glared back.

'Squall's tits,' Hitchmogh breathed, rubbing hard at his pock marked face. 'We're pushing it. Ye know that, don't ye, Cap'n?'

'I do, but an accord has been made and I am not about to break it at first step.'

Sighing hard, Hitchmogh nodded. 'On your, mine and the bloody crew's head be it.'

Answering the captain back in such a way, especially in front of others, was rare indeed for the first mate, but Mannino knew the cause and let it slide. He could hardly blame the man.

Moving to Croxon, who was now unconscious, Hitchmogh flashed Badham and a scowling Stone a stare that, despite their size over the small man, knocked them both back a step.

'Off to work we go,' Hitchmogh muttered before dropping to

his knees, wincing as he went. 'Let's give this a shot, eh?' he continued, to no one but himself it seemed. The other three lucid men in the room watched on as the first mate rocked back and forth, massaging the bloody rags about Croxon's stump-ended lower leg; an unpleasant tingling ran through all present and it built until they could taste sick in their mouths.

Licking his gums, Badham looked from Hitchmogh to Mannino, and when he saw the bitter expression on the renowned captain's face, he relaxed a little, clearly understanding that the effects of Hitchmogh's workings were felt by all.

Hitchmogh cursed, slapped the side of his head, which left a feint, bloody hand print, and threw-up to the side of Croxon, who began to groan.

Stone stepped forward, but Badham clamped a hand on the man, drawing his gaze before shaking his head.

'I don't like this, Cap'n,' Hitchmogh said, eyes back on the bound wound and his massaging hands.

'Needs doing, man.'

'He's an ugly bastard this one,' Hitchmogh went on, through gritted teeth. 'Inside as well as…' He threw up again and let go of the bandages, before climbing with a groan to his feet. When he turned to the three men staring at him, he looked drawn. Drawn and exhausted. 'I'm done,' he said, turning and leaving the room without another word; leaving Mannino alone with Badham and his officers.

'Well,' Mannino said, 'that's that, gentlemen. Now it's your turn. My men, if you please, and all this can be done with and we can all be on our way.'

Stone checked Croxon's wound, after unwrapping it, and Badham's eyes widened as Stone whistled at the healed flesh.

'You, Captain,' Badham said, turning back to Mannino, 'have a deal.'

***

Eyes wide, breaths and heartbeat quickened, Antreas, youngest brother of The Three, looked about his dark room, objects highlighted by the ambient light from the chamber beyond his own. His eyes were drawn to that light, through the lilac silk drapes that separated his bedchamber from that of his concubine's. Creases marred the otherwise smooth skin of his forehead and he

116

chewed his bottom lip before swinging his long legs out of the bed. Head tilted to the side, white hair hanging down to feather the sheets by his side, he took a deep breath and stood, arms wide.

Shadows moved as men swept in. They approached with deft skill, the contents of their hands closing on the ancient elf. As they reached Antreas he stepped and turned in a well-versed series of movements, passing close to but not touching those who moved about him. When he was done, stood by lilac silk, the shadows were whole once more, his servants out of sight.

Dressed in layers of white velvet and crumpled linen, Antreas strode into his concubine's chamber, dismissing the human men who were attending her, carnally.

'What is it, my love?' Rina said, pulling a gown about her black shoulders.

Lips working silently, Antreas shrugged before answering. 'I'm not sure, but it felt... dirty.'

'Well you look immaculate, darling.' Rina slid across the sheets and ran her fingers across his clothing and up to his pale skin, before resting entangled in his hair.

'I always do.' Antreas' pink eyes roamed Rina's room, his lips working once more. 'Where is Achiad?' he said at last, gaze lingering on thick velvet covering an entire wall.

'Behind the drapes.' Rina's honesty was refreshing, fearless, for a human.

'Come out, Brother,' Antreas said. 'I have news, I think.'

'What news?' Achiad's voice came from behind the drapes, a tone of boredom poorly hidden.

'I'm not sure,' Antreas admitted. 'We, all three, need to be together for me to make sense of it.'

'And it can't wait?'

A pale hand slapped away a dark one and Rina knew better than to persist, so repaired to her gargantuan bed where she crawled to the centre and lay sprawled amongst the voluminous covers and discarded clothes. Her brown eyes closed as the two brothers continued, Antreas now in the chamber's doorway, Achiad from behind the mass of vertical velvet.

'No, it cannot wait.' Antreas became weary and he swayed on the spot, moving the back of his right hand to his forehead. 'I tire. Attend me now.'

The drapes moved aside with a hiss, continuing on to reveal the open arch and balcony beyond. 'Lovely dawn,' Achiad remarked, his naked back to the room, skin matching the patterned velvet like the camouflaging of so many insects.

'I don't care!'

Achiad spun around, eyes narrow. 'Do not—'

'Apologies, Brother. I had a dream.' Antreas made sure his voice softened in a way he knew his older sibling could not resist. *If only it worked on Andarna as well.*

Pink eyes relaxed. 'A dream... of what, or whom?'

A deep breath. 'I shall tell you when we're all together.'

Achiad rolled his eyes and turned back to take in the view of the distant scales, or rather the flickering lights of the towns the scales suspended over the bay, one higher than the other.

'Are you listening?' Antreas practically glided back into the room and around the oval bed, to close on his naked sibling. He shuddered at the sight as Achiad's shimmering skin smoothed from the velvet mimicry to its usual pallid paleness.

'I will listen when you offer me something more specific. I was busy, you know?'

'With my concubine, yes, I'm fully aware. But I had a dream, Brother. Must I wake Andarna myself, or will you join me? Clothed, preferably.'

Releasing a weary sigh, Achiad turned to face. 'Stop eyeing my scars,' he snapped, pushing past Antreas and heading for coarse woollen clothes that lay scatted about the marble floor. He whipped them up and threw them on to reveal a confusion of colours and styles far removed from any current fashion in Brisance.

I hadn't noticed the scars, truth be told. Are they new? He'd considered asking aloud, but assumed he'd just forgotten the puckered criss-crossing marring his brother's chest.

Antreas moved to the outer door of the chamber. 'Let us see what state we find Andarna in, shall we?'

'Indeed.' Achiad followed in Antreas' footsteps, who halted suddenly.

'What now?'

'I tire of her,' Antreas whispered without turning.

'Rina? How so? I found her quite pleasing.'

'Her skin.'

'What of it? It is rare to see skin so dark, at least this far north.'

Screwing his face up, Antreas bobbed his head from side to side before going on. 'It is, but not as rare as white. *Pure* white.'

'Doesn't exist, Brother,' Achiad said, making to move past. 'Whether your new-found fascination with the neutrals recognises that or not. Our own skin is as pale as one could imagine, no?'

Taking one last look at his now sleeping concubine, Antreas merely grunted and left the room, hurrying to catch Achiad's long strides. 'It may not exist,' he said, once outside the earshot of Rina, 'but I do not much care for such trivial things as doesn't and can't and impossible, do I?'

'No. No you do not.'

'Exactly.' They walked down a curving, sloping passageway that revealed porcelain busts of both male and female elf, human and dwarf forms. Antreas stopped. 'So, I shall make one.'

Achiad stopped too, turning to look back up at Antreas from several paces further down the passageway. He held his scarred hands out, awaiting an explanation as to how that would happen.

'I'll have some porcelain skin made for Rina.' Beaming at the thought, grin stretched and wicked, Antreas continued on his way, a spring in his step, following the shaking head of his sighing sibling.

'I'd rather not know,' Achiad admitted, before changing tack. 'Now tell me more of this dream.'

'Can it not wait until we reach Andarna?'

'No, I tire of waiting, it's all we ever do.'

They turned a corner and two sentinels stood to attention, eyes diverted.

'Very well.' Antreas continued to follow Achiad down another corridor. 'I'll tell you who featured in it, but not what he was doing or where he was; I'll leave that surprise until we are all together.'

'It was a 'he', in your dream?'

'It was a 'he', yes, but not any old 'he'.'

Achiad's eyes widened as he looked back. 'You mean *Him*?'

A nod. 'Yes, I do mean Him.' Antreas shuddered. 'It was that beast of a human I dreamt of, Achiad, that shit of a mage. I dreamt of Master Hitchmogh, boil his rotten bones.'

Chapter 18 – Time to go

'We're leaving,' Correia said as she entered the tent, Fal and Gleave behind her.

'About time.' Sav sat up and stretched. 'This camp stinks.'

'Most do,' Gleave offered, dropping to a cot.

'I said we're leaving,' Correia repeated, glaring at Gleave. He groaned and pulled himself back to his feet using Starks' arm to do so.

'There's a spy in camp,' Starks said, crouching to pack his things. Correia sighed, Sav laughed and Gleave cursed.

'Starks, are you serious?'

'Why wouldn't I be, Gleave?' he said, looking over to the man. 'What did you think the hue and cry during the night was all about?' He shook his head with exasperation and returned to packing.

Gleave rubbed his face hard and forced another curse through his fingers. 'Squall's salty min—'

'Gleave!' Correia rounded on him, mouth open and eyes hard.

'Too much?' he asked, right cheek raised in amusement.

'Aye, mate,' Fal said, putting his weapons down and tending to his own belongings, 'a little.'

'Why's he so shitty with me again?' Starks asked without turning, thumb jerking Gleave's way.

'You don't get it, do you lad?' Gleave filled his saddle bags with increased gusto as Starks looked about the tent, brow creased.

'It was me, Starks.' Correia held her hands out to the sides and turned full circle. 'I'm the spy.'

Starks' furrowed brow was accompanied by an open mouth and wrinkled nose. 'Eh?' Eyes widened. 'Oh, you were spying on the Earl's son?'

Correia nodded, Sav laughed, again, and Gleave barked one of his own.

'She was—' Fal started, until Starks cut in.

'Then who've they got in the stocks, down the hill?'

All eyes turned to Starks. Correia swallowed hard.

'Explain,' she said, crouching before Starks, who shrugged.

'All I heard was they'd caught the spy, and had him trussed up in the stocks, awaiting questioning. They've sent a rider for a witchunter. Apparently, there's a camp of them nearby.'

'And we all know what that means,' Sav said, packing quickly, despite the fact everyone else had stopped to stare at Starks.

'How'd you find all this out?' Gleave asked, voice gruff as ever through lack of sleep.

'Never mind that.' Fal moved to the tent flap and peered outside. 'Where's Errolas?' he said, silhouetted as he was by the rising sun.

'Oh, shit!' Sav dropped his things and turned to Fal, then Correia, fingers dancing by his sides.

'When did you last see him?' Correia's question was open to anyone. All four shook heads.

'When we entered camp?' Gleave offered. 'You sent him and me off separately, didn't you, Correia, before we even had chance to re-dress our legs'

'And he's not been back since?' Correia shouted, glaring at them all.

No one said a word.

'Gleave, Sav, Fal, go get your friend out of the stocks. Starks, you're with me, where I can keep an eye on you.' Starks frowned and Gleave tutted. The other two armed themselves.

'Where're we going?' Starks said to Correia, as the others left the tent.

'Nowhere, Starks. We're packing, now get on with it, you've a lot to do.' Correia dropped onto her cot and closed her eyes. 'Another one of you gets captured and I'm leaving the idiot behind. Goes for you too, Starks.' Correia peeked at him through one half-opened eye.

Wrinkled nose matched wrinkled brow. 'But this is the first time one of us has been captured?'

'And the last, Starks. Now shut up and pack up. And quietly, I have a headache.'

From behind Gleave's empty cot and unpacked saddlebags, Pecker crowed, terribly, and Correia cursed poetically.

Wood smoke drifted across the muddy ground, filling the nostrils of the three men who walked – one limped – through it, hands on sheathed weapons. A dog barked off to the side, behind a row of campaign tents, another further up the hill. Jeering met the trio, the sound coming from beyond an off-white canvas corner. Jaws firm, they walked into a scene of pushing soldiers, some waving, many drinking.

'We have the bastard!' a scrawny lad shouted, nothing more

than braes and a ridiculously short linen shirt, all held together by a failing belt with a dagger slid through it.

'What bastard?' Gleave demanded, the grimace he'd worn with the pace they'd kept through the camp making him appear scarier than ever.

The lad shrank back and faltered entirely when he saw the spiral tattoos of Fal's face. He mumbled something.

'Eh? Speak up!' Gleave reached out, grasped filthy linen and dragged the lad along whilst approaching the back of the crowd.

'Elf, sir.'

'Elf, is it?' Gleave stopped and held the lad firm, Fal and Sav on each shoulder. 'And what's the name of the thick fuck who's in charge of the stocks?'

The lad's bottom lip quivered. 'Dunno,' was all he managed.

'Right, lads,' Gleave said, looking to the crowd whilst shoving the lad away; a stumble turned into a run, which was followed by two fingers held high.

'Looks like we're after a thick fuck called Dunno,' Gleave said. Fal and Sav shook their heads at that, although their smirks gave away their amusement.

'We go in hard and aggressive,' Gleave said, hands leaving his sword and axe, to hover away from his waist, chest puffed up to match the bravado he took on and showed off. Fal and Sav did the same, although not to the degree Gleave took it.

'Out of my way, fuckwits!' Gleave's deep voice moved men as might a city tavern doorman. Sav and Fal had to use elbows to keep up, despite their friend's injury, and Fal receiving more than a couple of bigoted remarks when folk saw who shoved them.

Before they knew it, they were through the throng of men and out the other side, curses following their forced path. All three faltered when they saw Errolas, legs and arms locked in thick wooden stocks, bruised face and shorn hair gazing back at them through swollen eyes. Three big men stood about him.

'Oh shit… Errolas,' Fal managed, before his stomach reached for his throat and his knuckles paled, fingers of one hand wringing his falchion's hilt, the others bunching to make a fist.

'Who's the thick fuck called Dunno?'

'I thought he was joking,' Fal said to Sav.

'I think he is. He's that bloody confident.'

Fal looked about the angry faces. Their fun had been interrupted; a whole army's fun.

Several had laughed at Gleave's words, laughs that died away when Gleave glared at the crowd.

'Well?' Gleave said, looking about. 'Who's the prick in charge here?'

'Lords above,' Sav muttered, before taking a deep breath and trying to look as confident as Gleave. Fal did the same.

'I am.' One of the three men stood by Errolas stepped forward, hand on belted war-hammer.

'You're this thick fuck Dunno I hear tell of?' Gleave asked.

Several in the crowd laughed, others crowed and shouted unintelligible things. Most of the bored men didn't care in what form the entertainment came, as long as something took their minds from their boredom; boredom bred dangerous men and the pathfinders knew it.

'Watch your mouth,' Dunno said, taking a step towards Gleave.

'You a sergeant, Dunno?' Gleave asked, not slowing his verbal and psychological assault one bit. He took a step forward of his own, leg paining him but ignored, Fal knew, hands away from his weapons, confidence radiating like heat-haze from a fire.

'I'm one of Sir Allon's ventinars. Who the fuck are you?'

Gleave spat. 'An fucking archer, typical...'

Sav frowned.

'...I'm Sergeant Gleave Picton of the King's Pathfinders, and he's one of ours.' Gleave pointed a grubby finger at Errolas. The crowd quietened.

'Ah,' Dunno said, grinning despite the situation. 'The Spymaster's pups. Well, this one lives up to your mistress' name. Been spying on our lord commander has this foreign bastard. So, I sent for the witchunters, as should be the way. Tis a shame we don't have a true inquisitor...' Dunno kicked Errolas' bare foot, not hard, but enough to elicit a response from the elf's friends.

Gleave rushed the man, leg be damned, Fal and Sav following suit, weapons drawn.

Before Dunno could respond, bar half retrieving his hammer, Gleave had him by the throat, up off his feet and slammed down hard into the mud. The other two by the stocks dropped their weapons as Fal and Sav held theirs within killing distance.

The crowd shouted, cursed and surged forward, a moment after the pathfinders. It wasn't quick enough. Before they could act, before they could use their numbers to best the three men who'd forced themselves through their lines, in their own camp, their self-preservation kicked in and stayed their hands. Many were drinking, but few were drunk enough to act on it. Most were unarmed and unarmoured, unlike the pathfinders, and more still were conscripts, not professional fighting men at all. What also stopped the tide was the bellowing voice of the sergeant who'd seen Correia and her men about the camp since their arrival. When he arrived, his own men in tow, the crowd, reluctantly but swiftly, departed, leaving three men at the mercy of three others.

'The elf leaves with the pathfinders,' the sergeant said, snatching the stock keys from the prone ventinar and opening the locks himself. 'My apologies,' he offered to Errolas, who looked back through slits, the merest hint of a nod noticeable. 'And you three,' the sergeant said of the ventinar and his two archers, 'get the fuck out of my sight.' They did as they were told, once allowed to do so.

'Do you expect thanks?' Gleave said, rounding on the man.

The sergeant laughed. 'No, but I do expect you three to fuck off too, with the elf, before the lads come back in force or the witchunters arrive. They ain't mine, you see, these archers, and I've trod on their toes in front of their men, so I'll be fucking off myself now.' Without a second glance, the sergeant motioned for his scowling men to follow and head off up the hill, back towards the colourful striped tents and banners above.

Heads shaking and curses flowing, Gleave, Fal and Sav helped Errolas up and headed back to their tent, marred all the way by glaring eyes and grunted comments and empty – for now – threats.

'The sooner we're out of here the better,' Gleave said.

The others agreed.

Starks half-drew his short-sword as he heard the commotion approach the tent. Correia held a hand up to stop him.

'That'll do us no good here, Starks,' she said, moving to the tent flap. Opening it, she sucked in a breath and moved aside as her men piled in, a battered elf held between them.

'What—' Starks started.

'Never mind what,' Gleave cut in. 'We're out of here, now!'

Correia nodded and motioned for Starks to do what they'd planned. He hauled two of the saddle bags he'd packed onto his shoulders and left the tent. The others lay Errolas on the nearest bunk, his previous slashed leg the least of his – or their – worries.

'Sav,' Correia said, eyes on Errolas, 'help Starks and make sure he's alright out there, I expect we could have company.' Fal and

Gleave voiced their concerned agreement at that.

'I'm alright,' Errolas managed through split and swollen lips. 'I feel better than I look.'

'Can you ride?' Correia wasn't waiting on pleasantries. She needed to know, and fast. Dogs barked and men shouted; the noises grew closer.

'We need to go to Sir Allon and...' Fal started, but Correia's shaking head stopped him.

'I was lucky to be spared the same fate,' Correia said, checking the elf's more obvious wounds, 'and I have the baron to thank for that, I'm sure. We can't risk putting on the young Bratby any more than we have. His father's knights will follow him, but the numbers out there will be hard to control should they decide they want blood. He'd be better giving it them rather than risking them turning on him, or leaving.'

'They wouldn't dare!' Fal tried.

'I've seen it happen,' Gleave said, pulling Errolas back to his unsteady feet. 'Not on this scale, but...' he left it at that.

'Gleave's right,' Correia said. 'Sir Allon isn't his father and many of these men know it. If Giles himself was here I'd have little concern about this, but Sir Allon? He doesn't hold the same authority. And we all saw those men he had executed and staked out, on show, for allowing his father to be captured.'

'Let's move,' Fal said.

Fal got under Errolas' other arm and he and Gleave walked the elf behind Correia, who led the way out the tent and into the light, where a crowd had gathered; faces stern and fists clenched, whilst some brandished weapons. Several dogs strained against the ropes their masters held.

A man pointed. 'There's the elf bastard!'

Shouts and curses followed, with calls to string up a gibbet tree.

'This elf is under my protection,' Correia said, looking for Sav and Starks. Before she'd scanned the surrounds, hooves thudded the earth and the two she looked for rode in, the rest of the group's horses held deftly alongside by Sav, awkwardly by Starks.

Sav pulled alongside Correia, with Fal's and Correia's horses, and leaned down to her.

'It's now or never,' he said, offering her a wink. She saw through the act of confidence, but nodded and smiled all the same.

The crowed surged and the dogs lunged, if but a little, until the pathfinders, Errolas included, mounted their elf-gifted steeds.

Once towering above the growing mob, few onlookers continued their courageous bullying of the few. They gestured and shook fists and weapons alike, threatened the release of their dogs and worse; much aimed at Correia herself, plenty of it lude, which pulled Sav's frown into a snarl. He drew his sword.

'Hold!' Correia said, forcing her mount towards the dogs and men. Pathfinders fell in alongside and behind her, their mounts snorting and huffing as they walked through, rather than around the gathered soldiers. Some shoved, some jabbed weapons half-heartedly towards the riders, but none came close to striking, most knowing that one word from one rider could send all horses kicking and biting and rearing. Those that didn't know were pulled back and told with harsh words or harsher fists.

The soldiers grew bolder as they stood and watched the riders walk their horses down the hill, away from them. Once far enough away, the insults turned to serious threats and talk of what they would have done should the scene have turned ugly. The following cheer bit at the backs of the group as they kicked their mounts into a canter through the white spread of campaign tents, scattering onlookers before passing the confused pickets to ride out into the meadows, to wheel and ride on into the forests of The Marches. Errolas looked half dead, but if that were the case it didn't show in his riding, for he not only matched his companions' speed as they charged on down the wide woodland road to Sirreta, but surged ahead, leaving the human camp and his abusers behind.

Chapter 19 – A well timed kick…

Joncausks sniffed, which sent his broken nose to pounding.

'If you sniff one more time…' Boxall said, chin resting on his knees, which he'd tucked up to his blood-soiled linen-covered chest.

Joncausks sniffed.

Tahir chuckled, despite missing teeth.

Boxall lifted his head from his knees and glared at Joncausks. 'I'm not sure how much more of that I can take, Jon.'

'I don't rightly care, Boxall.'

Tahir sighed. 'We've enough on, lads, without picking at each other. You ever heard what these Hillside gangs do to folk who wrong them?'

'Roasting pits.' Joncausks closed his eyes and prodded at his nose, grimacing as he did so.

'Roasting pits,' Tahir confirmed, nodding. 'Sick bastards the lot of 'em.'

'And whose idea, Tahir,' Boxall glanced at the man, 'was it to—'

'We've been through all this shit again and again,' Tahir interrupted, eyes locked on Boxall's, who sat opposite him in the foul chamber they'd been shoved in after being taken and beaten.

Boxall nodded wearily and planted his chin back on his knees. 'Aye, lad, that we have. Nowt else to do though, is there? We've tried and thought of every bloody way to get out. They may be scum, these gangers, but they know how to fight and I'm not for taking another gut punching. Reckon' I'll be shitting organs next.'

'Might be an improvement on what you're normally shitting,' Tahir said, glancing at the pile of excrement in the corner, the smell of which was overpowering, and getting worse by the hour.

Boxall couldn't help but laugh at that, as did Joncausks, who, once finished prodding his mangled nose, moved fingers up to press the lumps beneath his cropped white hair.

'Hush!' Tahir straightened and cocked his head.

'I didn't say—'

'Hush, I say,' Tahir said again, interrupting Boxall, who snarled at the Eatrian.

Narrowing his eyes, Tahir climbed to his feet and crept to the door. 'There's voices outside,' he whispered, loud enough to be heard by the other two, who climbed to their feet. Tahir pressed his small ear to the door and Joncausks stooped to pick up his green linen shirt, pulling it on to cover the map of Brisance that was tattooed across his back.

Boxall pressed up behind Tahir, who waved him back with a sneer. Looking to Joncausks, Boxall held his large hands up behind Tahir and mimicked throttling him. Joncausks smiled.

'Someone's coming,' Tahir whispered, backing away from the door. All three stood side-by-side, Joncausks and Boxall dwarfing Tahir, who stood in the middle. 'When it opens, I'm gonna have the fucker, even if it gets me killed,' Tahir promised.

'And us, ye prick.' Boxall's eyes remained on the grubby door.

'It'll be the captain, or Hitchmogh,' Joncausks said, like he had half a dozen times since they'd been incarcerated. He was the most relaxed of the three. *I just know it.*

Boxall looked over Tahir. 'That why you donned your shirt again, Jon, like the other times he didn't show up, because you're ready to stroll back off to *Sessio* with him, past all the bastard shite gangers?'

Joncausks looked back. 'Yes.'

'Fair one.' Boxall looked back at the door. 'Well, whatever happens, I'm not being roasted in a pit after having my long bits chopped off and fed to me or whatever it is Tahir keeps saying—'

'Shush,' Tahir hissed, launching himself at the door the moment it begun to open.

Joncausks and Boxall looked more scared than they had been since they were taken, as Tahir launched feet first through the opening aperture of the doorway, connecting with the sternum of their illustrious leader and captain. Their looks were second only to Tahir's utter terror as he, from the best angle it has to be said, propelled Mannino backward, off his feet and into the trailing Hitchmogh, who collapsed under the well-dressed captain, arms flailing and curses flowing.

Tahir at least had the intelligence to fall to the floor too, despite Joncausks knowing he could have landed squarely on his feet after the impressive kick.

Unfortunately for those present, both from *Sessio* and the Hillside gang, the hilarity of the scene, which should have caused great mirth amongst Badham, Stone and his now accompanying 'soldiers', was lost when the bastards, all of them, realised the superior position they now found themselves in. Not only did they outnumber the sailors before them, but three of those sailors now lay sprawled on the floor, two of them being the only two with weapons; sheathed weapons.

Joncausks cursed.

With a barked order, Badham's gangers surged forward, blades appearing in hands as they descended on the three men struggling to climb to their feet.

'Shit!' Boxall said, his aches and pains clearly forgotten as he too surged forward, leaping over Tahir to barrel into the nearest ganger. Joncausks followed close behind. He slapped his opened hands into two faces as he ran amongst the gangers, many of which were far from his size, both in height and width. His discombobulating slaps sent two stunned lads staggering away, their eyes rolling before closing for good; Tahir was up and at 'em.

Fists lashing out like the strikes of a mantis, Tahir finished the two stunned gangers with rapid strikes to their throats. Before they'd dropped choking to the floor, he was past them, his attacks finishing off those his companions stunned or knocked away from them in their bid to make the door and room beyond, where raised voices erupted.

Badham was already gone, Stone too.

With Mannino and Hitchmogh on their heels, no explanations or apologies necessary or suitable given the situation, Joncausks and his pals rushed through the second room, leaving two more bodies behind them.

'Ha!' Boxall shouted, bringing a knee up into the gut of a ganger that came at him from the third room. 'See 'em run now, eh?' he continued, charging through the empty room as Tahir finished the winded ganger, and out into the yard beyond.

Following Boxall, Joncausks reached the yard and sunlight, which blinded him temporarily. He slid to a stop, the sun not enough to obscure the large group of armed men he now faced.

'Lefey's in the street,' Hitchmogh shouted, the first Joncausks had heard him say, despite what had happened.

Joncausks felt his shipmates press up alongside him as he stepped forward again, giving them room to leave the building and enter the ganger-filled yard.

'Shit an anchor,' Tahir said, taking in the men arrayed against them, and the cleavers, basilards and other such weapons those men carried.

'That'd be less painful than this'll be,' Joncausks said.

'You three're gonna pay for this when we get ye back,' Hitchmogh said, pushing them aside. 'Lefey!' he shouted, hands cupped to his mouth. With a barked order from Badham, who stood opposite, the gangers charged. 'Now!' Hitchmogh roared.

Sailing over the tall wall like jongleur acrobats, came Lefey, Parry and two other sailors, cutlasses and a scimitar leading. They landed behind Badham and Stone who spun on the new threat and attacked, blades in hands, one of which flashed out from Badham's hand to take one of the sailor's throats, dropping him to the floor, leaving him gargling blood whilst he thrashed and died.

'We need weapons,' Boxall shouted, looking to the fast-approaching men and *their* weapons.

Mannino and Hitchmogh drew theirs, which included Hitchmogh's dwarf-crafted pistol; the trigger was pulled and the flint holding hammer struck the firing plate, resulting in a flash, bang and a plume of stinking white smoke. The lead ball the explosion propelled from the barrel entered the nearest ganger's freckled face before exploding out of the back of his skull, parts of which flew as shrapnel along with the continuing ball to drop the ganger behind him, who fell, screaming and clutching at his ruined teeth and collapsed left cheek.

The pistol fell to the ground as Hitchmogh stepped in, right leg leading as he flicked his cutlass this way and that, the tip of the blade scoring deadly hits on the next two men he met.

Mannino made such moves look effortless as he maneuverer through the hacking, stabbing group of men and lads, dropping all who came near. Making space so he could see the wall, Mannino sneered as he witnessed the sailor with Lefey and Parry fall. He caught Badham's eyes and the gang master withdrew, Stone between him and Lefey, as Parry moved on.

'Take him!' Mannino shouted, pointing his cutlass at the retreating Badham. Lefey obeyed without question, attempting to pass Stone and reach the gang master. It was her hasty move that allowed Stone to switch direction, from retreat to attack. He stepped in close and kicked out high and flat, launching Lefey backwards, much like Tahir had done to Mannino mere moments before. That brief respite gave Stone the time he needed to bundle Badham through a side gate.

Mannino growled through gritted teeth and gave chase.

'Shitting shite,' Hitchmogh said, seeing Mannino chase Badham and Stone out of the yard.

'We'll lose him,' a hard pressed Joncausks managed, doing his best to bat away a cleaver by repeatedly slapping the flat of the

130

blade. He managed to reach in, past one attempted hack and wrap his arm around his opponent's; the audible crack that followed dropped the howling man to the floor where Joncausks stamped on his head, silencing him for good.

Most of the gangers had been dealt with, and Parry seemed to be doing a sound job of butchering the rest from behind, whilst they attempted to take on a ridiculously quick Tahir and a roaring Boxall.

Joncausks caught Hitchmogh's eye and returned the nod. They both chased after their captain, or attempted to, for several more gangers entered the courtyard as they were approaching the gate. Lefey ran across to her companions, from where she'd been floored by Stone.

'Fuck!' Hitchmogh's fear and anger was visible and raw. He searched for a way through the gangers, Joncausks doing the same beside him, Lefey reaching his other side.

'The captain,' Lefey said, her breathing ragged, laboured; ribs surely bruised or fractured.

'I know,' Hitchmogh snapped. Gangers blocked the gate. Two of them had pit-dogs on ropes.

Joncausks breathed hard, unsure how to proceed. He hoped someone had an answer.

'They're stalling, and all the while—'

'I fucking know, Lefey!' Hitchmogh shouted, cutting the woman off. He looked to the sky and roared, a human roar that turned into something all the more animal. Looking back down, whilst Joncausks and Lefey stepped away, the gangers flinched at the twisted, flushed face of the man who'd released the beastly sound. Before the bastards could respond, and whilst their pit-dogs' tails fell between their back legs, whines replacing growls, the bloodshot eyes of *Sessio's* grizzled first mate locked on theirs. Their faltering resolve, their usual air of hubris and cock sure arrogance, fled, despite them being unable to do the same.

The earth before Hitchmogh shuddered. It shuddered, shook and erupted, all in but a few heartbeats, sending stone projectiles up from beneath the men and dogs, tearing them to bloody shreds that dropped like so many dead game birds, striking the ground in steaming piles of torn meat, muscle and broken bone. Before Joncausks could comprehend what he'd seen, Hitchmogh threw his hands forward and the wall and gate exploded out as if a wall of cannon strikes had struck it; the resulting noise was just as loud.

Chapter 20 – Can't be saved

'Hold!' Mannino shouted, following the gangers up a narrow alley, the white stone buildings of the Tri Isles giving way to tight-packed single story shacks with poorly thatched roofs. The stick-bound doors he passed were closed, although some revealed flickering fires inside.

The men Mannino chased disappeared around a corner to the left, slowing the captain, who didn't want to barrel into a trap, no matter his thumping heart and barely checked anger.

No one reneges on an agreed accord with me. No one!

Creeping up to the corner and placing his hand on the warm wattle and daub wall beside him, he stopped and listened. A dog barked in the distance, followed by a tremendous explosion that lit up a dawn-dim area further down the hill, drawing his eye.

Mannino cursed as someone rushed out from the side of the building, using the explosion to their advantage. Albeit a shock to Mannino, he managed to bring up his cutlass in time, his ornate basket hilt deflecting a knife that would have seen him drop his weapon. Before the young ganger could press his reckless attack, Mannino rolled his wrist and lunged through the lad's stomach. He twisted and ripped the blade free, spilling guts down striped pantaloons and onto bare feet. The lad said nothing as he stared down at his own insides, and as he looked up, swallowing repeatedly, the very cutlass that had opened him up took him neatly through the heart. He died as he slumped to the floor, and the captain who'd killed him moved on, cursing under his breath at the enforced loss of life.

'He's right behind us!'

Emms heard Stone's voice from where she sat in Badham's room, a cup of small-beer in her hand. Placing it down, she rushed to the door, continuing on into the next room where she collided with her lover.

Strong, bloodied hands took Emms' shoulders and shook her. 'What're you doing here?'

Heart thudding, Emms looked from Badham to a worried and bloodied Stone and back.

'What's happening?' she managed, searching Badham's wild eyes.

'Get back in that fucking…

132

'No, wait.' He let go of her shoulders but took her arm, forcefully, dragging her past Stone and into the yard. Stone followed.

Emms saw several gangers by the open gates, blades in hands. 'Sweets?'

'Shut up,' Badham said, bringing Emms round in front of him to face the gate, her back to his panting chest. Stone rushed to the corner where he retrieved a wood axe that was embedded in a log. He crossed back over to stand beside Badham and Emms, a well-dressed man appearing in the gateway, cutlass flashing left and right. The first two gangers to approach the stranger died quickly. The rest backed off, more than one glancing to Badham and Stone.

'He's one man, you shites!' Stone swung his axe at the closest lad, who dodged aside.

The stranger held his ground. Emms couldn't believe how calm he looked. Angry, yes, that was clear, but calm in comparison to everyone else in the yard.

A couple of lads puffed out their chests at Stone's words.

'These are our streets, Posh,' one said, holding out and turning a long knife this way and that as he strutted forward, another by his side. 'You know what we do to fuckers who come by here, eh, Posh?'

The lads laughed and more stepped forward, hands out to their sides, weapons on show.

'Yer gonna be roasted, old man,' another said, coming around to flank the stranger.

'It's Emms, is it not?' the man said, seemingly unimpressed, nor worried, by the approaching gangers.

Emms pulled her head back, which struck hard muscle. Her frown was her only answer.

'The girl's with me, Mannino,' Badham said, brandishing a knife Emms hadn't noticed before.

'Mannino,' she whispered to herself. Everyone knew of Captain Mannino. She swallowed hard and Badham cursed. His lads had stopped approaching the captain and were again hesitant, fearful even.

'Hand her over and I'll leave, Master Badham,' Mannino said, cutlass down by his side.

Emms found herself shaking her head. 'It's my choice, sir,' she said, eyes now locked on Mannino's. 'I'm here by my choice.'

'That's not what your last fuck-friend said, when we saw him.'

Stone looked to her with a scowl, and away again as Badham snarled back.

Emms' heart skipped between thuds as she thought of Quin.

'Quinnell is safe,' Mannino reassured her. 'I give you my word. He is with my crew.'

The hand holding Emms tightened, painfully so. She squirmed, to no avail.

'He shouldn't have sent you, Captain,' Emms said. 'He has no right—'

'To see you safe?'

'To dictate my life, my future.' Emms spat on the floor, eyes narrowed. 'He couldn't when we were together and he bloody well can't now. I chose Badham, and Quinnell needs to accept that.'

Mannino didn't seem surprised. He seemed frustrated and angry more than anything, but not surprised. Sighing hard, he rubbed at his face with his free hand and nodded.

'See, Mannino,' Badham said, 'you've wasted your time. And your life.'

Mannino looked to those nearest as they advanced once again. Grins spread across more than one face as the renowned captain stepped back, shaking his head.

'I'm sorry,' Mannino said, eyes on Emms once more, 'but I can't save you from yourself.' He turned to walk back down the street and the gangers charged.

Stone's grin faltered as soon as it appeared, for as the lads left the yard in pursuit of a walking Mannino, the sound of multiple boots reached their ears. The lads raced to get back into the yard, two of them dropping to crossbow bolts as they ran.

Emms felt her lover tense as those lads dropped. She also felt the knife he held press against her throat as *Sessio's* sailors rounded the corner, a grizzly old man at their head.

Stone pulled at Badham's arm. 'We run, now! Leave the bitch.'

Emms looked to Stone, incredulous.

There was no time for any response from Badham though, for when the pock-marked face of the lead sailor released a rippling bellow of spittle and rage, Emms, Badham and Stone dropped to the floor, vision blurring and hot blood running from their throbbing noses.

The deaths of Badham's soldiers came to Emms in sound alone; screams, guttural cries of sudden pain, grunts and curses, assaulting her ears. It all lasted but a short while and before she knew it, she was being pulled to her feet by a familiar hand. She glanced left to see a deathly, vacant gaze where Badham's mischievous look had once been, and right to the same death mask that was Stone. When she looked to the one holding her hands, tears filled her eyes.

'You're safe now,' Quin said, a pair of polecats bounding around behind him and climbing from corpse to corpse. He offered her a sympathetic smile and tried to pull her in.

Swallowing down the need to be sick, Emms felt heat rush through her as she screwed up her face, pulled her right hand from Quin's and slapped him as hard as she could. Turning away from the strike, Quin's left hand released hers to rise to his reddening cheek. Emms dropped to the ground, tears flowing and lungs burning from the screams she realised were her own. She fell about Badham's corpse, pawing at his broad chest and pressing her face to his own, pleading for him to awaken.

'I'm sorry, lad,' she heard Mannino say. 'They can't always be saved, no matter how much we wish it. Not when it's from—'

'Get out!' Emms shouted, face burning and red. 'Go!'

Quin staggered back, the hate in Emms' face hurting far more than the slap he'd received, that much she knew.

Before he or Emms could even break that love- and hate-filled stare, a panicked curse came from the gate.

'What is it?' Mannino said, turning to a female sailor – the one called Lefey – who looked down the hill.

'It's the bloody Adjunct's Guard, Captain.'

Whilst two sailors struggled to restrain the old man who'd annihilated her lover's soldiers, and her lover himself through magic, she was sure, Emms watched the rest rush to Lefey's side, bloody weapons at the ready.

'We're done for,' Emms heard one of them say. She couldn't help but smile at that, an awful smile that pulled at her top lip and revealed her teeth. Quin stood there, aghast, his eyes fixed on hers despite hers being fixed on the scene unfolding on the street. She cradled and stroked Badham's cooling face and chest, ignoring her former lover's pleading stare.

'Who are you?' Quin whispered. Emms heard it, but offered nothing in reply. She sat, stroking the body besides her as a sailor took hold of Quin and dragged him away. His pleading to be left with her also ignored, his attempts to fight the sailor off doing little better. Before any of it really sunk in, Emms watched the men and women who'd ruined her life flee from the yard; off up the road they ran, Mannino in the lead and the old magic man dragged along behind, a reluctant Quin at the rear. Her eyes dropped to the sable fur of Quin's polecats as they scampered after him. She looked back up, to the sound of thudding boots on hard-packed earth as two score Adjunct's Guards ran past, crossbows clicking and polearms bobbing like an iron forest a shrike would be proud of, that jerked its way across the top of the walls, past the open gate, to continue on up the hill, after the fleeing sailors. Not one guardsman paid notice to the carnage they passed, or to the sobbing girl sat amongst it.

Chapter 21 – The Adjunct's Guard

Eyes peered from behind shuttered windows and barred doors. Dogs barked, chained in unseen yards. A lone voice shouted a threat-filled order to halt and yet the men and women ran on, up through the shacks and hovels, around the crumbling walls and back down again through arches and derelict buildings where huddled families scattered like the rats before them.

'The bastards are closing.' Lefey barely managed to force the words past her laboured breathing.

'Why don't they tire, in that armour?' Quin, uninjured but exhausted, stumbled as he followed Lefey, a polecat hanging limp from each hand. One hand offered a hiss followed by the other, but on Quin went, doing his best to keep up with those in front and doing his best to keep all he'd witnessed from his tumultuous mind's eye. He'd asked, during the initial run, why they didn't stand and face, especially after what he'd seen them do to the gangers. Laughing, the ship's blade master, Parry, had informed Quin that the gangers, despite their best efforts, weren't soldiers. The Adjunct's Guard, alas…

'Hitchmogh!'

Quin rounded a corner and saw the sailor called Joncausks crouched by a fallen Hitchmogh. The man looked dead.

'Is he—?'

Lefey stopped and flashed Quin a dangerous look. 'No, Quin, he's not. Yet. We need to get him up and move on.'

'No shit, lass,' Parry said, jogging back to them.

'We surrender.'

All eyes turned to Mannino, who looked like a man who'd been through far less than he had. His breathing was calm but his worry was plain to see.

'After all that?' Quin looked from sailor to sailor, his incredulity clear in his wide eyes and limp jaw. He shook his head and lifted Guse enough so he could wipe his wet brow with his sleeve, rather than fur.

Mannino nodded. 'After all that, Master Quinnell.'

Whilst Lefey and Joncausks continued to check on Hitchmogh, who was mumbling, eyes closed, the rest of the sailors disarmed. They huffed, sighed, spat and cursed whilst doing so, but they did it all the same, as did their captain. Mannino placed his cutlass at his feet whilst the others threw their weapons down, and moved past his crew, arms wide, to stand on the corner they'd rounded.

'I'm Mannino,' he shouted. 'It's me you're after.'

'You can't be serious?' Quin looked from the back of the captain to the rest of the sailors, all of whom appeared defeated.

'Oh, he is, lad.' Parry sucked his teeth and sat, cross-legged on the floor. He closed his eyes and released a long breath.

'Halt!' a man shouted from the other side of the wall Quin was now leaning against, chest rising and falling heavily.

'I've already done that, man,' Mannino said, keeping his arms out wide.

'Where's your men?' The voice again, edged with suspicion.

'Behind me.' Mannino jerked his left thumb. 'We have injured. I insist on being seen by the Adjunct as soon as possible.'

'You'll do as I say.'

'I'll do as I damn well please, man. And you'll bloody well like it, or it'll be more than words we'll exchange, you and I.'

There was a pause, a shuffling of booted feet and metal on metal. Quin's heart thumped and he nearly ran, but caught himself in time. What good would it do to run anyway? Run to what? His life would never be the same. He'd played a hand in the destruction of a Hillside gang and despite the bastard who ran it being dead, the shite of a goblin he'd informed to get the message through to that bastard was still alive, and that shite of a goblin had the biggest mouth on the Tri-Isles. Before long, every gang on Hillside would be looking to roast him. As the thought struck, the realisation did too. 'I'm better off with the Adjunct's Guard,' Quin whispered to himself, eyes drifting to the guardsmen binding hands and gathering discarded weapons. 'I'd never make it off Hillside otherwise, not without the crew's help.'

'What you say, boy?' One of the guardsmen strode over, poleaxe lowered.

'Nothing.'

'Speak up!'

'Nothing,' Quin said, louder than before.

'What you got in your hands, rats?'

Quin sucked in a breath as he realised what would likely happen to his boys should the man get hold of them. He crouched and threw them away from him and the guardsman, who moved to grab Quin.

Arrik and Guse twisted in the air and thudded to the ground, before scampering off under the nearby rubble and debris of someone's former home.

Quin smiled with relief before a solid clout to the head brought nought but pain. His head whirled and throbbed as he and the sailors about him were hauled off down the hill, toward the Adjunct's fort.

Chapter 22 – To see The Three

'If that lad mutters about that bloody girl one more—'

'Tahir!' Lefey glared at the Eatrian, who leaned back against the stone wall of the cell they were in, tapping the back of his head against it. 'That muttering lad saved your life,' she added.

'Well,' Tahir said, head tapping away, ignoring the latter comment, 'even in his sleep he talks about her. It's been non-stop and we've been cooped up with him in this shitting cell for near on a day, by my reckoning. As soon as he wakes, I'm going to—'

'Keep your mouth shut.' It was Joncausks turn to glare at the man he'd been imprisoned with twice over. He grunted a laugh. 'Out of the frying pan...'

Tahir flashed him a dangerous look. 'What?'

'Nothing,' Joncausks said, prodding various bandaged wounds. 'Nothing.'

Lefey shook her head, looking about the sailors in the room. 'We need to put our heads together and think this through.'

'We're in The Three's fucking dungeons, Lefey.' Boxall got to his feet and rubbed his face hard before pacing between them all. 'What can we possibly do about that?'

'That's what we need to work out.' Lefey offered Boxall a snarl.

Parry opened his eyes from his cross-legged meditation on the floor and locked them with Lefey. 'Mannino and Hitchmogh will get us out, once they've sorted what it is they've been summoned to sort.' He closed his eyes once more.

'And you believe that do you, Parry?' Tahir again, head now forward, eyes down to the man sat on the floor in front of him. 'They've been gone long enough as it is. We ain't seen them since this morning.'

'I wouldn't have said it if I didn't,' Parry said quietly, dangerously.

Joncausks sighed hard. 'We're getting nowhere.'

'Well if it wasn't for you three—'

Lefey surged to her feet, eyes on Nessa. 'Let's not start that! I mean it.'

Nessa swallowed hard and nodded. She didn't look at anyone else after that, but several of the others looked at her. *Sessio's* crew members were a family. They certainly didn't abandon their own, so for Nessa to have brought up the fact they'd been on a rescue mission at all was a low blow, and wouldn't be forgotten any time soon.

Quin began to stir and Lefey moved to him. His eyes opened and Lefey smiled down, which triggered the same from Quin.

'Are we safe?' Quin's eyes were locked on Lefey's. Both smiles faded when the woman shook her head. Quin sat up quickly, wavered.

'Steady, lad,' Joncausks said.

'Where are we?' Quin looked about, the answer becoming clear to him as he did so. 'Oh yes, I'd forgotten. We're not safe at all, are we?'

'Course we are, lad. We're about to dine like a king and visit his fucking harem.'

Quin's face reddened as he looked to Tahir, who was glared at by Lefey and Joncausks.

Lefey sat beside Quin and placed a hand on his shoulder. 'The captain and Master Hitchmogh have an audience with The Three.'

Mouthing a curse, Quin held his breath and looked to the woman, who nodded to confirm her words.

Short breath released before taking in a deeper one, Quin asked, 'Are they mad, your officers?'

Boxall laughed, as did Tahir.

'Probably,' Joncausks admitted, drawing Quin's attention. 'Although it's not like they had a choice after the Adjunct's Guard took us.'

'But The Three?' Quin frowned. 'An audience with the Adjunct I would be surprised enough at, but The Three themselves?'

Joncausks smiled. 'It's not that surprising. Not when you factor in that the captain has a past with them, and Master Hitchmogh more so.'

Quin's eyes widened and the room fell silent as the implications sank in.

***

Surrounded by a score of Adjunct's Guards and The Three's sentinels, Mannino and a pale Hitchmogh stared at the elves before them, their thrones almost identical, as were the beings themselves.

'You have some nerve, returning here,' Achiad said, from the centre throne, pink eyes narrow.

'Which one are you again?' Mannino asked the one on the right, who hadn't spoken. Mannino's eyes widened in anticipation,

141

despite knowing perfectly well which elf had addressed him.

Hitchmogh's shoulders bobbed in amusement, regardless of the weakness, pain and dread permeating his self-tortured body and mind. 'At least my soul's not on my person to be treated so,' he whispered to himself, a little louder than he'd intended.

Antreas, to the left, surged to his feet, his white attire changing instantaneously to a depthless black, as did his previously white hair. 'You shall not speak here, worm!' His voice was shrill, although not quite a scream. Shaking with rage, he took his seat again, both hair and tunic returning to their previous pale states. The other two, having looked to their youngest brother, turned their attentions back to Mannino.

'What business do you have here, Mannino, that warrants such risk?' Achiad barely seemed interested in the answer his question demanded, his eyes focusing past Mannino and Hitchmogh to some distant memory or thought.

'Am I at risk, man?'

Even Hitchmogh filled his cheeks and held his breath at that, glancing sidelong at Mannino, not daring to meet the eyes of their captors.

Before Antreas could surge to his feet once more, the one on the right, the eldest, Andarna, spoke for the first time, his perpetual smile sending a visible shudder through Mannino, who locked eyes with the ancient being.

'You make light of your situation, Mannino,' Andarna said through his grin. 'I can appreciate that.' There was a long pause after he spoke, so long that all in the chamber finally realised Andarna wasn't going add any more.

Achiad shook his head and rested his chin on his linked hands. 'Whether Antreas likes your attitude or not is of no concern to me, Mannino. What concerns me is why you have returned to our Empire?' He gritted his teeth and forced the next words through them. 'With Him.'

Six pink eyes flicked to Hitchmogh, who'd looked forward again. He wished he hadn't and felt like dropping to the floor in an attempt to make them think he'd passed out through fear. It wouldn't be the first time that had happened in The Three's court.

'Repairs, man,' Mannino said. 'Repairs is all. Can't sail a damaged ship through pirates, blockades and the like without her fit and ready.'

'Even the renowned *Sessio*?' Andarna said through his oh-so-wicked smile.

Mannino nodded once. 'Even her.'

'Enough of this!' Antreas surged to his feet again. This time his tunic darkened to red, shifted, oozed; blood began to seep from the stitching, began to drip to the marble floor, pooling as the flow increased. White hair turned crimson and the elf's pink eyes blackened until to look at them was to lose all hope.

Achiad sighed. 'Enough, Antreas. Enough now. Your games bore us.'

The bloody illusion, which caused Mannino and Hitchmogh to step back, vanished. With a flick of his white-again hair and a snort, Antreas made for the door. 'This bores *me*.' He stormed past the Adjunct's Guard, all of which averted their gaze until Antreas passed.

A door slammed a moment later and Achiad sighed and continued. 'Where were we?'

'I have no idea,' Mannino admitted.

Andarna leaned forward at that, his smile broadening as he stared at a cringing Hitchmogh. 'It was our dearest brother who felt your return, Insect. It was he who was so affronted by it. If Achiad…' he indicated his remaining brother with a sideways jerk of his head, '…does not object, I would be more than happy to see you on your way. Your sailors too.' He looked to his brother on the centre throne.

Right eye twitching, Achiad merely shrugged. 'I can't even look at the Hitchmogh man, much less decide upon his fate. Things shift in Brisance, Andarna. Big things.' He shuffled in his chair, stood, turned and looked intently at the seat before turning back and sitting once more.

'Brother?'

'I felt a prick, Andarna.'

The grin slipped a little. 'A prick in your arse?'

Achiad nodded, eye twitching again.

'You're to wander, soon?'

'Seems so. Seems so. But first, these two…' Lifting his right hand, fingers splayed – for no apparent reason – Achiad looked past Mannino. 'Now!' he said, loud enough to be heard.

Mannino and Hitchmogh tensed. Nothing happened.

Achiad's arm came down. 'Understood,' he said to himself, before standing and leaving the room.

Mannino and Hitchmogh, both tense, looked to one another,

and on to the remaining, grinning, member of The Three.

'That's settled then,' Andarna said, spittle flecking his bottom lip. 'Big things move in Brisance, my youngest brother throws a tantrum, nothing new, and Achiad will go for a long walk on the mainland.' He giggled. 'Funny how things turn out, no? And all because you came back, Insect.' Standing, Andarna walked up to Hitchmogh, who shrank back despite a poleaxe levelled at and pressing into his back. 'Until next time.' Andarna turned to Mannino. 'Until next time, Captain Mannino, you charmer you! Look after Insect's soul, as ever, won't you? We didn't lose it to you for you to lose it to...' Andarna trailed off, sighed and giggled once more. And then he was gone. Just gone. As if he'd never been stood there at all.

Mannino and Hitchmogh looked to one another, brows furrowed both.

'What in Brisance was that all about?' was all Mannino could manage before gauntleted hands dragged them both from the room.

Chapter 23 – Sails unfurled

'Hurry, man,' Mannino said to the Adjunct's guardsman, who was fumbling a set of keys before a worn lock, the door of which was cross-hatched with iron bars over oak. Chewing on the end of his empty pipe, Mannino glanced sidelong at his wavering first mate. 'We need to get you back, Master Hitchmogh, and quickly; if this man would hurry The Three up.'

Keys fell to the floor with a tinkling thud.

'Apologies. Poor choice of words.'

Hitchmogh staggered to the side and caught himself on the stone wall, Mannino close behind and steadying him as the keys were retrieved and the lock opened. As soon as it was, the gaoler repaired to the guardroom, the fear in his eyes not missed by the shrewd captain now holding up his first mate.

'I'm fine, Cap'n.'

'Don't lie to me, man.' Mannino looked to the door as the first of his sailors emerged, eyes bleary.

'Captain?' Joncausks' frown made him wince and his hand moved to his broken nose.

'Clearly, man.' Mannino returned his attention to Hitchmogh, who'd slid down the wall to the floor despite Mannino's attempts to hold him upright. Joncausks rushed to help and the two men hauled Hitchmogh to his feet.

The rest of the imprisoned sailors left their cell as Mannino explained as much as he could.

'Master Hitchmogh hasn't had time to rest since the fight. We need get him to *Sessio*.'

Lefey came around to help. 'They're just letting us go?'

Mannino looked at her. Lefey flinched. 'They never *just do* anything, lass. They're mad. As mad as people say.' At a nod of Mannino's head, the sailors moved down the corridor towards the exit, Hitchmogh held between Mannino and Joncausks. 'I wouldn't be surprised,' Mannino went on, 'if all of this were a bloody game, drown my soul.'

The group approached half a dozen frustrated guardsmen, who'd laid out the sailors' weapons and gear on a long table in their guardroom.

'The Adjunct said you're to have this lot back, but no funny business. You hear, Mannino?'

Mannino snarled and lifted Hitchmogh's arm over and across

Boxall's broad shoulder, before picking up and sheathing his cutlass. The guard who'd spoken took a step back, hands out to the sides. The rest of the group took what was theirs and followed Mannino from the room and out onto the sunlit street. The heat of the sun hit them, as did the sea air.

'What about me?' Quin sped from the back of the group to the front.

'Oh…' Mannino pursed his lips as they made their way down the middle of the street, people moving aside to let the angry looking sailors pass. After an awkward pause, punctuated by curses from Hitchmogh as he stumbled now and then, relying on the two men either side of him to keep him going, Mannino said, 'I have to admit, I'd forgotten about you, Master Quinnell.'

Quin looked about, at nothing, as if taking in Mannino's meaning. Rounding a corner, he pulled on Mannino's sleeve, stopping him. The sailors behind halted too, but Mannino turned on them and with a whisk of his hand they continued on towards the nearby harbour.

'I'd appreciate you not doing that again, Master Quinnell.' Mannino looked at the lad, who looked down.

'I'm sorry. I—'

'Spit it out, man. The Three aren't fond of my first mate, nor me. I wouldn't be surprised if, after their tumultuous thoughts settle, they realise they want us after all. I wouldn't be surprised at all, Master Quinnell,' –it was Mannino's turn to take hold of Quin, albeit by the shoulders, forcing him to meet his gaze– 'if the very guards who rearmed us aren't receiving orders to do the opposite as we speak. Now are you coming or not?'

Quin rocked back, and stammered. 'Coming? Where?'

'Wherever it is I decide we're going.' Mannino looked back the way they'd come, to the corner they'd rounded, half expecting the polearm wielding troops of The Three to come charging around at any minute, horns blowing. He looked back to Quin, who was chewing his bottom lip, eyes flicking about as his options, or lack of them, raced through his head.

'I have a life here,' Quin managed after a shake from Mannino. 'My apprenticeship—'

'As a shipwright?'

Quin nodded. 'Yes, Captain.'

'*Sessio* could do with one. That's settled.' Mannino released Quin's shoulders, took his arm and dragged him along. The milling crowd parted as the opulently adorned captain barked at them to do so. He looked over his shoulder frequently, ignoring Quin's pleas to release him as he went.

'But my father?'

'Dead.'

Quin's eyes widened.

'He died two years ago,' Mannino added, halting as a cart passed in front of them. He also released his grip on Quin without looking at the lad, before setting off again, his long strides leaving Quin behind. The lad didn't see Mannino smile to himself, as he heard him follow.

'But how could you know that?'

'I don't recruit without knowing backgrounds of potential crew members, especially officers.'

Quin stopped. 'Officers?'

Mannino kept going. He caught sight of the backs of his sailors ahead, struggling as they were to carry an increasingly vocal Hitchmogh. His curses carried easily on the wind. Quin ran to catch up.

'You specified 'officers', Captain?' Quin kept pace now, alongside.

'I did. An on-board shipwright would be an officer in my eyes, on my ship.'

Filling his cheeks and holding his breath, despite the exertion of the fast pace they kept, Quin saw *Sessio's* masts as they rounded another corner and walked out onto the quayside. He stopped again. This time Mannino did too, a few paces in front of Quin. He turned and looked back, a genuine smile creasing his face.

'A beauty, isn't she, Master Quinnell?'

Quin nodded, eyes unmoveable from the ship before him. Quin closed his mouth, clearly realising he'd been gaping.

'Well, Master Quinnell?'

Quin managed to look at Mannino, finally. 'Sorry?'

'My offer? You have nothing left here I'm sorry to say. The girl proved not to want you—'

Quin winced at that.

'—the gangers on Hillside will be planning a roasting in your honour, and to boot,' Mannino turned and looked at the distant scales, the sun glinting off objects on the two towns they suspended, 'The Three will have you off to one of those suspended towns for associating with us.' Mannino looked back and offered a

147

sympathetic smile. 'And for that, lad, I am sorry.'

'It really is over, isn't it?' Quin ran the fingers of both hands through his hair and linked them behind his head. He stared off at the scales beyond Mannino and shuddered.

Mannino stepped closer, drawing Quin's eyes. 'Not if you join my crew, Master Quinnell. Not if you do that. I can't promise you a long life, for none of us know when we shall fall, but I can offer you an adventure, and training. Training to make those gangers you so rightly fear piss their pantaloons at the sight of your prowess with a bloody wooden spoon; when Master Parry is done with you. And on top of that, you'll complete your apprenticeship on board—'

'*Sessio*,' Quin whispered, eyes back on the glorious ship.

'*Sessio*, aye.' Mannino smiled and took Quin's shoulders once more. 'What say you, lad? What say you to a life on the finest ship you or I have ever seen?'

Quin nodded before he said a word. He started. 'My polecats? My boys?'

Mannino stepped back and squinted, his nose wrinkling for a second before he released a single snort of a laugh through his nostrils. 'They're on board, man. Now come, quickly!'

Quin's frown was brief as Mannino turned and ran full tilt towards his ship. The sound behind them allowed Quin a pace to match Mannino's, who didn't need to turn to know the Adjunct's Guards had come charging around the corner. People fled the square and *Sessio's* sails unfurled.

Chapter 24 – A warm welcome

'You're healing well.' Fal lifted Errolas' saddle bags for him. Errolas smiled and took the load.

'It was largely superficial, what they did to me. Bruising, grazes and the like. No bones broken, nothing more than bruised skin, scabs and muscular aches and pains left. The witchunter's cut to my leg was worse, but that heals well also. Thank you for your concern though, Fal, and thank you all for getting me out of there before it became something more. Before the Samorlians came.' Nods of welcome followed.

'It's taken you bloody long enough to talk about it,' Gleave said, hinting at the near silence the group had travelled in since their swift flight into the forest, two days before.

Correia scowled at Gleave, but Errolas laughed, knowing the people he travelled with well.

'It's taken you all a long time to ask!' Errolas winked at Gleave, who barked a laugh whilst mounting his horse.

'Fair one, elf,' Gleave said, leaning forward and patting the neck of his mare. 'Fair one.' He turned the animal as the others followed suit, and headed off along the road, Pecker in his lap.

'We'll stay together now,' Correia said, causing Gleave to reign in. 'No need to scout ahead until after the border crossing. We're close to Twin Inns and I want us together whilst we navigate the Troll Bridges.'

Starks turned in his saddle, eyes wide.

'It's a name, Starks,' Gleave said, nudging his mount to follow Correia, who'd taken the lead.

'Names are given for a reason, Gleave,' Starks said, pulling alongside and staring across at the man, who was picking away at his mangled ear.

'Well not this one. There's no trolls down this way. Moot Hills, lad, that's where they live. Maybe Chapparro Minor, too, but not The Marches. I'll wager you on that.'

'Done!'

Fal sighed. 'Starks!?'

'It's my coin, Fal.' Starks pulled a small pouch from his belt and weighed it in hand.

Gleave grinned. 'It's mine now. You wait and see, lad. You wait and see.'

'I hear something,' Starks said after several hours, the sun now past its zenith, continuing to poke beams of light through the shifting layers of branches above.

'Water,' Errolas confirmed. 'Waterfalls and rivers.'

'We're there.' Correia pulled ahead of the group. They encouraged their horses to follow, the animals snorting, whinnying and pulling at reins.

'Why The Three didn't we ride on last night?' Gleave said, pulling alongside Correia. 'We seem to be making a habit of camping early. If we'd ridden harder the past two days, we'd have made it to an inn instead of another bivvy by a fire.'

'Not that I need explain myself, Gleave,' Correia's accompanying look seemed to slow Gleave's mount, 'but I called camp last night because it's not wise to approach Twin Inns in the dark.'

'Eh?' Was all Starks managed.

Correia rubbed the back of her neck. 'Must I explain everything to you like a mother to children?' She turned on the lot of them. All eyes looked elsewhere, bar Errolas' slits, which barely managed to show his amusement.

'One inn serves travellers entering Altoln, the other serves travellers entering Sirreta.' Facing forward once more, she continued, leading her horse across a narrowing path that transformed into a wooden board-walk set a horse's leg above the rushing water that flowed through the undergrowth below. Everyone looked down, eyes tracking bits of detritus racing past, from one patch of open water to the next. Once all the horses clacked across planks of water spattered wood, Correia continued her explanation.

'Has no one heard of the Twin Inns?'

'I have,' Errolas said, avoiding a grin to save the pulling of his healing face.

'And me,' Gleave said, although he sounded less confident. 'Because I've been here before, albeit years ago, with you. But we arrived during the day.'

'And yet you asked... Never mind, Gleave. I'll go on and explain, shall I?' Correia went on without an answer. 'The inns are owned by the same family, albeit a split family. They're neither Altolnan nor Sirretan. Some say their ancestors lorded over these waterways before any borders were drawn here, and so it remains.'

'Why two inns?' Fal asked where no one else dared.

'Once the family split, generations ago and for whatever reason, one side built a second inn and declared it would outdo its rival. Both inns fought for a long time, enticing travellers in through offered wares and the threat of violence both. Trade died. Travellers tried to navigate the woodland waterways without passing through either inn. Travellers died. The family decided it needed a strategy, but none could be agreed upon, until, eventually, it is told that a wise old woman who lived deep in the woods—'

'Truly?' Starks narrowed his eyes.

Errolas laughed then winced.

Correia smiled. 'I don't know, Starks. All I know is they somehow decided to take trade on a directional basis. One inn takes travellers crossing the rivers one way, the other takes the opposite. The river being a natural border between Altoln and Sirreta means that to cross here, along the main forest road, you must cross through the appropriate inn.'

Correia guided her horse to the left of a cascading willow, around which another board-walk split, before meeting on the other side. A bloated frog hummed before plopping off the edge and into the water that slowed around the tree, pooling on the far side. All eyes watched the amphibian before looking back to Correia.

'Do they still fight?' Fal asked, when no continuation of the tale came.

Correia nodded. 'Oh yes. They try and steal each other's custom from time to time, when they think the travellers are wealthy enough to bother, or times are tough. They take pops at each other from the walls of their inns, too, when they can; in winter, mainly, when the leaves have fallen and the inns are visible to one another.'

'It's stupid,' Starks said. Most agreed.

'It's all they know.' Correia pointed ahead. 'And there's the one we're going to stop at.'

The Pathfinders looked through the trees, through the multitudes of greens to the grey stone beyond. Wood smoke caught their noses, drifting along on the breeze that shook leaves in a dance of shimmering emerald and rippled water on the surface of lily-covered pools criss-crossed by board-walks and stone bridges.

'Where's the one the Sirretan travellers use?' Starks asked, urging his horse to follow the others over the wood and stone spanned waters, iron-shod hooves clattering away.

Correia smirked. 'This *is* the Sirretan traveller's inn.'

Several brows creased. Heads pulled back and eyes met as the men looked to one another, unsure they heard right.

'Wait,' Errolas said, joining in with the confusion, 'did you say this is the one we should be using on the way back?'

'That's not what I said, but it's probably the case.' Correia nudged her horse into a proud trot. The others hesitated before doing the same.

'There's nowt wrong with breaking the rules once in a—'

A crossbow bolt thwacked off a tree beside Sav, cutting his comment short.

'Ride!' Correia shouted, her horse surging forward as she dropped low, head close to its neck. The others followed without delay.

'Quick, quick!' a thick accented voice called from above an opening gate. The stone structure came into view as the group rounded a trio of beech trees rising up from an island in the sweeping water beneath them.

Two more bolts rushed across the expanse of open water, shot from crossbowmen on a stone bridge that crossed the widening river. The unmistakable thunder of a waterfall accompanied the thunder of hooves as the riders closed on the opening gates.

The man on the stone gatehouse, for that's what it was – fit for a baron's keep – hurled abuse at the crossbowmen in a language none but Correia understood. Despite the unrecognisable words he spewed forth, the others knew from the tone and hand gestures that whatever he was shouting wasn't pleasant.

Crossbow bolts missing up to now, Correia looked left and saw more men crouch, aim and loose. She ducked low and waited for the dull thud or horse's scream and fall. Nothing came, from her, her mount or anyone else. She looked up to the man on the gatehouse, and before passing beneath the large keystone above, saw similar men to those across the way pop up along the wall. They returned crossbow bolts and insults both.

Breaths coming heavy to everyone, human, elf, hen and horse, Correia circled her mount and watched, along with her companions, as the heavy wooden doors were closed and barred. She looked up to the ramparts above the gate, where gaudily dressed men and women shouted, gesticulated and squeezed metal triggers, sending forth more bolts into the greenery beyond. Occasionally they ducked, as audible snaps and cracks came from the far side of the wall. More men and women rushed from surrounding buildings, to take reins and offer pots of ale, wine and mead.

A cheer erupted from the wall and the crossbow wielding folk filtered down the stone steps to greet their guests.

'Flay. Me,' Sav sounded out, snatching up a pot of ale and downing it in one. 'Whoah!' he added, looking down at the grinning girl who'd offered him the drink. 'That's no small-beer,' he said, sniffing the pot.

'Full ale, of course,' she said, her accent bringing a smile to Sav's mouth and eyes.

'Thought you didn't drink whilst in the field?' Starks said to Sav. Sav ignored him, eyes remaining on the serving girl.

'Dismount,' Correia ordered, her mount threatening to push the girl aside as it pulled alongside Sav's. 'The family will see to the horses. We need to talk, inside. Now.'

Sav grinned at the departing girl as Gleave, Fal and Starks downed what drinks they'd been given, licking lips and sighing with satisfaction before doing as they'd been told.

'Take care of my Pecker,' Gleave said to the nearest serving girl, who sniggered at his words, until a flapping lump of brown feathers and scaly feet struck her in the chest. Frowning, the girl struggled to keep hold of the large hen as she staggered away towards an outhouse. 'And you mind she's not harmed!' Gleave shouted, hands patting his belted weapons. The girl's eyes widened before she disappeared.

'Well,' Errolas said, whilst being helped from his saddle by two men in orange and red striped tunics, 'that was quite the welcome.'

'Apologies, Lord Elf,' one of the men said, although it wasn't easy to make out what he'd said, his accented Altolnan being so strong.

Errolas raised his hand, settling the man. 'No need to apologise. You defended our arrival.'

'Indeed, but my family attacked you, the bastard turds. They'll pay for that one.'

'We're honoured you made for our inn and not theirs,' an elderly woman called from an upper window, that overlooked the courtyard. Several family members cheered at that.

Errolas smiled and inclined his head. 'It was our fair lady here, not I, who led us to you.'

'Fuck me,' a beast of a man dressed in white linens said, from a doorway he had to stoop to pass through, 'if it isn't Lady Burr.'

153

All eyes turned to Correia, who smiled and spun on the man. 'Cook!' she shouted, running over to and wrapping him in a hug, her hands unable to reach around his broad back.

Cook laughed heartily and pulled Correia through the doorway.

'Wait for me in the tavern,' Correia shouted back, before the door slammed behind her.

'I hope he wasn't being literal.' Sav scowled at the tower-like building.

Fal and Gleave laughed, before pulling Sav along with them, following Starks and Errolas who were being guided into a thatched hall of a tavern, nestled in the sprawling expanse of courtyards and water bridging walkways.

'This place is huge,' Starks said, disappearing into the tavern.

'So was that bloke,' Gleave said, winking at Sav, whose response came in the form of two raised fingers and nothing more.

Chapter 25 – The calm before the storm

'I never thought it'd be like this,' Flavell said, eyes sparkling up into Croal's.

'And I never thought I could take any more of this sickening display,' Amis whispered to himself. Croal flashed Amis a dangerous look and Amis made a mental note to think things like that in future, rather than whispering them.

'Does he need to be here, my love?'

My love? Amis thought, baulking. *He's known her but a heartbeat in the stretch of a life and he calls her his love?*

'You know he does, Croal. He's my chaperone. My father would never allow such meetings between us without his presence.' She glanced at Amis, who continued to look forward, towards a light filled window. 'I'm surprised as it is that he left us alone in your reception room the other day, when he disappeared with the Earl of Bratby.'

Croal wrapped his arms around Flavell and squeezed her tight. 'Well, I for one was glad, and I hope it happens again; Giles can have him for good, for all I care.'

Flavell giggled as Croal moved in to brush her pale neck with his lips.

Amis rolled his eyes.

'I think perhaps you should leave us now, de Valmont,' Croal said, from beneath Flavell's curled hair.

Amis flashed Flavell a look. The woman smirked and winked. 'Mademoiselle?'

'Go on.' Flavell took a sudden, deep breath as Croal nipped at her neck. 'Go on, de Valmont. Please.'

With a huff, Amis turned and left the room, hand wringing the hilt of his sword. 'As you wish, mademoiselle,' he said, again, for his ears only. 'I know when my betters don't want me around.'

***

He wasn't sure why it made him sweat, especially when the cold wind sent chills through to his bones, but when the bile hung from his mouth like yoke from a cracked egg, Quin wiped his brow and heaved again, despite it doing no good.

'You've nowt left, lad.' Lefey appeared by his side to lean against the gunwale, which she spat over.

Quin groaned. 'I know.'

'You'll get used to it. Maybe.'

'Thanks.' Quin hacked up a cough as the wind caught and plucked the bile from his bottom lip.

'My pleasure.' Lefey patted him hard on the back, dropped to her haunches and ruffled the fur of Guse, who wobbled off down the ship, uninterested in the attention. As soon as the polecat left, his twin arrived, sniffing Lefey's hand before attempting to climb her leg. 'Ouch! Little monster.' She chuckled and stood, Arrik hanging limp from the hand that'd grabbed him. He hissed as Lefey stroked his back down to his puffed-up tail.

'He likes you.' Quin spat over the side after talking and heaved as *Sessio* rolled over a large wave, the spray taking what was left from Quin's cracked lips. He winced.

'He's hissing at me.' Lefey brought the animal up to face her, eye to eye.

'But he's not struggling. Nor has he sunk his teeth into you and locked on. And he certainly hasn't sprayed. He'd smell even worse if that was the case, and you'd bloody well know about it. We all would.'

Lefey put the polecat down and Arrik proceeded to bounce around, making a similar noise to that of a clucking hen.

'Saying that, you're more likely to get bitten by Guse, when you least expect it. At least Arrik is predictable.'

Lefey watched the spinning, jumping polecat at her feet. 'How do you tell them apart?'

Quin managed to look down at Arrik. 'See the black mask around his face?' Lefey nodded and used her hand to block the sun from her eyes. 'Well, Arrik here has white spots above the eyes. Guse doesn't. Well, he does, but they're less obvious.'

'If you say so.' Lefey turned, whacked Quin on the back once more and started away. 'Grubs up, Quin,' she said, turning and walking backwards with ease as the deck pitched and rolled. 'That's what I came to tell you, so head on down before you miss out. If you can stomach it, that is.'

Quin waved his thanks as Lefey grinned at him, and then she was off, off up the main mast to the fortified crow's nest above. Quin looked up and shook his head. 'I have no idea how she does that.' It was barely a heartbeat after that vocal thought before the apprentice shipwright was back over the gunwale and throwing up what little remained in his stomach, and all whilst Arrik attempted

156

to kill his shoe.

'Oh Emms,' Quin managed between gut wrenching heaves. His eyes watered, and not because of the wind. 'I'm not sure if it's the sea making my stomach twist so, or the thought we'll not be together again…' Quin sobbed.

Arrik hissed.

Chapter 26 – Twin Inns

Fal looked across the slab of food-scattered oak to the kitchen door, which opened with a squeak. Seeing who entered, and the look on her face, Fal hushed his companions, most of whom drained their preferred drinks before returning the pots, tankards and goblets to the table. All turned to look at Correia, who scowled back, before leaving the quiet tavern.

Sav grinned.

'I'll go talk to her.' Errolas slid his stool back and made for the door.

'And I'll order another round,' Starks said, dropping his heavier than usual coin pouch on the table.

Gleave grimaced.

'I would've bet the same way, if that's any consolation,' Fal said to Gleave, who stared out the small window besides them.

Starks placed their order with a girl who rushed across the tavern's stone flags, eyes lingering on the coin pouch longer than any man.

'I'm not convinced,' Gleave said, trying to make out the two warped figures on the other side of the small squares of bubbled glass. 'We never heard such a thing last time we were here.'

'Of which you admit to having little memory,' Fal said. 'Since, again by your admission, you ended up paralytic through the consumption of mead.'

'Bar girl said so,' Starks said, before Gleave could reply. He leaned into the high-backed chair he'd rushed for when they entered the tavern. 'Troll Bridges are named after the trolls that live under them.'

Gleave huffed. 'And I'm a billy goat wanting to reach a meadow on the other side.'

'If you say so,' Sav said, hovering over his stool, trying to look through the open-again door that Correia had come out of. The large cook peered through, saw Sav and winked. Sav surged to his feet and strode across the room, slamming the door on his way out of the tavern.

'Let's pretend he's off to tend the horses,' Fal said, failing to hide a smirk.

Gleave's mood seemed to lighten at that, and he slapped his dice pouch on the table as drinks were delivered.

'Time to win my money back, eh lads?'

Fal groaned and Starks' eyes glinted, as did the serving girl's as she spied the amount of coins the two gamers threw onto the oak space from which platters had been pushed aside.

Errolas and Correia heard the door slam and watched Sav storm past, heading away from them over a small stone bridge that led to the stables.

Correia sighed and Errolas smiled.

'You were saying?' Correia's arms folded across her chest, fists clenching.

'I was saying that for no messages, no travellers even, to be coming through this inn… Well, I don't know what to say. I've never heard the like. They're either taking a ridiculous detour west, via Royce, or east, via Stonebridge. Either way, it makes no sense unless something is stopping them on the other side of The Marches.'

'Eudes de Geelan?' Correia set off towards the stables at a slow pace. The direction wasn't lost on Errolas, who shook his head at the question.

'We can't be sure,' Errolas said. 'Besides, the marquis would surely lose a lot of trade by closing the border.'

Correia nodded at that. 'Could it have something to do with him holding Giles Bratby?' She stopped on top of the small bridge Sav had crossed and looked down into the channelled, fast flowing water below. Looking back up, she watched the slow, creaking motion of a wooden water wheel which turned milling stones on the other side of the wall it clung to.

Errolas stood beside her, watching twigs and such race beneath them. After a while, he shrugged before answering, 'We can't know. Did your man inside have nothing at all for you?'

'A recipe.' Correia's answer came with a smile, although it was short lived, despite Errolas matching it. She pulled her lips into a thin line and took a deep breath, before releasing it heavily. 'Nothing more than that. The recipe confirmed what I was expecting from our domestic reports.' She looked at Errolas, brow creased. 'Nothing, Errolas. No word from my man in Easson. I can understand that, perhaps, but no word from anyone at all? No travellers, pilgrims, traders? It makes no sense.'

'We're to enter Sirreta then? Do as you told Sir Allon and seek audience with Eudes de Geelan?'

Correia looked back to the water below. 'I couldn't *not* seek an

159

audience now, could I?'

'I suppose not. We need to know what hampers our neighbours, for it could very well darken our doors before long.'

Sighing again and rubbing at her scarred face, Correia left her head in her hands a moment before straightening and looking back at the tavern, then towards the stables.

'You go tell the lads we're heading into Sirreta, and get some more food and drink down you. I'll go tell Sav. Agreed?'

'Agreed.' Errolas smiled. 'We'll know more soon enough. Just hope we're the first back across these waterways, and not hounded all the way if we are.'

Nodding, Correia squeezed Errolas' shoulder before leaving the bridge and walking around the mill that the diverted section of river fed.

Errolas spent a little while with his tender eyes closed. The sound of the water below, the rest of the river and waterfall nearby, all washing through him, soothing his mind, his aches and pains. He smiled at the sound, a sound followed by the pleasant call of a bird. He opened his healing eyes, light flooding in, and looked down at the small, white-bellied brown bird that dipped up and down on a protruding rock. Ruffling its feathers as tiny droplets of water caught them, again and again, the bird looked up to Errolas, its head tilting one way, then the other. With no one else present, the dipper flew up to the stone wall Errolas leaned on before alighting on his shoulder.

Smile broader than it had been for weeks, Errolas leaned in and listened to the dipper's melodic voice. For several heartbeats, that soon quickened, Errolas listened to the bird and took in what it had to say. Its fear was palpable, its message filled with urgency. Errolas' smile faded.

'Thank you, friend.'

The dipper bobbed once, twice, thrice and was gone, down and under the bridge and away, back to its family in an area of the forest far from men.

Standing straight and looking to the tavern, and then towards the stables, Errolas swallowed hard before choosing the latter and making his way there with haste.

'I've told you, Sav, nothing happened. Not that I need tell you anything anyway.' Correia looked up to Sav, who was brushing down his horse, a chore he'd relieved the stable boy of.

'I know, and I never asked.' The horse was receiving a brushing like it'd never received before.

'Maybe not, but your bloody eyes did, and your expression. There's no time for this, anyway, we need to prepare to move, first thing in the morning.'

Sav turned to face her. 'Already? I thought we'd take a couple of days here, for Errolas at least.'

'Yes, and I'd planned to, but—'

'What?'

'Watch your tongue, Sav. You're pushing it.'

Sav inclined his head at that. 'Apologies. What's wrong?' He softened his voice, and his brushing.

'We need to go now!' Errolas said, limping into the stables, face ashen. Both humans frowned.

'What is it?' Correia said, moving to him.

'I've had a message. It's not good.'

'You've had a message?' Correia's question was full of scepticism. 'You've had a message,' she repeated before Errolas could answer, 'where I have not?'

'You've had nothing?' Sav asked Correia, dropping the brush and coming over to them both. 'You said that was what your meeting with the fat cook was.'

'I wouldn't say he was fat, just big,' Errolas said, receiving sharp looks from Correia and Sav.

'He's had no word from Sirreta for weeks,' Correia explained, before rounding once more on Errolas. 'But you have?'

Errolas nodded. 'A bird—'

'Blind me, Errolas,' Correia said. 'Another bloody wren, is it?'

'A dipper.'

'Whatever.' Correia's hands moved to her hips. 'Spit it out.'

Errolas looked to Sav before carrying on. 'It wasn't specific.'

'I don't care,' Correia said. 'I want some news, any news, from the far side of The Marches.'

'Animals are fleeing,' Errolas said. 'Fleeing north, towards and into this forest.' Both humans frowned. 'They are coming out of the Woolf Fells for certain, but I think some are coming from as far off as Lejeune Forest and the Chriselle Coast,' Errolas added, the bruise-free skin of his face remaining pale. 'As far as I could glean anyway, from talking to a dipper.'

'They're fleeing what?' Sav asked, leaning in.

'Armies on the march. They're burning as they go. They're

burning and logging, leaving death in their wake, bodies in the rivers, poison in the ponds and lakes and wells. Whoever moves through Sirreta, they're closing on The Marches and they're winning.'

Correia and Sav stood straight at that. They looked to no one but the horses and stable around them, before looking again to each other.

'We move now,' Correia said.

'Back to Sir Allon's army?' Sav asked.

Correia shook her head. 'On to his father's captor. On to Eudes de Geelan and his chateau.' Sav looked aghast.

'We need to get our marcher lord back, Sav, and ensure theirs is planning on holding the border, from those within Sirreta itself.'

'And the army we have at our back? The army we need protecting our borders, our towns?' Sav asked, holding Correia's gaze. 'Who will warn them what is to come?'

'I'll go,' Errolas said. Incredulous, both humans looked to him.

'They'll string you up, you fool,' Correia said, rolling her eyes.

'You concussed?' Sav added.

Errolas' cheeks reddened. 'Fair point, as Gleave would say.'

'No...' Correia made for the door. '...Cook will send word, if I warn him. I trust him and I know he'll have a way.'

'Perhaps he has a blue tit that can mime the warning to the whole army,' Sav said, following Correia, Errolas close behind.

''Morl's flaccid cock, Sav,' Correia said whilst walking, out of the stable and across the front of the mill, 'now isn't the time for shit jokes.'

The joke might not have drawn smiles, but Correia's retort did, although they were short-lived.

'I think I love her,' Sav whispered, knowing Errolas would hear it over the rushing water below the bridge they crossed, 'for that filthy retort if nothing else. I've never heard the like from her.'

Errolas said nothing, but his swollen eyes revealed the smile his mouth guarded.

Nothing else was said before they crashed through the tavern's door, warnings on their lips. After that, the tavern was awash with movement and chatter. Soon after, a pigeon left Cook's hands, followed by two others, all of which headed north, towards an army, and castles; everyone hoped the messages would be received, and received well.

Supplies were gathered swiftly, saddle bags packed even quicker. Weapons were sharpened by the inn's team of smiths – proficient in weapons due to their family's nature – whilst arguments were fought between Correia, Errolas and Cook.

'I've sent the messages, but there was no mention in them of support coming here, Correia?'

Correia placed a hand on Cook's thick arm. 'I know, but we can't risk funnelling an army through the forest road and across the board-walks to squeeze into Twin Inns—'

'Inn,' Cook said, staring at Correia. 'There's no need to protect those bastards over there.' He pointed at the wall behind him. 'Have Bratby's son send men to man *our* walls.'

Correia sighed and Errolas answered.

'You have a lot in your stores, but you don't have enough for a protracted siege, and that's what will befall you should you stay here; especially if you man the walls with more men.'

Cook's jaw bunched as Errolas spoke. 'We'll defend it on our own then. This is our home, our ancestral home. We're not leaving on the tweet of a dipper.'

'I'm not asking you to leave,' Correia said, placing her other hand on Cook and turning him to look at her. 'But I am asking you and your family, and those in the other inn...' She shook him. 'And those in the other inn, to prepare for a fighting retreat should we come back with gods know what on our heels. Or, should whoever or whatever is smashing through Sirreta be closer to The Marches than we fear, not return at all.'

Cook swallowed hard and sighed. 'I'll see what I can do, Correia, but I don't speak for the family. I'll need to request a family meeting for this and organise a parley with the shits over there.' Again with the pointing to the wall.

Correia stepped back and looked to the ceiling, head shaking.

'It's how it's been for centuries,' Cook said. 'I can't change the way it is on the word of a bloody bird!'

'Fine,' Correia said, the word little more than an exhalation. 'Do what you can.' She looked up into his dark eyes. 'But be ready, you and yours. Promise me?'

Cook nodded and pulled her into a hug before pushed her away and heading for the kitchen.

'You've done all you can,' Errolas offered, heading for the external door of the tavern. When Correia didn't follow him through the door, he turned and looked back at her. She faced him and offered him a tight smile.

Errolas' shoulders slumped. 'You wish me to stay here, don't you?'

Correia nodded.

'I won't slow you,' Errolas said, walking back over to her, his limp almost imperceptible.

'I know, but I can't afford anymore complications like we had at the camp. I need to be in and out of Easson with Bratby in tow.'

'I can't talk you around, can I?'

'No, Errolas, you can't. Besides, I'll feel better knowing you're helping guard our potential retreat.' Errolas was nodding before she finished. 'Hold the inns. Hold them until we return, but should an enemy march through these forests and reach these bridges and buildings, get out of here. Get back to Altoln proper and warn everyone. We may not know what comes, but if armies are sweeping a nation such as Sirreta, they won't stop at a border drawn on a map.'

'I know,' Errolas said. He surprised Correia with a hug before pushing her to arm's-length. 'Find out what we face,' Errolas said, holding her gaze. 'Find out and return here, with or without your marcher lord. Do you hear me?'

Correia offered a weak smile. 'I hear you.' Pulling away, she turned and left Errolas in the tavern, and sincerely hoped he would be there when she returned.

If we return, she thought, exiting the thatched hall and moving to the courtyard. She heard her pathfinders before she saw them. Iron-shod hooves on stone, whinnying horses and raised voices.

'Mount up, lads,' Correia said, reaching her own horse and taking the reins from the stable boy. She climbed into the saddle and threw the boy a coin. A flash of teeth was all she saw before he rushed off, eyes locked on the penny in his fingers.

'How'd he take your orders?' Sav asked, horse turning a full circle before walking over to Correia's.

'How you would expect.'

Sav nodded at that.

'I left him a surprise in his saddle bags,' Starks said, walking his horse over to join the others as the gates began to open.

'You shit in them?' Gleave said, grinning.

Correia's glare did nothing to deter the mirth in Gleave's eyes.

'No I did not,' Starks said. 'I left him half of my elven crossbow bolts—'

'The deer detonators?' Sav asked, grin matching Gleave's, who laughed at the comment. Starks scowled at the two men.

'I thought it best he had something, you know, something special should an army march on this place.'

'Clever,' Gleave said, watching gaudily dressed men and women of the inn running up stone steps to the ramparts above the gate, crossbows in hands. 'Shame he doesn't have a crossbow, you knob.'

'Like fucking children,' Correia said, moving ahead of the rest, through the open gate after an 'all clear' from above. Fal smiled and followed suit.

'No, you dick,' Starks said to Gleave, 'but the family have.' He pointed up to those above, as he, Gleave and Sav passed beneath the ancient archway.

Gleave rolled his bottom lip and turned in his saddle, looking back up to the waving men and women who'd served them in the tavern, tended to their horses and sharpened their weapons. He waved back, before turning to Starks, who rode beside him.

'I'll give you that one, Starks,' Gleave said, nodding and looking back one more time. 'Aye, I'll give you that one.'

'You seem to be taking all this well, Gleave?' Fal said over his shoulder.

'I wouldn't say that, but there's no point in letting it bother me, is there? I'm not one to piss and moan about life.'

Starks snorted and glanced at Gleave's bandaged leg.

Fal looked back, confused. 'No point letting it bother you? What, the fact there's an army, probably multiple armies, marching on Altoln?'

Green plate spaulders scraped as Gleave shrugged. 'Just another fight, Fal. It's what we do, isn't it?' He followed that with a wink. Fal followed it with a shake of the head and turned back to face front without replying.

'We're in Sirreta now,' Correia called back. 'Once away from the Troll Bridges, we're to have scouts ahead again, but not too far until we leave the forest and enter the Woolf Fells.' Everyone nodded their understanding.

'Sav, you're up first, followed by Gleave, then, by my reckoning, it'll be time to camp. Two days and we'll be off the woodland road and into the fells beyond. Fal will take point thereafter, range further out, make de Geelan's chateau and we'll head into Easson together. Understood?'

Another group acknowledgement.

It was soon after that Gleave cried out. Everyone turned to look at him, hands on weapons. He looked ill, distraught. He looked like the situation had finally struck him.

'What is it?' Correia said, reigning in and turning her horse. All eyes were on Gleave, who slumped in his saddle, shaking his head. He turned and looked back the way they'd come, across wood covered water and past weeping willows. He muttered something whilst turning back to the others.

'What is it?' Correia demanded, more than a little short tempered.

'My Pecker.' Gleave took a deep breath. 'That girl still has hold of my Pecker.'

Sav roared with laughter.

Chapter 27 – Fells, chambers and the open ocean

Correia groaned from the saddle as Gleave pulled alongside.

'What?' Gleave frowned as he looked across at her.

'Pull your hose up, Gleave.' Correia indicated the rolls of road-dusted black wool around his ankle-boots, and on to his bare legs above that.

'Why? It's bloody hot this far south and my legs were sweating like a man on a rack.'

'I don't give two shits, Gleave. I don't want to see your pale legs of a morning, nor your sweat-stained bandage and braes.'

Gleave grunted a laugh. 'You wanna see the sweat stains under my padding?' He grinned.

'I'd rather see nothing of what's beneath your padding, or anything else for that matter. Now hoist and tie up your bloody hose.'

Cursing, Gleave did as he was told, leaning one way then the other before fiddling with and tying the top of his hose to his braes, lifting his dark green padded gambeson to do so; his cursing continued and increased in vehemence as he rode along.

Correia smirked.

'Don't blame me if I stink tonight, Correia.'

'Tonight?' Correia laughed. 'You stink all the time, worse than our horses. There'll be no change there, Gleave.'

'No wonder,' Gleave called out, 'if you won't let me strip off!' He kicked his mount on to pull alongside Sav, who was leading the group.

'A wash wouldn't go amiss, Gleave!' Correia shook her head in disbelief at the back of the man's head.

'Clean folk are easier to track, and stand out a mile in the wilds, Correia,' was Gleave's over the shoulder reply. 'And we're potentially in enemy territory, so—'

'So you'll stink them to death will you? When they come for us; attracted by the noses of their swill-hunting pigs?'

Gleave offered up two fingers to Correia, and nothing more.

Correia smiled.

Sav laughed.

***

'You didn't think this possible, did you, my sweet?'

167

Flavell smiled, nuzzling her head into Croal's shoulder as they lay clothed on her bed. 'When my father told me I was to come here to arrange my own marriage, no, I didn't.' She looked into his eyes. 'But now?' Her smile broadened into a wonderful thing. 'I can't imagine anything else.'

'You are far more beautiful than I could have ever hoped for, do you know that?'

Flavell's high and wide cheeks flushed red. She buried her head once more into Croal's shoulder.

'Why so shy? You know how stunning you are. I see your confidence in my uncle's court.'

'Around men I care nothing for,' she admitted, voice muffled in his silks.

Croal half-rolled and grabbed her waist, pulling her closer. 'But you care for me, eh? Don't you, my sweet?'

She giggled, the sound magical to Croal's ears. To any man's ears.

'Yes. You care for me and perhaps… love me?'

She looked up at that, silent, eyes moist, wide; a single nod was her answer as she pulled strands of fair hair from her perfect face. Her emotion was plain for Croal to see, for him to drink in and absorb and love back.

'And I love you, my sweet,' he said softly. 'Though I know not how we both came to be like this, after so short a time.' She blinked up at him and he gasped. He leaned in and their lips met; his thin, hers full, the passion unbound. Croal's hand searched Flavell's body, hunting for an opening to the pale, smooth skin beneath.

Amis cleared his throat from the corner where he'd been standing, eyes locked on the courtyard below Flavell's window.

Dual sighs, and not of passion, came from the bed.

'You're killing our love, de Valmont,' Flavell said, serene face darkening.

'And you're killing me, mademoiselle.' Amis kept his back to them. 'Literally, should your father discover the sort of thing you were both leading to had I not cleared my throat.'

'Pfft.' Croal rolled onto his back and stared at the ceiling, hand clutching Flavell's. 'He could not know. And what does it matter, de Valmont, when we are to be wed? My uncle has already agreed to the proposal and accepted the dowry, at least verbally.'

'It matters,' Amis said flatly. 'And Messire Guiscard would

know, despite the leagues between he and thee.' He turned to look upon the scowling couple.

'Come, my love.' Flavell climbed from the bed and held out her hand for Croal to follow. 'Let us walk in the garden. This room suffocates me all of a sudden.'

'Go on, my sweet. I will follow.'

With an angry glance at Amis, Flavell left the room. The door slammed behind her.

Amis de Valmont and Croal de Geelan, Seneschal d'Easson, stared at one another; glared at one another.

'You take your duty too far, de Valmont.'

'I take it where it needs to go, messire.'

'Don't think that because you are of this distant, unknown Steedon, and not of my Easson—'

'Your uncle's Easson.'

Croal's face flashed murder as he surged from the bed, blue silks ruffled, but back straight. 'I am a good man, messire,' Croal said, fighting to stay calm, for Flavell's sake if nothing else. 'I do not intend to lead your beloved mademoiselle astray.' He didn't feel he had to explain himself to Amis, but he did feel like he wanted to. Wanted anything to do with his Flavell to be done right and done well.

Amis' eyes widened as the word 'beloved' reached him.

'Oh yes, de Valmont,' Croal went on, a little harder now his own good intentions were made clear. 'It's obvious to me that you lust after my betrothed. So many days on the road, likely watching her—'

Amis stepped swiftly forward, once, twice. As he half-drew his sword from its scabbard, the oval pommel of the weapon stopped a hair's breadth from Croal's face, leaving his heart racing and his mouth dry.

'Ware, Seneschal. This wedding has not yet happened and until it does, Flavell's honour is mine to protect. And I take that very seriously indeed.'

Breathing heavily, anger and a little fear flushing through him, which increased his anger, Croal batted the cold pommel from his face. He turned without a word, fists clenched at his unarmed sides, and made for the door.

'Remember the tourney, messire. Remember our joust.'

Croal growled as he slammed the door behind him and made his way to the gardens.

'Where to, Cap'n?' Hitchmogh focused on his pipe, glad to be feeling up to packing it again, let alone smoking it. His recovery had been arduous. He couldn't fathom why The Three had let them go, nor how *Sessio* fled the Tri Isles without any of the Adjunct's ships pursuing them. Oh, they had a ship following alright, but it wasn't one of The Three's, of that both he and Mannino were sure.

With me in the state I was, a Tri Isles ship would've caught and harried us, not followed a ways behind. Hitchmogh started, realising as he did that Mannino had answered his question and continued talking, to him. The captain now awaited an answer to a question of his own, that much was clear. Hitchmogh let his unlit pipe hang limp from his bottom lip as he stared at Mannino, Hitchmogh's expression as vacant as his soul.

'If you ask a question of me, man, make sure you bloody well listen to the answer and following efforts to enquire as to your health, both physical and mental. Eh?'

Hitchmogh's pipe bobbed as he nodded.

'Well?' Mannino rolled his eyes and reached for a clay pot on his desk. Hitchmogh rushed forward and snatched it from the captain, insisting on pouring the port for him instead.

'Physically I'm as plundered as ever. I feel like a troll has had its way with me. Mentally? I'm not sure I'm ever right with respects to that.'

Mannino took a sip of the port and swirled the remainder around in the glass. 'You know what I mean, man. How are your… abilities?'

Hitchmogh nodded, knowingly. 'I know what you meant and I don't like,' he lit his pipe, 'to admit it, but—'

'What?'

'We don't want no trouble, Cap'n.'

'I never want trouble, but it seems you get us into it.'

'Me?' The lit pipe slipped and hung from Hitchmogh's mouth.

Mannino sat back in his chair, glass held up, elbow on the armrest. 'You practically blew up a Hillside block of hovels.'

'Because you ran off, all hero-like!'

Mannino grinned. 'You think so?'

Hitchmogh barked a laugh. 'Stop fishing for such things. It was what it was and we did what we did. Question is—'

'Why did they let us go?'

'Aye.'

'Master Quinnell asked the very same of me.'

'And you said?' Hitchmogh raised his eyebrows, pipe now in hand.

'That they play games, The Three. Is there any other reason? Is there any other reason they do anything other than games and whims and sudden urges?'

Shrugging, Hitchmogh popped the pipe back in his mouth, puffed on it several times and walked through the resulting smoke to stand besides Mannino.

'They said something about the mainland. About something big being on the move, or something like that anyway. I wasn't exactly with it after out jaunt through Hillside.'

'No, you weren't. Fat lot of good you would have been if they'd intended us harm. What!'

'Oh, they intended us harm alright, Cap'n. Just seems they were too preoccupied, or too lazy, to do anything about it on that occasion. Anyhow, even if I'd have been my usual unfit self, rather than my wrecked unfit self, if The Three had made a move on us, I'd be about as useful as a eunuch in a brothel, or Squall in a desert. Or—'

'Alright man, alright. But with your soul—'

'They're The *bloody* Three, Cap'n! 'Morl's balls, but they're about as powerful as you can get without being a deity. In fact,' Hitchmogh turned to face Mannino, his fear plain to see, 'I'm not sure Squall herself, with the goblin Blood God and Sir Samorl riding Crackador like a bitch could take them down, not when they're together and not when they're treating something like it should be tret and not like one of their damned and blasted games.'

'Alright,' Mannino said, lifting a hand to calm the increasingly agitated Hitchmogh. 'Let's leave that one there for now, shall we? We were lucky, no? Let's put it down to that and put it to bed.'

Hitchmogh nodded and turned back to stare at the sea charts that were pinned to the wall.

After a pause filled with nought but pipe puffing and port sipping, Hitchmogh asked about the ship that continued to follow them.

'I have my suspicions, and such as they are, I'm not worried.'

'Fair enough, Cap'n. Fair enough. On to, or rather back to, my original question.' Hitchmogh looked at his captain once more.

Mannino pursed his lips and placed his glass back on the desk. Steepling his fingers, he tilted his head from side to side for a moment before speaking.

'Options aren't presenting themselves as readily as they used to, Master Hitchmogh. Neither is work. We've burnt bridges at the Tri Isles, but that happened a long time ago, we've set them alight again is all.' Hitchmogh grunted a laugh at that and nodded. 'We're best staying clear of Wesson for a while after running—'

'Oh shit, that reminds me.'

Mannino raised his brow and turned to face his first mate. 'Go on.'

'Master Spendley told me he saw a big bastard ship enter port, at night. Whilst we were playing chase to save our stupid trio.'

'And?'

'And he swears it was the very big bastard ship that nearly had us when we ran the blockade, escaping Wesson and her plague.'

Mannino took a deep breath and released it slowly, but said nothing.

'Strange it making port at the Tri Isles?' Hitchmogh moved back to the front of the desk. 'And stranger still...'

'Yes?' Mannino's eyes snapped to Hitchmogh's.

'Spendley also swears there was a bloody big flag flying behind it. He said the ship was lit like the northern lights and he caught a glimpse of that flag.'

'Aye, a king's ship. One of Barrison's own.'

Hitchmogh shook his head and drew long and hard on his pipe before revealing what Charl Spendley had seen. 'Wasn't the flag of *that* royal Altolnan, Cap'n.'

Mannino frowned. It didn't take long at all for that frown to give away to surprise. 'Edward?'

Hitchmogh nodded once. 'Aye. The Black Prince himself. Seems he's got himself a dwarven-gun toting toy, and I was wondering whether he thought himself a pirate hunter. And I was wondering, Cap'n, whether he classes us as such and whether he has *Sessio* in his mind's eye as a grand prize.'

Mannino filled his cheeks and released his breath with a pop. 'I sincerely hope not, man. I sincerely hope not indeed.'

'Well that makes two of us.'

Nodding, Mannino stood and moved to the very wall chart Hitchmogh had been staring at. 'She may be a big ship,' he said, tracing lines on the chart with his finger, 'but she's not fast. Not like us, and not like that ship following us.'

'I had wondered whether it was her or not, Cap'n, but also thought the same about the speed we've been making. Plus, the boy in the nest says the following ship is much smaller. A galley, he reckons.'

'No, it's not Edward's ship that follows, you're right there. And I'd have to agree it's a galley, too. Seems we have problems coming out of our ears at the moment, with little in the way of safe harbours to run to, what with the Chriselle Coast being patrolled by the gods know what.' Mannino turned on Hitchmogh. 'We could outrun whoever follows, give ourselves time to make plans.'

'You mean I could have us outrun them?'

Mannino nodded.

'And if we run into more trouble? I mean that seems likely of late, doesn't it, Cap'n?'

Sighing hard, Mannino turned back to the charts. There was a pause where neither said a word.

Hitchmogh savoured smoke then spoke. 'At least Master Spendley effected repairs whilst we were... on shore leave.'

'And they hold? They're lasting repairs?' Mannino said over his shoulder.

'Aye, seems so. The new lad, Quin, he's been useful and checked it all out. Seems confident. He may have been an apprentice but he knows his stuff it seems, and it turns out it was *his* master who assisted in said repairs, so he knows the man's work.'

'Good. He's a nice lad. He'll need toughening up though.'

Hitchmogh drew on his pipe and nodded. There was no need to vocalise his agreement. Pulling his pipe from his mouth, he hesitated before going on. 'Master Spendley spent a lot of what we had to make the repairs in such a time.'

'That's to be expected.'

'Well, so long as you know how little we have left, Cap'n.'

'Yes. Very good. Leave me now, Master Hitchmogh. I've charts to look at and thinking to do.'

'Very well, Cap'n. Shout if ye need me. I'll be down in the hold proper.'

Mannino waved his hand without looking. 'Will do. Will do. Glad you've recovered.'

'Thank you, Cap'n,' Hitchmogh said, before turning to leave.

173

'Let's hope we have a little more time though, eh? Before we run into owt else.'

'Of course, of course.'

Smiling to himself at his old friend's reply, Hitchmogh left the room.

***

'How's the chaperone business going, de Valmont?' Giles Bratby asked, appearing from a doorway reserved for servants.

Amis looked to the broad-chested Earl and smiled. 'As thrilling as you would imagine, messire.'

Giles grunted a laugh. They stood in companionable silence a while, watching Flavell and Croal whispering in each-others ears and laughing, as close as ever.

'They're like children.'

Giles looked to Amis and offered a sympathetic smile. 'You yearn for her, don't you, lad?'

Amis looked to the side and huffed. 'Why do people keep telling me that—?'

'Because it's true. I've said it before myself, to you, and you didn't deny it.'

The following silence was broken by a stream of laughter and nothing else. After the laughter settled and the watched couple returned to their whispers, Giles turned to face Amis – came around to block his view.

'You're a handsome lad,' Giles said, holding Amis' stare. 'You could enjoy a maid or two, or any lass, whilst here. And find yourself a wife when you return home.'

'I have a duty, messire.'

Giles smiled and looked over his shoulder. 'Aye, to see them two wed. A foregone conclusion is that and you know it.' He looked back to Amis. 'Relax, man. I'm the bloody prisoner here and I'm more relaxed than you.'

Amis couldn't help but smile at that. They again stood in silence, Giles turning to watch the young man and woman who were oblivious to the men watching them, as if the Earl and chevalier were but servants.

'Do you think he loves her?'

Giles paused before answering. 'I think he thinks he loves her.'

Frowning, Amis turned to Giles.

'They've not known each other long,' Giles explained. 'But I think they're intentions are genuine. Which says a lot considering it's a noble marriage; arranged.'

'Could be worse, I suppose.'

'Aye, lad, it could.'

'Were you made to marry your wife?'

Giles barked a laugh, turning the heads of Croal and Flavell.

'Apologies, messire, it was—'

A hand stopped Amis' apology. 'We were matched by our fathers, yes. However,' Giles smiled, 'we found love nonetheless, I'm happy to report. Took us a lot longer than these two though; I reckon they'll realise that this was lust before they're ten years together. Then they'll discover true love, if they're lucky and if such a thing exists outside my head.' The old Earl smiled softly, stealing a glance at the young man by his side.

'You sound sceptical?' Amis said.

'I know how I feel about my wife, Amis. What to label it doesn't concern me. True love is a fancy tag, but I know what it is, what she is, to me, and that's what counts. I reckon love could mean all manner of things to different folk. No?' He glanced at Amis once more.

'I suppose so, messire.'

'So, perhaps you don't lust after the lady Flavell. Perhaps you—'

'Don't. Please.' Amis kept his eyes front.

Giles grunted. 'Very well, lad. Let's go and drink, you and I, like last time. These two can't get up to much in here, surrounded by servants, though we rarely see them stood around, weighting on us…' For the first time in a long time, Giles noticed the half dozen men and women stood backs to the walls, eyes high, but centred on the room.

'Thank you, messire… Giles,' Amis smiled, 'but I must decline. I haven't heard the last of it for the previous drinking session you lured me to.' Amis looked at Giles and grinned.

Giles gave a hard look back and took Amis by the arm. 'I bloody well insist, lad. I need a supping partner or I'll go mad, stuck in this damned chateau. And it's about time you learnt to call me by the familiar. To me, that says you're ready for sharing another pot or two with me.' Without another word, Giles dragged Amis from the room and neither the servants nor the kissing couple batted an eyelid.

Chapter 28 – Wrong turn

The blustery morning wind hushed across scrubland and Fal's ears both, masking a sound Fal stopped to listen to. He rubbed his cold lobes and relished the warm kiss of the sun every time a gust fell, leaving a lighter breeze in its wake.

Turning his head to the side, Fal did his best to block out the wind, attempting to hear the noise once more.

His elven-gifted steed shifted beneath him as its ears pricked up, angled straight ahead. Fal turned his head further to the side, reducing the wind's voice to a whisper.

A dog barked in the distance.

Fal hadn't been told of any farms or hamlets ahead, by Gleave or Correia. He frowned and tilted his head again, trying to decide whether the animal was closing on him or not.

Large gorse bushes and small, twisted trees leaning with the wind blocked Fal's field of vision, but a second bark, closer now, confirmed what he'd feared as his steed pawed the ground.

Fal stood in his stirrups, trying to see across the yellow flecked gorse ahead, squinting against the wind.

Four great wolf hounds bounded around the thicket, accelerating towards horse and rider.

Dropping back into his saddle, heart thumping, lips cursing, Fal pulled on the reins and turned the magnificent animal on the spot, an action the horse needed no encouragement in performing. Heels struck horse's flank and the horse launched forward, passing a canter and swiftly reaching an all-out gallop. The sprawling gorse and gnarled trees rushed by, blurring in Fal's periphery.

The hounds continued their pursuit. Fal could hear them and so could his horse. They weren't gaining, but nor, across the rough ground, was the horse leaving them behind.

The dark green of The Marches stretched across the horizon like a sea of foliage as Fal crested and dropped down into a shallow vale. He remembered crossing the vale and was confident he raced towards his companions. Despite the distance he knew them to be, he was also confident he'd reach them before the hounds would him. Fal aimed for the narrow ford he'd used on the way out, eyes scanning the mottled vista for any sign of the stream it crossed.

Another sound reached Fal, and his mount judging by the flutter of her ears.

Turning in his saddle and trusting the horse, he looked back at the wolf hounds, which were closer now, able as they were to charge down the hill faster than Fal's mount. He spied thick leather collars; his eyes drew to the fleeting glimpse of a rider far behind both him and the hounds. A rider who'd disappeared into a gully before Fal could make him out.

Fal cursed and looked back the way his mount was taking him.

The nimble horse cut left as a man appeared from behind a squat tree to Fal's right. The sudden movement threw Fal from the saddle, his fall broken and life saved by the dense thicket his horse avoided ploughing into.

The sound of retreating hooves wasn't lost on Fal as he shook off the shock and impact of the fall. The nearby man on foot, closing rider and hounds flashed through Fal's mind and he fumbled for his falchion. Thrashing, he tried to pull his arm through the gorse to reach his weapon, but the only one he saw was the blade that pressed against his throat; a long blade, held by a man silhouetted by the sun and flanked by four wolf hounds. Fal's eyes looked from the silhouette to the grey furred animals, all of which sat at their master's booted feet, tongues lolling as they panted in the sun.

Before Fal could utter a word, something struck him on the side of the head.

His vision blurred, before blacking out altogether.

Chapter 29 – Our Queen

'Where have you been?' Flavell clung to Croal like a limpet to a rock. Knuckles white, she stopped him from pulling away as a shout for him to attend his uncle filled the corridor.

'I must go, my sweet. I'll speak to you—'

'Now!' Flavell demanded. 'You'll speak to me now, after disappearing for gods know how long.'

Croal frowned and looked to the woman holding him firm. He didn't miss the smirk that played across de Valmont's face, despite the chevalier looking through an arrow loop in the wall.

'We have a prisoner,' Croal said, reluctantly.

'Like the Earl of Bratby?'

Croal shook his head. 'No,' he said, eyes flicking to and from Amis' yellow clothed back. Flavell said nothing so he continued, pulled in by her green eyes. She always looked as if every word or sight or sound was a wonder. 'We've taken an Orismaran warrior,' Croal said, words tumbling from a mouth that wanted nothing more than to kiss his betrothed. 'He was riding on our lands.'

Flavell's concern was evident in her searching eyes and part opened mouth. Amis turned at the news, his own concern as evident as Flavell's.

'How is that possible, messire?' Amis asked Croal.

Croal sighed and looked back down the corridor to where a soldier in the blue and white chevrons of Easson stood, awaiting his company.

'Sirreta is invaded,' Croal said, to Amis more than Flavell.

'We know that, my love,' Flavell said, attempting to draw his attention back to her. 'But that is far from The Marches.'

Yes, including Steedon, your father's lands...

Croal shook the thought away as he replied. 'It seems they are moving up through Sirreta, my sweet. My uncle tells me he's had no word for weeks, but my own scouts tell me much.'

Amis stepped forward. 'And you've told your uncle of this threat to his lands? What is the marquis doing about it?' Amis shot the questions at Croal, his hand instinctively finding the hilt of his sheathed sword.

Croal swallowed hard and looked from Amis to Flavell and back. He shook his head. 'He does nothing, messire. Nothing.'

Baulking at the answer, Amis came forward yet more, narrowed eyes locked on Croal's. 'Nothing?' he said as if an accusation.

'Surely he gathers his forces to him, at the least?'

'No, de Valmont, he does not.' Croal shook his head once more, sighed and took hold of Flavell's cold hands. She said nothing, only looked between the two men.

'I have pleaded with my uncle to send me south, with his and my men—'

'And he turns you down?' Amis cut in. 'But it is his duty to respond to such news.'

'Yes, messire, it is, but he says he is to hold Easson against Altoln, Suttel to be specific, more than he is to move against Orismaran raiders harrying our country's centre; he claims that is the work of nobles elsewhere.' Croal was exasperated with it all and he let that show.

'Hold against Suttel?' Amis said, incredulous. 'Hold against the very man you have prisoner? Giles Bratby?' Amis scoffed. 'The Three with that, messire. Your uncle, the Marquis d'Easson no less, has no threat from a man he holds prisoner, Earl or not. And even if your uncle did and a Suttel army marches through the forest road crying for his head, I'm damned sure Giles Bratby, the Marquess of Suttel after all, would put those men to better use on Orismaran raiders, once he knew the situation.'

'I know that!' Croal shouted, releasing Flavell's hand as he did so. His frustration and anger and impotence at the whole situation burst forth into those three words. The relief of release was immense. 'I know all of that, messire,' he said, lowering his voice, which made him sound more dangerous than when he'd shouted. He stood toe to toe with the yellow chevalier of Steedon, and both men flinched not once under each-others regard. 'But what would you have me do? Eh? What would you have me do?'

Amis filled his cheeks and stepped back a pace before releasing his breath. The soldier down the corridor cleared his throat. Croal held up a hand to silence the man, eyes intent on Amis, who searched the low ceiling for answers. His eyes snapped to Croal's.

'Have Giles send word, by bird or rider, that he is safe and well and—'

Croal sighed. 'We allowed him that as soon as we took him. They'll be raising his ransom, collecting from their tenants and—'

'I know how chivalric ransoms work, messire, but did he say not to attack, in his message? Did he specifically say not to attempt a rescue? If not, have him do so now. Have him sign and send such a message, then, with that honourable agreement in place, your uncle might send you—'

'Stay!' Flavell blurted. She pulled Croal back round to face her. 'Stay, my love. Don't march. No matter what.'

'Mademoiselle,' Amis said, 'you know nothing of such matters—'

'De Valmont,' Flavell said with venom, without looking to him, 'you overstep your rank.'

Amis' face reddened as Croal glanced at him.

Flavell's face soften as she followed Croal's glance to Amis. 'Do you not talk to Earl Bratby, de Valmont? Do you not hear of his wife holding his castle whilst he resides here?'

'His son, Sir Allon—' Amis started.

'Commands his forces, yes,' Flavell interrupted, 'but his wife does indeed command Bratby Castle, I've heard it said.'

Croal confirmed it.

Gritting his teeth, Amis nodded, conceding. 'And your point, mademoiselle?'

'Her point, messire,' Croal said, looking down at Flavell in realisation, 'is that Flavell has a say in this whole affair, as my future wife.' They both smiled. Croal heard Amis grunt.

'Messire Seneschal,' the Easson soldier said, coming forward. 'I must insist you follow me to see your—'

'Alright,' Croal snapped. 'Go, I will follow.'

'Messire.' The man nodded and sped off.

'Stay,' Flavell said again, pulling Croal in close. 'I can't lose you now. Your Queen's armies will hold...'

Our Queen, my love.

'...Orismaran raiders will never pass the heart of Sirreta, will they? Stay and do your duty here: defend Easson, as your uncle wishes. Defend me!' She reached up on her toes and kissed Croal, and his heart fluttered and his body tingled. Oh how he wanted nothing more than to pull her away to his chambers and forget all of this.

'First,' Croal said as their lips parted, 'I will see what my uncle has to say. Then,' he continued, fingers interlocking with Flavell's, 'I shall pay this Orismaran prisoner a visit—'

'And?' Amis demanded.

Croal turned on the man. 'And I shall make a decision, along with my uncle. Watch your station, de Valmont. I shall ask for your advice should I need it, otherwise, hold your tongue.' Croal turned from a red-faced Amis, resolve filling him with his love at his side.

He kissed Flavell once more and walked away before she, or Amis de Valmont, could say anymore.

'You talked to him?' Flavell asked, sometime later.

'Yes, my sweet.' Croal sighed, rubbed his face hard and dropped into the chair beside Flavell.

'You're tired, my love.'

He smiled. 'I am indeed.'

'What did the prisoner say?' Amis asked from the window.

'We've talked about this,' Flavell said, glaring. She turned to Croal. 'What did he say?'

Croal managed to grunt a laugh at the repeated question. 'He says he is Altolnan. Orismaran by birth, but Altolnan nonetheless.'

Amis turned and frowned. 'Altolnan?'

'Yes, messire, that is what I said, is it not?'

Amis turned back to look out the window.

'He's lying.' Flavell reached across and took Croal's hand. She squeezed it and he smiled. 'You look more than tired, my love.'

A ragged breath left Croal's lips. 'I have a stomach for a fight, my sweet, but not for what Rasoir is doing to that man. Orismaran or not.'

'Tell me,' Flavell said, a little too eagerly for Croal's liking.

He shook his head.

'You don't want to know such things, mademoiselle, trust me,' Amis said from the window.

Flavell turned and scowled at him.

'For once, my sweet, I agree with your pet sword.'

Amis laughed.

'Fine.' Flavell let go Croal's hand. 'Protect the delicate flower, the two of you. I merely thought I could help glean something from whatever he may have told you, under duress or not.'

Croal reached across and took Flavell's hand as she had his. 'I will tell you all he says, my sweet, but not how and why he said it.'

Flavell offered Croal a tight smile, nothing more.

'Was he alone?'

Croal looked to Amis. 'Seemed to be, although he is likely a scout.'

'Certainly,' Amis said, beginning to pace the room's outer wall. 'They could be closer than we feared.'

'Perhaps,' Croal admitted.

'Certainly,' Amis said again, locking eyes with Croal. 'Has the marquis agreed to do anything about it? Send riders, scouts; agreed to let you ride out?'

Croal nodded, but grimaced. The memory of his uncle's words frustrated and angered him both. 'It's not good.'

'How so?' Flavell asked, her voice wavering at what was, perhaps, to come.

'My uncle has closed his borders completely.'

Flavell frowned. 'My love?'

'He has stopped all messengers, all comings and goings on all roads and tracks on his lands. He calls it a matter of defence, yet he sends no force out to defend what is his; what is ours.'

'When was this? When did he order such a thing?' Flavell asked, taken aback by it all.

Croal sighed. 'When I asked him to have Bratby sign an agreement—'

'You took de Valmont's advice?' Flavell cut in, amazed.

'I did, my sweet. Well, I tried.' He looked to Amis, who nodded his thanks.

'I don't understand,' Amis said after a moment's pause on all sides. 'He refused to have Earl Bratby order his own men back, on the off chance they were to march on Easson? And he closed all communication that he needs in such a time by ceasing all traffic across his borders? That won't stop an army, messire. In fact, it'll spread his men thin to hinder a travelling few.'

Croal pulled his lips into a tight, sad smile and nodded throughout Amis' words. 'I agree and I agree and I agree,' Croal said once Amis had stopped. 'Alas, de Valmont, my sweet,' he looked to Flavell, 'my uncle does not agree.'

'I'd say his brain is addled, if I didn't know any better,' Amis said, steeling a glance at Flavell. Croal watched his love glower back at Amis and the three fell into a contemplative silence.

***

''Morl's balls, Gleave, shut up about your Pecker will you.' Sav leaned back in his saddle and glared at the grey sky. The wind had died down, but not before dragging in heavy looking clouds that threatened more than dull shade.

Gleave snarled at Sav from alongside. 'It'd be different if you'd left Starks back at the inn, on the bloody border; in the middle of a bloody forest!'

Starks made to speak, but was cut off by Sav.

'The lad's hardly my pet,' Sav said, although the comparison tickled him.

'All of you shut up.' Correia reined her horse in and the others pulled alongside her.

Sav leaned forward, squinting. 'Isn't that...' He swallowed hard.

'Fal's horse,' Correia finished. Her own horse lurched forward before the others could reply, but they soon followed her lead towards the empty saddled, grazing animal.

Reaching the horse, Correia took hold of its loose reins.

'His saddle bags are all there, and his cloak,' Starks said, pointing to the woollen roll attached to the back of the saddle.

'Aye.' Sav looked from horse to dark horizon. 'But it's partly pulled from the straps, like he dismounted in a hurry.' He chewed his bottom lip at that.

'Or fell?'

'Gleave!' Correia rounded on the man, nostrils flaring.

Greened plate lifted as he shrugged. He too looked off to the horizon. 'The chateau's that way though, isn't it?'

'Yes.' Correia handed Fal's reins to Sav and stood in her stirrups. After surveying the area, she sat again and set out at a trot.

'No more scouting on our own. We're to ride together and find...'

Correia stopped talking at the appearance of half a dozen cloaked and hooded men, who came from behind gorse thickets. Most of them carried recurve bows, all of which were shorter than Sav's, but deadly all the same. Arrows were knocked and arrows were pointing their way.

Correia stopped her horse, took a deep breath and released it before holding her arms out to the sides.

Reluctantly, and with much cursing by Gleave, the others did the same.

'No harm if no trouble,' said one of the men, in Sirretan; one of only two without a bow. He stepped forward, the filthy fingers of his right hand wringing the long, hardwood haft and iron langet of the axe he carried. Correia slouched, trying to see into the shrouded hood with no luck. All the men were on foot, but the speaker's weapon was a horseman's axe and no mistake, the thin and light crescent blade perfect for lopping limbs and cutting deep into torsos with one hand, the spikes on the rear and top of the haft ideal for thrusting through gaps in plate. It was a well-made and well-kept blade, not a woodsman's axe and not a bearded axe of the north. So why wasn't the man mounted, and why did he and his men look so damned filthy and ragged?

A dark cloud blocked the sun, casting a deep shadow across the Woolf Fells. The hooded men looked more like spectres than brigands, their slate grey cloaks doing well to blend them with their surroundings.

'We have little to give you,' Correia said in Sirretan, walking her horse a few steps towards the speaker. She wasn't convinced they were brigands, but it was best to think that way until she knew more. 'We must move on with haste. A friend of ours passed through here recently. This is his… was his horse. I can pay you a small sum for information.' She motioned to the rider-less animal that pulled at a spray of tall grass. 'You wouldn't happen to know—'

'Not us, madame,' the speaker said. 'Any more information does require payment.'

He speaks very well, Correia thought. *As would a chevalier, or at least a long serving and educated retainer.*

'What a surprise,' Gleave said in passable Sirretan. The snarl pulling at his face had been present since the men appeared, Correia knew. She noticed Sav and Starks' confusion at what was being said, and their impressed glances at both her and Gleave when they'd spoken in the local tongue.

'I tell you, soldier man,' said the axe wielder, 'it was not us.'

'What wasn't?' Gleave asked, moving his horse forward.

'Enough movement!' The speaker shouted. Two of the archers flat-drew strings to chests and Gleave stopped. The strings relaxed again.

'We've no time for this,' Correia said. 'We're in Sirreta to see the Marquis d'Easson, but ultimately to find out why no word is reaching us from this side of the border. We've heard rumour of battles, of armies on the march. What do you know of this, brigand?'

The speaker lowered his hood. Black hair fell to the man's broad shoulders. He released his left hand from the horseman's axe and raised it. The hooded men vanished from sight, using the shadows and terrain to aid them.

'You have heard of the armies?' the axeman asked, incredulous. He approached Correia, arm and axe held wide. She nodded whilst lowering her arms to her sides. Her Pathfinders did the same.

184

'Eudes de Geelan, the marquis you seek audience with, has your man. He is Orismaran, no?'

Correia nodded eagerly. 'Yes, yes that's him.'

The man let the axe slide through his hand to thump on the ground. Leaning on it, he took in the Pathfinders before looking back to Correia.

'The marquis' men have been stopping travellers, traders, messengers; everyone, from leaving these lands. His troops range the edge of The Marches, ensuring no one gets through... as do other things.'

Correia frowned and shook her head. 'Why?' she asked, ignoring the latter for now. 'Why would he do that if Sirreta is in need of aid? Altoln would answer her plea if Queen Velenn asked it of us.'

'And you can say that, can you?' the man said, looking up to Correia from beside her. 'You can speak for Barrison on such a matter?'

Correia nodded. 'I can and I am.'

'Then ride,' the man said. 'Ride back before men of Easson return. Ride back and tell your King, tell him Sirreta does indeed require aid. Tell him Sirreta is falling back, back to its towns and chateaus and citadels, many of which are besieged. Many of which may have already fallen. Tell him Queen Velenn herself has pulled her greatest army back to the capital, back to Lejeune itself after losing her eldest brother, the Duc du Sud, in a disastrous battle earlier this year. She needs aid, now!'

Looking around to the others, Correia saw the concern in their faces, for even Sav and Starks had worked out what was being discussed, Correia was sure of that. She knew those looks though, those men. She knew their concern wasn't for Sirreta, not solely. Their concern, and hers, was for Fal.

'We need retrieve our man,' she said. 'We also need to retrieve an Altolnan Earl, Giles Bratby, for your marquis holds him—'

'He is not *my* marquis!' the axeman said, spitting off to the side. 'The shit calls his local peers to him, to host jousts and feasts and balls. Can you believe, madame? He hosts these things whilst his brothers and sisters go to war. Whilst they die in the thousands at the hands of—'

'Who?' Correia interrupted, leaning down towards him.

'Everyone and everything.' The man's voice caught in his throat, his face paling as he looked at Correia, eyes imploring her to act on his news.

'How do you know all this?' she whispered, reaching down a hand, placing it on the man's shoulder. She felt solid plate under the cloak. Gleave and Sav both moved their horses towards them, hands on weapons despite the arrows likely a draw and flight away from striking them from their mounts.

'I rode to Eudes de Geelan for aid. I rode, my men and I, by order of the Duc de Mallard, the Marshal of Sirreta no less.'

Correia pulled back, brow creased. Her eyes searched his.

'He turned us away, the marquis,' the deflated man said, head shaking in disbelief, the time between then and now doing nothing to make sense of it to him. 'I'm a chevalier of Sirreta, madame. A retainer to Queen Velenn's uncle, de Mallard... and Eudes de Geelan turned me away like I was a nuisance to his merry making.'

'Who marches on you? And be more specific.' Correia felt bad for the man, and scared for him and his country, but she was there for information and this man had it, so she pushed and pushed hard. 'Orismar?' she quested, when the man's glazed eyes offered nothing in return. He nodded, sighed and looked back to her, dark eyes focused once more.

'Them and more. Goblins, adlets and things I or my men have never seen before.'

'Like what?' Gleave asked, moving closer.

The man bit his bottom lip, much like Sav had been doing, and shook his head. He looked to Gleave, finally answering.

'Whatever haunts your dreams, soldier. Whatever nightmare you can conjure, they have brought upon us.'

'You faced them, in battle?' Gleave asked, fingers playing on the blade of his own axe.

'No. I saw them. I did not face them.'

Gleave's look was readable. He wanted the man to explain. He wanted to know if he was a deserter.

'My liege, de Mallard, knew it was folly. He sent me and my men here to Easson, as I said. The Duc told us that many from the north had ridden to his banner, but not all. He sent four of his chevaliers, me included, with our own men, north, to different seigneurs and higher nobles who failed to rally to his call. I don't know how the others fare, but us...' he turned, turned and looked at the cloud darkened scrub, at the darker shadows where his men hid. 'There was more of us when we rode away from the Marshal's army. Several fell within the first hour, more so within the first day.

186

After that we made good progress, animals running, fleeing, by our side at times, like you've never seen or would believe. We thanked the White Light upon our arrival to Easson.'

'And this is what is left?' Correia asked, her voice a melody of sympathy.

The man shook his head. He looked back to her. 'The marquis' men turned on us and we lost two more before we beat a bloody retreat. My men weren't conscripts, madame. My men were soldiers, liveried reeves and huntsmen of my house. I am a chevalier, as I said; second son to a comte and my men have served my family for years. I promised their wives I would return them after we put down the Orismaran tribes.' A breath shuddered through him and an unashamed tear fell. He let it. 'I have failed them. I have failed my father and I have failed the Marshal of Sirreta.' Correia made to speak but he held up his hand and shook his head once more. 'I have failed my Queen.' He looked into Correia's eyes, imploring her to send for aid.

'No, Sieur,' Correia said, motioning for Sav to bring Fal's horse forward. She took the reins and passed them to the distraught man. 'The Marquis d'Easson has failed *you*. Remember that; Eudes de Geelan and his peers, those who attend him now instead of your Marshal and Queen, they have failed *you*.'

More tears fell, on both sides. The chevalier was passed caring about losing face in front of a lady. He gripped the reins tight and he smiled, a thin line, but a smile nonetheless.

'Now take this fine, elven-trained steed and go with your men,' Correia whispered. 'Lead them from the saddle, as a chevalier should. Lead them home!'

Lip quivering, the man shook his head. 'There is no home left, for any of us, madame.'

Correia took a deep breath and sat up in her saddle. The wind was all that made a sound for some time. Sirretan and Altolnan eyes kept each other company, until Correia's broke painfully free to seek her own men. More passed between those looks, in that wind filled near silence, than any words could have bettered. Finally, Correia spoke.

'Will you honour your duty?' Correia asked, voice steady, back straight.

'I will.'

'Lead your men north, as you were ordered. You may not have found an ally in those you should have, but you've found one in me, in Altoln. We will honour the treaty signed centuries ago. Follow the forest road into The Marches, to the Twin Inns. There you will find an elf ranger named Errolas. He is our friend. He is *your* friend, Sieur. Tell him Correia Burr sent you and tell him what you have told me. Wait for us there. We're away to find our Orismaran friend. We're away to bring back our own marquess and by all the gods above and below, Sieur, if we can, we're away to see Eudes de Geelan pay!'

Correia looked back to her own, all of whom nodded to her, hands finally away from weapons, even Starks and Sav, who were being appraised of the situation by Gleave's hushed tones.

The chevalier looked south, to the shadows and then back to Correia.

'We should come with you, madame,' he said, lifting himself into Fal's saddle. 'It is *our* score to settle. It is Eudes de Geelan who betrayed *us*. And I have a horse to return now, to your man.'

Correia was shaking her head before he finished.

'Honour your orders, Sieur. Honour them and seek aid. An army sits on the far side of that forest,' she pointed behind her. 'An army ready to ride. Talk to my friend; talk to the elf. He will know what to do.'

With another tight smile and a respectful bow, the chevalier raised his axe high before pointing it north. Fal's horse walked on, through its former companions and towards the distant forest road. The shadows followed.

Once all had passed, the Pathfinders rode the other way, jaws set firm and determination set deep.

Chapter 30 - Avunculicide

Checking there was no one on the dark corridor, Amis moved down it, holding his scabbard so it didn't knock against his leg. Reaching his intended door, he checked once more before tapping on it. When no response came, he knocked harder. It was dark in the chateau and Amis carried no candle or lamp, so when the door opened, spilling a yellow glow into the corridor, he couldn't help but cover his eyes.

A hand took his arm and pulled him into the chamber.

'What are you playing at?' Giles Bratby's words were hushed, his rotten breath hot on the side of Amis' smooth face.

'Apologies, messire, but I have news I didn't want to discuss with you during the day.'

'Is that so?' Giles released Amis and Amis noticed the bollock dagger in the Earl's hand. The older man crossed to a side table and put the dagger down. Turning back, Giles rubbed his eyes and motioned for Amis to go on.

'Have you heard of the Orismaran they've captured?'

'Yes,' Giles said flatly, unimpressed. 'There better be more than that, lad. To wake me so.'

'There is,' Amis promised, voice low. He stepped into the room, fixing Giles' inquisitive gaze with a confident one of his own. 'The marquis has closed the borders to his lands.'

Giles shrugged. 'He'd already done—'

'No, Giles,' Amis corrected, before Giles could go on. 'He's closed them completely. To anyone! Even Sirretan messengers; even his own nephew, Croal.'

There was silence. Amis could see Giles milling over what he'd been told. He clearly hadn't heard the same.'

'Messire—'

Giles raised a hand and rubbed his face with them both. 'He has me trapped,' he said, with a finality to his tone.

Amis pulled his lips into a tight, sympathetic smile. 'No ransom will get through, no.'

Giles released a short, bitter laugh. 'The paranoid old shit of a man has done me over.' Giles looked back to Amis. 'If they truly have an Orismaran scout, a force won't be far behind, and no *border closure* is going to stop that. Not the sort of force that's made its way this far north. All it'll stop is the genuine messengers and poor bastard refugees.' Giles cursed and turned full circle, hands

189

linked behind his greying head.

'They're coming, aren't they, messire? The bastards are marching on us?'

'I think that they are. And I think that the old coot knows it. He's pulling his head and legs into his shell and hoping these fucking walls will protect him.'

Amis frowned. 'How though? How can an Orismaran army reach The Marches?'

'The coastal road is my bet, lad.' Giles crossed to a dresser and poured a glass of brandy. Turning, he gave it to Amis and poured himself one. 'The Sirretan pricks in Lejeune will have pulled everything back to them if their capital and queen are threatened. They care little if another force marches, or lands, on the coast; towards my borders and Royce. The Sirretan nobles likely expect Hugh Torquill to ride out with his army, Royce's Reds and all, to deal with Sirreta's problems for them.'

'But they're coming here, not to Royce, from what Croal has been told?'

'And why not, eh? This goat turd of a marquis is no Earl fucking Royce, lad. I tell you that.'

Amis nodded. 'And if they take Easson and this side of The Marches—'

'They cut much of Sirreta off from direct aid and have a lovely spot to launch an assault into Altoln; next campaign season, mind, we have that at least. It's too late in the year to do all they'd need to do now and march into Altoln proper.' Giles shrugged. 'Although, that depends how quickly they take Easson.' He sighed at the thought.

'We need to leave, messire. Leave before we're caught in a siege.'

Giles rocked back a bit at that. 'You'd leave Mademoiselle de Steedon?'

Amis rocked back the same. 'I'd do no such thing! We'll take her with us.'

'With guards about and roads closed?' Giles may have been questioning the idea, but Amis spied a glint in the older man's eyes.

'Where there's a will, messire…' Amis winked at Giles, who grunted a laugh.

'So they say, lad, so they say.'

Both men downed their brandy together.

'There's more,' Amis said after sighing pleasantly at the taste and burn of the spirit. Giles poured a second round and waited for Amis to go on.

'The Orismaran scout claims to be Altolnan, despite his darker skin and tribal tattoos.'

A bark of laughter this time from Giles, followed by a clink of glasses.

'Of course he did, lad.' Giles continued to chuckle at the thought. 'Of course he did,' he repeated, before locking a serious stare on Amis. 'I owe you for coming here, Amis. For telling me this.'

Nodding to that, Amis added more. 'The Orismaran claimed to be a pathfinder, I've not long ago learnt - there's benefits to standing in on Flavell and Croal's conversations.' He grinned. The grin passed as quickly as it'd come and Amis levelled a serious look on Giles once more. He'd seen the look of recognition the Altolnan had revealed to the *pathfinder* title. 'You know of what he speaks, Giles?' Amis switched to the familiar, as Giles had told him to do repeatedly during their time together. He hoped it would bring forth the truth of it.

Giles' brow remained furrowed, more so than normal. Several moments of nothing passed by and Amis let it, giving Giles time to think. When nothing came, he prompted the man.

'You're troubled by this news the most?'

Giles nodded. 'Troubled, aye. Troubled, intrigued and hopeful all at once.'

It was Amis' turn to frown. He swirled the second brandy around in the glass.

'If he's a pathfinder,' Giles explained, 'he is indeed Altolnan. And if that's true, we may have a way out, after all.'

'How so?'

Giles knocked back his brandy and poured a third. 'I shall tell you, my friend. I shall tell you...'

Confident in their plans should the opportunity arise, Giles and Amis settled into conversations of other matters.

'And what of her now, Amis? Do you trust she is safe in her room, in this chateau?'

Amis frowned. 'You think Croal would attempt to—'

'Croal?' Giles laughed. 'That'd be a matter of bringing things forward for future man and wife, nothing more. No, lad, not Croal. I'd be more worried about that old dog Eudes. You've seen how the marquis leers at your lady. You've seen how he paws at the maids. And that, my lad, is in front of his court, and his wife!

'Wait!' Giles wheezed the word as he pushed himself to his feet, in an attempt to chase Amis. The door hung open and all Giles heard was the echoing thud of boots on stone.

**

Flavell tried but failed to scream as the rough hand pressed hard against her mouth, the other pulling at her nightgown, trying to lift it. Eudes' weight pinned her body to the bed. Eyes wider than ever, Flavell stared at the bloodshot eyes looking back at her, accompanied as they were by the foul, rasping breath of the marquis. Her ears were filled with her own suppressed screams and the awful man's grunts and curses of exertion as he tried to part her legs and hold them out with his bared knees.

'You think,' he started, between grunts and curses, delicate hands slapping uselessly against his side and head. 'You think you can strut in here and wed my nephew… taking our wealth for your unknown family?'

The question was mute, for Flavell couldn't answer the man. Her eyes welled, her pale cheeks flushed red and her thighs burnt at the strain of keeping them together. Eudes was a much older man, but strong from years at the tilt and training yards, at hunt or at war.

'There's no way… I'm losing a valuable asset like Croal… to a title-less whore like you…' he managed, hands slipping further up, between Flavell's warm thighs, '…without,' he went on, spittle welling and dropping from his bottom lip, 'trying you out first… seeing if you—'

A shout and a clash of steel silenced Eudes' words and Flavell's struggles. They held their breaths as more shouts, a curse and a thud came from the far side of the door. Eudes' grip loosened and Flavell managed to bite the hand over her mouth before screaming as loud as she could. Eudes' shout of shock and pain joined hers to drown out the noise from the corridor.

Amis pulled his blooded sword from the blue and white chevroned gambeson of the second man at the door. Blood spilt and the guard attempted to stem the flow before Amis finished him with a pommel to the crown.

Steeling himself for what was to come, Amis noticed a confused and concerned maid appear from a room down the corridor.

'Fetch the seneschal,' Amis shouted. 'Now! Fetch Croal!'

The ashen-faced girl hoisted skirts and ran.

Amis turned the handle and threw the door open. With a snarl, he rushed into the room, sword leading. He hardly felt the dull thud across the back of his head, nor did he see where it came from. All he saw before the light faded was Eudes atop Flavell, her beautiful face a mask of fear.

Croal ran, two of his retainers at his back. The crying girl he followed, who he'd balled at for having his servants wake him, turned a corner, then another. His heart pounded. He'd got little sense out of the emotional maid, but he knew his uncle's chateau and he knew where the girl was leading him.

'That sounds like Bratby?' Croal said to no one in particular. The girl rounded a corner and Croal followed her. The screams and bellowing struck Croal as much as the developing scene in the darkened corridor they entered. The first person he saw was indeed Giles Bratby, who held one of the marquis' men by the throat, the man's sword arm gripped and held out wide by the large Earl.

'What is the meaning of this, Bratby?' Croal demanded, slowing to a fast walk as the maid shot inside a closer room and slammed the door. Croal's sword was in his hand, although he had no recollection of drawing the thing. Giles' eyes remained locked on the open doorway before him, rather than on the armoured man he held or the approaching men.

'Bratby!' Croal yelled, coming to a stop a swords length away.

Giles practically growled. 'Stay there, pup,' he said, without turning to address Croal and his retainers. The guard Giles held cried out in pain as Giles twisted his sword arm further, the wrong way.

'I've stopped,' Croal said, fearing the sound of soon to be breaking bones or joints or both. 'Now explain yourself, messire.'

'It's your bastard uncle who needs explain himself, lad.'

Croal frowned. A moment passed in which he heard his uncle's muffled voice from Flavell's room; the bottom fell out of Croal's stomach.

'Uncle?' Croal moved forward, chest heaving, regardless of Giles or his squirming prisoner. Heart thudding in his ears, Croal, loyal men at his back, forced Giles from his path, stumbled over a bloody mess of a man in the doorway and screamed his uncle's name as he surged into his beloved's bed chamber. Croal almost fell over another prone form: Amis. Eyes moving up from the downed chevalier, Croal took in his half-dressed uncle, who stood to the side of the bed, knife to Flavell's throat. Her face was red, cheeks wet. Her bosom heaved within her white nightgown and she struggled against Eudes' grip.

'Stop there, boy,' Eudes said. 'This doesn't concern the Queen's Seneschal—'

'Doesn't concern me?' Croal balked. He found it hard to talk, hard to breath. His palms were slick with sweat and he checked the grip on his familiar sword, the weight a comfort in the confusing, tumultuous situation.

'I needed to see what the little bitch was really about—'

'Don't lie to him, Eudes,' Giles shouted from the corridor, the marquis' man held firm. 'He's your bloody nephew, for 'morl's sake.'

'Croal,' Flavell managed, between sobs.

'Quiet!' Eudes commanded, his knife pressing in to her pale skin so much it was a wonder it didn't break.

Croal stepped forward, sword raised. He'd taken on an offensive posture without thinking. Years of training took over, his muscles comfortably raising the length of steel to such a place, ready to strike where and when needed, or defend should it come to it.

Eudes laughed at his nephew. 'Oh, come on, boy,' he said, spittle flecking his claret-stained bottom lip. 'You'll not act so over a bitch. Come to your senses. Half the shites running around Easson are mine. You think I would let this fine bit pass me by?'

Croal's snarl was enough to cause Eudes to take a shocked step back, pulling Flavell with him as he went.

'Harm her and I shall gut you, Uncle. You mark my words. I'll gut you and hang you from your own gatehouse, like you've done to others in the past.'

'You haven't the stomach for it, Croal. Now put that sword down. Now!'

'He's mad—'

'Quiet, Bratby,' Croal said, without turning. 'Or I'll gut you too so help me White.'

'You know what's coming, lad,' Giles went on anyway. 'You know the folly of your uncle's actions. Hiding away in his chateau

194

so he can rape—'

'I said quiet!' Croal screamed.

Flavell used the shock of that outburst to break free of Eudes' grip, but not before his knife scored a line across the side of her neck. Crying out, white gown spattered red, Flavell fell forward, into Croal's arms. Eudes lunged after her, knife leading, but Croal's sword was quicker. It jolted as it caught ribs and slid past vertebrae.

Eudes dragged the length of steel down to the floor, his own blade clattering on the stone beside him. Croal's arm and eyes followed it all down. He released the hilt of his sword and wrapped Flavell in a protective embrace as he watched his uncle curl around the bloody blade, attempting to pull at the hilt protruding from his chest. It was a while, without a word or move from any of the onlookers, until Eudes lay still. Silence followed. Even Flavell's crying had stopped, her hand pressed to the cut on her neck, her red eyes, along with everyone else's, on the body of the former marquis.

'Well… shit…' Giles said, breaking the silence. The man he held broke free and tried to run. Without an order, one of Croal's chevaliers chased and cut the man in the same livery as he down, the audible thud and following slaps of his sword reaching Croal. He couldn't even bare to imagine the thrice hacked man, for his uncle's bloody corpse stole all his mind could produce.

'Go for help,' the man with the bloody sword said to the other. 'I'll watch Croal.' He walked back to stand by the doorway, peering into the room. 'It's all yours now, Sieur—'

'Shut up!' Croal snapped, throwing a dangerous look his chevalier's way. The man nodded and stepped back.

Flavell buried her head into Croal's shoulder, floods of emotions breaking free. She shook and cried again as he held her, rocked her, told her she was safe.

'What will you do now?' Giles asked, leaning on the door.

'I don't know,' Croal admitted, eyes back on the body of his uncle. 'I don't know.'

Shouts came from a way off down the corridor.

'They're yours, Sieur,' the chevalier behind Giles confirmed.

Croal didn't care. He hugged his love and merely nodded at his man's words. Flavell continued to weep as multiple boots neared.

Amis groaned and stirred.

Croal's men were sent through the chateau, quickly, quietly and in some cases brutally. Their orders were simple: turn those men who they thought they could turn, and kill those they knew to be loyal to the late marquis and his wife. The marquise and her children were locked in their chambers as servants ran and cried, shouted and, again, in some cases died. Croal couldn't risk a knife in the back by one of his uncle's supporters, whether soldier or laundress. His men knew them all, knew who they could rely on and trust, or buy. There was no doubt in Croal's mind that some old scores were to be settled by his men, without his knowing, but he was, in a way, glad they would be dealt with, rather than hanging over him and his loyal few. There were troubling times enough heading their way.

'It's done, Sieur.' The chevalier was breathing heavily, the blue and white chevrons he wore spattered red.

Face grim, Croal nodded.

'Are the borders to remain closed?'

'Yes, for now at least. Send more men out in the morning though, at dawn's break. I want to know who travels my lands.'

The man failed to hide a smile.

'I did not plan this. Remember that. Have all remaining remember that.' Croal shook his head and began pacing the dark chamber. His uncle's body remained where he'd felled it.

'I know, Sieur, but the fact remains… Eudes had no sons. Sieur, you are the new Marquis d'Easson!'

Croal swallowed hard, his back straighter than it had been, despite his mental and near physical exhaustion at it all. 'Well, we'll have time to discuss such things at some point. It's not as simple as that and titles and such are not my concern right now.'

'Mademoiselle Flavell, Sieur? Is she well?' he said wisely, changing tack.

Croal turned and smiled at his man, his friend in comparison to everyone else he knew. 'Well enough, after all that has happened.' He looked again to his dead uncle, his dead father's older brother. His stomach threatened to empty itself, as it kept on trying to do. 'I sent her with de Valmont. Giles Bratby promised he would stay with them.'

A babe cried from somewhere nearby and Croal's eyes narrowed. 'I want no innocents harmed in this. Not unless there's no other way. I said that already, didn't I?'

The man raised his bloody hands. 'They won't be. I've warned the men. It's a babe wanting a tit is all, Sieur. I assure you.'

'Good. Good. Go, ensure all is as it should be. I'm to my aunt's chambers to... well.' Swallowing hard, bile burning his throat yet again, Croal offered his man a weak smile before they parted company.

Rubbing his face hard, Croal de Geelan, Seneschal d'Easson and now, potentially and by rights, marquis of the same, left the room he'd killed his uncle in and locked the door behind him. The thought of facing his aunt twisted his stomach more than anything else.

Chapter 31 – Enemy on the horizon

'How is your aunt?' Flavell's voice wavered from all that had happened. She'd been holed up in Giles' bed chamber all night, accompanied by Giles himself, and Amis, the latter pacing like a caged beast, hand on the hilt of his sword and, luckily, seemingly unaffected by the knock to the head he'd received.

Croal smiled weakly and leaned in to Flavell, touching his forehead to hers. He had to, for his eyes couldn't help but linger on the strip of blood-stained white linen around her neck.

'She struck me,' he said. 'Several times. And I let her. How could I not, after what I did?' The red marks on his face weren't obvious in the poor light, but they were there, he could feel them.

'I'm sending her away,' he said finally.

'Is that wise?' Giles leaned against the wall, brandy in hand. His words were slow, the brandy having an effect.

'You think keeping her here would stop her seeking support against me?'

'No.' Giles shook his head before draining his glass. 'I wasn't thinking of that. I mean because we don't know what's out there, on the roads you'll be sending her and her children down.'

'Giles has a point,' Flavell said, clutching Croal's sleeve. 'They've been through enough, your aunt and your cousins. This is their home—'

'I know that,' Croal said, a little sharper than he'd intended. He took Flavell's down-turned face in his hands. 'I'm sorry, my sweet.'

'Don't be.' She smiled at him like nought bad had happened, like nought had sickened him.

'Does your aunt know how it happened? Why?' Amis moved from the doorway to the raised window seat, nestled as it was in the walls of the chateau. He looked out of the lightening window, out and down.

'Obviously,' Croal said. 'That's why she struck me again and again.'

Giles filled his cheeks and let out a long breath.

'You have riders leaving the chateau,' Amis said without turning.

'I need to know who is out there. I need to know if there are more scouts, or...'

'Or whether their army has arrived,' Amis finished, turning finally, backed by the morning's light. 'Will you march out if there is? Will you send for aid, to Giles' family?'

Croal laughed at that. A bitter sound which caused Flavell to wrap herself about her man.

'Amis is right, messire. Send for my son. If I know him, and of course I do, he'll have gathered men already, after my capture. If I put my name to it, he will come to Easson's aid though. Of course, I'd expect the ransom—'

'Of course,' Croal said, looking to Giles, face softening. 'Of course. And I thank you, Messire Bratby, for…'

Giles held up his free hand. 'Your uncle was a gracious host, but no friend. You've always shown people far more kindness than he ever did. If all is well after this, I look forward to our cross-border relations.' Giles smiled and moved to pour himself another drink.

'Let's marry,' Flavell blurted, breaking the ensuing silence.

Amis spun, mouth open. The only thing that stopped his protest was Flavell's outstretched finger.

Giles chuckled and began pouring three more brandies.

Croal felt, and looked, shocked. 'I…'

'Don't say anything right now, my love,' Flavell said, the bags beneath her eyes doing nothing to stop the green sparkle. 'Think on it. I know it's too soon after… well, I thought it would be some happiness for all, especially us, after what happened. It's not like it hasn't been agreed upon already.'

'And if there is an army coming,' Giles said, dealing out the brandy filled glasses, 'and you do ride out, or they lay siege to Easson…' He let those possible futures linger in the room.

'That's optimistic.' Flavell scowled at Giles, the sparkle leaving her ever-wide eyes.

Giles held up his hand. 'If either of those things are to happen, and it's likely, Croal needs to unite Easson. The soldiers and the servants and the townsfolk. A wedding would help do that. That's all I meant.'

'It's not a bloody tactic—'

'Amis!' Flavell warned. 'It's alright, I know Giles speaks true. It might be what my father wanted, albeit quicker and without word sent back to him, but this town and chateau needs it. And it's what Croal and I deserve.'

'Then we shall,' Croal said, squeezing Flavell's hand and gazing into her re-sparkled eyes. 'We shall do it in the White Chapel, here in the chateau.'

Flavell nodded quickly and leaned in to her future husband,

fresh tears in her eyes; of joy, Croal hoped.

There was a sigh. 'I'm sorry to be such a shit,' Amis said, 'but I'm sure your mother and father and siblings would want to attend your wedding—'

'Don't spoil the moment, lad,' Giles said, a glint in his own eyes. 'Let them have this, eh?'

Croal opened his eyes and watched over his love's head as Amis sighed again, whilst nodding all the same. Giles crossed the room to pull him in close and chink his brandy glass. Croal took a deep breath of Flavell's lavender-scented hair and allowed himself a smile at the scene. He was to be wed, and the two men he watched were to be the witnesses. Oh how his life had changed in such a short space of time.

Chapter 32 – Loot

'Do you see them?'

'Yes, Gleave,' Correia said, 'they're sat atop horses, on top of a hill silhouetted by a red sky. How could I not?' She shuddered at the morning sky as much as the riders she was watching. A bad omen, if she believed in such things. Then again, if she didn't believe in them, why did it make her shudder?

'Tetchy.' Gleave nudged his horse on before *the* look came.

'We don't have time for this,' Correia said, under her breath. 'Fal, we're coming. Hold on in there.' Correia flicked her left hand twice, away to the flanks. Starks and Sav split and took one each, no words required. Correia followed Gleave towards the riders, tightening various buckles as she did so. She watched Gleave in his saddle, draw his hand axe and raise it to his lips. The weapon vanished. Correia smiled.

The ground sped beneath her as she urged her mount into a canter. The ground was hard packed, but she was aware of the risk such speed brought: rabbit warrens, rocks covered by tall grass; she wasn't about to walk up to the half dozen men on the hill though. She was going to make her intentions clear and see what move they made.

'We've no time for this,' she said again, through gritted teeth, thinking on the full day it had been since they'd last seen Fal, the long hours since the encounter with the chevalier and his men. Gleave, ahead of her, drew his sword, which appeared to be his only weapon. He steered his horse with his knees, despite holding the reins alongside his invisible axe. She'd seen him training like that several times of late, and knew it pained his leg, but the stoic man trained and rode through it all the same.

The men on the hill rode towards them. Down, towards them. Correia frowned, Gleave looked back over his shoulder, his features matching her own.

Why leave a position of strength? Correia thought, drawing one of her curved swords.

The sound of the approaching horses reached her over her own, and the rushing of the rain flecked wind. And the rushing of blood in her ears.

Those lads best have waxed their strings, or have spares. She looked left and right, to a rider-less horse each side. *Rain is not an archer's friend.*

She'd heard Sav and Starks say it many times.

'Shit!' Gleave's wind-carried voice found Correia, despite him looking forward once more.

More riders appeared on the hill, many more.

The first group is fleeing the second, Correia thought of the six riders fast approaching. They drew their weapons, falchions and the like, not a true sword amongst them. *They're Orismarans...*

Correia guided her horse left, Gleave right, as she knew he would. He leaned forward, into the surge his horse took on. Correia did the same, aiming for the lead rider. Risking a glance past her target, Correia saw the line of horsemen on the hill charge down, after the Orismarans, or so she hoped. She looked back to the tattooed man she closed on, who held a flanged mace out to the side. The rider to his right practically leapt back off his saddle, horse rearing and falling a moment later.

Heartbeats away from clashing with the warrior, Correia noticed the other rider, to her opponent's right, was also taken by one of Sav's arrows. Correia didn't have to look right to know that Starks had shot one of the riders near Gleave.

Correia leaned back, flat against the back of her saddle as the mace swung for her head. As soon as it passed, she slashed backhanded at the rider. Steel cut through leather and slid harmlessly across maille, the metallic swish unmistakable. Cursing her luck, she sat back up and wheeled round to chase down the man, aware of the riders closing behind her. They looked to be better armed, and armoured: Sirretans.

I'm not sure if that's better or worse anymore.

The man she'd harmlessly slashed hadn't slowed. He rode on, hard.

Unusual for Orismarans to run from a fight? Correia looked left, to where Gleave was hacking a tattooed rider from his horse with what looked like thin air.

The last rider on that flank, turning to take Gleave on, lurched forward as Correia watched him. She couldn't see Starks' bolt, but knew it to be the cause of the man's slump and fall; the horse fled, bucking and kicking as it ran.

Back to her own target, Correia saw another rider-less horse nearby and the mace carrier took one of Sav's arrows to the leg, pinning it and him to the horse, which let out a scream.

Correia slowed, knowing the rider would be finished before she reached him. She turned to the next threat, thundering hooves

202

drawing closer. Her periphery caught the fall of the last Orismaran, his mace dropping to the ground as he swayed left and right, falling and tearing free of the animal he'd been pinned to. The horse slowed, limped, came to a stop and stood panting, blood streaking its side.

The score riders approaching slowed, weapons sheathed and hands held high. The lead rider, caparisoned in the blue and white chevrons of Easson and bedecked in polished plate, lifted his visored bascinet and brought his destrier to a stop. The animal snorted and pawed at the ground, giving away its eagerness for blood. The beast was far heavier set that any the Pathfinders rode. Not big like a carthorse, but hard packed with muscle.

Correia raised her own hand and stopped her mount. Looking across to Gleave, she saw him riding over, sword now sheathed, other hand holding the reins, a nothingness present in the same hand, pressing against his palm. Correia nodded to him and he returned the gesture.

'Interesting,' Gleave said, reigning in alongside.

'Which bit?' She kept her eyes on the riders lined up opposite.

'Fair point. All of it?'

Correia nodded, but said nothing. *This bit's less interesting to me than the Orismaran riders, Gleave, but that's for me to know.* 'Stay here.'

Gleave turned on her, incredulous. 'You're going to parley? Sirreta's lost its mind and you're to have a chat, to trust them in doing that?' Correia rode on without a word. Gleave filled his scarred cheeks and let the breath out slowly. 'Your burial… and ours, I'd wager.' He hawked a gobbet of phlegm and sailed it out to Sav on the left. Eyes met over that distance, before both sets moved back to Correia, who'd turned to glare at Gleave.

Half way between Gleave and the men of Easson, Correia allowed herself a quiet chuckle, although she didn't let it show. *You're far more nervous than me now, Gleave. For this man, this man I know.*

The acidic burn of bile was forced back down Starks' throat as he pulled the maille mantle over the head of the first Orismaran he'd shot. He held the leather trimmed piece of maille in his hands, weighing hundreds of iron links as he looked at the spiralling blue tattoos of the corpse. Drying blood stained the man's teeth. Starks dropped back a bit, looking at that blood. Bile rose again and again he swallowed it down. The fact the Orismaran body had released its fluids didn't help, but Starks looked on, unable to tear his eyes from the lifeless orbs staring back at him. The whole body, and the land, after the brief shower, was drying in the appearing sun. The heat increased the stench threatening Starks' stomach contents, but thankfully the wind took most of it away. On he stared though, at blood and lifeless eyes. He'd killed before, of course he had, but taking from the dead? He took a breath in and wiped at his wind watered eyes with his free hand.

'You fallen in love, lad?' Gleave limped over and stood over Starks, who didn't reply. 'Correia's chatting to that Sirretan knight,' Gleave went on. 'With Sav hovering around the two of them like they'd rut in the grass if he didn't. Reckon he'd piss on the knight's leg if he thought it'd mark his territory where Correia's concerned.'

Still nothing from Starks.

Gleave grunted, annoyed his joke had been wasted. 'What you got there?' He crouched and nodded to the piece of armour Starks was running through his fingers. Starks nodded, eyes on the corpse. He wasn't listening to Gleave. He heard him, but he wasn't listening.

Gleave snatched the mantle. Starks let him.

'This is shit, Starks.' Gleave threw it and it twisted lazily through the air before flopping with a shush of links into long grass.

'Hey!'

'It got your attention off that fucker.' Gleave stood and kicked the body. Starks followed him to his feet. 'A maille mantle, Starks? Pointless.' Gleave set off towards the horses, held by one of the Sirretans.

'How's that?' Starks hurried after him.

'A bit of maille around your neck, weighing you down, without even protecting your bloody neck? I don't know, Starks, you tell me? A coif does a job, a mantle does fuck all.'

'It protects your shoulders and stuff.'

Gleave barked one of his laughs. '"And stuff".'

Starks scowled. 'Sorry, he didn't have posh spaulders for me to take.'

'And why take anything?' Gleave half turned, whilst they walked, so he could take in Starks' response: a shrug.

'Listen, lad…' Gleave softened his tone. 'There's no expectation from any of us for you to loot. Sav doesn't, Correia doesn't. And I'm damn sure good boys Fal and Errolas don't, so that leaves me.'

'And me.'

Gleave took a breath and changed tack, and direction, off towards a twisted lump of a man caught up in a patch of gorse. Starks followed.

'It's your choice, but if you're to loot and have it weigh on you...' Gleave stopped and took Starks by the shoulders, '...and it will!' Starks looked away, but Gleave turned his head back. Eyes met. 'It doesn't me, because I'm a shit, generally. You're not, Starks. You might not like to hear that, because you seem to think that you should be, but you're not.'

Starks was sick of being treated like a child and made to interrupt, made to correct Gleave, but Gleave continued before he could.

'However, if you want some good loot, you're going to learn from the best.'

A smile pulled at Starks' lip, drawn out by the one offered by Gleave.

'Now come, check this guy out, he looks funny all twisted this way and that.' Gleave turned and pulled Starks along behind him. 'And remember, this bastard would have stuck me had you not shot him. He's Orismaran, Starks, and Fal aside, those crazy tribesmen make me look like a fluffy bunny.'

Starks' crossbow bolt jutted from the Orismaran's neck. Dark blood coagulated around the wound. One leg pointed out of the gorse at a weird angle, bare as it was, tattooed as it was.

Gritting his teeth, Starks made himself look at the body, at the wounds, the broken bones, one of which stuck bright from olive skin and near black blood.

'Clots quick in this heat.' Gleave pointed to the gory wounds. 'Hottest it's been since leaving Wesson, ain't it, lad? Despite the cloud. Makes me sweat like an inquisitor's focus.'

Starks nodded.

'Now, what do you think I brought you here for?'

A shrug was all Gleave was offered.

'Eh?'

'I don't know, Gleave. He's got padding and scraps of maille, although not much. Boiled leather vambraces similar to Fal's...' Starks swallowed hard at that. 'We've no time for this.'

'You sound like Correia now, but you're right, so I'll crack on.' Gleave moved in quick, spun the body over and pulled at a bag the man had landed on. From the bag came a rusting, but modern hondskull bascinet.

'Ha!' Gleave grinned as he held up the Sirretan steel helmet, offering it to Starks. 'Now that, lad, is a find. Knew he had something heavy in that bag, the way it bounced on the back of his saddle and pulled at him as he fell.'

Starks turned the helmet over in his hands, eyes sparkling like, well, like polished plate.

'Needs cleaning up, Starks, but that there is worth more than King Barrison will pay you all year.' Gleave slapped Starks on the shoulder. 'And it's yours! And all for the price of a crossbow bolt.' Gleave pursed his lips. 'Unless you could retrieve the bolt,' he mused aloud, squinting at the shaft and leather fins of the thing.

Starks' lips spread into a full-on smile. He looked to Gleave and made to thank him.

'Ah ah,' Gleave held up a hand, looking at Starks in return. 'Thank me by looking after it. Mind you, first...' Gleave snatched the helm, crouched, drew his axe and proceeded to hack and bash the pointed visor from its mounts.

'Gleave!'

Hands slapped away with the flat of the axe's blade, Starks resigned himself to watch as Gleave hammered and pulled at the visor. Eventually it came free, and like the maille mantle had, sailed through the air and into the long grass.

'Here, you ungrateful shit. Shame it weren't the sort of visor that unpinned.' Gleave held the visor-less bascinet up to Starks. 'You're not a knight, you'll not be lining up in a cavalry charge, so you've no need for a visor to get in your way. Now come on, we're off to see what's going on.'

Staring at the back of a departing Gleave, Starks turned his frown to the helmet, back in his hands. The frown soon turned to a smile, despite his tumbling emotions over where the item had come from, and before Gleave made it to Correia and the others, Starks was fast on his heels, his prize held close to his chest.

'But you agree, Jehan?' Correia said to the chevalier she barely knew, but knew all the same.

A heavy sigh and a nod. 'I agree, madame. I'll take you to Croal de Geelan, but not his uncle, not the marquis.'

'The Queen's Seneschal will have to do,' Correia said, turning away from the man to look at her own. 'Hurry up, mount up and shut up,' she said.

Gleave closed his mouth, swallowing the question he'd been

about to ask.

'What's that?' Correia demanded, looking to a smitten Starks.

'My new lid,' Starks said, smiling up at her.

'That's Sirretan.' One of Jehan's men moved his horse close to Starks.

Correia wasn't surprised the man spoke Altolnan, this close to the border. Eudes de Geelan had his faults, but a lack of education for his men-at-arms wasn't one of them. She only wished Altolnan marcher lords would do the same.

Gleave mounted his horse and was beside the man looming over Starks before anyone else spoke. 'It's Altolnan now, that helm,' he said in Sirretan, holding the man's stare, a wicked, daring grin on Gleave's face.

Correia whistled and all eyes turned to her. 'If you're all done showing your cocks to one another, we'll move on, eh?'

Jehan, his own bascinet held in the crook of his arm, smirked and waved his men in the direction of the unseen town and chateau. With some reluctance from those nearest Gleave and Starks, the men of Easson did as they were ordered. Correia and her own followed close behind, Starks and his rust covered bascinet and hands bringing up the rear.

After a mile or two, with much Sirretan chatter coming from those in front, Sav pulled alongside Correia.

'Any word on Fal?'

Correia kept her eyes front. 'It's not good.'

Sav leaned across. 'But there is word?'

'Oh aye, Sav, they have him alright, like we were told by the Marshal of Sirreta's man, yesterday. I wish we'd ridden on instead of resting the horses for the night. I stupidly relaxed a tad, knowing where he was and who had him.'

Sav sat back and eased into the motion of his trotting horse. 'He's alive?' he asked, ignoring the latter. It was paining him as much, if not more, than Correia, she knew.

Correia squeezed her reins and nodded. *But they've had him over a day,* she thought. *A day that'll feel much longer to Fal.* She felt sick. *This isn't the Easson I knew. I should have ridden on...*

'He your man in Easson?' Sav didn't need to mention Jehan to make his meaning clear.

'No, not exactly.' Correia shifted in her saddle.

'You do have one, don't you? In the marquis' employ I mean.'

A nod.

'But it's not this knight, or chavilee, or whatever they call themselves?'

'No, Sav, it's not Jehan.'

'A cook, perhaps?'

Correia sighed, but shook her head.

'You're not going to tell me, are you?'

'No.'

Sav sighed and his free hand came up and rubbed hard at his face. After another quarter mile, he spoke again.

'Are they treating Fal well, Correia?'

She looked at him, words weren't needed.

Sav closed his eyes and cursed.

Correia wanted to cry and knew Sav would too should she tell him more. He'd also want to crack skulls. Correia wanted to do that as well, especially the bastard Rasoir's.

Chapter 33 – Black sails

The sun had hardly left the horizon when the call came from the fortified crow's nest.

'There! Another sail, coming in from the north!'

All eyes looked up, to the pointing finger.

'What is it, boy?' Mannino shouted, a frown pulling at his brow.

'Not sure, Cap'n. Sails are black though?'

'Squall skewer me,' Hitchmogh cursed, coming alongside Mannino on the aft-castle.

'She might if you keep tempting her, man,' Mannino said. He pursed his lips as Hitchmogh grunted a laugh. 'Black Guild, isn't she?'

Hitchmogh nodded. 'Alden-Fenn's floating castle is that, aye. Only Edward's beast is bigger, from what I remember of her.'

Mannino let out a long, slow breath. 'And so we have the next calamity to hit *Sessio* and her crew.'

'We can outrun her, can't we, Captain?' Spendley appeared next to Mannino. 'Can't we?' he said again, when no answer came.

'Well, we could, Spendley,' Hitchmogh said across Mannino, as the man twisted and looked to the stern, 'if we weren't being hounded by the one behind.'

Spendley frowned. 'We've dealt with more than one pirate before.' His shoulders bobbed in a laugh. 'We've dealt with an Altolnan blockade, for Squall's sake.'

'You've got Master Spendley using her name now, man.' Mannino looked forward again, eyes on his crew going about their business around the ship.

'Spendley,' Hitchmogh said, re-drawing the young officer's attention, 'the Black Guild's ship isn't some Altolnan naval vessel, or pirate bucket. With a ramming galley behind us and that thing closing in, we're stuck between a cock and a goblin face.'

Mannino and Spendley screwed their faces up at that.

Hitchmogh pulled his head back. 'What? You not heard the term before?'

Spendley shook his head. 'Not like that—'

'Enough,' Mannino said, in all seriousness. 'We act. Now.'

'To arms, to arms!' Spendley shouted, needing no more orders than that.

A bell rang and the decks exploded into motion, with sailors running about and archers piling onto the main deck before making their way onto the two castle-decks.

'They're a way out, Cap'n,' Hitchmogh said, frowning.

'They are, aye.' Mannino retrieved his pipe and shoved it into his mouth. Chewing the end, he turned once more and looked back past the stern. It was hard to see the galley since there was no obvious sail. 'That's the goblin ship, Charlzberg's.'

'That little shite?' Hitchmogh said, turning to look the same way, squinting as he did so. Spendley followed suit.

'Aye,' Mannino said, his empty pipe bobbing as he nodded. 'He has a net for a sail, remember?'

Hitchmogh barked a laugh. 'Oh aye. Prick.'

'He also had delivery of two new guns.'

Mannino and Hitchmogh looked to Spendley, who nodded his confirmation.

'These guns on deck, Spendley, as opposed to being pulled uselessly behind?' Hitchmogh asked. Spendley nodded. ''Morl's reekin' corpse.' Hitchmogh rubbed at his leathery face.

'You up for this, man?' Mannino asked Hitchmogh.

'I'm going to have to be.'

'Northern ship's closing, Cap'n.'

All eyes looked to the crow's nest and the boy. Two crossbowmen were climbing in next to him. Once in, they proceeded to check their windlass crossbows. The boy continued to point north.

'She's fast, for her size,' Spendley said, eyes wide, black sails fast approaching.

'She's fast for any size, lad,' Hitchmogh said.

'Are we turning side on, Captain?' the man at the whipstaff said, from behind the trio.

'No. If we do, we slow dramatically and expose our length to a ramming galley with guns.' Mannino cursed his lack of options.

'How are they so fast?' Spendley was leaning forward, over the rail. He squinted at the large cog closing on them, its nightmarish black sails bloating despite not having the wind.

'How are we, lad, when there's no wind?' Hitchmogh offered a tight smile when Spendley looked his way. The lad's eyes widened once more.

'They have a mage?' Spendley asked.

'The fuckers have two.' Hitchmogh slapped Spendley on the back and made for the steps down to the main deck. 'Time to tie me up, Master Spendley.'

Taking a deep breath and receiving a nod from Mannino, Spendley followed Hitchmogh down the steps and across to the main-mast, where Joncausks was waiting with a thick rope.

'You ready for this?' Mannino said, loud enough for the men and women on the aft-castle to hear.

'Aye, Captain!' the sailors and archers shouted as one.

'Are you all ready?' Mannino said louder, for all to hear.

Sessio's crew roared.

Chapter 34 – Boarders

Black ship and sails closing, Sessio ran straight and true, allowing the larger ship to approach on a course that would see the two pass side by side whilst keeping the goblin galley astern.

'Winds dropping,' Lefey shouted from the rigging above the forecastle.

Hitchmogh cursed, as did several sailors. 'You want me to put wind in her sails, Cap'n?'

Mannino shook his head at Hitchmogh's shouted question. 'Keep her as she is, whipstaff,' he said over his shoulder. 'Master Hitchmogh,' he looked back to the main deck where Hitchmogh was tied to the main-mast, 'be ready to unleash what you've got when it's needed, against their mages.'

With a deep breath, Hitchmogh nodded. 'Aye, Cap'n. I'll see what I can conjure up.'

'Literally, if you please, Master Hitchmogh.' Mannino stashed his empty pipe in a pocket and moved to the very stern of the ship where he could see the war galley, gaining on them as it were. 'Those hobyahs are unmatched on the oar it seems,' he muttered.

'Eh, Captain?' Tahir said, moving to his side.

'Nothing, man. Nothing. Observations and such, that's all.'

'Erm, right you are, Captain.' Tahir hesitated before departing the scene via the steps to the main deck, whilst Mannino returned to his usual position by the front rail of the aft-castle. The archers were on the port side, war bows strung and bodkin tipped arrows nocked in preparation for what was to come.

'Ready when you are, Captain,' Spendley shouted from the forecastle.

Mannino nodded. 'Let them fly.' His voice carried to all aboard, even to those below deck, and arrows flew, and Hitchmogh closed his eyes.

Spray rained down on the men and women of *Sessio's* forecastle. Arrows rained down on those of the Black Guild's ship, with surprising accuracy considering both the distance and the pitch and roll of both vessels.

Screams and shouts followed.

Hitchmogh opened bloodshot eyes, chest heaving. He looked left and right, to and from arrow nocking archers fore and aft. They loosed again, and again he closed his eyes. Droplets of sweat appeared on his forehead.

A cheer went up from the forecastle before more cries of outrage and pain filtered back from the black ship, fast closing.

'Leave the lads to it now, Master Hitchmogh.' Mannino leaned forward and rested his arms on the rail, studying the man tied below. 'Save yourself for what's to come.'

'Fuck off, Mannino!'

'He's ready, Captain,' Parry shouted from the main deck, scimitar in hand.

'Oof, what! Seems so, Master Parry. We're on now.' Mannino drew his cutlass. 'Hear your first mate and blade master?' he shouted to the crew. 'Time's come to get up close.'

The black ship was in range and the sky filled with arrows heading both ways.

Sessio's crew hurled abuse at the vessel about to pass by. The arrows of both ships struck. Sailors and archers on both sides fell, arrows jutting from fatal and none fatal wounds alike.

The tower-like side-castles of the black, modified cog reached over Sessio's forecastle as the vessel passed close. The windlass crossbows of the crow's nest clicked and two lives were ended on the enemy ship. Mannino didn't need to see it to know his men had taken two officers. That was their expertise after all.

A cloaked figure appeared at the edge of one of the side-castles passing by, the woman's black, bald head a stark contrast to the white, snarling faces of the assassins ready to jump down onto *Sessio's* decks.

'Master Hitchmogh!' Mannino pointed his cutlass at the woman, a hint of fear flecking his voice for the first time.

Hitchmogh cursed, spat on the deck and followed Mannino's pointing cutlass to the woman, who was shuddering violently, a sleek wand held out to her side.

Assassins jumped down from the side-castles. As they did, the female mage glowed like the sun itself. Many of *Sessio's* crew members fell back, hands covering their eyes as the assassins landed and struck. Two were met by arrows, which took them back overboard, but the rest landed true and struck true. Several archers fell, hands covering eyes. The light died as quickly as it flared and when Mannino caught sight of the bald woman again she was doubled over in obvious convulsive agony.

Hitchmogh screamed and the woman exploded in a mist of blood and a scattering of shrapnel-like bone. The Black Guild archers to her sides fell screaming to the deck.

Hitchmogh laughed.

Mannino looked up as the large ship glided past and he locked eyes with her captain. 'Alden-Fenn.' Mannino's voice was low; dangerous. He pointed his cutlass at the beast of a man, all tattoos and black armour. Mannino didn't have to say a word. As the man snarled back at him they both heard Hitchmogh roar. A stream of rippling air, like that of a hot summer's day, filled the distance between Mannino's blade and Alden-Fenn's tattooed face. The guild master fell back, howling with rage and pain as his skin seared. Mannino couldn't help but smile. Before he could witness Alden-Fenn's reaction, the sound of clashing blades drew Mannino's attention to the forecastle and main deck, where intense fighting continued between his crew members and the intruding assassins.

The black ship passed before more assassins joined the Black Guild's vanguard.

Mannino was eager to join his crew on the main-deck, but knew he had to command *Sessio* and plan for what was to come next. *That bloody war galley.*

Spendley ducked left and right, parried and lunged. The black-clad woman before him was quick. Too quick. He gasped, feeling her long knife slide across his outstretched arm. Despite knowing he'd been trained well by Parry, Spendley knew it to be the end as a second blade came in high and fast. He saw the point for the briefest moment and surprised himself by relaxing, knowing it was all over.

The female assassin collapsed with a jerk, her second blade nicking the bridge of Spendley's nose but no more, a windlass-crossbow bolt jutting from her shoulder. Through a drilled reaction alone did Spendley thrust down hard, finishing the woman before she had time to see it coming. There was no time to glance up, to thank the crossbowman above, and even if there was, Spendley knew the man would be within the crow's nest, cranking hard to reload his weapon.

Lefey rushed past, followed by Joncausks, both of whom launched themselves at a bearded assassin who pressed two sailors hard. The man went down before he could react to the new threat. The following blows and stabs left him unrecognisable as the sailors he'd pressed butchered him where he lay. Lefey and Joncausks had already moved on.

'I told you to stay below!' Parry dropped to his knees and slashed left to right, slicing the back of an assassin's legs who'd killed one of the archers. The man dropped to *his* knees and screamed before Parry brought his scimitar back around and cleaved the assassin near in two. Parry risked a glance at the lad he'd seen at the main deck's hatch. He grunted a laugh as he saw Quin throw up and go back down.

On his feet again, Parry raced across the wooden deck, sliding at the last moment to take the feet from an assassin who was hacking down two archers with a hafted-axe. As the man hit the deck, Parry dropped his scimitar and grabbed the man's head. He forced a thumb into each eye, blinding the assassin before pressing his digits deeper. The assassin thrashed and screamed.

'Teach you for boarding *Sessio*, you prick.'

The man stopped thrashing and the gore-slick face went slack. Parry withdrew his red and gelatinous smeared thumbs and retrieved his scimitar. 'Get me on that fucking boat, Hitchmogh!' he shouted. Hitchmogh's bloodshot eyes flashed to him. Parry grinned, turned, ran and leapt towards the departing cog. As the crew heard Mannino shout, 'No!' Parry vanished, although his shadow remained for a heartbeat longer.

'The galley's close, Captain,' Tahir warned, back by Mannino's side and pointing astern.

Mannino looked from the vanishing blade master to the closing galley. As he locked eyes on the black-clad goblin in the web-like sail, he heard a double crack and saw two puffs of white smoke, the rest obscured by the stern rail, which exploded in a rapidly spreading mix of shot and wood.

Mannino was tackled to the ground by Tahir, who grunted and coughed blood soon after. Men screamed and Mannino heard goblins cheer. He looked into the eyes of the man who'd sprayed the side of his head in blood and spittle; the eyes that looked back lost their spark whilst Mannino watched, helpless. Tahir was dead and Mannino was beside himself with rage.

Chapter 35 – A new debt

Mannino leapt back, as did the dozen archers around him, the twin guns of the galley firing yet again. Hitchmogh's arcane efforts held true though, the projectiles deviating and splashing into the sea. Climbing back to his feet, Mannino looked back at the scene before him., just as the loudest bang yet announced the firing of the galley's trailing cannon.

Mannino caught the swift approach of one of his sailors.

'They've turned on one another!' Joncausks shouted as he rushed to Mannino's side.

The black ship was turning in a great arc to port, listing all the way after being struck by the goblin galley's rear-facing cannon. Mannino strained his eyes in an attempt to see Parry aboard the black ship, but failed to do so. Chewing his bottom lip, he looked down to Charlzberg's galley and was surprised to see the goblin admiral waving with one arm from behind the galley's single mast.

'Hold!' Mannino ordered his archers as soon as they began to loose. All obeyed.

'Captain?' Joncausks dared.

'He's shouting something.' Lefey came alongside the two, squinting along with the rest.

'He's taking arrows aboard, from the black ship,' one of the archers said, pointing his bow to indicate the odd arrow flicking from cog to war galley, which was losing pace on *Sessio* and dropping back. Several hobyahs had fallen to arrows whilst some still rowed, many with arrows jutting from their chests and shoulders.

'Stubborn shites,' Boxall said. He'd appeared next to Joncausks, a chunk of his cheek missing.

'I take it *Sessio* is clear of boarders?' Mannino asked Boxall, eyes locked on a waving, shouting Charlzberg.

'Aye, Captain.' Boxall breathed heavily and held an arm across his ribs. He held a bloody hatched in his other hand, despite missing his little finger, the knuckle dripping blood onto the deck.

'And Master Hitchmogh?'

Lefey grunted a laugh. 'Cursing, Captain. A lot.'

'He's fine then. Don't release him yet.'

'Aye, Captain.' Lefey went to ensure no one else did.

'Any of you hear what the goblin is shouting?' Mannino leaned forward, head to the side.

Several of the men shook their heads.

'No, Captain,' Joncausks said. 'Not a word.'

'Shame.' Mannino stood straight and pursed his lips. He turned to Boxall. 'Go and tell Master Hitchmogh to get Master Parry back. Quickly, man.'

Boxall nodded and ran off despite the pain he clearly felt.

'They'll not catch us now, Captain,' Joncausks said. 'Neither of them.'

'I know, man. I know.'

Joncausks looked to Mannino. 'You're not thinking of coming about on them are you, Captain? Them turning on one another won't do us any good if we're in the middle of it.'

Mannino shook his head. 'I'm losing no more today.' He turned and took in the bodies strewn across his ship. His eyes settled on Tahir's, shredded as it was from neck to arse. He rubbed his face with his free hand and sheathed his clean blade.

Joncausks sighed and leaned back against the splintered deck. 'After all he went through with Boxall and me… After what we all went through on that island. It all feels for nought now.'

Mannino shook his head. 'Not nought, man. Never nought.'

Joncausks looked to his captain, but Mannino was locked on Tahir's motionless body.

They both started, as did those around them when they heard Hitchmogh erupt in a tirade of curses, shouts and surprisingly high pitched shrieks.

Another voice cried out, following a hollow pop that left a ringing in everyone's ears.

'Master Parry is back, I presume.'

'Aye, Captain. Seems so.'

'Go see to him then.'

Joncausks rushed off.

Mannino turned back and looked on the two ships they were leaving behind. The galley was peeling off, heading west whilst the Black Guild's listing ship seemed to be adrift. Its black sails falling limp.

'So, your remaining mage has a new task,' Mannino said to himself, eyes back on the modified cog whilst fiddling in his pocket for his pipe. 'Keeping you afloat until you can effect repairs.' He popped the empty pipe into his mouth and chewed on the end. 'Won't be the last we see of you, Alden-Fenn; seems I'm a mark.' Mannino released a single laugh and shook his head. 'Now who in

Brisance wants me dead enough to pay for it?'

'Captain?' An archer came close, brow creased.

'Nothing, man, nothing.' Mannino turned to him and smiled. 'You did well today. Extra round of rum for you all tonight, on me. Now get to it.'

The archer smiled briefly before helping the others shift bodies, of which the assassins went overboard – once looted, of course.

'And I,' Mannino said, looking back to the departing war galley, 'owe a goblin who thinks he's an admiral, despite him smashing up *Sessio's* stern.'

Shaking his head in frustration and disbelief at the brief encounter, he moved across to Tahir's body, crouched and placed a hand on the corpse.

'My biggest thanks to you, Tahir,' he said, empty pipe in hand. '*Sessio* doesn't forget her own.'

Hitchmogh's sudden string of shouted curses were followed by a chorus of laughter and a string of curses from someone else. Someone new.

Mannino stood straight and looked down to the arrow littered, blood soaked main-deck where a ring of sailors and archers stood, two men at their middle.

'Ah, Master Quinnell, you'll soon learn not to let him free so soon after such an event.' Mannino smiled. 'But you're a good lad and we like you. Don't we, *Sessio?*'

Patting smooth, sun-warmed wood, Mannino took one last look at it all before escaping to his quarters. It was all he could do not to wail and rail and turn *Sessio* about to avenge his dead.

Chapter 36 – Easson

'None have returned from the south-west, Sieur,' the captain of the watch told Croal, who continued to brush down his destrier as he let the news sink in. The beast snorted and stamped, the boy holding its head struggling to keep the animal steady. Croal found the chore calming nonetheless, which was why he chose to do it himself once in a while.

'You think an army approaches from that direction?'

'I do, Sieur.'

Croal's sigh shuddered as much as his destrier's flank. 'And what do you think I should do, Captain?'

The captain's moustache twitched before he took a deep breath, eyes searching the stable for an answer. 'Well,' he said eventually, 'we've clearly lost our scouts, so I'd advise against sending more. But we can't be sure aid will come...' he waffled, unsure as to what his liege lord wanted to hear, Croal knew.

That's why you're captain of the town watch and no more, Croal thought, brushing a little harder. The horse snorted and pulled its head up, lifting the boy off the ground for the briefest of moments.

'You think we should hold here? Prepare to defend?' Croal asked the captain, unsure why, but wanting as much input from as many angles as he could get. For he wasn't sure himself.

'Yes, Sieur. Perhaps the Marquess of Suttel's word will hold true and our message will get through to his son in Altoln.'

'Do you think he will come? And if the young Bratby does come to Easson's aid, do you think he will relinquish these lands after defending it on our behalf?'

There was a pause before the captain spoke. 'Would you, Sieur?'

Croal grunted a laugh at that. 'Right now? Yes, I think I would. I have enough to worry about without taking on more land and responsibilities. But I'm not so sure of this Sir Allon, despite my admiration for his father.'

The captain offered a smile barely visible under his bristles. 'I can see the load you have upon you, Sieur. I'm here, should you see fit to pile some of it on me. I would do all I can to assist.'

Croal turned on the man, ignoring the latter. 'And can everyone else? See the load on me I mean. Does it show so much?'

The captain shrugged. 'It does, Sieur, but it is understandable with all that has happened and is yet to come.'

'Still...' Croal passed the brush to the nervous boy and

219

motioned for the captain to follow him across the yard. 'I worry about trouble within as much as without.'

'That has been dealt with,' the captain said, placing a reassuring hand on Croal's arm. 'If there are any left who're loyal to the late marquis—'

'My uncle.' Croal offered the man a level stare. The captain removed his hand, but met the stare with one of his own.

'Yes, Sieur, your uncle. If there are any left loyal to him, they are few, and in fear. They'll also understand we have a potential siege to contend with. Any man with an ounce of brain will make that possibility their main concern and priority.'

'True,' Croal conceded, ascending stone steps to the chateau's curtain wall. Once at the top, he nodded to a guard in the blue and white of Easson, and leaned against the crenellations, overlooking his town.

'My town,' he whispered.

'Messire?'

'Pull everyone in, Captain. All the scouts, or rather don't send anymore out once those in the field return. Give the order to bring tenants in from the farms and hamlets too. Arm the militia and...'

'Sieur?' The captain frowned at Croal's pause and grimace.

'Have Rasoir drag some useful information from our prisoner. I have a wedding to prepare.'

With a grim smile and a nod, the captain descended the wall and headed for the barracks. Croal watched the man go.

'I spent years pleading with my uncle to let me command his men, and now...' he sighed and turned back to look over his town. 'Now I wish the bastard were here and his old self, to take command back again.'

A shout drew his attention, from further down the wall. Croal looked that way and saw sharp-eyed crossbowmen pointing. Shading his eyes from the afternoon sunlight, despite the clouds, Croal saw the dust of several riders approaching the edge of Easson.

Our scouts. Or... perhaps this is the start of it.

***

A smudge-topped hill revealed a grey walled town, centred by a white walled chateau with limp, blue and white pennants hanging from every tower; conical roofs a rustic red, in contrast to the green hills and grey, rain-flecked sky. It seemed to take an age to draw close to it, but now the riders passed through the earthen streets with crooked buildings either side, it wasn't long until they were looking up to whitewashed crenellations atop a gatehouse, in which an old portcullis hung like a poor attempt at a woman's clunky necklace.

'This it?' Starks nodded to the white walls and towers, their pristine nature a lie, revealed as they now were; age old stains and pitted stone and mortar.

'No,' Gleave said, 'this is the privy, the castle's around the corner.'

Starks frowned. Jehan smiled.

'No smile from you at that, Sav?' Gleave twisted in the saddle.

'Not until Fal is here with us, smiling too.'

Gleave nodded and frowned. 'I'll agree to that one. Never thought I'd miss good boy Fal, but I do.'

'So, let's get him out, shall we?' Starks looked to Correia and Jehan. Neither replied, but both kicked their horses on as the chain-rattling portcullis rose.

Knuckles rapped twice on rusted steel helm as Gleave overtook Starks. 'Don't lag behind, lad. You don't want to be under this thing when a chain breaks.'

Starks caught up quickly.

The deafening clatter of hooves in the high walled courtyard accompanied a barking dog and the smell of horse shit and smoke. It was a damn sight nicer than the smell of the town's streets though.

'Why is the portcullis down?' Correia asked Jehan.

'The seneschal's orders.' He halted his horse and slid from the saddle, passing the reins to a scruffy boy who appeared by his side.

'Not his uncle's?' Correia dismounted and Jehan shook his head.

A clatter and a resounding thud marked the dropping of the portcullis once all were through. All Altolnan eyes turned to the closing of the cage around them.

Horses taken, Correia and her men followed Jehan towards a set of double doors in the side of a large drum tower. The other Sirretans headed in a different direction, all chatter and laughs.

'Your companions are to follow mine.' Jehan pointed a gauntleted hand.

'Not likely.' Sav stepped alongside Correia. Jehan looked to Sav,

221

eyes creased in amusement.

'Do as he says, Sav.' Correia turned and placed a forceful hand on Sav's broad chest. She looked up into his eyes and drew them from Jehan's. 'Do as *I* say, Sav.'

Chewing his bottom lip, Sav nodded before following Gleave and Starks towards the tower the Sirretan men had entered.

'This way, Madame Burr. To Messire Seneschal.'

He opened one of the two doors and Correia followed him into the dark.

***

Stringy blood and snot hung and swung like a pendulum from Fal's broken nose. He tried to swallow, hoping some of it would slide down his throat, easing the woollen feeling that threatened to choke him every time he took a painful breath.

He cursed as another itch made itself known. What he would give to be able to pull his raw wrists through the iron shackles to scratch at the bastard irritation.

'Would that I had any nails left.' The croak of Fal's voice brought on a coughing fit that he instantly regretted. It wasn't so much the coughs, although they hurt muscles he didn't know he had, but the inhalation between each bark of blood and phlegm. If he ever told the tale, if he ever had the chance, he'd liken the feeling the deep breaths produced to the slipping of one knuckle across another: forefingers bent double, second knuckles pressed together, then slip. Slip them past one another, do it each time you breathed in and imagine someone sticking you with a bollock dagger each time it happened. That's what broken ribs feel like, he'd tell them. He'd had a lot of time to think such things. A lot of time to think a lot of things, although his thoughts didn't always feel his own anymore.

How long have I been here? he wondered again, opening dry eyes to gaze upon the smoke-filled chamber he was chained up in. Oh, how his shoulders burnt from the strain. The stonework was damp, nothing new there. The floor was straw, blood, urine and shit covered. Again, nothing new.

A rat! Fal traced the creature with his swollen eyes as it scurried across the floor, sniffing at the excrement slopped in a corner. Well, rats weren't new, but it was the first he'd seen in a while. *Days maybe?*

222

An appreciated breeze came through the barred slit of a window, bringing with it flecks of rain illuminated by the sun's light, which split on the iron rods meant to stop an escape Fal couldn't attempt even if the bastard seneschal holding him unlocked the shackles and gave him a leg up to the bright hole.

I'd wager that breeze smells a damned sight better than this place. Fal squinted as he looked at the white rectangle. There was no chance any smell could breach the stench that clung to him, let alone the chamber.

Closing his eyes again, Fal allowed his head to hang, chin on bare chest. Another itch sprung up. More of a tickle in fact. *A fly.* The pain his grunted laugh brought made him laugh all the more, until his grating throat released a rasp that resembled a coughing dog. The fly buzzed in his ear. Fal didn't flinch. He'd grown used to it.

'Quiet in there,' Sergeant Rasoir shouted from outside the door.

Fal fell silent.

'I don't want to have to come in there.' There was a pause. 'That's the truth of it, you know?'

Fal said nothing. He hung and licked at cracked lips, wincing as he did.

'As long as Croal stays away, I'll leave you be. You know that, Fal. So, until he returns, keep it quiet and I'll pretend like you're not there.'

Fal nodded pointlessly and chose to listen to the sound of his teeth scraping over his dry tongue. *It's surprisingly loud; I have my teeth!* He chuckled silently. *There is that, I suppose.* Fal ignored the pain, pulled back his lips and bared his blood-stained teeth. They felt like teeth tended to feel after a night on strong ale or mead. He moved his head left, right, up, down – chin on chest once more.

'Correia,' he mouthed, before moving on through his routine. 'Sav. Starks. Errolas. Gleave.' Slowly, Fal lowered his jaw, stretching it, moving it one way then the other, before closing his mouth again, mouthing the names again. His jaw clicked with each movement, despite the attempted stretches.

I thought they would have come—

Fal jumped as a dog barked on the far side of the bright oblong. Countless nerve endings fired, scolding darts through his entire body at the movement. The dog's barking was followed by clattering hooves and multiple voices, but he couldn't make out what was being said or by whom.

223

If he's back… if the bastard seneschal is back, I'll bite the fucker's face off for what he's had Rasoir do to me. I swear it on Samorl and Squall and all the gods between.

Boots on stone in the hallway.

Fal shuddered and the tears returned.

Chapter 37 – Preparations

'I'm so excited,' Flavell said.

Cateline, the young maid who'd run for Croal the night of
Flavell's attack, braided Flavell's golden hair, illuminated as it was
by the morning's rays, which cascaded through the window Amis
stood by.

'You should be, mademoiselle. Weddings in the White Chapel
are blessed from the start.' Cateline beamed into the silver mirror
and Flavell beamed right back.

'Will I have to dress up?' Amis said without turning from the
window.

Flavell rolled her green eyes. 'You'll be lucky to receive an
invite.'

Cateline all but tittered, eyes flicking between hair and the
handsome Yellow Chevalier, bester of the Seneschal d'Easson, as
Amis was being called throughout the chateau and town;
unofficially, of course, but it reached Flavell and Amis both,
amusing the latter.

'Oh, so you're sending invites to your family?'

Flavell huffed, her down-turned mouth more down-turned than
ever. 'Be quiet, de Valmont. You're spoiling it already.'

'Don't listen to him none, mademoiselle,' Cateline dared. 'He's
sore he won't be by your side all the time once you're wed to the
seneschal.'

'Watch your tongue, girl,' Amis warned.

Flavell and Cateline both laughed, despite the serious tone Amis
used.

He spun on them. 'What's so funny?'

'You,' Flavell admitted. She met Cateline's eyes in the silver
reflection and they laughed again.

'Care to enlighten me, either of you?'

'Girl talk, de Valmont.' Flavell failed to hide her continued
mirth. 'Girl talk.' She winked into the mirror.

Amis grumbled to himself and crossed the room. 'I'll guard the
door. From the outside.'

Both women burst into laughter as he left. Flavell noticed his
cheeks flush as he turned and slammed the door. There was a
moment of silence before Flavell spoke again.

'Do you think it all too quick?' she asked Cateline, in all
seriousness.

'The wedding, mademoiselle?' Cateline looked worried.

Flavell nodded.

'Life's a shit, mademoiselle,' Cateline said as a matter-of-fact. She blushed and hesitated, remembering who she was speaking to, but Flavell smiled and nodded for her to go on. 'What I mean is with what's rumoured to be coming, and what we can never know is on the morrow, there's never any time but the present to do what your heart desires. If I'm not being too bold in saying so.' She smiled and stepped back. 'There,' she said, hands clasped together before her. 'It's done. Finished.' She watched Flavell's reaction in the silver reflection.

Flavell beamed. 'It's wonderful. Truly.'

Cateline beamed also.

'Thank you! For my hair and… just thank you.'

'It was my pleasure, mademoiselle. Would you like me to send them in with your dress?'

Flavell nodded. 'Yes please.' Cateline turned to go. 'But please return, if you have the time for it. I would like you to see the dress and how it compliments your styling of my hair.'

Bubbling with excitement, Cateline nodded and rushed from the room to call for the dress.

Flavell looked at herself in the mirror and smiled once more. It seemed she would marry her seneschal, and that, after all, was all she had wanted from the start.

It was but heartbeats, or so it felt, before Cateline returned. Through the door she came, her smile less than before. 'The seamstress is on her way with your dress, mademoiselle.'

'Thank you,' Flavell said, turning to take the girl in. 'Now tell me, what has troubled you in so short a time? And be honest with me, for you can, you know.'

Cateline offered a tight smiled and curtsied her thanks. She hesitated, before steeling herself in the face of the noble woman not too dissimilar in age to her. 'My…' She swallowed hard and started again, moving over to fuss at the dresser before Flavell. 'My man is a scout, mademoiselle. A scout who went with the patrols the seneschal sent out. A scout who hasn't come back.'

Flavell gave a sympathetic sigh. 'Oh, Cateline, he may yet come back. We can't know for sure what has befallen those brave men. If anything at all.' There was a pause after that and Flavell knew her words sounded hollow.

'You're a brave one too,' Flavell said, taking and squeezing

Cateline's hand, 'carrying on like this. Stoic, I would say.'

Cateline looked Flavell in the eye. 'How could I not be? When he rode out into rumours as worrisome as The Three themselves?' A shudder ran through the girl.

'Indeed. Well, he's done you proud, your man. And you him!' Flavell squeezed Cateline's hand again, skin warm under her own, colder touch. The weather was warm, but the thick walls of the chateau let little of that warmth through. 'Rejoice in that, my dear. Rejoice in the fact that he knows he has a brave girl to ride home to and will be striving to do just that.'

Cateline nodded her thanks and Flavell released her hand. Both women started as the door banged three times. They turned and watched as the iron-bound oak swung in, revealing a handsome face in the opening crack.

'Your dress is here,' Amis said, eyes narrowing but a little on the red eyed maid.

Flavell's face lit up, as did Cateline's, despite her worry. Stoic for sure.

'Send it in, de Valmont. Send it in!'

Amis nodded and opened the door wide. Through came two dour-faced women carrying a shimmering, white silk dress that cascaded over their thick arms as if crafted from the finest snow.

Flavell gasped, hand to mouth. Cateline mirrored her.

'It's beautiful,' Cateline said. 'It's as if a dream came true, and no less.'

'Isn't it just,' Flavell breathed.

'It is… nice,' Amis allowed, from the doorway.

'And not for men to see.' The nearest women to Amis lashed out with her foot.

Amis grunted and hopped aside before disappearing back into the corridor, closing the door.

The two women busied themselves fitting the dress to a wooden manikin by the window, so the light from the tall patchwork of glass panes back-lit the magnificent garment.

'When Cateline is done faffing with the dresser and has gone, we shall—'

'You shall do whatever it is you were about to say you shall do, whether Cateline is faffing or not. Do I make myself clear?' Flavell's air of nobility took over from the soft tones she'd used with Cateline. Both women nodded, their faces as stern as when they'd entered with the dress. They reminded Flavell of the grotesques and gargoyles adorning so many cathedrals and churches and keeps. Cateline shifted, but Flavell's hand found hers and she soon settled.

'You were saying?' Flavell asked the seamstress, tone soft once more.

The one who'd kicked out at Amis and done all the speaking thus far cleared her throat, and proceeded to explain what they had done and what they would be doing regarding the check of the fit and so on. But Flavell was lost in the dress and what would soon be her wedding. She squeezed and pulled Cateline closer, eager to have a companion throughout. Eager to have someone share in the dream that was becoming a reality before her very eyes. *Oh, how the dress shines like magic itself,* she thought, as the seamstress prattled on. *My wedding dress.*

***

The blade was crude, the handle simple. Nothing more is needed when one thinks about it, and Fal did.

'My papa made me this knife,' Rasoir said, holding it in front of Fal. 'Truth be told, it's poor in quality, but...' Rasoir pulled his thumb across the blade, each ripple of his finger print flicking across the sharp edge. Rasoir swallowed hard, eyes flicking to the shadowed corner near the chamber's door before talking once more.

Fal blocked out the man's droning voice and lifted his gaze from blade to black, to the man he knew stood in the shadows of the doorway. Watching, waiting. *For what?* Fal thought. *I've already told them everything. And you...* Fal looked back to the sergeant in front of him. He held Rasoir's eyes for a heartbeat before the man looked away, back to his latest tool of torture. *You don't have the stomach for this, I know it, and yet you go on, poking me, prodding me, beating and slicing me. A sergeant following orders...*

Memories flooded Fal's mind, memories of orders given, orders accepted and the burning bodies that followed, throughout Wesson. *Is Rasoir any different to me? Is what he does here, to me, worse than the countless lives my actions took? I'd like to think so, but I'm not—*

The knife's point pressed up into Fal's left armpit. Not hard, the press wasn't painful, but it was there, it was threatening.

Sweat managed to appear on Fal's shaved head. From where, he didn't know, because he felt like there was no more water left within him. He winced despite himself as the knife cut sensitive skin. Ever so slight was the cut, but the pain flared as it always did. Rasoir knew what he was doing, whether he liked doing it or not. The thought of it was worse now. Fal's imagination attacked him as much as the Sirretans who held him captive.

I don't care what anyone says, Fal thought, sudden intakes of stale air pulling at and hurting various areas of his body, especially his broken, snagging ribs. *No one can take this and remain defiant. No one can go on without talking, without telling their captors whatever they want to know. Whether it be true or not. And I spoke quick, when they started all of this. Didn't I just. And still they ask for more.*

The blade came away from Fal's underarm. He allowed his aching muscles to relax, but for a moment; the knife only moved from one area to another, an area that made the painful breaths come quicker. He knew struggling wouldn't help, but his brain didn't have control over things like that any longer, his instinctive fear did. His brain was right, alas, and the struggles made the things that followed worse.

Crude blade parted bruised flesh and Fal let out a scream.

The shadows moved as the scream continued, and the Seneschal d'Easson moved to the door, a single Sirretan word passing his lips.

Fal's scream was no more than a whimper by the time the seneschal left the room. Free-flowing blood followed sweat to the floor, and Fal managed to drop his eyes to the man before him, his need to know what the seneschal said clear. The eyes that looked back were as pained as Fal's own.

Rasoir swallowed hard as he accepted that questioning stare.

'He told me to continue, Fal.'

Fal's released breath shuddered, as did his whole body as the knife came in once more. *I'm not sure I'll survive this.* The reality struck him harder than anything that came before. 'I'm sorry,' Fal said, his voice little more than a whisper, a whisper those he aimed his apology at could never hear.

'So am I,' Rasoir said, mistaking Fal's meaning whilst slicing fingertips from bone. 'Because he'll expect to hear you scream.' The seneschal wouldn't have been disappointed.

Chapter 38 – Sack of meat

'Good morning, Fal,' Rasoir said in his accented Altolnan, entering the chamber and huffing as he did so.

Fal opened his crusty eyes, thoughts of Correia and the others lost. A sack weighed heavy on Rasoir's shoulders, before thudding to the ground, scattering roaches and lifting dust into the air. The sack shook and thrashed, squealed even. Or whatever was captured inside did.

'Not sure you'll like this,' Rasoir said, eyes on the sack. 'Damn but she's heavier than she looks.'

Fal made to speak, but all that came out was a series of chesty coughs.

Rasoir sucked in a breath. 'Not good that, Fal. Fluid on your lungs, methinks. From the broken ribs, I'd say, and the shallow breathing that comes with such an injury. It was a cold night last night, too. All the worse for you, I'm sure. What you need do,' and Rasoir mimicked it, 'is brace yourself like so and take a deep breath or two. I'm told that clears the fluid. It'll hurt like a troll's grip though.'

Fal's voice was barely audible, so Rasoir came in close.

'Shackled, Sergeant. I can't.'

Standing back and sucking his teeth, Rasoir nodded at that. 'Right you are.' He looked over his shoulder at the door and back to Fal. 'The seneschal's been dealing with something up top and won't be down here for a while. So, aye, don't see why not.' He moved forward and Fal flinched, tensed and groaned through the pain it brought.

The sack shook, by the door, grunts now accompanying the movement.

'Steady, Fal.' Rasoir unlocked the shackles and lifted Fal to the floor where he helped him settle onto his side. 'That's it,' Rasoir said. 'On your side, so the weight's not on those ribs of yours. Now, brace like I showed you. That's it. Deep breaths now. Yes, I know it hurts but you must, for your health.'

Fal did as he was told, despite the snagging pain the breaths inflicted upon him.

'That's it, two's fine enough.' Rasoir sat back and rubbed at his face. Looking Fal in the bloodshot eyes, he offered a weak smile. 'I don't even know why he has me continue. We know your story is true.'

Head tilted, because it seemed to rest easier on his neck that way, Fal frowned.

Rasoir nodded. 'It's true. We discovered your Spymaster and her pathfinders nearby and, well…' Rasoir looked back to the sack.

Fal's heart thumped, stomach lurched. Mouth drier than it had been for what he assumed were days, his aching eyes found Rasoir's once more. The man offered another sad smile as the sack shifted, strange noises issuing forth.

Correia? He'd said her name, hadn't he, Rasoir?'

'And yet the seneschal sends me down here, with that.' He pointed over his shoulder. 'If it were me, Fal, I'd let you go. You know that, don't you?'

Fal nodded. He didn't know what he knew anymore. Although the flashes of pointless anger, rage even, felt more normal to him than anything else of late. Although they came when he was alone. He wasn't fool, or mean enough to let those episodes show in front of Rasoir. The man had it hard enough as it was.

Lips pursed, Rasoir climbed to his feet and crossed to the sack, before dragging it across the stone slabs to drop, grunting again, in front of Fal's tilted head.

'Time to get her out I suppose, like Croal ordered.' Rasoir took the closed end of the sack, lifted and shook. Another squeal and pink skin showed, followed by more of the same as a bound and thrashing sow shuffled and slid onto the floor.

Fal's painful breaths came fast. Confusion followed, mixed with relief. Relief it wasn't Correia. Guilt followed that relief, mixed with fear for the sow.

'I hate this bit,' Rasoir said. 'It's one thing doing what I do, but killing and cutting up an animal for nowt but show is wrong. Food wasted if you ask me. My wife would roast me alive if she knew this was going to waste.' He crouched down beside the pig's head, pulled it this way and that, looking into the terrified eyes.

'What—'

'What am I to do?' Rasoir said, cutting Fal's croak off. He shrugged. 'I don't know, Fal. He said to show you some tricks. Make you see what will come next. He reckons that works better than me doing it to you, but I'm not so sure. We'll see—

'Oh, I never told you, Fal. My boy started to walk yesterday.' Rasoir let the pig's head flop, causing fresh jerks and grunts from the animal whilst he dropped down onto his side, next to Fal. Looking across at him, nose to nose, Rasoir smiled. 'Can't believe I

231

forgot to say. Oh Fal, amazing it was. Truly amazing, like Madame White had shone her rays on him and given him the strength to take his first steps.'

Fal listened to the man over his own rasping breaths, pushing and pulling as they were through his blood clotted nose. It was too much to breathe through his mouth after the recent loss of his two front teeth. How they stung when cold air met them.

Rasoir talked, describing the event in detail. After a while, Fal realised the man had stopped. Opening eyes he now realised were closed, Fal saw Rasoir looking at him, smiling.

'You drifted off there, Fal.'

Fal made to apologise.

'Ah ah, no need.' Rasoir surged to his feet, causing Fal to grimace at the pain which followed his defensive flinch.

'Oh Fal, it pains me so to see you react like that. I don't do this out of choice.' The pig rolled, exposing its belly.

'That bastard seneschal, Fal.' Rasoir sighed and shook his head. 'I believed you right away, you know?' He took his papa's knife and proceeded to skin the animal, slowly, skilfully. Its screams could have been human. Rasoir didn't flinch as he worked, eyes on Fal more than the pig's peeling skin. 'One of the infamous Correia Burr's pathfinders,' he said, taking great care in pulling long strips of skin off at a time and laying them out on the floor. Blood oozed and the pig pissed and shat itself. The stink was overpowering, but Rasoir continued regardless.

Fal looked from the cutting knife to the man, who looked back and nodded.

'Oh aye, I know her alright.' Another sad smile. 'Another reason this pains me so, but it wouldn't look good if I went easy on you, Fal. You said it yourself, Correia has men everywhere. How would it be for all of those men if they were found, eh?'

Heavy, painful breaths.

The pig looked wet now, glistening as its skinless flank shuddered in the torchlight. The smell worsened and that was saying something indeed. Fal ignored it all. He concentrated on the man, who continued working on the living carcass between them both, as would a practiced butcher.

'I find,' Rasoir said, heaving the pig about so the thrashing, squealing head was again visible, 'that the eyes are the key to a lot of things. To lies, that's true enough, but to fears too. The pain is one thing,' he said, bursting one of the wet orbs, 'but the

232

knowledge they'll never heal, never be restored. A bit like your front teeth' He sighed and stopped what he was doing, halting his torture of the poor beast. He sat back, pressing the point of his jelly- and blood-soiled knife to his forefinger. Minutes passed in silence, apart from the noises coming from the agonised sow, and those outside the bright window high in the wall.

Fal jumped when Rasoir started his work again, muttering about his son liking pigs and what, again, a waste it was.

With a show of anger, Rasoir jabbed the blade into the pig's remaining eye, gouging it out before throwing the knife across the room. He'd gone deep, Fal knew, for the pig, after a final spasmodic jerk, fell silent and stopped moving all together. Nerves twitched a foot, but that was it.

'Waste of good fucking meat,' Rasoir complained, surging to his feet and storming from the room. The door slammed behind him and Fal jumped once more, left as he was, staring at the eyeless animal.

***

'So… this is it then?' Amis raised his eyebrows. Flavell pulled her full lips into a tight smile and nodded, patting down her white silks.

'Well, mademoiselle, you look—'

'Stop it, de Valmont,' Flavell's smile widened and near on stunned Amis. 'You'll make me cry.'

Amis grunted a laugh at that.

'Are you going to do me the honour, since my *father* isn't present?'

'Whether it's my role or not, I cannot deny you your wish, mademoiselle. If you want me to, I shall.' He dropped into a low, respectful bow. A rare sight indeed.

Flavell beamed and clapped her hands together.

'Are you ready, mademoiselle?'

Flavell turned to Cateline, who'd stuck with her throughout the preparations.

'I shall ever be ready for my wedding,' she said to her, a twinkle in her green eyes.

'I can lead the way,' Cateline offered, with a curtsy as low as Amis' bow.

'Please do, my dear. De Valmont?' Flavell held her arm out to Amis, who dropped into another, albeit shorter, bow, before taking

233

her arm and leading her to follow Cateline towards the White Chapel.

'Who do you suppose will be present?' Amis asked, eyes front.

Flavell frowned. 'I'm not sure?' She looked sideways to him.

'Well, Croal's family certainly won't be, being that most of them are dead or locked—'

'Please…' Flavell squeezed Amis' arm. 'Not now, Amis. Not now.'

Inclining his head in an apology, the three continued on down an unusually deserted corridor.

A bell tolled in the distance.

Amis turned to look at Flavell, the light of the day filtering through blue and green stained glass, followed by ruby-red, painting her dress crimson as she glided along beside him.

'You've come a long way, mademoiselle,' he said, eyes searching hers.

'As have you, Amis de Valmont; with me, besides me, guiding and guarding me all the way and seeing me right.'

Amis smiled. 'As my family has yours for generations.'

Flavell nodded. Another bell tolled, closer than the first, which continued, creating a distant cacophony of bells that worked not together, creating no melody nor tune.

'The White Chapel's bell?' Amis asked. Flavell chewed her enticing lips and shrugged.

'No, messire,' Cateline said over her shoulder, her frown and fear plain to see. 'The first were town bells. The last from the chateau's gatehouse, I'd say.'

Flavell's eyes widened. 'Could be your man! Back to whisk you off your feet.'

Cateline's breath caught as she walked, her frown lost to the excitement and wonder of possibility and hope. She turned back to check their path and turned a corner. She looked back to Flavell once more. 'You believe it could be, mademoiselle?' She stopped, despite herself, to take in Flavell and Amis fully, hands clasped before her, worrying at a white, wooden disk that hung from her neck.

'Let's go see, shall we?'

'Mademoiselle—'

'Not now, de Valmont. My love can wait a little longer. This girl has been kind to me, after all that has happened. It's the least I can do, and will make the day so much more to me to see her reunited with her own love.' Amis made to speak but Flavell put a finger to his lips and silenced him. He squirmed at the touch, but said no more as the finger fell away. 'If her love has returned...' she removed herself from Amis and crossed to Cateline, taking her hands, '...I insist they attend the wedding, as my guests.'

Cateline balked, disbelief slackening her jaw. 'And if you're late, mademoiselle... because of me?'

Flavell laughed. 'It shall be fashionably, my dear, as a bride should be.' She pulled Cateline by the arm, suddenly and sharply. Pulled her and ran, laughing, back the way they had come. Back passed a stunned Amis and on towards the yard, where they could move to the outer bailey and the returning scouts.

Amis followed, his curses reaching both the girls as they ran, skirts held high, revealing pale calves Flavell knew would have a certain chevalier colouring red, rather than yellow. She laughed all the more at that.

***

'How's your nerves, Sieur?'

Croal looked across the White Chapel to Giles Bratby, who'd agreed to wear the traditional white of a Sirretan wedding. Croal smiled at the large Earl, whose greying hair complemented his white tunic and hose. Only his brown ankle boots and green and gold-plated belt stood out, but Croal could forgive that of the man. He smiled at Giles, though it was strained.

'Nerves that bad, eh?'

Croal swallowed and glanced about the white walls and white ceiling before answering. 'Is it normal to feel thus, messire?'

Giles laughed. 'But of course! The benefit you have, though, is that you've met the lady.' Giles laughed again, his baritone rumble filling the household chapel. 'It's rare to already love the lass as you do, or seem to.'

'I do,' Croal promised.

Giles was already nodding. 'I can see that, messire. We all can.'

There was quiet for a time, with the shifting of the white priest the only thing to break the silence of the candle-filled, windowless space.

'I had thought it would be different, messire: my wedding day.'

Giles offered a sympathetic smile. 'I'm sure you did, lad.' Giles looked about the chapel, festooned with carvings of Croal's family

235

members long since passed. It lacked the late Eudes de Geelan. The man hadn't even had a pyre yet, as was the Sirretan way. 'I expect you thought you'd be surrounded by family, approving and loving.'

Croal nodded, head down whilst he fumbled with his already buckled, looped and tied white belt. He went on to smooth down the tiniest of ruffles in his velvet coat, brushing the material this way and that, grey then white, grey then white; rough then smooth. He felt sick. Sick with love in the best way possible and sick with anger and regret at the death of his uncle and the internment of his aunt and cousins. He thought of his father, his dead uncle's younger brother. Had he failed his father, who'd died so his older brother, Eudes, could live? It'd been a cold day, snow blessing the ground, covering everything in a virgin snow. Much like the white of the chapel where he awaited his bride, Flavell de Steedon. His love. Croal's stomach twisted, fluttered, and his heart sang. So many emotions, from memories of his father dragging Eudes from the frozen pond, only to fall back under himself, to the eyes that now graced his mind's eye; beautiful, depth-less greens, leading to a soul he wished to bind to his own. As he wrestled with the memories new and old, good and bad, Croal was snapped from his reverie by the faint ringing of a distant bell, from the town if he had to guess. He frowned.

'That's a gods-awful bell?' Giles said, hand on the sword he'd been allowed to carry since aiding Croal on the night of Eudes' death; on the night Flavell had been saved. Giles squinted, as if it'd help him hear the distant clanging.

'I owe Amis de Valmont, you know,' Croal said. It'd spilled from his mouth with little intention.

'You do,' Giles agreed, relaxing at Croal's inaction to the bell's toll. 'He got to your lovely lady in time to save her... well...'

'In time to save her sanity is how I would put it, messire.' They locked eyes.

'Aye, lad. That'd be the right way to put it.'

Another bell, closer. Both men frowned and the white priest turned, head cocked.

'The outer bailey?' the priest asked, although his eyes were on a wall, rather than a person.

'I would agree.' Croal walked to the arched doorway and pulled it open further, spreading the dark gap that had been there and further breaking the white of the cube they stood in. He looked out onto dark stone slabs and colourful tapestries either side of the corridor.

'Messire?' one of his two chevaliers said. They moved as if to listen to the bells more clearly, hands on swords, tense for what it might mean.

'Go and see what is amiss. For the bells to toll like so...'

The man who'd spoken nodded before rushing away, maille rustling and plate scraping.

'It could be an army approaching,' the other man said, face set like the stone he stood against.

Croal shrugged. 'I cannot know. But of all the days, it best not be today, or they will receive my wrath tenfold. By White I swear it!'

The chevalier broke his stern expression and revealed a grin before nodding. 'And mine, messire. And mine.'

Croal gripped the man's steel vambrace in thanks. He smiled, nodded once and turned back into the chapel.

'You can postpone, Sieur,' the priest said. 'Pray for what is to come instead, should it be what we fear—'

'I do not fear it,' Croal lied. He licked his drying lips and turned to Giles. 'What would you do, messire?'

Giles' eyes widened, greying eyebrows lifting and brow creasing with the action. He filled his cheeks before letting out a long breath. 'You're asking your late uncle's rival? His enemy?'

'The enemy of my enemy—'

'Alright, lad.' Giles held up his large hands to stop Croal. 'Don't finish that line. He was your uncle, after all.'

Croal managed a smile. 'I was talking of the Orismarans as our mutual enemy, messire, not my uncle.'

Giles grinned. 'Ah, yes, of course.'

Both men allowed true mirth to show through. The priest scowled and moved about the chapel, laying petals from white lilies on the few pews that were there.'

'The choir will be here soon,' the priest said, killing the mirth and drawing both sets of eyes to him. 'And the equerry to record the marriage contract—'

'Marriage will do, priest,' Croal said. 'This is a binding of love, not papers.'

Giles didn't even attempt to hide his smirk as the priest blustered and scoffed. 'Well, that may well be, Sieur, but procedures must be followed and events documented. Now, if you would…'

Someone screamed. The sound came from a way off, but it was clear that whomever released the sound was terrified, or dying. Likely both if the latter.

The door swung in fully, revealing Croal's remaining man. 'Stay here, messires, and lock the door.'

'I'll do no such thing.' Croal fired the words and drew his sword in one. Giles followed suit.

The priest rushed down the chapel's short isle. 'You'll put those blades back—'

'Not now, priest.' Croal turned on the man, free hand forward, index finger pointed to accentuate his point.

The priest's face being the reddest thing in the chapel at that point, he merely huffed and went about scattering more petals. He hesitated when a second scream reached them, closer this time. His fearful eyes searched Croal's, but Croal turned to look down the corridor, along with Giles and the chevalier.

'I need to go for Flavell.' Croal made to move, but the armed and capable men now either side of him clamped hands on his arms.

'Not now, messire,' the chevalier said.

'The lad's right, Croal. Let me go in your—'

'I should go,' Croal's man said, eyeing Giles with distrust. 'And you should disarm, Messire Bratby.'

'Flavell is my responsibility,' Croal said, ignoring the latter. 'She is my betrothed and my love, gentlemen.' His heart skipped, stomach churned all the more, breaths quickening and chest heaving beneath white linen and velvet; he was suddenly and acutely aware of his lack of armour, lack of padding even.

'We all go,' Giles said, releasing his grip on Croal's arm.

Croal looked to Giles, who stared back before taking a step towards the door. The only thing that stopped him was the maid who ran around the far corner and into the corridor, the red she was covered in a stark contrast to the chapel from which the three warriors watching her stood, and the white two of them wore. Croal knew, from her blood-soaked clothes and spattered, terrified face, that their fine clothes wouldn't remain white for much longer.

''Morl's fucking arse,' Giles breathed, the curse matched by two more, albeit them of white and light and not a long since dead knight.

Croal's heart stuttered, his stomach lurched. 'That's Cateline, the maid assigned to Flavell.'

Cateline continued on towards them, tears mixing with the blood on her cheeks. The three men beckoned for her to hurry. The chevalier took two steps into the corridor, towards Cateline, the only thing stopping him being the thing that came into view next. The thing that chased the poor girl.

With bile rising to burn his throat, Croal was pulled back from the doorway by Giles. Before he could protest, before he could see what the approaching horror did to Cateline and his loyal man, the dark scene was blocked by the shutting and barring of white.

A guttural scream... no... two screams, ripped through the hearts and souls of those inside the chamber of purity.

Strong arms held Croal firm as those of the priest slammed a second locking bolt across the portal. All Croal could do was picture his love, his wife to be, torn to pieces like those beyond the door. Heart thudding as if to break free, or break at the possibilities of what was to come, or what was already there and happening, he released the tears and a throat grating scream of anger.

'Flavell!' he screamed, after the first incoherent roar. 'Flavell!' His struggles to break free of the man holding him failed, and that man pulled him in closer, nose and mouth pressing against the top of his head. Croal sagged. He hung from the big man who held him as would a father, as would have his father.

'Flavell,' he said this time, rather than shouted or screamed, the fight in him falling away at the thought of what lay beyond that door, likely devouring Cateline and his loyal chevalier. 'My love...'

Chapter 39 – Besieged

'Is he finally ready for me?' Correia said to the knock at the door. She'd been tapping the back of her head against the stone wall behind her, fed up of sitting and drinking and eating alone; fed up of sleeping and pacing the chamber with nought but arrow slits for poor light, now that morning had come. It'd been a long, largely sleepless night, but what could she do? She couldn't very well demand an immediate audience with Croal de Geelan. No. As much as she'd wanted to do that, as much as she was dying to go in search of Fal, she knew she had to be careful. She risked more than Fal alone if she wasn't. Correia had heard a commotion build outside over the past... however long. Time had slipped from her. She was used to waiting, used to being asked to wait, but this was different. A whole night? Something was wrong. Her heart skipped in a sickly way when the door opened and she saw the chevalier who'd guided her and her pathfinders into the town, the chateau and then her into the keep itself. His face was a mask; a mask attempting to hide a panic she knew a man such as he was unused to feeling.

'What is it, Jehan?' Correia dared, when he failed to answer her previous question. The opening of the thick, iron studded door had brought with it sounds. *Shit.* They weren't good sounds.

'Messire Seneschal is... indisposed—'

'Gods above, man, spit it out!'

Jehan straightened, but his steel encased fingers continued to worry at the hilt of his sheathed sword. 'We're to be besieged.'

There was a silence, or rather there would be if it weren't for distant bells. Alarm bells, from the town she reckoned. Correia licked her lips, eyes straying from Jehan, albeit briefly. 'By whom?'

'Orismarans.'

'An army?'

He nodded, jaw bunching, hand wringing his hilt, his frustration and want to act apparent.

Correia nodded and came away from the wall. Her own hands moved to her own swords, either side of her. She paced once more, eyes flicking left and right, brain working, spinning. *How have they reached The Marches? Is Lejeune lost? It can't be...* Jehan said nothing, let her pace. She stopped, looked at him. 'How is Croal indisposed? What of the marquis, what of Eudes de Geelan? Are you to ride out and meet them? Why a bloody siege?' She fired the

240

questions at him.

He swallowed hard. 'I wasn't to say, but it seems ridiculous not to now.'

'What does?' Correia sighed, exasperated. 'Tell me!'

'Eudes de Geelan is dead.'

Correia rocked back but composed herself. 'By whose hand?'

'The seneschal's hand—'

'His nephew? His bloody nephew killed him? How? When?'

'Madame, it is not my place—'

The sword-tip pricked Jehan's throat before he'd had chance to half-draw his own, and he was quick, a tourney winner, Correia knew. He ground his teeth and snarled, but made no move to counter the threat; she knew that he knew he'd be gushing red on the floor before he could act. A good fighter knew another good fighter, and Jehan was very good. Correia knew that and she knew he knew that, so she knew how good he knew her to be. The swift thought process she'd just ran through near on addled her. *I know he knows she knows, so say all of us.* An old ditty, from her childhood with Edward.

Correia sighed and Jehan made no move to counter as she lowered and re-sheathed her sword.

'Eudes was attempting to bed Croal's betrothed, forcibly.'

'And who might she be?'

He frowned, as if her name was unimportant.

'Humour me.' Correia paced once more.

'Mademoiselle Flavell de Steedon, daughter to Guiscard, the Sieur de Steedon.'

It was Correia's turn to frown. She looked to him. 'Never heard of her, or her father.'

Jehan shrugged. Maille rustled. Plate scraped. 'Nor had I. Nor,' he said, 'had Croal, or his uncle, until Flavell arrived for Eudes' festivities, a single chevalier in tow. She stole Croal's heart though, and he hers. I know him, madame. We fed from the same wet nurse. He's in love. The fairy tale kind.'

She held his gaze. 'Even so. Betrothed? That doesn't happen within families such as his without proper arrangement.'

Jehan nodded. 'Eudes' doing, as far as I know, but that's rumour. I'm not privy to all the details…'

'Madame, I think we'd be better addressing the army—'

'And how is Croal indisposed?' Her glare forced Jehan's hand. He knew when he was beat and answered the latest question.

'He and his betrothed are to be married.' He left a pause, but Correia said nothing. 'Now.'

'Now?' She blurted the word, hands on hips. After a nod from Jehan, she moved towards him, towards the door. He stepped aside and followed when she passed through. Bells continued to ring and a girl ran past, crying. Correia and Jehan ignored her.

'Where are we going, madame? I'm needed in the yard.'

'To the White Chapel.'

Jehan's eyes widened as he kept pace with Correia's stride. 'But—'

'Nothing. But nothing, Jehan. You're to accompany me there whilst I slap some sense into the Queen's bloody Seneschal...' She trailed off as someone screamed, outside. The sound came in through an arrow slit. All she saw was blue sky. Blue sky and... black: smoke. Correia stopped and held her hand up. Jehan might as well have been an Altolnan Pathfinder, not a Sirretan chevalier for all the protest he gave at the order to halt. He drew his sword, Correia doing the same to both of hers.

'They can't be through the town and in the chateau already? They were miles off...'

Steel met steel somewhere outside, in the yard, the ring of it clear. It was distant, likely in the outer rather than inner bailey, which gave them time, but it was in the chateau and that was surprising and worrying indeed.

Correia snarled. 'An advanced party set to disrupt? Maybe they're attempting to open gates or set fires.'

Nodding, Jehan made to move forward, but Correia stopped him with an outstretched sword. She shook her head. 'Take me to my men.'

He looked at her, anger reddening his face. 'They're in the outer bailey. If there's enemy there, they're already taken.' His stare was intense. Correia's more so.

'Take me...' Correia's words were slow, deliberate, '...to my men.'

'And the seneschal, in the White Chapel? I'm sorry,' he shook his head, eyes locked on Correia's, 'but my place is with Croal if the chateau is breached.' He pushed through Correia's sword – the flat of which had been held against him – and made down the corridor, backed by fresh shouts, screams and fighting. Correia followed.

'Tell me a way out, at least.'

He grunted a laugh and shook his head.

'You think me a coward?' Correia said, reaching Jehan's side and matching his pace.

'No. I think you a demanding bitch, if I'm honest. There seems little point in politeness now.'

Correia grinned despite the situation. 'I'd agree with both of those statements.'

A smirk pulled at Jehan's mouth. 'There's a tunnel on the ground floor, south side of the keep. Find a tapestry…' Two page boys raced around a corner. Faces set in fear, in horror, they barged past the sword carrying man and woman, their tilted run unbroken as they disappeared down the corridor. Jehan continued, accelerating to a jog. '…a ceiling to floor tapestry of Eudes de Geelan on a boar hunt. You won't miss it, it's garish and hideous. After all, he insisted on a true likeness.' Correia failed to hide her smile at that.

They rounded a corner onto a wider, door lined corridor. One of the doors nearest to them opened as closer bells tolled, from somewhere within the chateau itself. A man stumbled through the opened door, knotting his sword-belt, head down. When the maille-clad man looked up, he straightened.

Jehan pointed his sword at him. 'Fllened, with me, now.' The man-at-arms nodded and fell in behind them, finishing off his belt as he did so. At the end of the corridor, Jehan paused and turned to Correia. 'Go to the tunnel, I'll have your men meet you there. If they live.'

'They will. Now go to your liege, drag his arse out of that chapel and bring him to me at the tunnel. All's lost if they reach the inner bailey, so we need to get him out.'

Nodding, Jehan turned, hesitated. He looked back, past Correia. 'Take Madame Burr to the passageway behind Eudes de Geelan's tapestry. Do you know the one?'

Correia didn't turn, nor did she hear anything so she assumed the soldier, Fllened, nodded.

'Good. When she's safe, come to the White Chapel and bring whoever you can find along the way. Go, now.'

'This way, madame.' Fllened's voice was smooth, young. Correia hadn't paid much attention to him as he'd stumbled from the room, but his voice gave away his lack of years. A squire, perhaps. She heard his boots heading back the way they'd come.

Jehan turned to leave.

Sword held thumb to palm, Correia placed the hand on Jehan's armoured shoulder and stopped him. He looked back, over shoulder and hand.

'Bring Croal and his wife and—'

'Your Earl?'

'I was going to say anyone else along the way, Jehan, but yes, Earl Bratby would be pleasing.' Jehan nodded and smiled. 'Bratby's son has an army,' she added, before he turned away, 'camped on the other side of the border. If we make it to them quick enough, Easson may not be lost entirely.'

Smiling again, tightly this time, Jehan nodded once more, turned and left.

Correia ran to catch up to Fllened, who neared the far end of the corridor.

More bells rang, closer; from above. From the top of the keep.

They've breached the inner bailey…

Correia and Fllened ran.

***

The Sirretan soldier fell back, stunned, attempting to keep his insides from spilling to the floor. Gleave pushed past him, knowing the lad to be lost. Sword arm leading, he whispered to his axe and it vanished, his hand looking like it'd been broken and set wrong as it appeared to grip nothing. The Orismarans had come fast. Through the town they'd raced, not stopping to ransack, rape and burn as was their way when raiding. Doors slammed shut and were bolted, shuttered windows offering those inside a slim sense of protection as the tattooed warriors piled through the streets, dozens of boots, bare feet, carts and mounts making short work of the wet-from-the-night-before road and turning it into little more than churned earth. It was as if a drunken ploughman had been up and down, up and down, slewing this way and that to ruin the road years of feet had worked at, to hard-pack and create.

Once at the main gate, bells tolling and women and children of the town wailing, the guards atop, crossbows clicking and insults flying, had balked as men they'd known years drew blades and drove them deep, whilst others worked cranks and lifted door-bolts. The portcullis rose and the gates opened. The Orismarans entered like guests to one of the late marquis' balls, all confident and cock sure.

The room the Altolnan Pathfinders had been playing dice,

sleeping and drinking in had erupted in a table-turning scattering of knife drawing men on both sides of the guardroom. Blood and piss flowed quicker than the ale had leading up to the event. Sirretans murdered Sirretans and Altolnans finished off those left.

Sav and Starks, bells ringing on the chateau's inner walls now, followed Gleave as he ran awkwardly for the inner bailey, the length of visible steel in his hand hacking into the side of an Orismaran passing close to the door they left. The gut-spilled Sirretan lad who'd left ahead of them was prone now, dying as Starks ran past, slipping on the blood.

Starks hadn't had time to make his crossbow ready, but had picked it up. Carrying it in one hand, he held his short-sword in the other. Sav, on the other hand, had strung his bow before Gleave had finished the last Sirretan turncoat, and now proceeded to place white feathered shafts into the olive skin of any Orismaran that came close, spinning one and punching another from his feet.

Starks nearly slipped on horse shit, but managed to right himself whilst avoiding the swing of an axe from a roaring tribal warrior. The snarling face of Starks' attacker caved in, the image stranger than ever, white bone poking through tattooed skin and red flesh as the invisible weapon that caused the wound sucked free, dropping the man to the dirt.

'Go, go!' Gleave yelled, waiting until both his companions had passed before following, howling Orismarans in pursuit.

'Fucking coward bastard Sirretan traitors,' Gleave shouted, each word punctuating a pounding, painful footfall towards the closing gates of the inner bailey. 'Wait, wait, wait!' he shouted louder, waving his invisible axe carrying hand at the crossbowmen above. Bolts flicked down, dangerously close. Gleave bit back his vocal retort to the men looking down at him as he heard a grunt close behind. He ran faster, despite his bastard leg, not realising he'd slowed to shout and wave. Starks made it through the gate and Sav turned to loose one more arrow before doing the same. Green paint scraped from iron spaulders as Gleave sucked in a breath, squinted and dived through the closing slither of a gap between the oak barriers, which thudded shut behind him. The thud was followed by many smaller thuds and bangs. The Orismarans were hammering on the barrier.

Not relaxing, the three pathfinders kept their backs to the gates, eyes out, weapons at the ready. There was no way they were going to let anymore traitors approach.

Gleave's leg flared, as did other aches and pains. He gritted his teeth and pushed it all from his mind.

The two Sirretans that had closed the gates fell back against them, panting. One was in a state of half dress, one hose on and crumpled around his ankle, the other missing altogether and his chest bare. He wore a belt with an iron loop, through which hung a war-hammer. He looked to Gleave and nodded. Gleave nodded back.

'That's the fastest take of a gatehouse that I ever seen... or heard telling.' Gleave spoke in Sirretan, albeit poorly. The half-dressed solider nodded before moving off, companion in tow, ascending stone steps jutting from the side of the wall. They joined more men on the ramparts.

Shouting came from the far side of the gate and wall, as well as from the wall above. Gleave, Sav and Starks turned their heads to an opening door to their left, from which four armoured men ran, weapons drawn. The soldiers glanced towards the Pathfinders, stood backs to the gates, but paid them no more heed. They didn't make for the wall, but ran around the back of the keep itself, the great white stone block reaching up several stories to crenellations hiding the shallow-pitched red roof on top.

Gleave filled his cheeks before letting out a ragged breath, heart hammering in his chest.

'How did this happen?' Starks looked to Gleave, expectant, as ever, of an answer from the older warrior.

'Sirretan incompetence... and treachery,' Gleave said, eyes scanning the yard as a renewed pounding begun on the gate at their backs. 'That's something big, heavy,' he added, stepping away.

'Let's get inside the bastard keep,' Sav said, setting off. 'We've Fal to find yet, and Correia now too. I knew being told to wait all night wasn't right.' Sav spat and sped up. The other two followed, heading for the main doors which stood tall. As they neared, those doors opened. A wide-eyed boy of twelve years or so stepped through, eyes searching the walls above. The boy's gaze fell to the three men approaching him at speed. He tensed, then relaxed a little.

'Pathfinders!' The word tumbled from him, more a statement than a question, his Altolnan better than Gleave's Sirretan. The three Pathfinders skidded to a halt before him.

'Where's Correia?' Sav wasted no time and towered over the boy. He and the others were rewarded with a hasty answer, which

246

they just about understood.

Thanking the boy and urging him to follow – to which he denied, claiming he had more messages to pass on from Jehan of all people – the Pathfinders continued on into the keep at speed, weapons drawn, Correia's position now known to them.

Chapter 40 – Points and pricks

Locating Correia led to her barking orders at Gleave and Sav and sending them away again, to scout their retreat; the chateau was in turmoil.

'That masked helm he wears,' Gleave said, eyes wide in adoration. 'Look at it!'

'I take it you like it?' Sav screwed up his nose, trying to make his mind up if he did too.

'Oh aye, it's as clever as a mage is that.' Gleave pressed his fists to his cheeks and frowned, looking about as if he wore it himself. 'Ornate to the point of being king-worthy,' he said. 'Yet defensive because, well, it's a visor in all intents and purposes. But most of all,' he went on, lowering his hands, 'it makes the bastard look like a fucking demon. I want it.'

'Ask him for it.' Sav stared at the armoured Orismaran brute wearing it.

'I would, but...'

'But what, Gleave?' Sav grinned.

'Well, it's too ostentatious.'

'Big word for you.'

'Fuck you, Sav.'

'Sorry. Go on, it's too ostentatious...'

Gleave nodded, eyes on the mask and its wearer. 'It's so damned pretty, it makes me want to shove something through it more than it makes me want to wear it, now that I'm thinking about it.'

Sav grunted a laugh. 'I'm worried what you want to shove through it, looking at that grimacing mouth vent, and the way you're gushing over it.'

Gleave turned to Sav, who grinned and winked.

'You're funny today,' Gleave said, 'especially considering the shit we're potentially in and this bollocks-of-a-scouting mission she's sent us on.' Gleave looked back to the masked Orismaran, so did Sav. 'Perhaps I'll shove your face through it.'

Sav frowned. 'My face? Through his... face?'

'Alright, I didn't think that retort through, too intent on that bastard I am. Point is... well, that *is* the point, isn't it?'

'Eh?'

'A point. That's my point; that's what I were on about.'

'You lost me.' Sav shook his head and rested it on his thick arm, looking back out at the masked man from the grassy mound they lay on. The commander, for surely that's what he was, paced the open space of the outer bailey at the back of the keep.

'A point, Sav. The bloody mask is so fancy, makes me want to shove the point of… I don't know, something sharp and preferably made of iron through it.'

'Ah, now I see. Nice.'

Gleave nodded. 'Aye. Stick the prick inside. Perhaps I could have it after that. Clean it up, patch it up and such. Ostentatious loot, I like that. And with the hole the random point made, other bastards I faced would know I fucked over the original wearer and took it for myself.'

'That they would,' Sav agreed. 'And said bastard, some hoary warrior or grizzled maniac facing you, will want to do exactly the same to you.' Sav grinned and looked to Gleave once more. 'You know? To make a point…'

Gleave nodded. 'Point taken.'

'There's that point again.' Sav frowned as he saw the masked man make a series of hand gestures to one of his warriors, who rushed from the yard and out of the postern gate.

'I think we should crack on, Gleave. Get back in to Correia and Starks.'

Gleave took a deep breath. 'I think you're right, Sav. The mask will have to wait, so will sticking that ostentatious prick.'

Sav slapped Gleave on his back and slid back down the mound. Moving away, and once he was satisfied Gleave had followed, Sav turned back to Gleave whilst they made for the hidden door to the tunnel their companions hid in.

'You know, Gleave…'

'Yeah?'

'You take anymore plate off folk and you'll clank louder than that prancing prick of a Duke, Rell Adlestrop.'

Gleave laughed. 'Aye, maybe, but I won't polish it to within an inch of its creation, unlike that hubris filled posh prick. I'll green anything else I get like I did these here spaulders upon my broad shoulders.' He grinned at Sav and slapped him back like before, on the back.

Sav nodded as he bent to pass through the door. 'Points and pricks. It's all about the points and pricks today, isn't it?'

Gleave followed Sav through into the darkness. 'Aye lad, today it is. And tomorrow, and the next day. As long as it's shoving points through pricks, rather than them shoving 'em through us.'

Sav stopped, looked at Gleave and smiled whilst closing the door behind them.

'Now that, Gleave, we can agree on.'

Correia was crouched in the tunnel with Starks as Gleave and Sav returned.

'How is it?' she asked.

Gleave shook his head. 'Not good. They have men guarding the postern gate. This siege is a setup, Correia, I'd wager on that. They're walking around that small gate like it's their own, with little to no resistance at all from Easson's soldiers, and those Sirretans we witnessed turning on their own, opening gates and such?'

'There's something wrong with it alright, that much is clear,' Correia agreed. 'I still haven't seen the seneschal either. Alright,' Correia said, looking up, decided, 'we're moving. Gleave and Sav, go and get Fal. We know where he is now thanks to the lad that brought me to this tunnel, and it's time to have him here with us.'

'And the way out, once we have him?' Gleave looked back down the tunnel towards the small door he and Sav came from.

Correia's stare was not to be questioned.

'We'll go now,' Sav said, pulling Gleave along and shuffling past everyone.

'And me?'

'You're staying here with me, Starks. If we lose this way out, we're lost altogether, so we're to hold here and wait for them to fetch Fal.'

'Do you think this Croal bloke is against whatever's happening?' Starks asked.

'I know he is,' Correia said. 'That's why I was so intent on seeing him personally.'

'But you said you wanted to see the marquis?'

'Of course I did, Starks. It'd be weird if I'd told the Sirretans I wanted to see their liege lord's nephew, wouldn't it?' She offered Starks a rare wink.

'He's your man, isn't he?' Starks leaned forward. 'Isn't he, Correia?'

'Well it's all gone to shit now,' she said, resting back against the wall. 'But yes, Croal de Geelan is my man. Believe it or not.'

'The bloody seneschal himself!' Starks was clearly impressed.

'His title means nothing to me if I can't get an audience with

250

him, in private.' She rubbed her face hard.

'And if you did?'

Correia spun on him. 'I don't know, Starks! Alright?'

Starks swallowed hard and nodded.

'I don't know,' Correia whispered, head back against stone.

Chapter 41 – White wedding

White priest hid behind white lectern as a continuous hammering made him flinch repeatedly.

'Oh for 'morl's sake, man,' Giles said, pacing the White Chapel, sword in hand. 'You're making my arse twitch more than that thing out there.'

'I need to go out,' Croal said, breaths quick, frantic. Through gritted teeth he growled, a poor attempt to match that which came from the far side of the door.

'And I told you, Croal, you're not.'

Croal spun on the Marquess of Suttel, his late uncle's counterpart and rival. 'You do not order me, Bratby. Especially in my own home.'

'No, but I'm advising you, lad. She'll be safe, I promise you that. Amis will see to it—'

'I should be seeing to it!' The sound outside the room stopped at the shouted words, then started again with renewed efforts.

Giles sighed, Croal too. The priest mumbled prayers of light and white.

All three men hesitated, held their breaths at a new noise: shouting and metal on metal.

Croal's face lit up. 'My men!' he said, eyes on the door. He rushed for it, throwing the locking bolt across, Giles too slow to stop him. The priest's prayers turned to whimpers.

The banging and growling stopped before Croal opened the door. It had been part of his reason for opening it.

The beast entered at speed, knocking Croal back and to the floor, its blood-red bulk a stark, horrifying contrast to the interior of the White Chapel and the attire of the three men it towered above. Like a blunt faced, over-muscled human without skin and with canines protruding from its fat mouth, the gore soaked beast stood on two legs and hammered its chest with a ferocity that stunned the onlookers.

'We're fucked…' Giles stepped back against the wall, sword lowering, face paling.

'No,' came a throaty, accented voice from the doorway, 'this one's fucked, if any of you raise those swords.'

An Orismaran in maille and plate, who stood nearly as tall as the panting beast in the centre of the chapel, held Flavell by her throat, his other ham of a hand pulling at her hair so her eyes weren't much more than slits across her tear-soaked face.

Silence. Sudden and heart stopping. The scene before Croal flooded him with dread, with a hopelessness that wracked his chest with a single sob like he'd not felt since he'd lost his father. Despair took its hold, its talons surrounding his heart and squeezing with an ice-cold grip that dropped him to the stone slabs. Distantly, through the previous silence, Croal heard the metallic clatter of steel on stone; his sword. Heavy breaths came and went through his nose, lips pressed together, eyes wide. He stared, locked on green eyes he'd come to know so well. Come to love.

'My sweet...' The words came as a breath, fuzzy to his inner ear. Flavell struggled within the hold of the tattooed brute. The Orismaran's leering grin was lost on Croal, as was the red beast that closed on him. Giles roared something, to him, Croal thought, but it was as if a dream, hazy, unreal... slow. All so slow. Strong hands, huge hands, closed around Croal's unarmoured arms and wrenched him to his feet. The beast lifted him free of the floor. Flavell screamed and thrashed in the Orismaran's embrace. The man laughed, her struggles doing nothing to hinder him as he dragged her across the White Chapel. Her dress, her beautiful white gown only now became apparent to Croal. His eyes dropped for a moment and a smile pulled at his dry lips. She stunned him more than all else, her beauty and the love they shared.

'Flavell.' The word rolled off Croal's tongue, bringing forth a smile broader than any he'd ever given. He heard her voice, clear, like crystal. It rang out; she shouted his name, pleading, crying out in fear and desperation.

'My betrothed,' he said softly, weakly. 'My love.' All was well with the world, because they'd found one another, discovered the truest love. If it all ended now, Croal knew they would both die knowing they'd found true love in one another. Like the tales sung by troubadours and the like. A love such as legends describe.

Giles' shouts, full of anger and incredulity, were lost on Croal, dumbed down by the thumping of Croal's heart in his chest, his ears; everywhere, throughout his body and beyond.

'Croal!'

Her voice again, as the beast dragged Croal to the quivering, pissing priest behind his lectern. The priest's knuckles matched the chapel, his grip on the lectern was that fierce. He'd been forced to stand, a knife at his back. Croal hadn't even seen the other two tattooed warriors enter. Female, he noted, with dark skin and long white hair, grinning-skull-like tattoos to match, the contrast fitting in the White Chapel.

'Croal, please!'

Croal's eyes snapped back to Flavell's. Those wide eyes, perfect as they were, were red rimmed, wet, her face screwed up with fear, panic and more.

'Flavell.' Croal whispered her name and it all struck home. The Orismarans, the red, glistening beast that set him down and stained his white velvet crimson; his throbbing arms where the creature had gripped and lifted him. A heat surged through him, flashing white hot in his veins, through his heart and head. 'Flavell,' he said, louder now. She was held before him, before the lectern.

'Marry them,' the Orismaran said. 'Now!' His Sirretan was terrible, but Croal understood it and knew the priest would too.

Sucking in a lungful of air, Croal's eyes widened, the scene hitting home. He snarled.

Flavell was yanked away, yelping in pain as rough hands swung her round. The Orismaran was flanked by two sickle wielding men.

Croal stopped his surge of anger, his rush forward, as those blades filled his vision, their wicked curves good for slicing and lopping men with no armour, Croal knew. Incredibly strong hands took his shoulders and forced him to his knees. The grunts and bass growl behind was lost on him. Tears filled his eyes and he cursed himself for it, blurred as his vision now was. He didn't want it to end like this, apart, his vision of her watered down and unreal.

'You'll be wed apart then,' the Orismaran officer said, eyes narrow. 'And I'll fuck the bitch whilst it's done.'

'No!' Croal tried to surge forward once more, heard Giles attempting the same, but Croal was held firm by the beast. He winced at the pain it caused and saw Giles knocked back, the female Orismarans close to skewering him with long knives.

'Play nice and I won't be too rough,' the officer said, pulling at Flavell's dress as she failed to fight him off.

'No!' Croal screamed, willing the word to halt the man who was aggressively hoisting up Flavell's beautiful dress from behind.

'Croal...' Flavell struggled, but it was for nought.

Giles made to move again, Croal saw in his periphery, but was pushed back once more, blades pressing against his chest until his back met the white wall. He glared at the women and they glared back.

'Wed them,' the officer growled, and it was a growl, guttural and animalistic as he tore shimmering white silk and forced Flavell over, her hands gripping the lectern, stopping herself from falling forward. She looked through red eyes at Croal, at her husband to be, as the Orismaran's large hand reached round, under her dress. She gasped, no pleasure in it, bit her lip, face contorted as the brute looked over her shoulder at Croal, a wicked grin playing across his inked face.

Croal thrashed despite the pain. He thrashed as the priest reluctantly read aloud from the blank pages of the White Book. The priest couldn't look up. His voice shook but he went on, reading aloud the vows hidden, white on white, pure on pure.

'Louder!'

The priest's breath shook as he spoke up, the marriage words, ancient, unsullied until now, flowing from him as they had a hundred times before, albeit not accompanied by pleading cries and cursed denials. The ceremony reached its conclusion as the big Orismaran forced his way into Flavell, taking her breath as the binding words were spoken. Giles roared an Altolnan curse. Croal struggled and thrashed and fought against the grip and the pain. He cried and yelled and hurled threats as his beloved was raped before him. She was forced forward yet more – connected to her captor – who brought a serrated knife around, forcing it into her hand.

'Now slice your husband's throat, bitch.'

Flavell's attempted refusal was halted by a thrust.

Croal roared in the purest rage, face red, spittle flying.

'Do it or you'll have more of this from my men. Maybe even the beast that holds your husband. Do it, or the town folk of Easson will have the same, the women and the children, no matter how young. Do it and you'll rule here. You'll pay your tithes to my master, but you'll live, and so will your people.'

'Do it,' Croal whispered to her, wincing each time the officer squeezed her flesh or jerked her forward with one of his thrusts. Croal fell back against the bloody wetness of the creature holding him. He even lifted his head with a stoicism he didn't know he had. 'Do it, my love. Free me. Free yourself!' He couldn't go on. No matter the times he'd told himself he'd do this, that or the other come the end; come the fighting, glory-filled end. He never thought sitting back and accepting it would have factored. But it did. It was all he could do now. Accept it.

'Listen to him,' the officer breathed.

Giles' protests and curses were lost to them all, the man forgotten in the corner, as was the whimpering priest.

Flavell shook her head, her sobs hindering her breathing, along with the grunting thrusts coming from behind her; violating her.

'Croal...' she wept, taking hold of his hand despite what she endured. 'My love...'

Croal came forward as much as he could, took her slender fingers in his own, gripped them tight. 'Do it,' he whispered to her. 'Set us free. Remember me from before this... before my failure.'

She was shaking her head before he finished his words. Their heads closed, met, before she was yanked back. She screamed.

'I'll kill the bitch instead.'

Croal lashed out, took the serrated blade held between them and drew it hard and sure across his own throat, jagged iron snagging as it went, his life's blood hot on his hands and chest as it turned his wedding coat red.

Flavell and Giles screamed their denial.

The tears wetting Croal's cheeks seemed more real than the throbbing agony of his neck as blood pumped free, the pressure of it released from his body as his hands fell by his sides; his life released into the White Chapel. He felt his energy, what little remained, failing completely.

We'll always have our love, he thought, for he couldn't force the words out past wet gurgles and rasps. He looked into her green eyes and released himself to her. He gave her his soul in that one true connection.

Croal's heart stuttered as he watched his love being raped. He watched on as his vision blurred, darkened; he watched on as he felt himself letting go of the light, of the White of the world. Croal watched as the woman he'd given himself to smiled. Smiled!

Flavell smiled wickedly as she began to pant and gasp, not in pain and horror, but in pleasure. He watched as she dragged her captor's free hand up and onto her covered breasts, laughing with ecstasy as the man ripped her wedding gown down to reveal a breast, pale skin and pink, erect nipple pawed at by the tattooed hand.

Croal died in an agony far greater than that of the knife tearing across his throat.

As Giles Bratby's horrified roar of anger found Croal's ears, the young man's life left him, his final sight that of his beloved's eyes gazing up at the grunting man with a hand around her throat, licking the side of her face as her tongue reached to meet his.

Croal died a married man. A married man who'd left the world amidst the purest of horrors. The purest of betrayals; his soul destroyed.

Giles stood, back to wall, chest heaving as he sucked in one great lungful of air after another, incredulous to the sight he'd witnessed. The White Chapel was flooded with offending odours and colours, mostly red; the red of the beast at its centre and the red of Croal's blood as it worked its way across stone slabs, travelling further along the grooves between stones, spreading out, pointing accusingly towards Giles and Flavell.

'I should have done something,' Giles whispered, eyes returning to Flavell at the sound of a low grunt.

'Get off me, you filthy cur,' Flavell hissed, planting an elbow into the Orismaran's padded and maille clad gut. The big man felt the impact, that much was clear as he backed away and doubled over, trews up and belted, cock stowed away as it had been throughout the feigned rape.

Giles frowned, snarled.

Flavell looked to Giles and grinned, her top lip bulging as fangs slid into view. 'It seems,' she said, walking around the lectern and the sobbing priest, 'that I am now the Marquise d'Easson, especially since I had that bitch, Croal's aunt, butchered, along with her three brats.' The red beast stepped away from her, cowering as much as the white priest.

'Succubus.' The word tasted bitter to Giles, although he had to admit, it made more sense than what had been the truth a moment before. 'You played us all—'

'For fools, yes.' Flavell glided up to Giles in her torn and blooded white gown, biting her bottom lip as she neared.

The Orismaran officer straightened, muttering a foreign curse. His two female warriors watched Flavell with a mix of awe and terror, their eyes as white as their tattoos; pupil-less. The two sickle-wielding male warriors stepped from the chapel and closed the door behind them, to guard the corridor or flee the succubus, Giles couldn't know.

'Oh, how I was moved by your anger at what the savage was doing to me, Giles.' Flavell practically purred as she spoke, lifting up onto her toes to make herself level, eye to eye, with the large Altolnan Earl. She hissed as Giles spat at her.

257

The strike he felt across his face might as well have come from the red beast for the strength of it. Spitting and adding more offending red to the chapel, Giles made up for the imbalance and added two white teeth to the floor, his mouth numb, the loss of the teeth and the knowledge they would never grow back angering him further. He prodded at the bloody holes they'd left, the feeling alien to his tongue. As alien as the creatures in the chapel with him, Flavell included. He steeled himself and grinned red at the bitch.

There were shouts and the briefest clash of weapons that silenced the room. Everyone, everything, held their breaths, surprised. Then came the sound of iron on wood, three times the knock.

'Mademoiselle de Steedon? Messire Seneschal?'

The Orismaran officer moved for the door with intent, but Flavell lifted her clawed hand to stop him. 'Amis?' she said, voice weak, soft, like it had been before her change. She clamped her other hand across Giles' mouth.

'They're in here!' came a muffled reply. 'Open up,' Amis shouted. 'There's not much time.'

Flavell frowned before motioning for the officer to open the door. Giles didn't miss the frown. As the tattooed brute reached the door and opened it, Giles drove his knee forward and up, enough to stagger the succubus, dislodging the blocking of his mouth.

'Trap!' Giles felt relief as he heard himself shout the word; he flinched as the door burst open.

A length of steel was the first thing through the portal. The sword twisted and came in at the officer, followed by Amis and a black-clad woman.

'Correia!' Giles' mouth was uncovered as Flavell leapt towards the door, claws outstretched, fangs bared and wings tearing free from the back of her dress.

The red beast roared and charged, flicking pews like driftwood.

Amis' eyes widened. He rocked back as if struck by the multiple horrors before him. 'Flavell,' he said, more a gasp, whilst fending off a counter-attack by the large Orismaran.

Giles winced, but when he recovered, his eyes were drawn to two white-hot swords. Everyone's eyes were drawn to the glowing blades.

Correia raced past Amis, taking a thrusting arm from the officer, who fell back, howling and holding his partially cauterised stump.

Flavell struggled in the face of the assault. The revelation of her wings had caused strips of silk from her gown to hang, tangle and hinder her. She tried to step back as Correia attacked with both swords. Flavell managed to bat the blades away, screaming in anger and searing pain as she did so.

More pews crashed and tumbled as the hulking red beast powered through them, towards Correia and Amis both. It made it halfway before Giles' blade arced out, opening up a line in the creature's shoulder. He hadn't even planned the attack, had hardly thought it; years of training and hunting and fighting had launched him into action as soon as the Orismaran bitches made for Amis.

With a roar, the beast turned on Giles, swinging mighty fists. Giles stepped out of the way in time, experienced as he was. There was no skill to the creature's attack, just raw aggression and strength. Despite its sheer horror and bulk, Giles took two more attempts to put good steel through the monster's face, pushing crushed bone and more from the back of its thick skull. The red beast left a bloody smear across the floor as it fell and slid, momentum carrying it a heartbeat after Giles jerked his sword free of the falling beast's head. He wasted no time and charged into the continuing fray, aiming for the back of the nearest Orismaran. She turned and avoided the unseen attack, but backed away, her knife a poor match against Giles and his sword.

Amis, confusion plain to see, regained enough of himself, if not all, to hold off the tattooed women. Seeing Giles come to his aid bolstered him and he thrust anew.

Giles used Amis' renewed efforts to step in close to the nearest Orismaran, avoiding a hasty thrust from Amis himself. With a growl, Giles shoved the woman back onto her arse, grabbed Amis and dragged the smaller man out into the corridor, confident enough in his King's Spymaster to know she'd be close behind. He'd seen the nod from her, despite their predicament.

The two men manoeuvred around the dead Orismaran guards and ran down the corridor, Amis looking back over his shoulder more than ahead. Correia followed them at full tilt, a screeching succubus and two screeching Orismarans on her heels. The black armoured officer stood in the doorway of the White Chapel, clutching his stumped wrist and glaring at the escapees with unbound hatred.

'A succubus?' Amis' words were breathy, heavy as he ran. He

glanced over his shoulder again, eyes meeting the green of Flavell's. The look that passed between them brought tears to his eyes, and Giles didn't miss it.

Flavell halted in her tracks. 'Run, little people!' She tore the rest of her wedding dress off with an otherworldly shriek of hatred and malice and amusement rolled into one.

A horn sounded somewhere in the near distance, replacing the bells that had long since stopped clanging their warnings.

The three companions ran on, Giles dragging a stunned Amis by his side, Correia bringing up the rear, swords cooling.

'My lord Bratby,' Correia said, loud enough for Giles to hear, 'take Amis to the stables…' she sucked in a breath as she ran, '…and meet us at the postern gate with mounts. As many as you can find.'

'And you?' Giles struggled with the words, his age and the shock of all that had happened doing its best to hinder his every breath.

'I'm to gather my men. I'll meet you there.'

Giles needed no more than that. With a silent curse and a groan, he fled down a set of stairs as Correia ran on, unsure whether he or she were pursued or not.

Chapter 42 – Droning

The route down to the dungeons had been surprisingly uneventful. No soldiers hampered Gleave and Sav's way. The only people they'd seen had been servants, all of which were scared by the events unfolding outside the keep; events they would be hearing about, but not seeing. Yet.

'Which one?' Sav whispered to Gleave. The two of them looked down the corridor, a row of closed cell doors on either side.

'Damn but this dungeon's big.'

'Gleave? Which one?' Sav shook Gleave's maille sleeve.

'Dunno. Let's knock on a few, eh?'

Before Sav could react, Gleave did just that.

'Wakey wakey!' Gleave hammered the back of his axe blade on every door he past.

'Lords above,' Sav said, 'he's going to get me killed.

'Fal!' Sav shouted, rushing from door to door. 'Fal, it's Sav!'

'Fal!' Gleave joined in, hammering and shouting.

'And if this draws the marquis' men to us?' Sav shouted down to Gleave, who was nearing the end of the corridor.

'I'll ask the limp dicked shites why they're not at the postern gate, shoving a point through that ostentatious prick's face!'

Sav laughed, then froze. The shout they heard come back at them was more of a scream.

'Was that him?' Gleave rushed towards Sav.

'Fal!'

Another scream, guttural, painful.

'That was.' Gleave pulled on Sav and ran to a door they'd passed near the beginning of the corridor.

Before they could even attempt to open the door, booted feet on stone turned their heads back to the steps they'd descended.

'I'll take them,' Sav said, motioning for Gleave to continue. A nod and Gleave opened the door and rushed inside the dark chamber.

Gleave had to throw himself right, avoiding the jab of a blade. He swung his axe around behind him, hoping to deter any further attack.

Someone grunted something from the other side of the stinking room, but it wasn't clear what was said, or who said it.

Movement again and Gleave swung wildly before shifting his feet and hitting something soft yet heavy on the floor. He fell, striking stone, thankfully not with his head. He rolled immediately. A spark kicked out from the knife strike that would have bit into him had he not moved.

Another grunt from a deeper shadow amongst the others. Someone huddled in the corner?

'Fal?' Gleave managed, swinging with his axe and jabbing with his now drawn sword.

'Gleave?'

It was barely recognisable, but Gleave knew it to be Fal.

'You're dead,' Gleave said to his opponent, who was circling whatever was lying on the floor.

'No,' Fal protested, or rather croaked.

'Yes!' Gleave surged forward.

The knife flicked out and across and Gleave did the same with his axe, struggling in the dark. He held his sword back, hoping it was out of sight, there being no lamp or candle light to catch on its blade.

Shouts from the corridor. Sav cursing. Sav yelling in anger.

'Sav?' Fal said, voice little more than a whisper.

'Yes, mate.' Gleave hopped back, hoping he didn't trip again. 'We're all here for you.'

A shuffling from behind Gleave.

'But I need to kill this twat first.'

A shout and a lunge from the man Gleave spun to face.

Knife slid across steel.

'Spaulders to the rescue!' Gleave stepped into the attack and kicked forward, connecting with something hard. A knee? His attacker shouted and dropped to the floor. Good light wasn't needed to know he'd gone down hard.

'Don't,' Fal said, coming away from the wall and stumbling into Gleave.

'What?' Gleave dropped his sword to stop Fal from falling.

'Correia's man,' Fal said, although his voice sounded different.

'Him?' Gleave pointed his axe to a lump on the floor.

Fal nodded: Gleave felt it against his own head.

'The Queen's Seneschal makes him do it,' Fal whispered.

'What, torture you?' Gleave frowned and shrugged. 'Fucked if I know whether that's right or not, but even so...' A dull thwack sounded as Gleave swung his axe down and into flesh and bone. Once, twice. 'He ain't gonna do it now,' Gleave said, pulling Fal along. 'We're leaving.'

Fal panted, cheek wet against Gleave's as Gleave tried to pull him along.

'Don't cry for that bastard, Fal.'

'Tried helping me,' Fal managed, between sobs. 'Didn't want to. Has a son.'

'Gods below, he's messed you up good and proper.' They reached the doorway.

Fal squinted against the dim torchlight.

Sav appeared, sword blooded.

The bells at the top of the keep began to toll once again.

'Shit,' Gleave said. 'It's starting.'

'Fal!' Sav took Fal's free arm. 'Oh shit, Gleave, look at him!'

Gleave cursed and urged them on, towards the steps. 'We need move, now.'

'He helped,' Fal said through blood crusted lips. 'Food and talk. Rest and smiles.'

'Sav,' Gleave said, 'ignore it for now. Let's move. Let's keep going, we've no time to listen.'

The trio stepped over four bodies before the stairs, and as the bells continued tenfold, Gleave and Sav helped their friend ascend. Every step brought another painful word from Fal's lips, the majority about how his torturer had been Correia's man.

Again, luckily, the path between the dungeon and the tunnel was uneventful, this time due to the masses of people, not the lack of them. Servants and soldiers alike, rushing past the three pathfinders, none of which had any time to spare on the two men carrying another who looked like a walking corpse.

Once at the tunnel's entrance, Gleave and Sav made sure it was clear before exposing the hidden doorway and helping Fal inside.

'Who goes?' Starks hissed from further into the tunnel.

'Who'd you think?' Gleave said back, whilst Sav closed the door behind them.

'Is that Fal?' Starks asked.

'Mostly.' Gleave shuffled along, Fal behind him, helped by Sav.

The faint light near Starks illuminated the extent of Fal's wounds. Starks gasped.

'You said it best, Starks.' Sav checked Fal over as best he could. 'He's bad, really bad.'

'But he's back with us,' Starks said, the relief showing through in his expression.

'Wait, where's Correia?' Gleave looked past Starks.

263

Starks took a breath. 'Yeah, well, she headed back into the keep to find her man on the inside.'

'Shit!'

Sav rounded on Gleave. 'What?'

'I think I hacked him up a bit.'

Sav's eyes widened, as did Starks'.

Iron spaulders rose and fell. 'He's the shit who tortured Fal.'

Wide eyes remained as Sav and Starks nodded their understanding.

'Can you blame me?'

'No, Gleave,' Sav said, 'but it means Correia's risking her life to find and question a corpse.'

'Sergeant Rasoir,' Fal said, through missing teeth.

All eyes turned to him.

'He didn't want to...' Fal started sobbing once more. 'His son...' he managed, although it was hard to hear it.

'Rasoir?' Gleave's brow creased. 'I slotted that bastard?' He barked a laugh.

'You know him?' Starks said.

'Oh aye, but he's not Correia's man and he's no fucking sergeant-at-arms, although he'd kill to be. Literally. He's a sadistic rodent is what he is. A shit who can't own what he does to people. He's certainly not an Altolnan spy, I can guarantee that.'

Fal turned his wet, bloodshot eyes to Gleave, his painful breaths coming quickly; shallow, but quickly. 'Not... her... man,' he said, each word causing him obvious pain.

'The seneschal is,' Starks said matter-of-factly. 'She told me the Queen's Seneschal, Croal de Geelan, is her man.'

Fal's shallow breaths turned to a shudder as he started to thrash, started to snarl and shout and lash out at anyone and everyone.

'It's all that was keeping you going, wasn't it?' Sav breathed, helping the others restrain their friend. 'Rasoir following orders was the only way you managed to go on, the only way you could make sense of what he was doing to you.'

Fal stopped struggling. He stopped and he sagged, letting his head fall against Sav's shoulder.

'Starks,' Gleave whispered.

'Yeah?'

'We need to go for her, now.'

Starks said nothing, but managed to squeeze himself and his crossbow past Fal and Sav, following a wordless Gleave back towards the tunnel entrance.

Distant horns sounded, foreign horns, along with shouts accompanying the sounds of clashing weapons.

'I'm here, now run!' Correia shouted as she rounded a corner and saw Gleave and Starks. Both men slid to a halt and turned without hesitation.

'Is the keep breached?' Gleave shouted, Correia close behind him.

'Yes.' She stopped, so did her men. 'Croal de Geelan, my man... He's dead, and some bitch—'

'What?'

Correia continued despite Gleave's incredulous interruption. 'His betrothed was the one to turn folk, to allow the enemy into the outer and inner baileys, or so I reckon. This keep is the only part of the chateau not to have fully fallen yet, and that's due to Croal's loyal men. I've barred the doors and ordered them to hold it, but I don't know—'

'Ordered the men?' Starks shrank back from the look Correia gave him.

'On the word of their seneschal, yes. They don't know he's dead yet.' She rocked back. 'Wait, where's Sav? Did you get Fal?'

'Sav has him,' Gleave said, shaking his head, 'but he's in a bad way.'

Correia nodded and looked back the way she'd come. 'What's that noise?'

Several people ran around the corner, servants and soldiers both, their faces a collage of disbelief and terror.

'This doesn't look good.' Gleave drew his weapons.

Correia did the same and Starks crouched and spanned his crossbow.

Two of the approaching people shouted for them to run, in Sirretan. Before Correia and her pathfinders could turn, the droning hum they'd heard increased. An enormous, black cloud of wasps swarmed around the corner and into the wide corridor, catching the trailing men and women and driving them to the floor; hands swatted, limbs flailed and screaming mouths were filled with the insects, their rear ends repeatedly driving stings into flesh.

The remaining people fell as they attempted to flee, the swarm faster than any of them could run. Looking back at the doorway they needed to make, Correia, Gleave and Starks launched themselves towards it, the horrific sound of an agonising death closing on them.

'We won't make it,' Gleave shouted, risking a glance behind as his feet pounded the stone slabs.

Correia didn't speak. She kept her head down and tried to use the pendulum motion her sword carrying hands created. It wasn't enough.

'Shit, shit, shit,' Gleave said, his injured leg flaring up, causing him to lag behind. He locked eyes with Starks, who turned back to look for him. Those eyes looked past Gleave and widened as the droning buzz neared. The screams behind Gleave died, as did those releasing them.

Another surge and Gleave continued, although the realisation he was lost struck him harder than any blow ever had. The only thing to strike him harder, as he saw Correia make and open the door, was seeing Starks turn and run back towards him.

'No!' Gleave shouted, reaching for the nearing lad, who shrugged off Gleave's grasping hand to run towards the swarm.

'Starks!' Correia screamed, half way through the doorway, looking back.

Before Gleave could slow enough to turn back fully, Correia's hand grabbed him by the nearest spaulder and pulled him through the door and off his feet.

The last thing he saw was Starks skidding to his knees and loading a bolt into his crossbow's groove in one fluid movement. He looked back and gave them a brave smile, whilst pointing and loosing his chosen bolt at the ceiling above his head.

Correia screamed as she heaved the door shut.

The following thump shook dust from the ceiling and set a ringing in Correia and Gleave's ears, both of whom lay on the floor, eyes on a door they knew wouldn't be opening any time soon. A door that would not see the passing of Starks.

Gleave's roaring denial was soundless as the aftermath of the concussive explosion stole their senses.

'He's gone,' Correia mouthed, tears flooding her cheeks. She looked to Gleave, who'd watched her mouth the words, his face white from shock, his head shaking in disbelief; his eyes watering as much as hers. 'Starks is gone...'

Chapter 43 – Furious grief

The door at the end of the tunnel opened and Correia crawled in, followed by Gleave. They shuffled down the passageway, not a word between them; there hadn't been a word spoken since they'd left the destroyed corridor behind. They'd have struggled to hear it even if there had been.

'Finally.' Sav craned his neck to try and see past Correia whilst cradling Fal, who stared at the stone wall. Sav frowned as Correia and Gleave drew close.

'Where's…' Sav's voice trailed off when he saw Correia's tear-streaked face in the dim light.

Before anyone else spoke, Gleave shoved past Correia, Sav and Fal, shuffling along aggressively, surely wearing holes in his hose and taking skin from his knees, never mind paining his injured leg.

'Gleave?' Correia said, voice unreasonably loud, yet somehow, at the same time, weaker than normal.

'What's happening?' Fal managed, although his voice was the weakest of all.

'Gleave!' Correia shoved past Sav and Fal, the latter's recent capture and torture forgotten in the face of what was happening, what had happened.

Sav was shaking his head in disbelief. No one needed to tell him what had happened. 'Can you follow?' He looked to Fal, who looked back and after a moment's pause, nodded. The two of them followed behind Correia, Sav helping his pained friend. It was impossible to match Correia or Gleave's pace.

Light lit the far end of the tunnel.

'Shit,' Sav said, knowing Gleave had reached the outer door.

'He's angry,' Fal said, followed by a pause in his movement and a string of coughs. Sav waited with him, before both continued.

Correia reached the end and saw the mound that blocked the view of the outer bailey's yard and postern gate. Gleave was cresting that mound, both weapons drawn, both weapons visible. Correia looked back into the darkness of the tunnel.

'Hurry!' she shouted, although it was hard to know how loud her shout had been, ears ringing as they were. She heard Gleave roar though. She'd be surprised if the whole of Easson hadn't heard it. 'Hurry!' she shouted again, at the top of her voice. Sav and Fal obliged, the grunts and curses evidence of that.

'What's he doing?' Sav said as he reached Correia, Fal propped against him.

'He's getting himself killed is what he's doing, if we don't act now.'

Weapons clashed from over the rise.

'Fal, stay here,' Correia said. 'Sav, string up and follow me.'

'I'll guard the rear,' Fal said, with a wry and wicked smile.

Sav managed to bark out a laugh at that. 'Glad to have you back,' he said, stringing the bow he'd had in the tunnel. He grabbed the linen bag of arrows and followed Correia without strapping on the bag.

Cresting the hill, he saw the chaos beyond. He also saw Correia sprinting into it, both swords drawn.

The linen bag tumbled across the mount as Sav threw it. He also threw the contents to the ground, each arrow sticking into the grassy knoll, holding them upright for his retrieval and dirtying the arrowheads for good measure.

'Whichever bastard doesn't die immediately,' Sav said to himself, nocking the first arrow, a needle-tipped bodkin, 'will hopefully,' he aimed and loosed in one, 'die slowly later on.'

The arrowed whirred through the air, turning two spiralling arcs before easing itself through, at great speed, the small, riveted iron link attached to thousands like it. Before the link split through the force of the impact, the needle tip of the arrowhead pierced flesh. Of course, the victim didn't feel that, so close was it to the final thudding impact of the rest of the arrow, which compressed on impact before flexing and passing clean through the Orismaran warrior's maille covered throat, erupting from the other side in a spray of iron links and blood. The man fell to the ground, thrashing and pawing at his agonising wound. At the same time, another arrow was already falling towards the dying man's nearest countryman, who fell soon after, screaming this time, an arrow jutting from his groin.

Sav pulled, nocked, drew and loosed time and again, not waiting to see his victims fall before moving on to the next. He aimed for those a way away from Gleave and Correia, not wanting to risk hitting his friends in the confusion, although he did keep them in his periphery, needing to know how they fared.

Gleave heard Correia approach as he hacked and slashed, lunged and parried. He stepped in, backed off, but largely stayed still or moved slowly, despite his welling anger. He knew he needed to conserve his energy. He knew he needed to outlast the greater numbers coming at him, all shouting and whooping as Orismarans were wont to do. He also knew he had to be cautious of his shit of a leg.

He stepped back once, twice, avoiding the swing of a falchion without exerting himself. There was something about that weapon being used against him that made his anger flare all the more; the thought of Fal took Gleave's mind to the loss of Starks, and on to the losses of Mearson, Tom and all the others he'd known and fought alongside.

Axe to lips and a word hissed through teeth. The falchion wielding warrior frowned as Gleave's elf-rune inscribed axe vanished from sight. The tattooed frown transformed into a grimace when Gleave stepped in and thrust his sword into the man's belly, distracted as he'd been with the magical axe. The falling body sucked off Gleave's sword, which he turned on the next man running at him. Iron clanged and Gleave felt it through his arm. He cast about, seeing Correia in her dance of swords, men falling about her. Gleave almost lost the side of his face as his eyes lingered on the woman's twin blades, which glowed orange to white, like they'd been pulled from a raging forge.

So that *was your gift from the elves…*

Twisting away from the slice that swished past his face, without turning his back on his attacker, Gleave used his translucent axe to tie up the offending weapon. The surprise in the Orismaran's face was doubled when Gleave's sword found that man's stomach too.

'And down you go,' Gleave said, his words little more than a growl. He turned, heart thudding in his chest, pulse in his ringing ears, looking across men dropped by arrows and back to Correia slicing through maille like it was leather. He looked past her and saw approaching riders.

'Shit,' he said, before shouting the very same.

Correia heard him and glanced the way Gleave pointed. She looked back to her nearest threat, dropping low and taking the leading legs from two men. Down they went, twisting and screaming.

'They're with me!' Correia shouted, first back to Sav to stay his hand, then to a hard-pressed Gleave, who back-stepped out of immediate danger, swinging his sword as he did, muscles burning at the effort. Training was one thing, but the swift desperation of

269

actual combat was another, especially with recent wounds not yet healed.

'I'm getting too old for this.' He spat the words as he changed direction, back at his enemy. The two tattooed warriors tried to adjust to Gleave's sudden attack, but there was no defending against a weapon they couldn't see. Both fell as the riders Correia had vouched for reached Gleave's side. He looked up to the two men, both knights, although one, the older, wore fancy white clothing and no armour. *Giles Bratby*, Gleave thought, relieved to see the Earl's faintly familiar face.

'Amis de Valmont, at your service.' The yellow knight looked to the Orismaran warriors now massing at the postern gate.

'So, that's where we're to go through?' Giles asked Correia, moving his sword about at the side of him, loosening his shoulder.

'Aye,' Correia confirmed, 'that's our route out.'

Another arrow arced overhead, taking down what looked to be an officer in the enemy ranks.

'There must be two dozen and growing; massing before their assault,' Amis said from his horse, standing in his stirrups. 'And they're coming through the gate we're to leave by.' He laughed nervously.

Another arrow and another man fell screaming to the ground.

A commotion from the back of the Orismarans and through came the beast of an armoured man with the ostentatious masked helmet, its grimacing visage panning left and right, taking in the people holding his own men back. As he emerged from the warriors around him, it became clear he was being pulled forward by two animals which he struggled to hold by their thick ropes.

'What the fuck are they?' Gleave said, eyes locked on the masked man's pets.

Amis screwed up his handsome face before answering. 'Honey badgers, I believe. Vicious little bastards.'

Gleave strode forward. 'Look like overgrown polecats to me.'

'Gleave!' Correia surged forward, but Giles leaned down and took her arm.

'Your man challenging that man is the only thing holding the rest of them back, I'd wager,' Giles said, eyes back on Gleave, continuous groans and screams of pain coming from the multiple arrow-studded, slashed and pierce wounded scattered about the yard.

'He's right,' Amis said. 'As much as it pains me to say so.' He turned to Correia. 'I'll ride out. I'll challenge him.'

'No, you won't!' Gleave shouted back, within earshot, the ringing subsiding. He continued on, meandering around dead and dying men, not passing close in case a knife found its way into his leg – again – or worse.

The Orismaran commander came forward, honey badgers bearing teeth and attempting to surge forward, their master straining to keep a hold on them.

Gleave glanced back and saw Correia turned to Sav and nod. An arrow followed that silent order, a swallow-tailed arrowhead, made to punch large and bloody holes in the heaving muscular chests of charging destriers. The arrow corkscrewed lazing through the air, or so it looked, but when it passed Gleave and punched into the honey badger on Gleave's left, it churned its way deep into the animal, slamming it hard to the ground.

Gleave sprinted forward, aches and pains once more forgotten as fear and anger fuelled adrenaline flushed his system.

The downed honey badger shrieked, hissed and climbed to its feet, arrow jutting from a bloody hole in its thick, furred side.

'Shit,' Gleave said, another arrow speeding past him and slamming into the stuck animal. The first arrow downing the animal had shocked the onlooking tattooed warriors, the second sent them to roaring and running towards Gleave and the others behind him.

Gleave heard Correia shout and he heard hooves pound the earth as he reached the ostentatious commander and his pets. At the same time, a third arrow punched into the same honey badger as the first two. The animal dropped again to the floor, remaining there this time, hissing and thrashing and not dying, but remaining on the floor at least.

Both ropes were released by the man Gleave aimed for and the remaining honey badger lunged forward at a surprising rate; the speed and aggression of the animal put any hunting hound Gleave had ever witnessed to shame. Gleave dodged right and lunged left, his sword tip piercing hide. The steel blade snapped. Gleave cursed and leaped aside as his opponent drew a giant scimitar, which swung out as the man powered forward on a set of trunk-like, armoured legs.

The curved blade swished across Gleave's maille-clad back. As he slid to a halt and turned, an arrow thumped into the remaining honey badger whilst it jumped at him. As if pricked by a thorn and no more, the animal struck Gleave, teeth snapping and long claws raking. Those claws cut through woollen surcoat, split iron links and padded gambeson to do the same to the skin and flesh beneath.

Falling back from the raging animal, Gleave dropped his broken sword and clutched his side despite his want not to.

The scimitar came in again, with a grunt of contempt from the armoured man. Gleave managed to avoid its bite, but not that of the honey badger, the powerful jaws of which clamped onto his bad leg.

The grunting animal on Gleave's leg continued to thrash to and fro, mangling the limb as Gleave cried out in pain, the agony the worst thing he'd ever endured. He saw the grimacing mask of his opponent stood over him, looking down, eyes shrouded in the darkness of the iron helm.

Gleave steeled himself and grinned up at the man, causing the brute to hesitate.

'You'll get the point!' Gleave said through gritted teeth as the honey badger continued to savage his leg, his invisible axe now embedded in it, not that it seemed to do any good.

The moment of impact was a glorious sight for Gleave to behold as one of Sav's arrows entered the ostentatious visor through the gaping mouth grill, before exploding out the other side. Head snapping back, the Orismaran toppled backwards and hit the ground with a clattering thud, horrific gurgles coming from behind the convulsing brute's mask.

There was no time for celebration. Gleave turned his painful cries into shouts and curses of anger. He began hacking at the animal with renewed gusto as it broke bones in his leg. He hacked and hacked until he feared he couldn't lift his axe anymore, but finally... finally, after two more strikes of the axe, the honey badger died.

The pain pulsing through Gleave's leg matched his quickened heart. He bent and pawed at the wounds as a horse charged past, the yellow rider slashing left and right with sword, ending those warriors closing on Gleave, who, teeth grinding against the pain, was now attempting to leaver the locked jaws of the honey badger from his destroyed leg.

'They're still coming in!' Amis shouted from above Gleave, who looked with tear filled eyes to the tattooed warriors pouring through the gate.

Sav was there, sword drawn and arrows spent. 'We're fucked,' he said flatly, eyeing the Orismarans lining up for another charge. The gravity of it struck them all; deflated them.

A horse whinnied from the strangest angle, an impossible angle. All eyes, on both sides, looked to the sky.

Chapter 44 – Royce's Reds

From the blinding light of the sun came eight riders, their crimson caparisoned horses bearing feathered wings like those of a teratorn; all bar the leader, whose mount was both equine and raptor, horse and giant eagle.

'Well, blind me,' Correia whispered, unable to control the smile pulling at her blood-spattered lips. 'Royce's Reds,' she said, looking about her companions. 'It's Royce's bloody Reds!' she shouted, waving her glowing swords to draw their attention.

The winged mounts landed at a canter, which took them clean across the centre of the yard, avoiding the wounded and dead as they did so. Pulling up near an outbuilding, the riders turned their mounts on the spot; they turned them to face the Orismarans at the gate.

The knights atop the pegasi charged, lances lowering as their mounts surged forward. The winged horses were as heavily muscled as any destrier. The bay beasts thundered across the yard, bearing their riders into the scattering enemy with destructive abandon.

As combat was joined, Amis and Giles kicked their own mounts on into the fray, swords rising and falling alongside the seven red knights, who'd dropped their soiled lances in favour of swords, axes, a mace and a hammer.

Correia made to follow the two horsemen, whilst Sav tended to a cursing, snapping Gleave, but before she could get close, the side-saddle riding woman atop the hippogriff barred her way, the beast looming over Correia, beak snapping as its front most talon clawed the ground.

Weapons clashed and men roared and screamed across the way. Correia looked up to the woman wearing red-died wolf fur. From beneath the wolf-headed hood, a badly scarred face stared back down.

'Lady Burr, we need leave, now!' The woman issued the words as a command, not a request, and Correia knew the captain to be someone who wasn't accustomed to having her orders declined.

'How did you know I was here?' Correia asked.

Turning her great mount a half circle, the wolf-clad woman looked to her men, who were pushing the Orismaran warriors back through the gate.

'Captain Hud?' Correia said, anger flecking her voice. 'Answer me, damn it!'

The woman turned back to look down on Correia, but not before issuing a shrill whistle through finger and thumb. Her mount shrieked high-low, matching the whistle, which was followed by the swift return of the rest of Royce's Reds, along with Amis and Giles.

'We've seen your elf friend,' Hud said, eyes locked on Correia's. 'He told us where to find you, but there's no time now. You're needed in Wesson.'

'Wesson?' Correia said, brow creased.

Gleave cursed louder than normal and Correia looked to him, an unavoidable wince showing on her face as she took in his wounds.

'They'll push back through at any moment,' one of Hud's knights said, coming alongside his captain, who nodded and looked to the gate.

'Correia,' Hud said, looking down once more, 'climb up behind me. We leave now.'

'What's happening?' Correia demanded, whilst moving to Gleave. 'Sav,' she said, not waiting for a response from Hud, 'go and get Fal.'

'I'll help,' Amis said, pulling Sav up behind him and riding over the mound.

The hissing hippogriff walked up to Correia and Gleave, the latter of which had passed out from the ongoing pain. Correia looked up. 'Help him!'

'I have my orders, Lady Burr—'

'From who? Royce?'

Hud nodded. 'Through Royce, yes, but originally from Will Morton, I believe. Now come, I'm to get you out and get you back, nothing more.'

Correia snarled. 'Help this man or fail in your mission, Captain!'

Hud spat and slid from her mount, which lowered to the ground of its own accord.

Crouching over Gleave, she lowered the red-furred wolf's head from her own and began chanting over Gleave's shredded and broken leg, a redwood wand appearing from her voluminous sleeve.

Correia looked back at the sound of hooves. Sav ran beside Amis' horse, atop which Fal clung to Amis' back, wrecked face pained through the motion.

'What happened here?' one of Royce's Reds said, eyeing Fal. 'Is he a prisoner?' He pointed his bloody mace to Fal, who was helped from Amis' horse by Sav.

'No, he is not,' Correia snapped, looking back to Hud, who was practically touching Gleave's wounds with her moving lips, wand held to the side.

Hud pulled back and glanced at Correia. 'He'll live and is fit to ride—'

'To ride?' Sav cut in. His wrinkled nose and open mouth attested to his incredulity at the statement. 'He's not fit to stand.'

'We'll leave him here then, shall we?' Hud looked up at Sav, her features drawn after the use of magic.

'No, no of course not,' Sav said, shaking away his disbelief.

A bestial roar erupted from the far side of the gate.

'They'll be in here in moments,' Giles said. 'Whatever we're to do, do it now.'

'My lord Bratby,' Hud greeted, turning to Giles. 'I'll return you to your son and army, before continuing on to Royce with Lady Burr.' The man merely nodded at that.

Shouting and another roar drew close and all eyes looked to the gate.

'Mount up. Now!' Hud said, to Correia.

Correia nodded. 'You heard her.'

Moving quickly, Correia, along with Sav, helped Gleave up over the lap of the nearest red knight, whilst Amis did the same for Fal, before climbing up behind another rider himself.

The rest of them followed suit, with Correia riding behind Hud on her hippogriff.

'Where from here?' Correia asked, as they made for the far end of the bailey, avoiding bodies as they rode. The smell was cloying as bodily fluids stained the ground about them, mixing with the smell of wolf fur and mounts.

'Bratby's army, in Suttel,' Hud said, slowing and turning her mount back to face the other side of the compound, along with her retinue. 'Then west, to Royce.'

'We need to stop at Twin Inns first,' Correia insisted.

Pulling her wolf-hood back up, Hud said nothing before spurring her screeching mount on, hard and fast.

As the riders surged across the hard-packed earth, the Orismarans entered the yard in numbers. The nearest bore polearms long enough to snag the closest riders. Correia clenched her teeth and held her breath.

Wand out once more, Hud pointed it towards the tattooed warriors and uttered a series of unrecognisable words.

Orismarans fell face first, their limbs limp as they crashed to the ground, heads striking the floor more oft than not; several slid or rolled as they fell. Those behind stumbled or pulled up, not one able to strike at the winged mounts already taking flight, out over the wall and away from the roaring enemy below.

The sight the sudden lift allowed was of devastation and all out ruin. Homes burnt in the town outside the chateau. Dozens of townsfolk – shrinking in size as the group rose in altitude – scattered where they could, chased from all directions by Orismaran warriors and their various beasts. One bipedal creature dwarfed the rest, its metallic armoured hide glinting in the sun as it crashed through the walls of homes, leaving collapsed buildings in its wake. Thick black smoke rose like columns to hold up the clouds above.

The awful noises from below quietened as the pegasi and hippogriff rose higher. It eventually died out altogether, replaced by the sound of rushing wind.

No one said a word. Shock had taken hold. Noses streamed, gripping fingers and ears numbed, and eyes watered; for more reasons than the bite of the wind as the pathfinders left behind not just the sacking of Easson, but the body of one of their own.

The adrenaline had passed and heart rates dropped. An unusual calm settled across the group as their eyes settled on nought but distant valleys and scrub-land below, and it hit them all.

Starks was gone.

***

Mandibles working, the wasp sliced a perfect sphere of red flesh from beneath charred skin. Using one of the still-warm metal rings as an exit, it crawled up and out into the lingering smoke filled light. Meat sphere held between six legs, the wasp lifted into the air and away, oblivious to the groans of the man it and its companions were ever so slowly butchering.

The groans of the man increased as, from under a blackened iron helm now welded to his scalp and scorched face, the realisation of what had happened sank in. Unconscious bliss fell away, revealing a searing agony from head to, well, where his feet should have been. Attempting to move resulted in fresh flares of pure agony through limbs that were little more than immolated strips of bone and blackened muscle, the tops of which were fused into and around a mass of iron links barely touched by the brief inferno's heat.

Footsteps approached and the man-come-corpse attempted to turn towards the noise; attempted to look upon whom he hoped were his friends. The fact he'd somehow protected his eyes, sore as they were, was almost a blessing in comparison to the rest of his body. Almost.

When unknown tattooed faces loomed over him, Starks' painful breaths caught in his raw throat. He succeeded in releasing a scream as one of the onlookers prodded his wasp strewn flesh with a road dusted boot; the pitiful scream was little more than a rasp, a rasp that, if the witnessing warriors knew what to listen for, may have been recognised as a name: Gleave.

Chapter 45 – A forceful connection

'How's she faring?' Quin ran his hand along the port gunwale of *Sessio's* main-deck. He appreciated the craftsmanship that had gone into the vessel.

Lefey sighed. 'Seems whenever we get her back to how she should be, we're attacked.'

'Reassuring,' Quin said, smile forced.

'Nothing for you to worry about, Quin.' Lefey placed a hand on his shoulder. Needle-like claws dug into her shin. Lefey cursed and hopped away.

'Arrik, no!' Dropping to his haunches, Quin took hold of the polecat and scanned the deck for the other. 'Sorry, Lefey,' he said, rising to his feet.

Lefey grunted a laugh. 'No bother. They're too cute to be mad at, and excellent ratters to boot. The ship's hold has never been so clear! Puts our fat cat to shame.' She dared stroke Arrik's head and grinned when the animal closed its eyes and allowed her to do so.

'That's likely where Guse is.' Quin joined in the stroking of the polecat hanging from his hand. 'Either that or asleep after feeding.'

Lefey looked up at that. 'I've hardly seen them since you've been aboard.'

'That's because they sleep most of the time. Can't be bad, eh?'

Lefey smiled. 'Not much chance of that for me or thee.'

Arrik started to struggle so Quin put him down. With a hiss, Arrik waddled off along the gunwale, sniffing anything and everything he passed.

'You'll be working on the stern I expect?'

Quin nodded, eyes on Arrik as he fell down a hatch. Both Quin and Lefey laughed, along with another sailor who'd seen it.

'I will,' Quin said. He looked back to Lefey. 'I'm looking forward to it. Well, now we have clear horizons and my stomach has settled.'

'And has it? Sea aside, you've been through a lot, not to mention a recent battle against the Black Guild of all organisations. That's not something that sits well with any of us.'

'Any idea where we're heading, Lefey?' Quin's avoiding of the subject was obvious, even to him; especially to him.

'Nope. No clue. I can fathom direction and hazard a guess at a port or two, but there's been nothing from the officers as to where.' It became apparent as Lefey talked, that Quin wasn't listening. His eyes had glazed over and focused on nothing in particular.

Lefey tried to make eye contact, leaning round into Quin's line of sight. 'We'll be alright though, Quin, you'll see.'

A tight smile was all Quin could manage.

Lefey sighed. 'She's not worth dwelling on, that lass.' She reached out for Quin's shoulder again but he pulled away, face dropping.

'I best be off to the stern, see if they're ready for me to help with the repairs.' He nodded once before turning away.

'Of course,' Lefey managed, leaning back against the gunwale. 'Of course,' she whispered, once he'd gone. 'Why am I not surprised that after several near-death experiences, it's the bloody girl that hurts him the most.' Shaking her head, Lefey turned, hopped up onto the smooth rail and jumped up to the rigging above. It wasn't long until she was high above the deck she'd been stood on, sat on a spar.

'You soft on that soft-lad?' Boxall shuffled across the same spar, heading towards Lefey, who flicked two fingers at him.

'I worry after him is all, you fat prick.'

Boxall laughed. Lefey grinned.

'How're you holding up?' Lefey asked.

A shrug was all Boxall offered.

'There's nothing wrong with feeling, Boxall.'

'Oh, here we go. I'm not that Quin lad—'

'That lad saved your life. We've been through that more than once.'

'Doesn't mean he's not a soft-lad, though, does it?' Boxall sidled up to Lefey and draped his arm over her shoulders.

'Never said it did.' Lefey stared at the stern, where Quin worked alongside a couple of other crew members. 'I do think we owe it to him to help him deal with it though.'

Boxall sniffed and nodded before replying. 'Help him toughen up, like?'

'Exactly. It'd benefit us as much as him.'

'True that, lass. True that.' Boxall pulled her in close and squeezed her tight. 'You miss him?' he said, eyes on the stern.

'Tahir?'

Boxall nodded.

'You know I do and I know you do.'

'I don't deny it.' Boxall pulled in his lips and rubbed at his eyes with his free hand.

'Wind getting to you?' Lefey made no attempt to hide a smile as she glanced sidelong at her friend.

'Aye, lass, reckon that's it.' He looked back at her and matched her smile.

Heads together, the two sailors watched the other crew members on the decks and listened to the familiar sounds of the sailing ship. It was all they'd known for a long time, and despite the loss of Tahir, as well as others, they'd grown used to that too. It was that knowledge that made it all the harder at times. The knowing that by the next port, those they'd lost would be replaced. Jobs needed doing and that was that. They were all expendable and they all accepted it; didn't make it any easier though.

***

The airborne journey had taken nowhere near as long as it would have on land, but still, Correia felt like it'd taken an age and it'd certainly taken the group through the freezing night. She'd wished she'd been wearing the wolf pelts of the riders that bore the group, to reduce the wind and the cold that bit at her extremities like the winds of winter passed.

'We're nearly there,' Hud said over her red-furred shoulder.

Correia nodded, chattering teeth failing to allow any words to pass between her blue lips. The ground gradually came up to meet the descending cavalry. Correia looked upon the vastness of the forest of The Marches, spreading like a dark spillage upon the land. It took her breath more than the cold. *It resembles freedom: home.* She knew now that the green horizon was Altoln, and on that horizon an encamped army. The tears brought on by the wind and the loss of Starks began anew, but she saw an end to it all, although she couldn't fathom why she was being pulled back to Wesson. Did her father know of the northbound Orismaran army? Her thoughts lingered on her father, on the plague he'd succumbed to and been rescued from, and on to her half-brother, Edward, and the man he'd become. She shuddered, the wind-chill only half of it. The hippogriff beneath her circled down, towards a walled opening. Correia leaned to the side as much as she dared and squinted as the wind calmed. *Twin Inns,* she thought, the fear of Edward's future reign lost to the possibilities a landing would bring. *How fair you, Errolas?* The elf's pleasant features painted in her mind's eye, warming her heart and soul. He would have answers; even stuck here, in the inn, the elf ranger would have answers. And maybe Cook, too.

Pegasi whinnied and snorted to the left and right and Correia looked both ways, a smile pulling at her lips as she settled on Fal, despite how bad he looked; worse even, for the ride. *But not as bad as you would have been, Fal, had we left you.* Her thoughts came easier now, as the buffeting winds died off and the tall trees rose above them all.

Correia squeezed her knees into the flanks of the beast and clung onto Hud as their mount struck the ground at a jolting, decelerating run, wings flaring to slow them quickly enough so as not to strike the wall on the far side of the yard they'd landed in.

Seven pegasi followed their lead.

Men and women in garish clothes ran from doorways and around corners. They took reins and helped lift the injured down to be placed on carts. Ale and wine, bread and a rich terrine was brought forth on platters as if a dinner party had arrived for a planned banquet. Correia stood, once dismounted, hands on knees as she sucked in horse- and wolf-scented air to fill her aching lungs. The tinkling, familiar laughter of an elf drew her gaze, for Errolas rounded a corner, a young woman linked on his arm and a large brown hen clucking and ducking about their feet. His laughter died away, face fell in fact, as he counted the number accompanying Royce's Reds. The realisation of Starks' absence staggered him, quite literally. After a moment in which he composed himself, Errolas left the woman's side and moved to Fal, laid on a cart as he now was, Sav by his side.

Correia turned and followed Hud from the yard, leaving the boys to their stories and lamentation. She couldn't bear it; not now. Besides, she had plans to make, questions to ask and warnings to give.

'What's the plan?' Correia attempted to rub life back into her arms. The action was noticed and acted on by one of the inn's womenfolk, who chased them both with thick woollen blankets. Correia smiled and took both, wrapping them about herself as she followed Hud.

'I need some time.' Hud lifted the red wolf-head over her own and strode off, behind the stables.

Correia stopped, mouth agape at the rudeness of the captain.

'Where's she going?' Sav said, appearing at Correia's side. He already sported one of the inn's blankets, which he'd pulled up over his head like a cowl.

Correia shrugged. 'I don't know, but there's no time for whatever it is.' She turned to take in the walls and buildings. 'We need to help them prepare, if they're too stubborn to leave.'

Sav took a deep breath and nodded his accord.

'How did Fal fair, during the flight?'

Sav's face dropped. 'Not good. He mutters, mumbles. His face lit upon seeing Errolas, so I deemed it best the elf accompany him to the chambers they have ready for us. Perhaps he needs someone who wasn't there when... well, just there, in Easson.'

Correia nodded but said nothing. They stood for a while, Sav's arm wrapping around her shoulders, pulling her tight.

'And Amis de Valmont?'

'What of him?' Sav frowned, grip loosening.

'Does he have any answers about the bitch he escorted across Sirreta?'

A shrug was Sav's only reply.

'I'll need to question him.'

'I bet you will. Handsome man is de Valmont.'

Gods above, Sav. Not now. Correia shrugged off Sav's hand and strode away, the lanky scout close behind.

'If you're going to follow me, Sav, at least have something useful to say.'

'Words won't help us—'

'I don't mean that.' She sped up. 'I wasn't talking about Starks.'

Sav swallowed and licked dry lips as Correia glared back at him. He followed wordlessly, until Correia spoke once more. They'd arrived at the door to the kitchens.

'Who's the woman with Errolas?'

'I don't know.'

Correia snorted as she turned and looked up at Sav. 'A pretty, capable looking woman like that and you don't know anything about her? I am surprised. You're losing your touch.'

Sav's face flushed. 'We'd only just bloody landed, for 'morl's sake. I had more on my mind than a pretty face and a nice backside.'

'You did look then?'

Sav flashed a grin. 'Why? You jealous?'

The punch was a blur, only given away by the sudden shifting of two blankets. Even so, Sav failed to avoid it completely. As he doubled over, gasping for air, Correia disappeared inside the kitchens, slamming the door before Sav could follow.

Hud looked about before crouching to the hard-packed earth. She'd chosen a shaded spot behind the stables, of which there were plenty, this one black from multiple shadows caused by numerous overhanging branches and tall walls.

Scratting in the dirt with her wand, she scrawled out a series of symbols before rearranging herself to lie amongst them, finishing the image the symbols created.

With her wolf covered head the centre of a large paw print, Hud closed her eyes, held her wand with both trembling hands and hummed. Low at first, the magician's humming began to build, build until the disturbed earth surrounding her vibrated, shuddered even. Horses whinnied and nickered on the other side of the stable wall.

After several quickened heartbeats, Hud's humming reached a reverberating crescendo that finished with a hollow pop, her eyes opening wide, orbs grey.

The horses fell silent. As did the birds in the trees and the insects all about.

The connection had been made, the channel opened; forcefully. Now all she needed was for him to respond, and kindly. Not a guaranteed outcome considering her unannounced, and dangerous, method of contact.

'As long as it doesn't harm him permanently,' Hud whispered, not wanting the thought forming in her mind and slipping into his. 'I don't want him to think I've turned soft, after all.' The slightest smile pulled at her lips. The same wouldn't be happening on the other side.

***

Hitchmogh stood and staggered to the side, hand out, reaching for the nearest crew member.

'Master Hitchmogh?'

Shaking away the dizziness, he righted himself and waved away the sailor's concern.

'Stood up too fast,' he lied, offering a grizzled smile. 'Nothing to worry—'

'Shit!' The sailor rushed to break Hitchmogh's fall.

His descent slowed by grasping, calloused hands, Hitchmogh succumbed to the spinning of the room, to the thudding threatening to split his skull; to the voice becoming more apparent in the back of his mind. No, not *his* mind, hers...

I hear you, Hitchmogh thought, although the thought was a slippery thing, like trying to land a squirming eel.

I was worried you weren't going to accept me, the voice said, clearer than before.

I didn't have much of a choice and I certainly didn't want to, Hitchmogh replied into the blackness about him. *It hurts... a lot.*

Apologies, old friend, but I had no other choice, we *have no other choice.*

A swirl of smoke-like translucent memories came and went, like the passage of jutting, mist born rocks as a ship sails on by. What felt like a smile played across Hitchmogh's thoughts, *her* thoughts; someone's thoughts.

Hud? Hitchmogh ventured tentatively, grasping at the eel and taking hold.

Aye, it's me, old man. I need Sessio *in Royce, and I needed her there yesterday. Can you persuade Mannino?*

Why? Hitchmogh allowed his confusion to flood the black void he was fearful of becoming lost in. A great sense of urgency and fear was all that came back to him.

I'll persuade him, Hitchmogh sent, simply. *Now get the fuck out of my head!*

The pain-filled mirth of the thought was hard to project, but it got through to Hud, who broke the connection.

Voices. Creaking. The rush of blood in his ears, oh the thumping of it...

'Flay me!' Hitchmogh surged into a sitting position, bumping heads with someone who'd been looking over him. Faces moved back, concern evident on every one of them. Hitchmogh waved them away aggressively.

'I need Mannino, now.'

'Captain's not awake yet,' a sailor dared.

'Now!' Hitchmogh shouted, spittle arcing from his chapped lips. Sailors scattered.

***

'What do you mean, nothing?'

Cook winced at Correia's barbed tone. He held a cleaver in his

285

lump of a hand, bloody from the dead goat he'd been hacking into. He placed the cleaver down. Both hands held out, placating, Cook repeated himself.

'They've sent nothing in reply, Correia. I can't do anything about that.'

'And no riders have come out of Sirreta since we left? No mounted chevalier with archers in tow?'

'Only the woman who's attached herself to your elf friend, although she'd been here, left and returned, from your side of the forest.'

Correia leaned forward, brow raised, head tilted to the side but a little. She blocked the pressing thoughts about the chevalier who'd ridden away on Fal's horse. She couldn't bare thinking what might have happened to him and his men, not now.

'I don't know who she is,' Cook said, his exasperation clear. He picked up the cleaver once more and took his frustration out on the carcass on his chopping block. Thwack, thwack, thwack...

'Must you do that now?' Correia attempted, but Cook continued. She'd pushed him too far too fast. He was a sensitive soul. She huffed, turned and left the kitchen, blankets pulled about her. 'I'll find out for myself.'

'Well he *is* your frien—'

The slamming door cut off Cook's retort.

'Well?' Sav leaned against the outside wall.

Correia wasn't in the mood. She thumped him and made for the tavern hall, where she hoped she'd find the others. Sav cursed and followed and cursed some more as he attempted to keep pace with Correia, despite his longer legs.

Hood appeared from behind the stables, looking downright ill.

'We need to talk, now.' Correia shot the words at the captain and motioned for her to follow. Correia didn't wait to see if the woman did.

'You alright, Captain?' Sav asked.

Correia didn't slow to hear Hud's response. She didn't care at that moment. She pounded on towards the hall, two sets of footsteps following behind. 'We're all going to gather, now, and sort this shit storm of a situation out,' she blurted.

Hud's response to Sav had been cut off by that, and before the woman could answer Correia, they were at the doors to the hall, which were opened by two gaudily dressed men who bowed to the trio.

'Your companions are inside—'

'I know,' was all they got from Correia as she barged past, Hud and Sav doing the same.

Chapter 46 – Family meeting

'You're sure?' Stubley dared ask Correia, squeezing his bulk into an ornate chair at the head of the tavern's table.

Correia released a heavy sigh and dropped onto the bench between Errolas and Sav, before flashing the inn keeper a dangerous look. 'Yes, Master Stubley, I'm sure.'

'Why here?' Stubley looked about the soldiers lining the long table, Correia's look having no effect on the old man.

'Because you're on the border, of course.' Sav was filling his face, although a fair bit came back out whilst answering the question. Gleave and Fal were elsewhere, being tended to by the inn's capable barber-surgeon. It was said he had powers akin to a cleric, as well as skills with needle, razor and saw.

Stubley snorted and waved his arms about, his voluminous orange and purple sleeves hanging low from over-fleshed upper-arms. 'We've always been on the border, since the border began, and before that some say. It's never meant we've been in danger when the Marquess of Suttel here and his—'

'This isn't a war of The Marches, my dear fellow,' Giles said, baritone voice reaching everyone. Royce's Reds sat in silence, bar the noises they made whilst eating, which was similar to Sav's dining percussion. Giles rubbed his face and leaned back against the wall. 'This is something far worse. They have beasts the likes I've never seen. They've employed long-played deceit, turning men on the inside. For all we know, you're a bloody demon—'

'How dare you!'

Giles raised both hands. 'Apologies, Master Stubley, but that's how it's made us all feel.' Giles seemed to notice Amis' vacant stare and offered the chevalier a tight smile, forgetting the pompous inn keeper opposite. 'You couldn't have known, lad. I keep telling you that.'

'And you'll have to keep telling him,' Correia said, eyes on Amis. 'It'll kick him in his chest for a good long while, as events in Easson have done us all, but it's happened and that's that, as hard as I sound.'

'Correia's right.' Errolas' usual lightness of tone and mirth was gone, his healing face darkening, and not just because of the remaining bruises. 'With what's happening, we don't have time for 'why' or 'if' or 'but'. We hardly have time to act, but act we must. That includes the Twin Inns.' He looked pointedly to Stubley; he looked from him to the other family members of the inn, who encircled the long table, jugs and platters in hands. They all met Errolas' gaze, one by one.

'What would you have us do?' Stubley pleaded, over-expressive hands off on the move once more.

Hud looked up from her goblet of wine. 'Unite with your family across the way and pull back. Back to the army in Suttel. It may end up a fighting retreat if you don't act immediately.'

'Never!' A bar girl stepped forward, anger in her face. 'My brother was shot dead by those shites, I'll never—'

'That's enough, my dear.' Stubley's words weren't loud, but they were listened to.

'We've wasted enough time already,' Correia said, 'and hardly brushed on any of what's been going on. Like who this is, for starters?' She motioned to the dark-haired woman on the far side of Errolas.

'Of course,' Errolas said, before the woman could answer. 'This is Salliss de Pizan of Velenn's Witchblades.' There was a gasp in the room. Three red cloaked knights stood, hands on belted knives before Hud waved them down. She glared down the table at Salliss though, her suspicion there for all to see. The witchblade had half risen too, halted only by Errolas' outstretched arm.

'I was sent north,' Salliss said in passable Altolnan, sitting back down. 'I am sorry for not speak finer.'

'It is fine.' Correia nodded for her to go on.

'This army that has taken Easson is but one.' All eyes were on Salliss now, whether suspicion filled or not.

'Go on.' Correia encouraged Salliss with a nod.

'A much large force was marching on Lejeune when my cabal and I were sent north. Sent to see why Eudes de Geelan had not replied to Queen Velenn's shout for aid. We were pursued, all the way.'

'By Orismarans?' Hud leaned forward, intently.

Salliss shook her head. 'By something else.'

One of the red knights snarled. 'One thing?'

'Yes, one,' Salliss snapped, returning the knight's snarl.

'Tell them what happened.' Errolas spoke smoothly, quietly.

Salliss took a deep breath. 'We were cut down, one by one, as we rode for Eudes' court. We…' she thought about the words she required. '…attempted countermeasures and traps. Nothing worked. On it came.' Her jaw bunched, steeling herself against the memories she was reliving. 'When we reached Easson we had it the worst. Sirretan men attempted to ride us down, despite our word as to who we were and who sent us. The beast struck—'

'A red beast?' Giles blurted.

Salliss frowned and shook her head.

Air escaped Giles' lungs. He waved her on.

'Caught between who we thought to be our own men and that... thing, we fled. We did all we could to make it to the border, knowing how... dire,' she nodded at the word, 'our Queen's situation was. To make it to Altoln.'

'To Altoln?' It was Hud's turn to frown. 'Why not—'

'I don't care why,' Correia said, cutting the captain off, much to her knights' disgust. Two pairs of knightly eyes were on Correia now, the others on Salliss. 'You made it to the border and then what?'

'I alone made it here, to this inn. I stayed, before you arrive. I stayed a day and I ran again, for two days, into... Suttel?' Giles nodded at her pronunciation. 'After encountering witchunters...' she made to spit, but thought better of it. Sav cursed at the mention of the witchunters. 'After encountering them in a dangerous way, I fled back into forest. I fled back here, unsure what I am to do. I almost failed in my mission by their hands.' Salliss took a breath and went on, 'And by the beast's own—'

'So how did you manage to escape?' one of Hud's knights said, accusingly. 'Beasts and witchunters and armies and such. Eh?'

Without looking at the man, Salliss continued. 'I threw all I had into that final stand, in Suttel.' She glanced at Giles again as she named his lands. The marquess frowned.

'The beast was in Suttel?' he asked, leaning forward.

Salliss nodded once. 'The beast was in league with the witchunters,' she said flatly.

'Fucking pricks—'

'Sav!' Correia snapped. 'Go on, Salliss.'

Taking a breath, Salliss did just that, eyes flashing to the red knight who'd asked her how she'd escaped. 'I used the memory of all those lost along the way, Sir...?' Errolas squeezed her hand and Salliss steeled herself once more. The knight she addressed made to speak, but Hud motioned for him to stay silent. 'I was welcomed,' Salliss went on, 'once I found my way back here, and was introduced to Errolas.' Salliss smiled. 'He bade me wait, wait for you, Madame Burr. He said it would be best course of action to witness aid to my Queen.' She held Correia's gaze. 'I too fear we are running out of time, Madame Burr.'

'We are,' Hud said, 'but on more matters than your queen and capital's fate.'

Salliss made to say something, venomous by the looks of it, but Errolas stopped her.

'What else?' Correia looked to Hud, brow knitted, hands on the table, balled into fists. *Bad news is ceaseless of late,* Correia thought heavily. She flinched as her mind flashed back to the concussive thud of Starks' end.

'We leave for Royce in the morning,' Hud said, eyes on Correia in a way that made Correia feel like it was but the two of them in the hall. 'A reliable ship is on its way to escort you and your pathfinders to Wesson.'

'But why?' Correia fought to keep the anger from her voice. 'I've worked hard,' she said, before Hud could answer, 'to learn what I've learnt through hardship and loss; to learn of a great threat to which I have a chance, with the good Earl here, to attempt to thwart before it—'

'The King is in danger,' Hud cut in. 'And that is more than I should have said, so do not try and pry more from me, Correia Burr, for it will not work, I assure you.'

Correia struggled not to let her fear show at the news and her heart faltered, stomach twisted. *In danger, how?* She wanted to scream the question and made to ask it, before catching herself, believing Hud would say no more. 'Will Royce tell me?'

Hud shrugged. 'That's up to him.'

'Can you not fly us there now? Is that not quicker?'

Surprised and questioning eyes turned to Correia, especially those of Sav, Errolas and Giles Bratby.

'But Correia…' Sav started. A raised hand stopped him.

Correia turned back to Stubley, who'd been quiet as he took it all in. 'You need to consolidate your forces with your family across the way and fall back to the waiting army in Suttel.' He made to speak but Correia lifted a finger, stopping him dead. 'Failing that, since I know how stubborn you all are, you need to brace for an assault. They *are* coming, I guarantee you that, and you *will* be overrun. They don't want to buy breakfast, Master Stubley, they want to skin and eat you themselves.' She wasn't sure about that last part, in fact she doubted it entirely, but she did need to scare the man into action; the family into action and she noted more than one set of eyes widen, even a gasp from one of the stripe-dressed serving girls.

'Should you decide to stay, Master Stubley,' Giles said, drawing attention to him, 'I shall have men ride to bolster these defences, for it is a strategic location like no other along this border. The longer it holds, the longer I'll have to manoeuvre my forces for a counter-attack. I told Croal de Geelan, before I watched him tear his own throat out on the words of this foe, that I'd ride to take Easson back from those bastards, and I bloody well meant it.' Giles finished by looking at Salliss. 'I truly meant it,' he said in Sirretan.

Salliss smiled and nodded her thanks. 'I will join you, messire—'

'No,' Correia said, drawing the woman's hard eyes. 'You're to fly to Royce with us, then on to Wesson—'

'Like shit she is!' one of Royce's Reds said. Hud didn't stop him. 'I'm not carrying some Sirretan witch—'

'You bloody well ride with the like!' Giles rounded on the man beside him, arm outstretched, pointing at Hud.

The knight whacked Giles' arm away and made to surge to his feet. Only a well-placed forehead crunching nasal cartilage stopped the action. The knight's top lip matched his red surcoat before he could do anything about it.

'Outside, now!' Hud shouted at her man. He looked more shocked than when Giles had head butted him. With a bloody snarl and a hand to his broken nose, he obeyed.

'My apologies, Earl Bratby.'

'I've never experienced the like from a knight,' Giles said, huffing before carrying on, 'but I accept your apology, Captain Hud. I won't mention your knight's outburst to Hugh when I see him next. We're all heated here, with all that has happened and all that is to come.'

They both nodded at one another, a clear agreement to leave it at that and not involve Hud's – and so the knight's – liege lord.

Correia rolled her eyes. 'If this is how we're to continue the evening, I suggest we don't. I have much to discuss with Errolas and Master Stubley's family. Captain Hud, you're welcome to assist in the planning of what's to come before we take our rest, otherwise, I bid you good night.' Correia locked eyes with Hud, who stared back wordlessly for a moment.

Everyone watched the two scar-faced women, until, after some time, Hud nodded. 'I'll stay and offer what advice I can.' She looked to her men. 'Go check on the mounts,' she said, whisking them away. They left with frowns on their faces, unable to drag their eyes from Salliss until they were walking out into the night.

'Sav,' Correia said, without looking at him, 'go and check on the lads, I'll be through to do the same when we're done here.'

Sav nodded. He knew when to keep quiet and do as he was told, most of the time anyway. With a shallow bow to all present, Sav left the room.

'I think I'll turn in,' Amis said, voice saturated with melancholy.

'No, you won't.' Correia fixed Amis with a look that halted his half-risen departure, causing him to drop back onto the bench. Giles shuffled along to sit next to him, wrapped an arm around the man's shoulders and pulled him in close as a father would a son.

At that point the inn folk chose to depart, leaving Stubley and two others, who worked the room, clearing dishes and re-filling pots and goblets.

'Now, before we go on,' Correia said, to Amis more than anyone else, 'I'd like to hear all Amis knows about this Flavell de Steedon he escorted across Sirreta.'

Swallowing hard, Amis de Valmont nodded and began his tale.

Chapter 47 – Fight or flight

Eyes swollen from a smoke-filled night's sleep in the tavern, Sav woke to the sounds of shouting, whinnying horses, barking dogs and a tolling bell.

'Always a bloody bell,' he said, climbing to his feet from the straw covered ground next to the hall's hearth. He'd been supplied a bunk, but after everyone else settled – as much as they could – for the night, he'd come back to the hall for a snack, unable to sleep; thoughts of Starks haunted him. He should have been there, with them. Thoughts of Fal and the torture he'd endured had followed. It had been a rough night. He'd lost track of the time he'd spent staring into the glowing embers of the hall's fire and hadn't realised he was falling asleep there. Taking in the space about him, Sav checked his person to make sure he had everything he should. It wouldn't be the first place he'd woken to find a lack of coins in his pouch.

'Sav!'

He jumped and spun to see a sunlight-framed Correia in the doorway.

'What's happening?'

'The bastards are here. Move, now!' She disappeared into the light.

'Shit!' Sav hurried after her.

Despite sleeping next to a fire and the hoarse throat and sore eyes that followed, the smell of wood-smoke struck him more than ever when he reached the yard. Colourful inn-folk ran to and fro, carrying buckets of water, bundles of crossbow bolts, and saddles. He turned and saw flames licking up from the thatch of the stables.

'Double shit!' He raced towards the blazing building where Correia stood, helping with a distressed pegasus, the red-clad knight whose mount it was doing his best to calm the beast. Correia took hold of the reins as the knight attempted to mount the animal, its wings shuddering as much as its bay flank as it pawed the ground and pulled its head away from the reins Correia struggled to hold. Sav reached her side and leaned over her, placing a palm on the animal's white-starred forehead. He whispered to it, easing Correia out of the way whilst taking the reins from her with his free hand. She raced off to help lead the rest of the animals out of the burning building whilst men and women did their best to douse the spreading fire with buckets of water.

The pegasus settled, slowly but surely. Once in the saddle, the knight leaned forward, patted its neck and took the offered reins from Sav. 'Thank you, Sav.'

Sav smiled up at the man who had carried him from Easson, but said nothing. There was no time. As the bell continued and the animals and people added to the din, Sav caught Correia's eye and pointed to the bunk-house. She nodded and Sav set out towards the building. He crossed a waterway to get there, the sound of the rushing river beneath the stone a pleasant contrast to everything else. Two inn-folk ran the other way, crossbows cradled in their arms. There were no words said between Sav and the men as they crossed paths. All hands were to the defence of the inn, he knew that and knew he needed to get to Fal and Gleave, to secure them, ready to be moved.

A chilling roar came from the forest, to the south. Sav shuddered before ducking into the bunk-house through a door a young girl held open for him. His imagination conjured all sorts of things that could produce such a roar. Perhaps one of the bipedal beasts that crashed through homes in Easson as they'd flown from the scene? Perhaps something worse!

'Fal? Gleave?' It was all Sav said to the barber-surgeon as he raced into the second room, where he knew his friends to be. They weren't there.

'Gone already,' the scrawny man said without looking. He was applying a salve to a red raw burn which covered a woman's hand. She bit her bottom lip and sucked in breaths as the man smoothed the ointment over the blistering flesh.

Sav winced and shook himself free of the sight. 'Where?'

'The Sirretan witch took them.'

Sav frowned, nodded his thanks, turned and ran once more, through to where his bunk had been set. He grabbed his bow and quiver, sword and pack and raced through the building and out to find his companions. He ran back across the bridge to the stables, the yard of which was a chaotic mix of people, horses and winged beasts. 'Where's Fal and Gleave?' he shouted, for anyone to answer.

'What do you mean?' Correia came running from the back of the stables, instinctively ducking as a burning wooden beam made an almighty cracking sound.

'Everyone out!' shouted an ageing man, who held his hand out to shield his face from the intense heat radiating from the stable.

'Out, now!'

Two more inn-folk ran from the stables, which were close to collapsing. No sooner had they left, another loud crack preceded the caving in of the burning roof.

Sav caught Correia's arm, his sword now sheathed at his side. 'Who started this?'

Correia looked panicked, which in turn panicked Sav. 'A girl—'

'The one with the burnt hand?'

Correia nodded and Sav frowned. 'She claims to have no recollection. Listen, there's no time for this, we need to leave.'

'Salliss took Fal and Gleave, but I don't know where?'

It was Correia's turn to frown. 'She can't have moved them on her own?'

Hud rode up beside her on her hippogriff. 'We're off to the Altolnan gate. We can't take off in any of these yards, there's no room to get to speed and there's arrows coming in. It's too big a risk.' Hud leaned down, offered Correia her hand.

'Not until I know where my men are?'

'We have them, at the gate. Now come on. We may have to ride if there's no room to take flight outside the compound, and the enemy is closing.'

'Could've bloody told us,' Sav said, scowling at the woman pulling Correia up behind her.

Hud didn't respond, and as if to accentuate her point about the enemy closing, warning shouts came from a watch tower.

'Did she say goblins?' Hud looked round to Correia, brow furrowed.

'Sounded like it.' Correia looked equally puzzled. 'Ride on, Captain, there'll be time to ponder it later.'

Sav made to talk, but jumped when the eagle-headed beast the women sat atop snapped its beak at him.

'I'll meet you there,' Sav said, shaking his head at the mention of goblins and running off towards the main gate. 'Bloody bird-horse. Stupid creation.' He ran as fast as he could, passing more inn-folk along the way, their faces a mix of grim determination and fear.

Hooves and talons thudded behind, alongside and away from him as Hud and Correia rode past, over one of the multiple bridges and off to the Altolnan gate, Sav cursing as he followed. 'Orismarans and now goblins?' He shuddered at the memories of Beresford.

Fire arrows came in, whooshing overhead and striking roofs,

296

walls and the ground around Sav. He cursed and ran on, head
down. Someone screamed from a way behind, followed by more
hooves clattering off the stone of the bridge he'd crossed. He
turned and saw one of Royce's Reds approaching at speed. As the
knight neared, he slowed and motioned for Sav to climb up.
Another wave of fire arrows flew overhead and Sav took the offer,
climbing up behind the red-cloaked knight.

When the two of them arrived at the gate, they encountered the
rest of Royce's Reds milling about atop their mounts, shields held
above their heads. Correia's pathfinders, Giles Bratby and Amis de
Valmont sat behind them. Gleave looked and sounded more
himself, colourfully cursing the continuing pain in his broken and
torn leg, despite the barber-surgeon's ministrations, whereas Fal
looked like a husk of a man, leaning against the back of his knight,
head to the side, eyes staring up at the smoke-filled patch of
otherwise blue sky. Salliss de Pizan, the Sirretan Witchblade, was in
the process of climbing up behind a frowning Hud, as Correia
made her way over to and climbed up behind another one of the
pegasus riding knights. It was clear none of Hud's men would have
Salliss with them, and it was clear Hud had been ordered to do so
by Correia. The atmosphere around the three women was tense.

Drums sounded from the woods, on more than one side of the
inn.

'Goblins move well through forests,' the knight carrying Fal
said, turning his mount and searching the tree framed sky beyond
the wall. 'I'm not convinced the pegasi will be able to lift off, not
with so many branches overhanging the road and not with extra
bodies.' He looked to Hud, squinting against the bright sky. 'You
might manage it, Captain, on your mount.'

Hud shook her head. 'Not without the rest of you. We ride
together, as always.'

The knight nodded, lips a thin line as his mount snorted, eager
to move on. He pulled across and tied his maille aventail, as did
some of the other knights.

Sav felt suddenly vulnerable without the maille and plate the
knights wore. He looked to the Earl of Bratby, who still wore the
blood-spattered white he'd donned for a tragic wedding. *A bright
target if I ever saw one.*

'You're leaving?' Master Stubley came out of a stone building,
sword and buckler in his hands, kettle helm on his head. The dull
steel of all three items looked strange indeed compared to his

outrageous pink and yellow long-coat and mix-matched hose. Cook followed close behind, a windlass crossbow resting across his thick arms, obscuring his apron covered chest. Sav noticed the man locking eyes with Correia, but Cook broke the look soon after.

'Ride away, now,' Correia said to Stubley. She leaned from the back of the pegasus, imploring him to do so with her eyes. 'Bratby's army won't make it in time, but if you ride out, all of you, even on foot if you've not enough horses or carts, you have a chance of outrunning them and making it to safety should we fly to the army first and send them your way.' Correia looked across to Giles, who nodded from behind the knight he clung to.

Sav knew Correia well enough to know she wasn't convinced of that.

Stubley was shaking his head before Correia finished. 'My place is here, Lady Burr. We will defend our home as you would your own. There are tricks you know nothing of within these waterways and woods. We'll hold them. Ride... fly,' he grinned, 'and send soldiers to aid us. We'll be here, waiting, I give you my word.'

'And I mine!' Cook said, eyes locked on Correia's once more.

Nodding, Correia offered a tight smile. 'I'll hold you both to that,' she said. Sav couldn't help but notice the glistening of her eyes; a rare thing, but not of late.

'We're going,' Hud said, rounding her mount towards the gates. 'And we may need those tricks, in case flight isn't possible.'

The drums were now accompanied by shrieks and hoots Sav knew to be goblins. Some of which came from beyond the Altolnan gate. *On the road?*

Inn-folk on the walls shouted warnings and loosed bolts from crossbows. Cook took one last look at Correia before running to the steps that took him up to the ramparts. His curse was audible even to those in the yard as he loosed his bolt at some unseen target.

'They're coming around both sides!' Cook shouted. 'They're traversing the waterways and...' he ducked and several arrows whistled over the wall. A young man in purple and green grunted and fell back, hitting the ground with a thud, dead, a crude arrow jutting from his chest.

'We'll not make it to wing,' Hud said, looking about frantically.

'And there's no room out there to manoeuvre,' Cook shouted down, loading his crossbow with the windlass cranks attached to it, his shoulders rolling with the effort.

'It's time,' Stubley said, a ragged breath leaving his lips. He pulled a polished tuning fork from his gaudy coat and crossed to the nearest waterway, a channel that rushed along the edge of the courtyard. Twanging the tuning fork on a stone wall, he leaned over and placed the fork into the water.

No one heard a thing, bar Errolas it seemed. Sav saw the elf wince, saw his eyes widen as the realisation of what was to come struck him.

'Errolas?' Salliss said, noticing his expression.

Everyone turned to Errolas as Stubley withdrew the fork, twanged it off stone and again placed the fork back into the water.

Cook popped up from his crouch and loosed another bolt through the gap in the crenellations. 'Ha!' he shouted, before cranking again.

'Trolls!' Errolas said, breaths short, head scanning the tree-line above the wall as if it'd reveal the beasts.

'Silt trolls,' Stubley confirmed, stowing away his glistening fork. 'And they should buy you some time. Just…' He flicked the seriousness of his look between Hud and Correia. '…don't linger on the bridges.' At a nod, before anyone could respond, Stubley waved his sword in the air and two men rushed forth to throw off the locking bolts of the Altolnan gates. They heaved the gates inward as more crossbow bolts whipped out.

A cacophony of shrieks, howls, grunts and roars met the group, but before any of them dared take the time to think about what they were to do, Hud drove spurs into her hippogriff's flanks and the beast surged forward, five pegasi struggling to keep up.

Sav turned and saw the inn-folk watch them leave, a line of them coming to stand beside Stubley, weapons drawn, spears lowered. Sav's heart lurched. 'Yet again we leave folk behind,' he whispered against the wind. 'Fair thee well,' he said a little louder, still for his own ears. 'Your ale was grand and your hospitality grander.' He turned back the way they were charging, him, his knight and their mount acting as the sternguard, alongside Hud, Salliss and the shrieking hippogriff. A racket joined the rest as shod hooves launched into a gallop across the first bridge and beyond, water rushing beneath them more often than not; goblin arrows flicking past, one thumping into a knight's shield, another glancing off Gleave's left spaulder to be swept away in the fast-flowing waters.

'Too many trees,' Hud shouted, riding down a goblin that dared

299

step out in front of them, a pathetic spear levelled.

A loud splashing and a guttural bellow drew all eyes right as a mud-like monster rushed from beneath a bridge, taking a goblin's head in its webbed hand and popping it like an egg. Saliva strung between thick incisors as it stretched its maw, shoving the blood-gushing goblin in and swallowing it as a heron would a fish.

More trolls emerged, moving with incredible speed considering their blubber and paunch. Goblins shrieked and broke cover, falling to crossbow bolts from the walls of the inn, the gate of which was being hauled shut as half a dozen of the little green bastards swarmed it. More goblins fell to the hooves and weapons of the fleeing cavalry. It rankled every man, woman and elf that they were fleeing the fight, Sav knew, but seeing the horrific destruction the massing trolls were now reaping on the swarming goblins gave him heart that the inn-folk may survive long enough for Bratby's reinforcements to arrive.

Crossbow bolts came in from another angle, from the second inn, whose walls had ladders thrown against them, goblins scaling the shifting wooden pieces of siege equipment before they came to rest against stone.

Sav swung his short-sword from the back of the pegasus he clung to with knees and thighs. It wasn't a clean hit, more the flat of his blade striking a leather-helmed head, but it had the desired effect and the goblin target stumbled and fell before being dragged under a fallen tree by a slimy hand. The goblin's shriek struck Sav as it disappeared. He shuddered and clung on all the more as the group accelerated onto the road-proper. Towards Altoln and Bratby's army.

The last thing Sav heard before hunkering down was another guttural roar. His stomach churned from both flight and fear, for the men and women left behind and for Sirreta as a whole. For whether the trolls aided the inn-folk or not, he was sure the goblins were but scouts compared to the force that would come; compared to the force they'd witnessed taking Easson.

Chapter 48 – Deceive the best of us

There had been nowhere to take flight since leaving Twin Inns. Correia and Hud had talked at length about what happened and what was likely happening elsewhere. They'd stopped to camp on the first night in the forest, for Fal needed much rest, as did Gleave, despite his arguments to the contrary. It may have been a risk, with goblins afoot in the territory, but it would have done them no good, they'd agreed – nor their mounts – to ride on through the night.

Much suspicion surrounded the Sirretan witchblade, Salliss, but Correia's concern lay with Amis de Valmont, who seemed distracted, distant; melancholy to say the least.

'You can't take your eyes off him, can you?' Sav said, as they made a second night's stop; their final stop before reaching Suttel and the army camped there. It rankled to stop once more, with potential enemies on their trail, but the mounts were weary despite the previous night's rest, two up as they were, and it wouldn't do to push them. Everyone knew that.

Correia sighed and looked sidelong at Sav.

'Well, it's true,' Sav said, crouching by Correia, eyes on Amis who sat by the fire Errolas and Salliss had made. 'He's a pretty boy, I'll give him that,' Sav conceded, turning to watch Correia's reaction to the words.

'Give it a rest, Sav,' she said, weariness flushing her more than anger. There was none of the usual hardness to her tone. She sounded defeated and hearing that in herself, feeling that in herself, made her feel more so.

Sav chewed his bottom lip, but said nothing.

'Whatever it is you're thinking, don't.' *Just don't.*

'It might be something useful.'

'It won't.'

Sav smirked. They shared a companionable silence for a while, watching the others about the camp. Light was fading swiftly, as it did in the great forest. One minute an illuminated green canopy, the next, darkness.

The mounts snickered and snorted before they fell asleep, and then the owls started, where the other birds had given up on the day. Insects came out in number too, the warm air of The Marches at summer giving life to countless scuttling and winged beasties that liked to nip and irritate bared skin. Sav slapped at the back of his neck and cursed. Correia managed a smile at that.

'I thought the midges up north were bad,' Sav muttered. 'Days of this...' –another slap– '...and I'm still not used to the little bastards that swarm this forest.'

Correia let out a choked sob as the words and the high-pitched buzzing about the camp reminded her of the swarm that had... *Oh Starks,* she thought. *You stupid, stupid... brave, brave boy.* She wiped her eyes, hoping the poor firelight would hide the reason why.

'They biting you too, eh?' Sav asked, mistaking her movements. Correia said nothing, half-listening to the various conversations instead. She took in the faces she could see, orange light playing across them enough to see their sullen expressions, tight smiles and slow nods as questions were asked and small talk was forced.

'How's Fal?' Correia asked, eyes back on Amis despite the question. Sav spent the most time with Fal since Easson. Correia felt guilt for not being able to do the same. She grunted to herself, drawing a frown from Sav. She felt guilt for Fal being taken in the first place.

'He's...' Sav took a deep breath and eyed Correia some more. 'He's Fal.' He shrugged, clearly unsure what else to say. Correia looked at him and he shifted uncomfortably. 'He'll pull through, once home. Which is where we're heading, it seems. Earlier than planned, too.'

Correia did her best to hide the smile that pulled at her mouth. There was no mirth in it, only a knowing of the man by her side that triggered it.

'I know as much as you, Sav.'

Sav grunted a laugh and there was mirth in that. 'I'd be disappointed if that were true, you being the King's Spymaster and all.' He grinned at her now, firelight glinting off his teeth.

Looking away, back to Amis, Correia offered a shrug of her own, knowing Sav was watching.

'All's well, Correia, as long as you know more than us. Well, that's the way I look at it.'

'And is Starks well because of what I know?' The words left Correia's lips before she could stop them. They were quick, sharp, and she regretted it. She turned to Sav but his smile remained. Sympathetic, but there. It stopped her apology dead. She knew it wasn't needed and looked around the camp again, taking in the scarlet fur cloaks and surcoats bent to varying tasks. *They're used to this warmth, to be wearing those cloaks all the bloody time,* Correia mused, eyes finishing on Hud, who was curled up close to the modest fire, wolf-head atop her own. Sav startled her by answering her rhetorical question, the one she'd wanted to forget as soon as she'd voiced it.

'We've been lucky,' he said. 'We could have all ended up alongside Starks.' Sav placed a hand on her shoulder, squeezed. He stood and moved across camp, back to Fal's side, who was sleeping amongst a bundle of blankets people had offered him as he'd muttered himself to sleep. He held the blankets like a babe would its comforter.

Amis caught Correia's eyes. The man was approaching, leaf-litter crunching underfoot. He looked nervous, hands wringing together before him. 'May I?' he asked when he came close, motioning to where Sav had been sitting. Correia nodded. Amis sat and stared at the fire. Correia did the same. They sat in silence for a time, listening to the hushed tones of Hud's men and the occasional grunts and curses from Gleave as he shifted constantly, failing to make himself comfortable because of his leg and various other stitched and patched wounds.

'They're a hardy bunch,' Amis said, eyes leaving the fire to take in the pathfinders.

'They are indeed.'

'You risked all to come and find Giles. Your dedication is admirable, madame.'

Correia's shoulders bobbed. 'Correia, please.'

Amis smiled.

Correia couldn't help but smile back, although it was short lived as the dull thud and soundless screams of Starks' explosion came back to her once again, triggered by the quiet or the guilt of her smile, she couldn't be sure. She knew Gleave would be reliving it too, which was likely where his moments of none-cursing came from. Some things were too painful to curse, too raw to attack with words and grunts and the like. *He'll be adding Starks' explosive end to Mearson's now, in his mind, in his dreams. And feeling the guilt for both... as I do,* she thought, watching her restless pathfinder. Her friend.

'I'm sorry for your loss, Correia,' Amis said, eyes on Fal's prone form.

'Starks?'

'And the rest. Your Orismaran friend and the gnarled one, Gleave.'

Amusement threatened to take Correia's pain, but she didn't

303

allow it. 'They're hardy, as you say. And Starks…'

'There's no need.' Amis glanced sidelong at her. 'Such things are best left unspoken, for quite some time.'

Correia nodded at that. 'And is that the case with Flavell?'

Amis took a deep breath and looked away, cheeks flushing a deeper red in the firelight.

'You're embarrassed?' Correia searched the man's face. He didn't respond.

'How long did you know her?' Correia's tone was soft, searching, but not demanding.

'Too long and not well enough, it seems.' He glanced at her. 'But we talked of this, at Twin Inns,' he said. There was no venom in his tone, only a weariness Correia understood.

'We talked as a war council, for want of a better term. And you told us of an uneventful trip across Sirreta and of her personality change within the chateau. We never talked of before.'

Amis took in a shuddering breath, nodding slowly. His embarrassment and frustration were obvious, fingers pulling at dried leaves from the ground.

'Succubi deceive the best of us, Amis. My lads can attest to that.' Correia looked to Sav and noticed, in her periphery, Amis looking now at her, searching. 'A tale for another time,' Correia said, offering a weak smile. *I've enough to think on without dredging up what Sav did in Broadleaf Forest.*

Nodding, Amis continued, voice low, like the words tasted bitter as he heard them. 'I've known her since I was a squire. Years, Correia. Years. I was sent to her father, Guiscard de Steedon, by my own, as are the ways of such houses. You will know that, I'm sure.' Correia nodded once as he continued, his eyes without focus, lost to memory. 'My father had the better of it, Flavell's…' he grimaced, '…Flavell's family being of higher standing than ours; Guiscard being a seigneur and mine a vassal of his.'

'A prestigious position and a great opportunity for you.'

Amis nodded. 'So I thought.'

'She may have been replaced, Amis, within Easson. I'm not sure, but a Succubus may have been able to take her form.' Correia wasn't sure, that was true, but she saw the hurt in the man and couldn't help but try to fix it.

Amis nodded again. 'Perhaps. Truth is, I never knew her in her father's chateau. I saw her about…' He grunted a laugh. 'She caught my eye as much as any other man's, but I didn't know her, not until the journey north.'

'Why were you her only escort?' It sounded like an inquisition and Correia bit her lip, worried she'd overstepped the mark.

'She's Guiscard de Steedon's third daughter, Correia. Truth is, he never much cared for her, hence sending her so far away to be wed.' Amis shrugged. 'Seems he didn't think much of me either.'

Correia placed a hand on Amis' arm and squeezed, much like Sav had done for her. 'You don't know that, Amis. The way I see it, he felt safe with his daughter in your hands, so he only needed you. A long way from home, a woman like that could fall prey to the very men sent to protect her. I believe he had a great deal of trust in you, this Guiscard. Take pride in that, messire. Take pride. We have to find the light in the dark sometimes, all of us.'

Amis smiled, eyes and all. 'Remember your own words, Correia Burr.' He squeezed her arm in return, stood and left for his bedroll.

Correia took a deep and shuddering breath. *Would that I could, Amis. Would that I could.*

Chapter 49 – The field lay bare

The trees overhanging the road gave way to a slate grey sky, heavy with distant rain. Weather aside, the opening of the forest gave the riders pause, causing them to squint against the wind as they shielded their eyes to look upon an army that was not there.

'I… I don't understand?' Giles Bratby stared at the hill before them, to hundreds of circles and rectangles of yellow grass, intermingled with much smaller dark disks where campfires had warmed soldiers and boiled pots. Three white campaign tents remained, one with Bratby's own banners snapping in the rising wind. His eyes moved to the men crossing the distance between, two on horseback, shields and padded gambesons in his own colours, the other dozen carrying war bows, their garb plain, drab. He frowned. 'Why so little?' He urged the red knight he sat behind to ride on, but Hud and Salliss came alongside, Correia and her red rider mirroring the two women off Giles' other shoulder.

'Wait,' Hud said, arm outstretched. 'Let them come to us. Despite our red livery, I don't want your archers mistaking us for an enemy.'

Giles chewed his bottom lip but nodded.

'Fall back a bit,' Correia said, turning and waving at the rest of the mounted group. They did as they were told, leaving three men and three women atop two pegasi and a hippogriff. The sight was impressive indeed, much more so than the mounted men-at-arms and their archers, six to either side of the two riders.

As Giles' men approached, the first droplets of rain fell, or rather whipped about in the wind. No sooner had the sky begun to spit, did it unleash all it had on the hill, sweeping down like a diaphanous grey veil being drawn towards the forest.

Hud smirked. 'Your archers wouldn't do much good now anyway, milord, even if their strings are waxed.' The wind howled as if to accentuate her point.

'Perhaps we should be thankful of that.' Correia pulled her gifted red cloak about her shoulders and drew up the hooded mantle. She shielded her face with her hand as the wall of rain struck. 'Welcome to Altoln, Salliss,' she said, without sarcasm. Oh, how she loved the rain; the life-giving, revitalising and atmospheric stuff of dramatic stories and vistas and adventure. Well, perhaps not in winter when each strike of a droplet sent a chill through to one's soul, but summer? And especially after the insects and clammy warmth of Sirreta and the forest. She relished the torrential greeting Altoln offered her. Although the smell of wet dog that permeated the air after the sudden soaking the red wolf-fur about her shoulders took didn't impress.

The pegasi snorted and the hippogriff snapped its beak, the mounts shifting under their riders.

Correia could see the two riders drawing near, their kettle helms doing a better job of running rivulets of water away before it found their faces. They came to a stop, backs to the worst of the weather, waxed canvas cloaks protecting them, for the most part. The closest one, by half a horse-length, rocked back in his saddle as his eyes locked on his liege; mouth previously agape, likely because of the strange mounts, the soldier snapped it shut as he took in the Earl of Bratby.

'My lord!'

Giles grunted a laugh and smiled. 'Mits,' he greeted, recognising his ageing retainer. 'You look like shit, as always.'

Mits laughed. 'And you look well, my lord. Considering—'

'There's no time for this,' Correia cut in. 'There was an army here?' She knew she needn't say more than that.

Mits grimaced. 'They've moved north, to march on the threat there.'

Correia looked across to Hud, who shrugged.

'What threat, Mits?' Giles said, wiping water from his brow. He'd not drawn up a hood, like most of the others, and clearly regretted it. Mits nudged his mount closer. It whinnied and threw its head back, a greeting to the beasts before it.

An equine salute across species, Correia mused.

'Adlets.' Mits spat the word, like he'd chewed on something bitter before saying it.

Everyone frowned at that. 'You don't need such a force for Adlets,' Correia said. 'We saw how many gathered here, to potentially ride on Easson.' She didn't miss Salliss' look of surprise at that, a touch of anger to the Sirretan's face. 'Such numbers,' Correia continued regardless, 'such an army, aren't needed for the dog-legged raiders of the Toye Hills, surely?'

'Normally I'd agree, my lady,' Mits said, hunkering down in his saddle after swinging his shield round onto his back. He needed it more against the rain than those facing him.

'But?' Giles this time, eyes boring into Mits.

'We had a warning. Came from what remains of Stonebridge…'
Mits' eyes darted between those present, letting the implications of
that sink in. He finished on Correia, who offered the next question
with a shake to her voice.

'Remains? Explain.'

A gust of wind had three mounts sidestep, none of them the
hippogriff, which seemed as solid as ever, talons sunk into soft
earth.

'May I suggest we continue this in one of those tents?' Mits said,
slouched down as he was, arms folded.

'It makes sense,' Giles agreed. 'Ride on, Mits, and we shall
follow.'

Mits nodded and turned his horse, cursing as he took a face full
of rain. He waved his arm three times and the archers turned and
leaned into the wind, making their way back to the tents, a variety
of mounts carrying a variety of folk at their backs; making their
way to the succour of the campaign tents the army had
purposefully left behind.

The sides of the white tent bellowed and shook, rain hammering a
ceaseless beat on the canvas, intensifying as gusts battered all but
those inside.

Fal watched the stinking tallow candles glowing within glass
storm lanterns that ensured none turned over and caught light; a
tent aflame was a magnificent sight to behold. *As long as it's not your
own*, Fal mused. He shuddered at the thought of flames licking up
about him, hot, painful; deadly. He shook the sudden memories of
his parents away and looked to Giles Bratby, whose baritone voice
was booming once more.

Giles ran his finger across lands he obviously knew well,
depicted on a single map from the Cartographers Guild. He cursed
their inaccuracies as his fingers drew imaginary lines. 'Would that I
had my own maps,' he said, before reaching for a skin of watered
wine and taking a swig. He wiped his mouth with his sleeve and
turned to Correia as she spoke.

'It'll do us well enough,' she said, leaning over and looking to
where Giles pointed. 'How did they cross?' she asked, clearly
sceptical that Stonebridge could be taken by Adlets.

'By all accounts… well, one, my lady,' Mits said from the
shadows, the candles offering insufficient light to illuminate the
tent's corners, 'they took it with siege engines and great numbers.'

Mits shrugged to the faces frowning at his answer.

Hud stepped forward, hands on the table. She looked around everyone. 'Adlets rarely band their clans, or packs rather, since that's what they are, let alone move in great numbers and wage siege warfare.'

'But they have!' Errolas came to the end of the table, locked eyes with Hud. 'As have Orismaran tribesmen. As did goblin tribes from the Norlechlan Mountains, which went on to take Beresford of all places.'

'And likely the Twin Inns, although I know not where those goblins came from,' Correia said, voice low; several of the heads looking her way hung lower after that. Correia took in a deep breath and released a deeper sigh. She stood straight and ran hands through her lank hair.

'That sigh says it all.' Giles offered Correia a sympathetic smile, then looked to Hud. 'Do your borders remain clear, Captain?'

'For now,' Hud said. 'Although that's the land border. Our ships have stopped sailing south, to and along the Chriselle Coast. Strange ships, small fleets even, have been spotted and narrowly avoided. There's more to this than a wicked coincidence.'

'Of course there is.' Errolas' words were short, unlike him, and Fal watched him intently. 'Succubi in Broadleaf Forest,' Errolas went on, his tone little better, 'and now in Easson, taking a marquis' chateau? There's a lot more to this, and we knew it, hence our trip down to The Marches, no? But this,' he said before anyone could speak, pointing to Stonebridge on the map, then Twin Inns. He hammered his finger down on a third spot: Lejeune Forest and Sirreta's capital city within. 'This is far worse than we feared. This is war on a scale we have not witnessed in an age. For all these races to be acting at once, co-ordinated – for that's what it is, a co-ordinated attack, starting in Wesson, with the plague. Someone, or something, is behind it all, and that means they have messengers, agents on the move; on the roads or seas, or air.' He looked up to the tent ceiling, to accentuate the point. 'You don't co-ordinate such movements, such activity, without communication.'

Fal watched Giles begin nodding before Errolas finished.

'Errolas is right. He must be, for all this to be happening the way it is.' Giles looked up from the map, met the eyes of everyone present. 'I need to ride for my army, but we will be leaving this border crossing unguarded.' He pointed to the tent wall, in the direction of the forest and its road. Fal looked that way as a reaction. It wasn't as if he could see through the canvas.

Errolas lent across and ran his splayed fingers through the map-drawn forest as Fal looked back, from Twin Inns on the map, to their position in Suttel. 'Goblins attacked Twin Inns and goblins move through forests largely unhindered, such is their way. They could come out anywhere along the tree line, and likely will. They'll fear an ambush on the forest road. You can't defend the whole border from here, anyway, and by the sounds of it,' he added, as Giles made to speak, 'the adlets pose the most immediate threat.' He finished with his finger on Stonebridge and the road that ran from it, into Altoln.

That spot on the map will be worn through by the time this lot are done, Fal mused from his corner, eyes now on the map and folks' fingers more than their faces. He listened on, although he couldn't quite feel the emotion about it all that they seemed to. He continued to feel pain, that was true enough, despite the Twin Inns barber-surgeon's ministrations, but worry and fear for what was to come? He merely shrugged and pressed his bound fingertips together. *Some pains you have to prod and prod.* He silently laughed at that before listening to what was being said.

'…the Orismarans come through the forest,' Hud was saying, 'along the road we're to leave unattested?' Hud raised a single brow, scars creasing.

'Can Royce not send aid?' Correia looked to Hud, who shook her head and offered a frown.

'Earl Royce will look to his own defences. If armies are marching on the other two border crossings, we have to assume they'll march the coastal road too. Or land by sea.'

'Or both,' one of Hud's knights said. Fal looked to the man who, until now, had held his tongue behind his neatly trimmed black beard. He'd been the knight who'd carried Fal from Easson to the Twin Inns. Fal decided he didn't like the man. He didn't know why, he just didn't. Shrugging it off, he looked back to the officers, Correia central amongst them.

'Your man's right, Captain.' Giles nodded sideways to the knight and chewed his own lip, all eyes upon him, knowing there was more. After a pause, he released his lip and said, 'What of the whelp, Rell Adlestrop?'

Fal smiled at that. *I like Giles Bratby.*

'The young Duke,' Giles went on, 'can muster a decent force, and Adlestrop itself isn't too far north of The Marches.'

Correia shook her head this time. 'He called for his men to march on Beresford, to aid his father in retaking the town. I believe the duchy of Adlestrop has been emptied of its levies.'

'As well as his northern holds and the Reaver families?' Hud asked, brow creased, scars deep once more.

Correia shook her head. 'No, he's kept them there, for fear of more than goblins moving down from the mountains.'

'Or to harry the Northfolk, as is his way,' Hud muttered. Correia shot her a look.

More secrets, Fal thought, scowling at Correia despite her not looking his way.

'Unfortunately for us,' Giles lamented. 'Yewdale then, surely?' he asked, moving on, eyes flicking from Correia to Hud and back. 'Now *there's* a Duke who'll trounce what's to come; he's not Lord High Constable of Alton for nothing!' He beamed at that, like he'd solved it all.

Correia shrugged. 'He'd be willing and eager, I'm sure, but his closest estates are a long way from here. It would take weeks of marching and the emptying of food and supplies from many an estate along the way. His peers, and other minor lords, would not take kindly to that.'

'Weeks may do, if he acts now,' Giles said, ignoring the latter. 'We're in mid campaign season, there's plenty of time for this to drag on. A late coming army from Yewdale would be better arriving for nothing than not coming and being desperately needed.'

'Perhaps,' Correia said, 'but an army being formed, marched south and back north without a fight is a dangerous army, Will Morton's or not.'

Fal noticed Correia glance at Hud. Was it nerves he saw in her expression as she changed tack. 'I can try and talk to Royce, once there.' Hud's head snapped up from the map. Correia held up a hand, placating the woman. 'I know he'll need to secure his own lands, but he may be able to spare barons from his eastern holdings, like Baron Arrisal and others of his ilk. It's worth asking, surely?'

Hud swallowed hard, annoyed at Correia putting her on the spot, Fal was sure, but she nodded all the same.

'What of Piggett?' Correia suggested, giving no one else time to talk. She frowned at Giles' scowl. 'My lord Bratby, Piggett's earldom is part of Altoln—'

311

'Well he's done fuck all to stop an adlet incursion into Altoln proper. Has he, Correia?'

By the look on Correia's face, she'd expected Giles' outburst at her suggestion. Fal really did like the man.

'Call him from his mountains, my lord,' Correia went on, determined. 'Call on him to aid you.'

Giles sighed and rubbed hard at his face, at the bags under his bloodshot eyes. 'Fucking gnomes,' he said through his hands. 'He's a belligerent little bastard and we don't need him,' he said, locking eyes with Correia's stern stare.

'And if we do and didn't call on him?' Correia left it at that; let the implications sink in to the stubborn man.

'I'll think on it,' Giles said, before changing tack, his following words coming from nowhere. 'I've decided to ride to Bratby Castle and co-ordinate from there, rather than riding to my army. I can trust my son to deal with adlets. I need muster a defence and fortify the old towers along the forest's edge. Bring the villages into the walls and such.

'Mits.'

Fal had forgotten the old retainer was in the tent. He was quieter and even more absent from the conversation than Hud's knights, Sav and Gleave; two who seemed, for all intense and purposes, to be asleep at the back.

'My lord?' Mits stepping into the light.

'These archers, where do they hail from?'

'Old Bailey, my lord.'

Giles nodded, satisfied. 'Good. Have one of them ride back there and give my order to Lord Teshe to mount patrols and prepare for a possible siege. Tell him to send birds to Bratby Castle and await their return. I shall have orders sent back with them once I arrive. We're going to man the old watch towers and he is the anchor point between Royce and Suttel. Understood?'

Mits nodded once. 'I know the man to send. Want me should get on it now?'

'Aye. I know it's blowing a shit out there, but send your man immediately, and tell him to make haste. Tell him to walk his horse through the night if he needs to.'

Mits left the tent without another word.

'Can you garrison the watch towers?' Correia asked.

Fal had never heard of them. He certainly hadn't seen one whilst in the area. *You'd think they'd have one by the bloody road,* he thought, shaking his head.

'I don't need to garrison them, Correia, just man them with enough to keep constant watch. I'll have a bird or two at each, or a pair of fast horses. Anyway,' he said, shrugging again, 'the bastard things practically garrison themselves. They're more of a net than anything else. Should one be attacked, they'll send word and I'll act with whatever aid comes my way.'

'It's settled then,' Correia said. 'We'll ride, or fly,' she looked to Hud, who nodded, 'on the morrow, once you've dropped camp and moved on. I'll petition Royce and continue to Wesson, doing the same to whomever I see at court once there; with King Barrison's backing, of course.'

Giles smiled. 'And I thank you for it, Correia. Ever have you been a friend to my family.'

Correia smiled in return.

Fal scoffed and sneered, the action pulling at healing wounds on his face. *She seems to mean that smile, too,* Fal thought, as Correia spoke.

'Send my regards to your wife,' Correia said.

'I will do.' Giles smiled all the more, although it turned into a stifled yawn. 'I'm for the archers now, to talk to them. After which I'll take some sleep, despite the early hour. Good day to you all.'

A chorus of replies followed Giles from the tent, Fal watching the big man leave.

Fal realised he'd not seen Amis de Valmont present. He'd assumed the fresh-faced chevalier would be staying in the tent gifted to Correia and Hud, but clearly not. Brow creasing, Fal looked back to the two women stood by the map table, Hud's knights now moving about in the background, removing each other's armour and preparing to take some rest.

As Fal tried to watch, tried to listen from his bunk, the women's voices blended together, dulled; lulled him into a deep sleep he'd needed for too long. He'd tried to fight it, but it took him all the same. As did the horrific dreams that followed; flames and blades, cuts and burns, the smashing of his two front teeth which pained him whenever he breathed in, ate or drank. Family lost in the past, friends lost in the present, and future. Dignaaln's face appeared in the haze of the swirling images, and whilst Fal slept, he smiled at the memory of the pleasant man who'd visited him in Easson's dungeon, between Rasoir's horrific ministrations.

Chapter 50 – Planner of fates

Fal woke with a start. Raised voices pulling him from his slumber. He looked up to the pitched canvas above, white with the morning light beyond; his eyes flicked from stain to stain, some of which were the red-black of dried blood. The voices continued, but he didn't listen, not yet. He focused on the bloody patches, mixed with damp and mould. A surgeon's tent once upon a time, of that he was sure. Spurts of blood arcing from severed limbs and the bleeding of every ailment the hackers could get away with bleeding.

Tentatively biting at his bottom lip, which felt strange to do these days, and ignoring the pain, Fal continued to study the inside of the tent, wiping sleep from his tender eyes as he did so. After a while he sighed and rolled onto his side. His ribs pained him more than anything else at that, but he was becoming used to it, numb to it. Gleave was arguing with Correia, as was Sav, although Sav used words whereas Gleave used grunts and curses and shouts, as he had a lot since Easson. Fal heard it all, but didn't truly listen. They'd asked his opinion about this and that since they'd landed in Twin Inns and travelled and camped the forest road, trying to include him, trying to act like all was well. He shrugged, if he answered at all, much like he had the thousand times Sav had tried to engage him in conversation or jest, or when Correia had asked him questions about questions asked and answers given.

What had it all been for? he wondered, as the others talked about hidden dangers and not so hidden ones. The wind and the rain did its best to drown out their monotonous goings on. He huffed. Eyes turned to him.

'Fal, you alright there?' Sav asked, brow knitted, concern evident.

Fal nodded and smiled, although his eyes didn't match his mouth. Reluctantly, Sav turned away, back to his protestations over someone being left behind. Fal couldn't make out who they were arguing about. He snarled, but hid it quickly so as not to draw attention. He couldn't fart at the moment without them rushing to see if he was well or not.

Course I'm not fucking well! Dragged away in the dark by Gleave, iron spilling blood. Shouts around me; screams and death and the orphaning of a little boy, whose father tended to me and showed me mercy where he was meant not to. And what were they saying since they fled? Since they left another town to horrors unbound. Easson; like Beresford. What did they try to make him feel better by saying: that Sergeant Rasoir was a sadistic bastard? That he wasn't one of Correia's own? That he wasn't even a sergeant-at-arms, like Fal!? Well of course they'd say that. Correia didn't like anyone knowing her men and women on the inside of places, did she? So, it was convenience that had them telling him Rasoir wasn't one of them. It was convenient to Gleave that he'd had a chance to kill the poor man, telling Fal that Rasoir was an enemy to cover it up. Fal nearly spat. *Correia and her lies.* But what had they achieved through it all? Through going to Easson and killing Rasoir? Nothing. No, not nothing, quite the opposite. They'd stirred up a bloody hornets' nest, literally by all accounts, and left Starks behind in the process. Poor Starksy lad, the only decent one amongst them. Now dead. Dead and gone and left behind.

Fal sighed again, rubbed his face hard this time, catching scabs newly formed with bound, tip-less fingers. He sucked in a painful breath and held it. No one turned. He released the breath and tapped his head against the tent pole he lay against. He preferred the floor to the crates and boxes the others sat on. Cold. Damp. He'd grown used to that in a short time. Short time! His ribs snagged and pained him through a silent chuckle. *I swear they left me there days, weeks even, and yet they tell me it was far shorter a stay in Easson's dungeon. How can I believe that? Convenient again for them that I cannot know for sure.*

Raised voices and gesticulating hands drew Fal's attention back to the centre of the tent. Gleave was cursing again. He'd done nothing but since his roar and charge at the Orismaran commander in the yard; since losing Starks. Starks had been with Gleave, and Correia, so he, they, had lost him. It was only right that the man should piss and moan and feel ill about it. Correia thought? No. The hard-faced bitch continued on as ever, shaken little by the loss of yet another one of her pathfinders.

Fal grunted a laugh, quiet, so as not to be heard and harassed. The mirth lasted but a moment. Their words spoilt it. He was to be left. With Gleave, it seemed. To be taken to Castle Bratby, unfit to ride atop winged horses despite their successful flight from Easson riding the very same. They were probably right, mind, considering the many stitches he and Gleave sported. And getting left behind was nothing new, although Gleave bleated continuously about it. Correia was to take the new one, Amis de Valmont. He was fit, strong, handsome even. Correia would find use for him; chew him up and spit him out like Tom and Mearson, and Starksy boy. And now Gleave and… 'Me.'

Eyes turned to Fal.

He looked away from those stares, his own eyes rolling. He heard something said – missed it, although he thought it sounded like 'walk'.

Walk, Fal thought, staring into what had been; darkness, a friendly voice. *Walking,* he thought, remembering the joy in the tale told. Rasoir's little boy had begun to walk. Incredible! Such little legs. Such will. To stiffly charge forward, barely able but doing so anyway. A brave new world for him to discover. Fal swallowed and licked his lips, slumping further, albeit tentatively, eyes closed now, lost to welcomed darkness. That poor boy. *Orphaned… like I was.* He sneered. *And we left him and his mother, to them. To my bastard kin.*

He opened his eyes, turned his head and spat.

Everyone turned to him. Sav made to speak, to approach, but Fal waved him away, turned and curled. The pain flared in various places, but he ground his back teeth and closed his eyes.

I hope they're all gone when I awake, he thought, remembering Dignaaln's soothing voice in the spaces between Sergeant Rasoir's own.

Dignaaln: teller of truths and opener of gates, whisperer of strategies and planner of fates.

Chapter 51 – A hammer blow

Sav stepped out of the white tent and took in a lungful of wood-smoked air, the camp's fire nothing but smouldering embers as the men of Suttel dropped camp. The vale descended before Sav, ending abruptly against a wall of trees. He looked upon the dense forest of The Marches and smiled, the scene taking him back to Woodmoat and Broadleaf Forest. His smile faded as quickly as it appeared, thoughts switching to darkness, flashes of light and bangs, one of which had taken Mearson's life. 'And now Starks is gone too,' he whispered, steeling himself and shaking the memories away. He took in another breath and walked over to a canvass laden cart, where Bratby's men-at-arms were fussing over straps, securing the load.

'Morning, lads,' Sav said, grin wide. He nodded to the cart. 'Your lord left you to it?'

'As usual,' the younger of the two said, eyes on his work.

Mits looked to Sav and smiled. 'Morning. Earl Bratby left at first light. Took our horses and half the archers. Nothing changes, eh?' Mits laughed and continued securing the cart's load. There was no grievance in his words, only jollity. 'Once the rest of your lot are packed and ready, along with Hud's own, we'll have yours and their tent down and packed away. Then we'll be off too. Your elf friend and the Sirretan lass left at first light with two of Hud's knights,' Mits added, as if Sav didn't know.

'Aye,' Sav said, looking back to the forest below. 'Hud said we'll be swift to Royce, but need to stop half way. She wanted Lord Temn ready to receive us at Landon Hill.' Mits nodded and Sav went on. 'Anyhow, the others shouldn't be long. You taking Fal and Gleave?'

Mits nodded. 'The injured lads, aye. They'll be good with us, don't you worry. It's a short journey where we're heading. A day at a slow walk with but one stop off overnight, so they won't be on the carts for too long. Better than aback a winged beast, methinks.' He laughed again and slapped the white canvas he'd finished securing. 'Well,' he said, smiling once more at Sav, 'must crack on. Need to whip those archers into line.' He winked and headed off behind Hud's tent, where Sav could hear laughter.

Sav smiled and wandered away, hearing voices behind his own tent. Moving around the back, he caught sight of Correia talking with Amis. Sav wasn't sure whether hunger churned his stomach or something else as he watched them together.

The sun appeared in the sky to the east as a cloud shifted aside; a mist began to lift from the wet grass as Sav strode towards Correia and Amis, jaw set, eyes on the man squeezing Correia's arm. Amis turned and walked away before Sav reached them.

'Sav,' Correia greeted, turning his way. She nodded curtly. No smile, not even in her eyes.

'Correia,' Sav said back, trying to keep the shake from his voice. 'How's Fal?'

'How's de Valmont?' Sav said before he could stop himself.

A frown was his only reply. Correia grabbed Sav's thick arm, hard, and pulled him away down the hill. She didn't look back at him as she walked, fast. His frown matched hers, before turning into a wry smile.

'You finally in the mood?' he asked. It was mostly fun. Mostly. It's not like he thought she was actually going to jump his bones on the side of the hill, below the camp. One could hope though.

She continued on, without a retort, without even one of her famous glares. They reached the bottom of the hill and continued on a while, on a level with the forest and within clear view of the dark tunnel that was the forest road. Finally, Correia turned to Sav, released his arm and took hold of his face in her hands. She raised up to him, on her toes.

Sav's smile disappeared. As did his nerve. His stomach churned all the more and his heart quickened. He didn't even return the kiss Correia planted on his lips. There was more truth in that kiss, from her, than Sav had seen or felt from the woman since they'd met. He stood there, frozen to the spot as she dropped back down and stood looking at him, hands now on hips, a neutral expression on her hard face despite the passion she'd revealed to him. He couldn't speak. He couldn't react at all. Sav just stared at Correia. He licked his lips.

'Is that what you wanted, you fool of a man?'

The words struck him and he took a step back. 'I...' was all he could manage. He searched her face, her eyes, for any sign of emotion. He'd felt enough of it in the kiss, but she seemed void of it now.

'We've been through this, Sav, not that long ago, after Towton and again at Twin Inns.' She sighed and shook her head a little. 'I've too much in here,' she tapped her head, 'to add anymore.' He made to speak but she continued. 'I need you to trust me—'

'I do!'

'So stop with the glares and the huffs and the pining, Sav. Stop it, please.'

Sav shifted, said nothing.

'I need you to be there, as my pathfinder, as my trustworthy man.'

'And I am,' Sav said quickly. 'I...'

'You puff your chest out whenever I talk to Amis... See!'

Sav had tensed, clenched his teeth at the mention of the handsome chevalier. He shook himself loose and smiled weakly. 'I'm sorry.'

'I don't need sorry, I need—'

'Trust. I know.'

'Well, give it to me. Flay me, Sav,' Correia flung her arms out and turned a circle, coming around to look up at him again. 'If you're like this now, before we're even... anything. Before I've even confirmed we *can* be anything—"

'But—'

'No! Don't speak, Sav. Listen,' Correia said, eyes narrow, finger pointing. Sav did as he was told, though his mind raced with all that was happening; his heart and stomach and soul raced with all he felt. 'If,' Correia went on, 'you're like this now, with me talking to Amis, a man we barely know, but one I need to know much more if I'm to trust him, what The Three will you be like when— *If* we're together as man and woman. Eh?'

Sav swallowed hard. 'I don't trust him,' he said, and began to fill his lungs, push out his chest. He caught himself and relaxed, a little.

Correia grunted a laugh. 'Why? Because he talks to me, looks at me; because he's handsome? Or because I smile back at him once in a while?'

'I just don't,' Sav snapped, leaning down towards Correia, face reddening with more than a little anger. He pointed up at the remaining tents, illuminated by the sun. 'He arrived in Easson with the damned demon bitch you said slit the seneschal's throat!'

'Well, you'd know all about demon bitches, wouldn't you, Sav?' It was Correia's turn to flush red with anger.

Sav sighed hard and stood straight.

'Listen, Sav,' Correia said, softening her tone. She closed her eyes and took a breath before going on. 'All I need...' Her face paled as her eyes focussed past him.

Sav frowned. 'What is it?' He turned to look behind him, towards the forest road where Correia stared. 'Shit,' was all he could manage. He reached out and pushed Correia without looking. 'Go,' he said, eyes on the three riders emerging from the darkness of the forest road. 'Go!' he shouted, shoving her harder as he turned and saw her standing there.

'They're Sirret—'

'I know,' Sav interrupted, 'but we can't trust that.'

Correia glanced back, up the hill. 'We won't make it,' she said, panic in her voice. Eyes wide, she looked at Sav, took hold of him with both hands, head shaking. 'We won't make it!'

You will. Sav grabbed Correia's arm, much like she had his, back at the camp, and he launched into a run, pulling Correia along beside him. The sound of hooves thumping the ground reached them, but they couldn't quicken their pace, the ground wet and uneven. To fall was to be caught; to die.

'Goblins!' someone shouted from the camp above.

Sav risked a glance back and sure enough, scores of goblins were emerging from the trees, a dozen riding great boars that followed the charge of the three approaching chevaliers, two with lances pointing to the sky.

'Go!' Correia shouted, shoving Sav away and turning towards the men closing on them.

'Sav!' The shout from above turned his attention from Correia, who found her footing and stood ready, twin swords drawn against the three riders bearing down on her. She'd not even made the base of the hill.

A familiar unstrung bow and linen quiver sailed down through the air towards Sav, thrown by Amis, who was following his throw down the hill, drawing his own sword as he descended. Sav sprinted and caught the well-thrown bow, but had to take two more long strides to retrieve his arrows, all of which took him further away from Correia.

There was no time to worry. No time to curse or shout. Stringing the bow, Sav took three arrows from the quiver and threw two of them into the earth at his feet. The first of the three he'd taken from the bag was nocked, drawn to his cheek and released before the first rider reached Correia. It corkscrewed through the air and struck the roaring man square in his chest. The coat-of-plates the chevalier wore under his striped surcoat failed to stop the armour-piercing bodkin tip Sav had selected.

Unintentionally pulling on his reins as he was punched backwards, the chevalier forced his mount up into a rearing-tumble. Man and beast crashed backwards, horse screaming, man dying as his neck snapped upon impact with the ground.

Correia took the opportunity Sav had given her to turn and run, back towards him, the hill and a carefully descending Amis, the man's feet slipping at least once through haste.

Sav forced himself to breathe and attempted to shake away the fear that threatened to take hold of him. He'd been in worse situations, much worse, but not with someone he cared so deeply for relying on him to aim as true as he needed. He'd taken the second bodkin and nocked it. The next rider pointed his couched lance towards Correia. Sav watched as the chevalier drew blood on his white destrier's flanks with bodkin-like spurs, causing the animal to surge into a galloping charge despite the uneven ground.

Sav exhaled, narrowing his eyes, willing the rune-carved bow to do his bidding. He loosed the arrow at a seemingly impossible angle to strike the rider closing on Correia, yet the arrow arced and arced true. Whistling through the air along a sweeping trajectory, Sav retrieved the last arrow from the ground as the second split iron links on both sides of the rider's maille-clad neck. The chevalier spun to the side, pulling his mount round in a leg-breaking turn that saw both crumple to the ground. A second horse screamed and a second man likely died; Sav didn't pay attention after his arrow struck to know or care.

Sav cursed as he hastily released the third arrow at the dangerously close remaining rider. He cursed, threw his bow and ran towards Correia.

Goblins hooted and howled as they approached the action, boars snorting with the effort.

Correia turned as the second rider fell to Sav's arrow; she turned, tripped and stumbled forward. Sav watched in horror as the third rider, which his arrow had missed through his fear and distraction, hung off the side of his high-backed saddle, war-hammer raised ready for the stumbling woman. An arrow from the hill glanced off the chevalier's shield, another off his pointed, pig-faced bascinet as he brought his hammer down in a skull-crushing arc.

The chevalier roared and Correia screamed as Sav ploughed into her and sent her tumbling away from the swinging hammer. They were the last sounds Sav ever heard.

The hammer crumpled the side of Sav's skull in an explosion of pain, and his world faded as he watched the woman he loved tumble away from him, her face contorted through terror and disbelief; he didn't even have time to form a thought before the end.

Chapter 52 – Feathers and scales

Gleave watched as Sav fell, was hammered down; killed in the field below him. Gleave lay on the cart he and Fal had been helped into and screamed. He screamed in shock, horror and anger at himself and the enemy. He sat there, useless, too injured to assist as the enemy charged Correia. He looked to Fal, who looked back, a bitter sneer pulling at his mouth. None of the shock or immediate grief Gleave was feeling was present in that bruised, scarred and tattooed face. None of the anger and frustration and horror at what they'd witnessed, what they were witnessing. Fal merely looked at him and then back down the hill, seemingly in disgust.

'Give me a crossbow!' Gleave shouted, throwing his head this way and that, looking for someone who might listen, but all were engaged, either hastily harnessing and mounting winged beasts, or loosing arrows down towards the growing numbers of goblins approaching Correia. Gleave watched as her swords glowed through red and orange to white. White hot. He watched, impotent in his inability to help, railing at himself internally. He couldn't even bring himself to curse aloud. He watched as, wails of loss and anger reaching his ears even from her distance, Correia surged to her feet, ducked low and turned from the path of the chevalier who'd slew their friend, his mount rounding in a tight circle to bring its rider and a bloody hammer to bear. The horse accelerated towards its target and screamed as its front legs fell away, crashing it face first into the ground, sliding as it went a little past Correia, who turned back as quickly as she'd turned away, driving the points of her curved swords down and through the maille covering the rider's neck. Gleave watched the glow of the blades disappear into the man, halfway to the hilts. He watched the steam rise. Screaming, shrieking even, Correia withdrew the blades before shifting her stance and slicing at the corpse, ignorant or uncaring of the vile horde fast approaching her from the forest.

'A crossbow!' Gleave shouted again, although he doubted his request would be heard or acted upon. He didn't even know if there was one. He felt the rush of wind as two of Royce's Red's launched into the air, off the hillside, atop their winged equine beasts. He watched them in awe as they glided down towards Correia, low to the ground, shadows darkening the dawn-bathed grass they skimmed.

A guttural roar pulled Gleave's eyes up, past the bay pegasi, past

Correia who continued to hack and slash at the armoured lump of meat like a butcher taking out her anger on a side of armoured beef. He looked up and past the goblins, to the treetops where great leathery wings preceded the mottled brown of a snaking tail. He focused on the beast's head as bowstrings twanged, arrows thrummed.

'We're fucked,' Gleave whispered, eyes wide as the approaching beast released another roar. Horses nickered and neighed, causing the brakes on the cart to squeal as they tried to drag the cart behind them to escape.

'Wyvern!' Captain Hud shouted, finally climbing her harnessed hippogriff. Gleave looked to her and wondered what match her and her remaining knights would be against such a beast. 'Two!' Hud yelled, forcing Gleave's eyes back to the forest. He caught Correia slicing into the nearest goblin, its spear falling in two before it did the same. He watched the knights in red crash into the line of goblins, their mounts' hooves and wings smashing the creatures from their feet whilst biting others. The knights skewered the enemy on fresh lance tips gifted them from Bratby's camp supplies, then threw aside the long weapons to draw swords which smashed heads as much as cut limbs.

Amis was with Correia now, moving through a series of sword sequences like he was in the training yard, taking lives with every one or two moves as easy as a squire might best a page with a wooden sword.

Goblins fell in good order to the archers near Gleave, but it was the incoming wyverns, the second larger than the first, that stole Gleave's breath. He cursed, looked to Fal who seemed to watch with interest rather than fear; fear for himself or his friends.

The shriek of Captain Hud's hippogriff grabbed Gleave's attention once more and he turned in time to see the woman release a swathe of what looked like pebbles from a bag on her mount's saddle. The smooth white stones lifted into the air as if feathers on a breeze and scattered as if launched from a trebuchet: slow at first, before shooting off into the goblins, taking many from their feet.

Following the ranged assault, Captain Hud launched her mount into the sky, flanked by the rest of her knights. Their mounts' wings beat the air as they climbed away from the pathetic arrows the goblins loosed at them. Royce's Reds were flying hard and fast to regroup with the other two knights, who launched once more into the sky, swords leading, goblin corpses left in their wake. Gleave saw Correia and Amis fighting together in a retreat towards the small camp. He knew she'd be screaming within as much as without, for losing Sav and, now, for leaving his body behind. Gleave shook with rage and bit back a sob as he saw goblins stopping to hack, loot and pull at Sav's corpse. He roared at them, everything else forgotten, as one of the goblins pulled down its trews and defecated on his friend's body.

Gleave surged to his feet, or tried to, crying out in pain as much as anger and frustration as he crashed back down into the cart. Fal stopped him falling from the side. That was something at least, but the man seemed to watch on without any passion, anger, sorrow or fear, of the situation, if nothing else.

Gleave righted himself, shrugged Fal off and watched the sky in sickening horror as the wyverns collided with Royce's Reds. A cerulean flash blinded him for a moment, and when he lowered his instinctively raised hands, to the accompaniment of equine and human screams, Gleave saw the smaller of the wyverns plummeting to the ground where it slammed into a dozen unsuspecting goblins, crushing them all. Gleave looked to Royce's Reds and realised two of them had fallen in the time it'd taken him to raise and lower his hands. He caught glimpses of them amongst the goblins, of twisted limbs and wings; one knight lost to the rising and falling of goblin weapons whilst the other stood, swinging his mace awkwardly, his injuries hindering his hopeless defence. A lucky arrow-strike saved the knight from one goblin's spear-thrust; lucky considering it was at the edge of the war-bows' range. The knight fell after that, too many spears and pole-axes for him to swat aside with his mace, which appeared to gain in weight as his swings slowed, inevitably opening him up to his death. Gleave heard archers curse from off to the side. They were running out of arrows. They'd sent a hail of them down into the massing enemy.

The remaining wyvern roared as it banked, approaching the three remaining red knights, who landed in a thudding of hooves and beating of wings to effect Correia and Amis' exhausted retreat up the hill.

'Run!' Gleave shouted. 'Run!' His voice was hoarse now. He could see how close the goblins were; how close the wyvern was. The remaining arrows arced up towards the beast, which grunted as one found a soft spot. The grunt was like the impact of a trebuchet launched rock upon a wall, and the beast let out three more grunts in quick succession, causing Gleave to flinch at every sound; each flinch marked flashes of pain as he tensed at the same time, reminding him of his wounds and uselessness.

The wyvern crashed into the last two lance tips of the three red knights, snapping them like twigs as it bit through one, the other tearing through its sail-like wing, ripping a hole big enough to ride a destrier through. The large talons at the end of its two legs sunk one into the rider who'd torn its wing, the other into the pegasus of the knight whose lance the wyvern had bitten through. Gleave heard all four, mounts and men, cry out as they crumpled under the weight and blades that were the wyvern's talons. He heard Captain Hud shout too, although her command sounded weak and he feared her magical release had taken more from her than they could afford.

'Run!' Gleave shouted again, to them all; despite knowing they needed no encouragement.

Goblins hung back now, loosing pathetic arrows at the camp, all of which fell short. They were as fearful of the frenzied wyvern as the humans. At least that was something.

Gleave looked across camp and saw archers stood, arrow-less and stunned at what came before them. 'Help them up, you fools!' Gleave shouted, wanting to have their energy and health so he could charge headlong into the fray to protect Correia. She was half way up the hill, swords shining steel once more – clean of blood despite the front of her, face and all, being spattered with the stuff. Amis was much the same, both armour and sword black with the lives he'd taken. He sucked in breaths and blew out hard, as did Correia as they powered up the uneven ground. The sound of chanting goblins, screaming pegasi, barked orders from Hud, and the deafening roar of the thrashing, snapping and lashing wyvern following them up.

Gleave sensed movement to his side and shouted for them to wait as the archers left the camp. None came to his or Fal's aid. They just ran, and part of him couldn't blame them. Correia and Amis neared Gleave's position and Correia yelled at the archers to hold and make a line. Two obeyed, the rest fled across the fields, bows forgotten.

There was a concussive thud that Gleave felt in his chest. He flinched again, from the impact of it, and when he looked back down the hill, he saw the wyvern climbing back to its feet, surrounded by flattened, unmoving goblins in a twenty-foot cone from Hud's position. The captain sagged in her saddle. One of her own rode up alongside her, his left arm hanging limp at his side, his bascinet's visor lost and his face awash with blood. Yet he managed to stop his captain from falling. Gleave realised they were the only two left from Royce's Reds. The pegasus and the hippogriff were well trained and ascended the hill, their reins loose. Gleave balked at the destruction, at the loss that had occurred in such a short space of time. He balked all the more when he saw the wyvern advancing once more, when he heard it roar as it tried to beat the air with its wings; the hole in one like the clipping of a hen's flight feathers. It tried to lift from the ground and lurched to the side, crashing into the earth, its teeth-filled maw scooping sods of grass and dirt as it ploughed a short furrow. It roared again and rather than trying to take flight, locked its tiny eyes on its escaping prey and charged. Gleave knew it to be over. There was no way the winged mounts of Hud and her man would climb the hill before the beast reached them. There were no arrows left for the two stoic archers, not that it would have done much good against the wyvern from what he'd seen. The only fighting men and women left were spent, and—

A pathetic crow startled Gleave. The sound came from behind him and again from beneath the cart he sat atop. With a mix of joyous confusion, incredulity and fear, Gleave watched as Pecker emerged from beneath the cart on a wing-flapping ridiculous charge down the hill. She half-flew and half-bounded towards the ascending wyvern, its muscular legs propelling it up, its head low and neck straight like the biggest – living – ballistae arrow.

'Pecker!' Gleave found himself shouting as Correia and Amis made the cart. Gleave looked at Correia, but she didn't meet his eyes. He noticed Fal glaring at her, but she seemed not to see that either. Fal's eyes bore into her back as she took the driver's seat, Amis slumping onto the bench beside her. As Correia relieved the break and snapped the reins, the cart lurched forward and Gleave rocked as he looked back towards the mixed sound of a roaring wyvern and a crowing, overgrown hen.

'We won't make it,' Amis said, more to himself than anything, as he looked back past Gleave, who'd glanced at him.

Gleave swallowed hard and felt a shudder run through his body. His eyes welled and he failed to bite back a sob at it all. Hud and her man reached the top of the hill, where the wyvern closed on them, a hen the only thing between it and its prize.

'So, this is it…' Gleave slammed his fist into his own leg and raged against it all. *Torn to shreds on the back of a fucking cart, my body broken and friends lost—*

Gleave practically choked as he saw the wyvern lunge towards the tail of Hud's hippogriff, the vile beast ignorant of the fat, brown hen in its path; Gleave practically choked as the flapping feathers and grass-flicking feet of his hen, his Pecker, exploded in a rapid expansion of wings and torso, beak and talons. Gleave gasped and cried out in both surprise and awe as Pecker grew in a flash of feathers and scales to barrel into and turn over the lunging wyvern, her now equal size a match for the reptilian beast. Her giant hooked beak and lashing talons ripped scales from flesh, dug rents of red into the brown hide of the wyvern. Her crow caused everyone to duck, be them men, women or goblins below, their renewed advance halted as the cockatrice tore shreds from the surprised wyvern beneath her.

Hud's mount shrieked and bucked, and her knight's pegasus attempted but failed to throw him because of the sounds coming from the titanic battle behind them. Bolting, with renewed energy, Hud and her man reached Gleave's cart as he watched large scales and feathers fly; blood and flesh doing the same. The two beasts tumbled down the hill together in a fight like none he'd ever seen. It reminded him of the very cock fighting pits he'd rescued Pecker from. The fact that the so-called hen was a legendary, shape-shifting cockatrice… Gleave shuddered.

Their cart pulled away as fast as it could, Hud and her man riding close behind, with Mits and his remaining men running to catch up, their tent-laden cart and supplies forgotten. Almost all of them watched the continuing brawl between beasts below, but Gleave turned to Correia and saw that she looked not back, at what most of them couldn't draw their eyes from, but forward, to nothing; to the road and nothing more. And he knew her pain. He knew the love she had held for Sav, and so it was, despite the cheers that arose about him as he turned back to see the scattering goblins below, that Gleave felt none of the joy the others felt as Pecker finished the wyvern with a stretching, tearing and rending of thick head from scaled neck. For Gleave had lost too much to rejoice now, even at the sight of his incredible pet turning for and running to catch him up, shrinking back to her former state as she did so, despite the lack of feathers and open wounds she sported.

Chapter 53 – No matter the cost

Hud half-turned in her saddle as she heard footsteps approaching from behind the group. The movement pained her, and as soon as she saw who it was – as soon as she was satisfied it wasn't a renewed attack – she faced forward and slumped once more, clenching teeth against the wounds she'd suffered both physically and mentally whilst battling the wyverns.

'They're not pursuing,' Mits said, as he caught up to the cart and hopped onto the back. He started when he saw the battered and bleeding hen in Gleave's arms.

'It's alright,' Gleave reassured Mits. 'Trust me.'

Mits nodded, although he looked far from convinced that the hen wouldn't explode into the beast it had been and tear him to pieces.

'Then we stop,' Correia said, without turning from the driver's bench. 'Bind wounds. Make plans.'

Mits scoffed. 'I say we continue and deal with such things whilst on the move.'

'We stop and someone else might get left behind,' Fal said, eyes boring into Correia's back. He turned and snarled at a nudge and glower from Gleave.

'Correia's right,' Hud said, slumped in her saddle, alongside the cart. 'Your elf and the witchblade have a head start on us to Royce. We need to rest up and get you there too, Correia.' The women met eyes.

Correia swallowed hard, her stern visage set in place, as if sculpted. Not a feature twitched or moved as she nodded her accord. After stopping the cart, causing gasps for air and prayers of thanks from the remaining archers who'd been dog-trotting alongside, Correia jumped off and approached Hud. 'With me,' she said. It wasn't a request. She walked off the road, towards a standing of thick gorse, and Hud followed, or rather her mount did, Hud doing little to guide the intelligent creature. *I need to take her to Royce and yet I'm struggling to stay in the saddle.* She accepted the pain that came whilst leaning forward and stroking her mount's feathered neck. The hippogriff let out a sound not too dissimilar to a cat's purr. Hud knew it to be understanding from her mount.

'How do we do this?' Correia said, eyes past Hud, to the group parked on the road.

'Correia—'

'What?' Correia glared at Hud. 'Don't,' she said, before Hud could say anymore. 'Just don't. Plans are what we need, what we'll discuss, not feelings or emotions or losses…'

Hud watched the war within the women she barely knew. She watched the hardness crack, but no sooner had those cracks appeared had Correia smoothed them over. *Smoothed over,* Hud thought, *not hardened or repaired, despite Correia's face. She wears her mask well. Too well.* Hud thought of her own face. Scars and such. So different to how it had been years ago. She thought about the mask she often wore too, to hide her fears and hesitations, to ensure her knights, men all, followed her without question. She thought of the few she let in. The knights closest to her that she allowed the mask to fall away for, on occasion, so they knew she was real, human, vulnerable even. They had to know. They had to feel for her as she felt for them, to know that she valued them and would die for them as they would for her. As they had… She fought back tears at the thought of those lost. Her closest. There was but three left, the two who'd flown at first light and the one slumped in his saddle alongside the cart on the road behind her. She had brought her best, her longest serving to retrieve Correia and now, with war looming, she felt alone. Despite the numbers she commanded in Royce's Reds, all but three of her true friends were gone. Her brothers. For that's what they'd become. Steeling herself, like Correia was, Hud gritted her teeth and nodded once. *Perhaps she's already lost the ones she'd reveal her true self to, as have I. There's no time for it now.*

'We need to get you to Royce and on to Wesson, no matter the cost.'

'I'm aware of that.'

You're not making this easy, woman. Hud sighed. 'And do you think I look like I can make that journey, Correia? Does my one remaining man look like he can?'

It was Correia's turn to grit her teeth. Jaw muscles bunching, she shook her head.

'I'm suggesting something I've never done before, nor even thought of.'

'Go on,' Correia said, blood-soiled arms folding across blood-soiled chest.

Hud winced and leaned forward, patting the neck of her hippogriff. 'Take my steed and choose one other able bodied man to take my knight's pegasus. You don't need to guide them, they know their way and are fit enough to carry you.' Correia made to speak, but Hud continued. 'They'll not fare well in another fight, nor are you trained to fight aback either mount—'

'I know that—'

'Listen, will you?'

Correia snarled, but she nodded all the same.

'Avoid any contact with any enemy, Correia. No matter how easy it may look to be; no matter how tempting after what we've… well.'

'Well,' Correia repeated.

Both women took in deep breaths and held each other's gaze.

'What will you two do?' Correia asked, arms remaining folded; defensive.

She's not arguing the point or questioning my idea then. 'We'll stick with Mits and your men for now and I'll figure out what to do as I go. I'm not sure when I'll be fit to do anything but sit on that cart. I took more damage than is visible in—'

'I understand,' Correia said, not coldly, but it was clear she wanted to get on with their plan.

Hud slid from the saddle, painfully, and was surprised to have Correia help her to the floor. 'You understand you'll be leaving your injured,' she said, passing the reins to Correia.

'I was anyway. Seems to be what I'm good at.'

Hud scoffed. 'Please.'

Correia rocked back.

'You're not the only commander to leave injured and move on. You're not the only one to lose men in the field. I lost—'

'The man you love?' Correia snapped, face red, bottom lip quivering. 'The man you just realised you loved. *Just* realised, Hud. Too late!'

Hud's stomach turned. *Oh love,* she thought, feeling her own lip going. She shook her head. 'Not quite,' she managed, 'but close enough. Brothers lost, practically.' She could tell Correia didn't dare speak for fear of breaking. For fear of losing her mask completely. Correia nodded and chewed her bottom lip, nostrils flaring in grief more than anger. Hud wanted to hug the woman, which wasn't something she wanted to do often, of anyone, but she wanted to. She needed it herself, after all. But she didn't. They both stood strong, eyeing one another, helping one another find their stoicism and resolve once more.

'It's decided,' Correia said.

Hud had waited for the woman to speak first, for fear of breaking her with any more words. 'It's decided,' Hud agreed, nodding with it. She felt incredibly weak. She hated the thought of her mount being ridden away by another. Not even her knights rode her. She feared never seeing her again, but forced it all down and away. It was the only way. Royce had ordered Correia to him before she was to move on to Wesson, and Hud must have it done, if not see it done. She also knew she could ride no more. Nor could her remaining knight. She looked over the red fur of her wolf-skin and saw the man standing, stroking his mount. Stroking it and leaning against it, left arm hanging at his side, useless.

'Dislocated?' Correia asked.

'He thinks so. I think so and you do too.' Hud turned and offered Correia a weak smile.

Correia nodded. 'Best see to him then, and yourself. You'll be able to strip armour and do that on the cart. Mits and his men can help with that. I'm taking de Valmont.'

It was Hud's turn to nod. 'Come,' Hud said, turning and heading back to the road, 'I shall tell you what you need to know so you can ride her to Royce, successfully.'

'I appreciate that,' Correia said, leading the hippogriff, which pulled at the reins as they walked.

'It's not for your benefit, but hers,' Hud said, a wry smile playing across her scarred face at the fond memories, recent and old, of her mount's quirky ways.

Fal watched Correia and Amis launch into the sky atop their gifted mounts. It made him think about the gifted mounts they'd received in Broadleaf Forest, from the elves. Correia seemed to do well at being given things despite the amount she took from people. The lives she took and threw away. Dignaaln had been right to tell Fal to watch how she used folk. The emissary had been right to tell Fal that she would lose more of his friends, leave more behind, if she ever came for him at all. *Well,* he thought, watching the winged beasts carry her and her new companion away, *she might have come for me, or rather for information, but it didn't take long for her to prove Dignaaln right. Starksy boy and then Sav. And now? Now Gleave and me too. Left again, and for what? Because the Earl of Royce has clicked his fingers, sent his red dogs to fetch her. How quickly we are forgotten.*

'What?' Fal snapped, realising Gleave had been trying to talk to him. Gleave flinched then scowled, although the expression was replaced with one of sympathy. *Oh, here we go,* Fal thought. *He's going to attempt to engage me in friendly chat or banter, as if all was well, as if—*

'Fal?' Gleave said again, brow creased. The cart lurched forward and they rocked at the motion. 'You keep disappearing somewhere; drifting off.'

'And?' Fal said. *What The Three has it to do with you?*

Gleave heaved in a breath.

'Leave him,' Hud's knight said, wincing as the archers helped him off with his armour to see to his wounds. His words were weak. He was weak. 'He's clearly not wanting to talk.'

'What's it to you?' Fal said, turning on the man. He snarled at him, scoffed and laughed. 'You're all the same,' Fal said, slumping back down into the cart to watch the clouds.

'All the same how?' the knight said, iron in his tone.

'Steady now.' Gleave held his hands up, one per man.

'Since when were you the peacemaker, Gleave Picton?' Fal couldn't stand hearing Gleave's voice, let alone have him try to talk to or defend or placate, or *anything* him. 'Leave me be.' Fal heard Gleave start to say something else, but Hud cut him off with a comment Fal missed. He'd given up bothering to listen, for now. Watching the clouds, he thought about the instruction he'd overheard Hud giving Correia and her new man, Amis de Valmont. Fal grinned. Now there was a man that interested Fal. *Not as clean-cut as he makes out,* Fal reckoned. A fair fighter, that much had become clear, but not as emotionally delicate as he likes to project. *To get the women?* Fal shrugged. *Do I really care?* Sighing and tapping the back of his head against the wood of the cart, Fal thought about his shorn hair, which matched the stubble of his face. He brushed at the bristles with his fingers and winced, catching nail-less and mangled tips on the sharp bristles; he'd removed his bindings, sick of how they made him feel. *Shut up and keep your head down, Fal,* he thought, cursing himself for snapping so much at everyone. *Keep your head down and do as Dignaaln asked you, nothing else.* And so he waited, for the cart to cross the miles and the sky to darken until they made camp, where he could listen to the group's innate babbling about shit and bollocks before grabbing some much needed sleep. For there was a lot approaching in his life. Deeds to be done and masters to please.

***

333

Errolas was worried, Salliss could see it in his eyes. Eyes searching the white clouds and blue skies above Landon Hill for sign of Correia and the others. Salliss was happy to have been accepted into Lord Temn's castle and the earldom of Royce without trouble. It helped that they had two of Royce's Reds escorting them, although the men were far from friendly towards her. She couldn't help but laugh at that, being that their captain was also a mage. *Witch.* She ran the word around her mouth, whispering it to herself. She was indeed a witch: a witchblade. The Queen's elite, witches all. But so too was Captain Hud. They just used different terms for what they did in Altoln.

'Salliss?' Errolas asked, looking across the bay pegasus they were brushing down.

They don't mind me grooming their mounts, she mused, before smiling at the handsome elf. *Handsome?* The thought shocked her. Not because he wasn't, but because it had popped into her head, after all the time she'd spent with him. 'Yes?' she said, sure her face flushed red.

'Your whispering, I…' He trailed off and smiled.

'Could hear it,' she finished for him. Errolas nodded. 'Musing aloud,' she said. Her Altoln was flowing better than ever. It was one thing to be taught it and to speak it on occasion, it was another thing entirely to be surrounded by it.

Errolas smiled again and continued brushing the proud pegasus. The animals were calmer when he was around. Bred in Royce and trained in the same ways as destriers, the beasts were positively terrifying up close. Snapping their teeth at stable hands, at anyone that passed for that matter, and threatening to lash out with iron-shod hooves at any given opportunity. Even their thick wing-arms, for want of a better name, could land quite the blow. Salliss had seen it already. The poor lad who'd attended them as soon as they'd landed in the castle's yard had been knocked from his feet by one. Salliss could have sworn she'd heard ribs break. She fretted about the young lad now she came to think of him. He'd been rushed off to the infirmary after the incident, although the knight whose pegasus had lashed out seemed more concerned with the animal's wing than the boy. *Bastards,* she thought, and brushed a little harder at the beast's dark brown neck. The pegasus huffed, its hide shuddering, right across its flank.

'It's been too long,' Errolas said, eyeing the sky once more.

Stopping brushing, he walked out into the centre of the yard and squinted.

'What is it?' Salliss asked, doing the same. She shielded her eyes with her free hand, a cloud revealing the late afternoon sun.

Errolas sighed and shook his head. 'Nothing.' He pulled his delicate lips into a tight smile and looked at her. 'Let's eat,' he said, taking her by the shoulder and guiding her towards the food hall where the knights had gone.

'I thought you would never ask.' She smiled back. Smiled too much, she feared, flushing once more. 'They will be here soon, I am sure,' she said, trying to comfort Errolas. 'Correia probably wanted to spend more time with Gleave and Fal before leaving them...' She noticed Errolas' face drop at the mention of his Orismaran friend. 'Errolas?'

He wore his tight smile again and motioned for her to enter the hall. 'I'm fine,' he said, following her in.

I don't need to be a witchblade to know that's untrue. 'Alright,' she said, leaving him to his worries. 'Let us eat.'

Chapter 54 – Landon Hill

The hippogriff started to descend. Correia was doing her best to snuggle into the red wolf furs Hud had given her. It was freezing, almost literally, despite it being summer and southern Altoln. The sun was dropping to the horizon, so she figured it would be getting colder as they flew on, but she wasn't sure how much more of it she could take; how much more of anything she could take. Correia shook that sort of thinking away and moved her shoulders under the furs, doing her best to stop her teeth from chattering at the same time. The wolf fur stunk, but she was glad of its warmth.

'There!'

Correia looked across to Amis, who was as wrapped as she was, albeit less slumped and huddled in his saddle. His back was straight, arm outstretched. She wasn't sure how he dared let go to point. Correia had flown with both gloved hands on the reins the entire journey. Steeling herself and leaning out a little, vertigo threatening to take her, she looked down, squinting against the wind, and saw the shape of a castle on the horizon. Not a huge one, but a castle all the same, a spread of buildings falling away from it, the town rolling down the hill like a spillage of homes and stores and smoke producing smithies.

'Landon Hill?' Amis shouted, both hands back on the reins of his pegasus, despite the animal, like the hippogriff, deftly guiding them towards the castle below.

'I don't know where these animals have brought us,' Correia shouted back, too cold to think of memorised maps or topography. She was too cold to care. 'I don't know,' she shouted again, 'but it's red brick, so it's in Royce's earldom for sure.' The red bricks of the structure looked like the castle was made of iron and rusted solid as they glided towards it.

'I keep thinking they'll start to shoot at us.' Amis laughed with the shouted comment. The laugh was half humour, half fear, Correia knew.

'I'm sure they'll know,' she replied, unsure of her own reassurance. *I hope they do.* The thought of arrows spiralling up to meet them, perhaps even ballistae, made her think for the umpteenth time of Sav. And each time it took her a heartbeat to get to his fall; his death... his sacrifice for her. Each time she had a flare of wonder and excitement and warmth at what they could be when all this was over. And, every time, came the fall and the cold and dread and emptiness— no, not emptiness. Guilt. Guilt and hate and self-loathing for his loss; for Starks' loss too, and Mearson and Tom and the rest. But most of all Sav's. Her Sav. The thought kept coming to her: her Sav. Kept slapping her in the face and threatening to throw her from the saddle to plummet to the ground that now rose to meet them. The furs did nothing to take the chill from her tear-streaked cheeks. Sniffing for the hundredth time, Correia pictured her father, and brother, Edward, and what was to befall Altoln in the coming months, if not years of war. *Stop your selfish melancholy, woman.* Anger washed through her like liquid fire. *There's more to all this than you and your feelings. It's why you shouldn't have let yourself—*

The hippogriff screeched high-low, startling Correia from her thoughts.

'Here we go,' Amis called.

Correia gripped the reins tighter than ever, knuckles surely white under her near on useless-in-the-cold gloves, and gritted her teeth. Red walls with patterned crenellations shot up to meet them as the beasts flared their feathered wings and spiralled down into the outer bailey, where Correia breathed a sigh of relief to see familiar faces looking up at them: two stern faced knights, a woman and a relieved elf. She heard a bell ringing and realised it must have been for them. Crossbowmen dotted the walls, tracing their descent with loaded weapons of varying sizes. Mounted men-at-arms sat atop destriers at one end of the yard, moving away only when one of Royce's Reds shouted that all was well.

As the crossbowmen stood down, the winged mounts touched down, and Correia felt an overwhelming rush of relief. It had been different with Hud in control of the hippogriff. Scary, but exhilarating, whereas this time it had been plain terrifying. 'Errolas!' Correia heard herself shout through numb lips.

Errolas ran ahead of the two red knights, using his elven ways to calm the hippogriff and pegasus he rushed towards. Reaching them, he took both sets of reins and the animals settled, nuzzling equine head and giant beak against his neck and chest.

'Errolas,' Correia said again, as he frowned, eyes turning skyward once more. She saw the witchblade and knights do the same.

'Correia…' he began to ask, before drinking in the emotions playing across her face.

She fell from the saddle, the weight of it all, and her injuries, proving too much. She'd had the chance to fall and she didn't stop it, couldn't stop it. The last thing she felt and saw was Errolas catching and cradling her like a babe, before exhaustion took her.

'Well, Lady Burr?'

'I don't know, Lord Temn.' Correia felt anger more than frustration now. She didn't have all the answers and she was becoming sick of everyone demanding them of her. She'd slept well – that annoyed her, angered her – and she'd eaten well. Had the others, back on the road to Castle Bratby, or wherever Mits was taking them? Were they even on the road, on course? She shuddered and she drank, yet another glass of southern red.

Temn of Landon Hill, Baronial Marcher Lord of Altoln, opened his fat mouth to speak. He shut it again at the raising of Correia's free hand. His nostrils flared and he chewed his wine-stained bottom lip, but he held his purple tongue.

'I've decided...' Correia said, although she admitted to herself that she was making it up as she went; the time to weigh all the odds as she usually would, the time to plan, was lost to her. She'd paused and Temn had leaned forward, chewing stopped, piggy-eyes wide. 'I've decided,' she went on, 'to fly north with—'

'On Captain Hud's mount? With her *company's* mounts?' Temn sat back in his protesting chair and huffed.

'Yes!' Correia snapped. He'd told her, when she'd woke, that a rider had come in that night with news for her. For her! There, in Landon Hill. The urgency in which she needed to go to Wesson had increased. No reasons were given, but nor did she need any. Her father needed her, according to Will Morton, and so she would fly. There was no time for Royce, for petitions and for journey by ship, where weather could hinder her far more than it could across land... albeit in the air. Still, it became clear as she decided it that even if a storm blew up across Alton, Correia and her companions could ride rather than fly. Swap mounts even, if it came to it, unlike travelling by weather dependant ship. Hud would understand. She'd have to.

'Well, Lady Burr, I'm not sure what the captain—'

'I don't care what she'll think or say or do, my lord Temn.' Correia stood. 'Your King requires my presence immediately. Would you defy him?'

Temn shot to his feet. If you could call it a shooting. 'Of course not! How dare you—'

'I dare a lot and I win a lot, my lord. Now do as I command you on our King's behalf and send riders as we discussed. Send riders and make ready for war. I have no time to discuss this further. You must act and Royce must act. We all must act if we're to hold the borders, The Marches, as is your duty and his; it is what Giles Bratby is doing. Now have me attended whilst I see to my own.'

Blustering and flapping and practically bursting at the seams, the red-faced baron stormed from the room, servants hurrying before and after him, curses flowing from him.

After a ragged breath, Correia reached over and finished the last of the man's wine before striding from the room.

***

Booted feet and iron spurs echoed off the courtyard's tall walls as half a dozen green liveried men-at-arms walked from the stables to the door of Wesson's magistrates court.

'Hold.' The sergeant of the court stepped out from a second doorway, a man on either side. All three wore burgundy, two padded gambesons and the sergeant's brigandine. All three touched hands to sheathed swords.

'This is Stowold, now fucking move,' the hard-looking man at the front of the approaching group said, without slowing. His richly embroidered, long green surcoat was bested only by the man behind him, whose eyes were the only pair not on the three guardsmen.

The court's sergeant stammered a protest, but ultimately followed as the Earl's men marched past and into the magistrates' building.

'Not sure that was quite necessary, Sir Bryant,' Stowold said, once inside.

Sir Bryant shrugged as he continued leading the way down a corridor. 'You said there's no time to waste, my lord.'

'That I did, Sir Bryant. That I did.'

They turned a corner and moved down another corridor. The sound of maille and plate marked their path. Employees of the magistrates moved aside and bowed respectfully as the men walked with speed and purpose.

Knight at his front and retainers and magistrates' men at his back, Stowold strode towards a cluster of guards and clerks, all of which turned in surprise at the procession heading their way.

'Move aside,' Sir Bryant said, waving his hand as if bothered by flies.

'You can't go in there,' one of the clerks dared, narrow eyes flicking from armoured man to armoured man.

'He's the Constable of Wesson,' came a shout from the back, from the court's sergeant. 'Let him through!'

The two new guards stood firm, barring the way. 'Sorry, milord, but court's in session. No one passes but the King.'

The clerks pressed themselves against the walls either side of the corridor and doors, as most of the approaching men made to draw swords.

'Move aside, you cads.' Stowold shouldered past Sir Bryant, taking the lead. His lack of acknowledgement that the guards were even a threat was what moved them in the end, for Stowold was the only man not to have hand on blade. They turned in time to open the double doors for the Earl, who entered the courtroom beyond to a series of gasps and cries of outrage.

Stowold's eyes locked on the lead magistrate's, who shrank back under the visual assault. Stowold pointed to a lone man stood in the centre of the room who looked filthy, dishevelled, but determined, stoic and strong with it.

'This man is under my protection and employ. Release him at once so I can get back to my estate. I have wasted enough time this day.'

The room fell silent. The man in the centre of the room turned, eyes wide.

'Well?' Stowold said, hands on hips. He looked at the red bearded man stood alone and winked, before looking about the room. 'I'm the Constable of Wesson and I demand his release. Now!'

'You heard my lord Stowold,' Sir Bryant said, walking the perimeter of the room, staring down any who would dare look at him.

'This is the magistrates' court, my lord.' The magistrate to the left of the lead magistrate stood, face reddening. 'I don't care who orders this man released. If you're not King Barrison, this criminal stands trial and that's the end of it. I won't be shouted down in our own court—'

'You will and you have.' Without so much as a glance to the magistrate who'd addressed him, Stowold turned and left the room, muttering one last thing to one of his men before he left. 'He's all yours, Biviano.'

Biviano nodded once and looked to his shackled friend.

Sears grinned.

The magistrates and their assembly descended into verbal chaos as their sergeant and guardsmen stood by and watched the Earl's liveried men escort their prisoner out of the courtroom and away.

Chapter 55 – Reunion

Sears grimaced as he looked down the devastated street. Hollowed out and blackened homes flanked them as they rode along. The remnants of black crosses on doors were visible, although some had been painted over, the wood fresh and clean in appearance.

'Can you believe it?' Sears said, a tumultuous flow of memories assaulting him as he rode beside his friend.

'Believe what, ye cock? You getting arrested?'

Sears glanced sidelong at Biviano. 'No, ye weasel. All of this.' He waved his thinner-than-normal arm to encompass the destruction about them.

Biviano grunted. 'It was worse, wasn't it, mate. Least it's improving, slowly.'

There was a pause filled by the near-deafening sound of iron-shod hooves on cobbles and the chatter of the surrounding men-at-arms.

'Where's our new employer gone?' Sears asked.

'Back to his city estate I presume, Sears, and he's not our employer. That position is still held by the King and his City Guard, for now.'

Sears turned to Biviano, a frown creasing his filthy brow.

Biviano looked back at him. 'Stowold only said that to get you out, you ungrateful prick.'

'You're wearing his colours, Biviano.'

'Wouldn't have looked much like Stowold's retainer if I weren't now, would I? Ye puss filled bubo. Ye certainly stink as bad as a plague victim.' He grinned at that one.

Sears sneered. 'Hardly funny considering—'

'What, the plague?' Biviano barked a laugh and looked to the riders in front again as they rounded a corner, scaring a cat from where it sunned itself in the middle of the road. 'Making jests about what's past won't change owt, Sears. Ye gone soft in that red head of yours whilst incarcerated by the good magistrates of Wesson, for however many days and weeks? I couldn't be bothered counting.' He looked back to Sears. When no reply came, not even a glance, Biviano huffed and looked forward once more. 'Thought it'd be fun to break you out. Thought it'd be fun to have you back.' He looked at Sears yet again, awaiting a response.

'I don't want to talk about any of it. Not right now.'

Sniffing and shrugging, Biviano nodded. 'Right ye are man, right ye are. Well, it's to the tavern for us. Stowold reckoned ye could do with a good watering before we decide what we're to do next.'

'And that is?' Sears said, eyes locked ahead.

'Well I don't know, do I? Ye shit. Hence the need for a drink first. I reckon the good Earl thought it'd be a celebration. More like a wake if ye keep this crying up.' That got a response.

Sears turned in his saddle, reached across and thumped Biviano on the maille covered arm.

Biviano cursed, then smiled. 'That's more like it, big guy.'

Stowold's men peeled off down a side street, waving their goodbyes. Sears frowned after he waved back.

'They're off on errands for Stowold. It's just thee and me again, Sears. And as for what we do now, that's down to us two.'

'And he's alright with that, the Constable of Wesson? Insists on my release and goes back to his own business, all casual like?' Sears shook his head and grunted a laugh. *Not likely,* he thought. 'There'll be repercussions for him, doing that. Even him.'

'Let's just say, ye ungrateful ginger get, that Stowold likes me enough to let me owe him a favour in light of what he did back there, for you!'

'For you, ye mean. Ye'd be lost without me, Biviano, and ye know it.'

'Enough farting from ye mouth. We can talk between supping ale.' Before Sears could reply, Biviano kicked his heels into the flank of the horse Stowold had loaned him and aimed it towards the nearest tavern, Sears a horse-length behind.

***

A colourful gaggle of courtiers and other hangers on shuffled through the formal rose gardens of Wesson Palace, their King at the head, an armed and armoured Earl walking by his side, hands clasped behind his back. Crossbowmen in Barrison's red and blue livery adorned the surrounding ramparts, eyes watchful for any sudden or suspicious moves; half the crossbows loaded, half not, switching on a rotational basis.

'At a time like this, Bagnall?' Barrison asked of Stowold. They stopped to appreciate a white marble fountain, the water of which caught the summer sunlight as would a troop of glittered faerie-folk.

'I am afraid I must, Your Highness.'

Barrison moved on, Stowold matching his pace, the garish gaggle following.

'We need the City Guard at full strength, Bagnall, as you very well know. Wesson is at its worse: lawless in many parts, vulnerable as a whole. Guilds war with one another for new trade rights as new gangs try and assert their dominance in Dockside, and beyond! Can you not recruit for your household from outside the city?' Barrison looked to Stowold, who returned the look with a solemn shake of the head.

'Sire, the City Guard recruit men to crack the heads of louts and layabouts. I'm recruiting men to fight an ongoing war beneath our feet; the biggest threat to Wesson, to Altoln, in my eyes. I haven't the time nor the men to train fresh recruits from the counties and shires, nor those plucked from the streets of Dockside. I cannot effectively go on with my duties as both Constable of Wesson and Watcher of the Deep without experienced men at my back.'

Barrison pulled his lips tight and nodded. He stopped to stare at a rose bush with white petals. The shuffling behind him stopped.

'And your removal of a prisoner from the magistrates' court, Bagnall?' Barrison's eyes remained on the white ruffles of roses.

Blued plate scraped as Stowold shifted where he stood. 'Ah, yes. News travels quicker than I can, it seems,' he admitted, drawing a smile from Barrison. 'Well, Sire, he is one of the ones I would recruit. Invaluable he is, to me.'

'As is his friend?' Barrison glanced sidelong at Stowold, who nodded once.

'As is his friend, yes.'

'Whom you attempted to knight, not so long ago?'

'The very same, Sire.'

Hiding his true feelings, as a good king oft should, Barrison showed a face of disapproval and continued to walk, the roses changing from white to powdered pink, red to orange and on to yellow as they walked in silence, the shuffling and murmuring behind them ceaseless.

'Tell me,' Barrison said as they walked, 'of the accusations concerning the one called Sears; he breathes fire, they say.'

'He does, Sire.'

Barrison hid his smile and stopped. He rounded on Stowold, eyebrows high. He was curious as to what Stowold thought of the fire breathing man, and whether it would match the thoughts of Barrison's brother-in-law and friend, Will Morton.

'It is true, my liege. He does indeed breathe fire, although I have yet to witness it for myself.'

'And you want him free? You want him in your keep, this man who breathes fire?'

A nod. 'I do, to both. As I said, he is invaluable to me. Imagine that skill in a tunnel defence.'

Barrison licked his lips at that and nodded. He did indeed imagine it, as vibrant and orange as the roses they passed. As violent and red as more of the same. 'And that's what you want him and his companion for, is it? That's why you broke the law, my law, to free him? You want him for tunnel clearances in the Deep?'

A pause and Stowold pursed his lips. 'Amongst other things, Your Highness.'

Barrison sighed. 'Do I even want to know, Bagnall?'

Stowold smiled. 'Probably not, Sire.'

'Would Will want to know?'

'Definitely not, Sire. The Duke has enough to tend with, although I'd wager on him smiling at the possible outcome of what I have in mind.'

Barrison sighed. 'You two will be the death of me, and constables both.'

'Don't say that, Sire.' Stowold took a step forward, hand held out as if to comfort his King.

Barrison waved the hand and words away. 'Very well,' he said. 'Your word, and Will's, are good enough for me. I've enough to worry about without you two adding to it. So, I shall leave my constables to their business whilst I tend to my own.'

Stowold bowed his head. 'Of course, Sire. Thank you.'

There was a pause again, within which a falcon screeched from the opposite end of the garden. The courtiers mumbled and whispered and Barrison looked about, from crossbowman to crossbowman, halberdier to halberdier, stationed here and there as they were; hardly noticeable when seen daily, like furniture or servants of the palace.

'I'm surprised Sergeant Grannit allowed you an audience, armed and armoured as you are, Bagnall.' Barrison rose one eyebrow and took in Stowold's impressive battle-scene-inscribed plate and the serpent coiled drum tower on his green silk surcoat.

Stowold smiled. 'Grannit and I have an understanding, Sire.'

'Go on,' Barrison said.

'He lets me pass and I don't push a length of good steel through

345

his hard face.'

Barrison couldn't help but snort a laugh. 'Well quite,' he said, shoulders bobbing with continued mirth as he played Stowold's words over in his mind. He sighed, then smiled at Stowold. 'I need more humour about me, Bagnall,' Barrison admitted. 'It seems to have left my court of late... since the plague that nearly stole my life.'

'Alas, that is not surprising, Your Highness, with all that is going on. Although,' he said, a smirk pulling at his lips and eyes, 'I wasn't entirely joking, regarding your good sergeant.'

Another smile graced Barrison's face and he felt the warmth of it flush through him. Shaking his head through nought but amusement, he whisked his hand in the air at Stowold. 'Now be off,' he said jovially. 'Be off to do the things I'd probably not want to know about.'

With a low, slow bow of the head and a sincere smile of his own, Bagnall Stowold turned and pushed through the gaggle of followers who'd been doing their level best to listen in.

Barrison sighed once more, relieved to have such men as Stowold and Morton about him. He continued his lonely walk, despite his courtiers and chamberlain, who was swift to his side.

Chapter 56 – Cruel to be kind

Sears swayed a little and grimaced. 'Fucking sun,' he slurred, lifting his hand to shield his eyes. 'S'pposed to be night.'

'Shut up, prick.' Biviano bustled past him, Stowold's dark green livery augmented with patterns of sick, an orange chunk or two stuck like poorly adorned badges of honour.

Biviano led the way, feeling along the wall of the Guild District tavern, the stone and lime-mortar exterior smooth in places, rough in others. Biviano stumbled, stopped and frowned, eyes wide as his hand brushed across a wool-textured, double-bumpy surface.

'Hey!' A shrill woman's voice.

Squinting, Biviano looked to the wool, the bumps, above which the voice had come from.

'Unhand me at once!'

Biviano looked up and sucked in a breath, cried out as the powerful slap stung his cheek and turned it in one. Sears sniggered from above and behind him. The woman whose breast Biviano's hand remained clamped on was glaring from red-rimmed eyes that hung in a face of blotchy scars, presumably caused by the recent plague. She slapped his hand away when he failed to move it himself. The following, second facial slap spun him, nearly floored him.

Sears laughed, hands on belly. He didn't see the knee coming up, but he bloody well felt it crunch his prize goods.

Spinning on Sears as the woman cursed and pushed the big, bent over man to the ground and stormed off, Biviano felt his mouth water, the sudden turn being too quick for his vision to keep up with. As Sears pulled his knees up into a foetal position on the ground, Biviano decorated him in patterns to match his own augmented livery. They may not have *both* been wearing Stowold's green, but at least they both wore patches of the same lump and chunk textured orange.

Biviano couldn't be sure whether it was the knee to his friend's tackle, or his own spraying and the smell that followed, that caused Sears to follow suit. Less of a projectile spray than Biviano's, Sears' sick simply splattered on the cobbles next to his head, followed by a stringy gobbet of vomit which slid down and through his red bearded cheek, matting it and joining red hairs here and there with yellow and orange web-like patterns. Biviano found himself leaning in, crouching unsteadily. He squinted and studied the patterns, for

347

no reason he could fathom, before finishing off what he'd started and covering Sears in the rest of the contents of his stomach. The hard work done, Biviano took a deep breath, stood, held his arms out to account for the shifting of the street and building before him, and continued on his way, calling for Sears to follow.

Somehow, Sears did, although his eyes were but slits and his steps those of a toddler braving a new world at a slightly higher altitude.

'Is good have ye back, shit,' Biviano said, mouth now dry rather than wet, his teeth the driest of the lot and feeling as furry as Sears' face.

'Tis good be back, Bivs...'

Biviano held both arms high in the air and meandered his way down the road, Sears' hands now resting on his shoulders. 'Onward!' Biviano shouted. 'On, to vic'ry and honour!'

Sears roared and pushed Biviano on, oblivious to the dozens of disgusted – some amused – eyes upon them. And on they went, heading towards... well, neither of them had the faintest clue where, but it was good to be back together, despite having lost the Earl of Stowold's horses and the saddles and harnesses that came with them, in a game of poorly played nine men's morris that would come to cost them more than a year's wages each.

Chapter 57 – Bender

'It's your bastard fault, Sears. Not mine, will ye be told!'

Sears sneered at the little man walking ahead of him. 'No, I bloody won't. Ye bust me out of court and took me to a tavern which turned into a three-day bender. Ye supplied all the drinks since I had no coin. And you, *you* Biviano, ye plague touched prick, you produced, if I recall, the nine men's morris board and stones that lost us the fucking horses—'

'And saddles and harnesses.'

'Yes, and saddles and—'

'And the board and stones themselves.' Biviano patted himself down as he walked. 'Yup, not even the stones are left.'

'Aye, and the magistrates have my arms and armour too.' Sears shook his head and sneered some more.

'What we gonna tell Stowold? About his horses and shit. I don't want to imagine how many years' wages that lot was worth.'

'You mean your good Earl, Biviano? The Constable of Wesson? The Watcher of the fucking Deep?'

'Aye, that bastard.' Biviano's voice sounded pinched as he rammed a finger up his nose, had a good dig around.

'How should I know, Biv? You're his damned pet, not me.'

Biviano grunted a laugh, produced a bloody crow from his nose and flicked it out into the street. It stuck to a passing coach, which had him turning to face Sears, grin wide. Sears rolled his eyes and Biviano turned back and turned a corner.

'I'll think of something, Sears, me old mucker.'

'That's what worries me.'

They walked along without talking for a while, beads of sweat appearing on their brows and necks as they walked a wide street with no shade. The sky was blue and summer had arrived in full. Biviano wore his maille hauberk and padded gambeson, but had rolled his hose down to his ankles, to air his legs, off-white braes baggy and flapping as he walked. His liveried tabard was gone. It'd had too much sick staining it to wear now the two of them had sobered up. Biviano sighed and mopped his brow with his shirt's filthy cuff, which poked from the maille of his sleeve. He'd lost his maille coif and helmet early on in their drinking binge. A good sight more money lost in those items, but at least he had his short-sword. How he'd been allowed to stagger about with that he had no idea. Perhaps, he wondered, slightly amused by the thought, no one had dared take it from him. He grinned once more and cleared his other nostril with a push, hook and pull of his forefinger's black nail. He looked back and flicked the sloppy bogey Sears' way, delighted as it stuck to the big man's linen shirt.

'Cock!'

Biviano shrugged and carried on walking. 'You look weird, Sears, in braes and a shirt and nothing more. People are staring. This isn't Dockside. Folk don't walk around bare footed in this district.' They'd entered Park District, their old haunt and patrol area.

'And it's got nowt to do with you flicking the contents of yer conk here there and everywhere? Anyhow, ye shit, it's your damned fault the rest of me clothes, and boots, are gone. Just like the horses and—'

'Yes yes, Sears. 'Morl's floppy cock but yer a miserable get these days.' Biviano winked at a woman walking towards them. She crossed the street, averting her eyes. Biviano huffed and Sears laughed. 'Shut it, Sears. Ye wanna cheer up, anyway. Think it was me ma who used to say—'

'Ye never knew ye ma, Biviano.'

'Again with spoiling me anecdotes and advice and proverbs and such. I swear, once—

'Oh, we're nearly there!' Biviano sped up, arms pumping at his sides like he'd been told to run without actually running.

Sears sped up to match, cursing and wincing as his bare feet found stones along the way.

'Ye'll cheer up when we get in and speak to Stowold, mate, I'm sure of it.' Biviano pointed to a long stone wall twice as tall as Sears, with a solid looking arch covered gateway further along the street. 'He told me we'd be stunned with what he has to tell us, should we decide to meet.'

'That before—

'Ouch, fuck!' Sears hopped, skipped and stumbled along after a now jogging Biviano. 'That before or after we tell him we—'

'Don't you dare mention those animals, Sears! I've got the only bastard sword between us, remember that!'

'Whatever.'

Biviano slowed as he approached the tall gates and stone arch. There was no sign of a guard. No sign of anything but stone and solid oak, re-enforced with black iron bars and studs.

Sears and Biviano stood there, side by side, looking left, right and up, and panting all the while. Both men pressed hands onto hips, bent forward a little, Biviano's sweat dripping from his nose. Sears' lip twitched, eye twitched. He sniffed once, twice, reached across and wiped the sweat from his friend's nose with his own sleeve, like a father would a child.

Biviano slapped his hand away. 'Get off, ye ginger get.'

'We gonna stand staring at wood and stone, or we gonna knock?'

Biviano nodded. 'Guess we knock, aye. Don't see any other—'

The gates opened inward. Both men raised eyebrows and stared through the widening gap.

Half a dozen green liveried men-at-arms stared back.

Biviano frowned as Sears glanced sidelong at him; frowned and jerked his thumb at his friend.

'Sears here lost the horses.'

The punch to Biviano's shoulder damn near floored him.

Chapter 58 – Underkeep

'Now this, Sears, is the life. No?'

'I don't like it.'

'Oh for 'morl's sake, ye great oaf.' Biviano rubbed hard at his pock-marked, but clean face as he moved away from Sears. 'Is there no pleasing you?' He crossed the grand chamber and stood by the only wall without a door. He stood and admired a wide tapestry depicting a scene shifting from naked, curvy – in some strange places – women on one side, to a raging subterranean, or so it looked, battle on the other. 'What do ye suppose this is all about?'

'Wealth,' Sears said, sitting in a wooden chair and squirming in the clean, crisp clothes he, along with Biviano, had been given upon their arrival. His red hair fluffed out at all angles after the wash they'd been forced to take and he glowered as he swilled his wine around the glass he'd been given. 'Glass,' he said, before Biviano could say any more.

'Eh?'

'Wealth,' Sears repeated the former. 'Too much and ye buy rot ye don't need. Tapestries picturing deformed women flowing into fights between pale-skinned, hairless dwarves, or whatever they are, and stick-thin men. And wine served in cups made of clear stained-glass windows.'

'So, just glass then.'

Sears ignored Biviano and sipped the wine. He winced. 'Tastes like…' He shrugged again. 'I don't know, but I don't like it.'

Biviano turned, arms out wide. 'What *do* ye like, eh? Gods below, Sears. What did the magistrates do to ye whilst in custody? Sap yer sense of humour, yer sense of adventure and—'

'It was before that, Biviano,' Sears said in all seriousness, locking eyes on his friend across the lamp-lit chamber. There were no windows, or none to speak of. A wide strip of black glass ran along the bottom of the tapestry wall, a contrasting smooth base to the textured art above. 'Pointless thing, that,' Sears had said of the black window, as soon as they'd been brought to the room, seated and served. Sears sighed heavily and smiled weakly. 'I left them, Biv. I left Longoss and Coppin to a pursuing gang, to take a message to Will Morton of the Black Guild's mark on the King. And for what? To be arrested by the King's bastard magistrates. The very men we served for gods know how long as City Guards.'

He looked down to the wine and swilled it around some more.

Biviano sighed as loud as Sears had. 'Fair one, mate. Fair one. I can see how that would grind on ye. Heh. I can see how it *is* grinding on ye.'

Sears nodded. 'All I wanted to do afterwards was go back into Dockside. Find and help my friends.'

Biviano offered a sympathetic smile. He crossed the chamber and sat opposite Sears. 'Like I wanted to, with Ellis Frane at the cathedral, and then, especially then, with you in Dockside when Buddle the bloody dog somehow called for Effrin.'

Sears nodded some more. 'I know, and I know ye know.' He looked up, locking eyes with Biviano. 'Let's do it, now,' he said, leaning forward. 'Let's ask Stowold for men and ride in like ye had him do for me—'

'Alas, gentlemen,' a woman said from the doorway to their side. They'd not seen her enter, but there she stood, floral-patterned open surcoat revealing a white gown cut low at the front, falling to the floor all about her. She held a glass in her left hand and gathered and lifted her skirts with her right, enough to walk across the floor towards them, her smile disarming and stunning them to silence. 'My apologies for not arriving sooner. I have been a poor hostess.'

'Not at all, my lady.' Biviano stood. Sears did the same.

A servant in the doorway cleared his throat.

'Introducing The Lady Elsane Stowold,' the man said, in a matter that was clear he was annoyed not to have announced her before she had spoken. The servant disappeared thereafter.

'Biviano, my lady.'

'Sears, milady.'

Both men offered a bow, Biviano deftly and Sears awkwardly. Sears hadn't missed Biviano's switch in accent either, from lower to upper district.

Elsane's smile broadened and she bobbed the briefest of curtsies in a manner that seemed nothing but a fine courtesy to the two guardsmen.

'May I offer you my seat, my lady?' Biviano asked, moving to slide the wooden chair nearest him to accommodate her.

'Thank you but no, I prefer to stand.'

Biviano bowed his head as she thanked him.

Sears glanced past Elsane to the far side of the wide tapestry, taking in the unsightly curves of the depicted women in ridiculous poses, and back to Elsane, whose curves were... he released the breath he'd been holding. She met his eyes and he knew his cheeks now matched his red hair and beard. He swallowed hard, mouth dry and suddenly the wine was the sweetest of nectars.

'My husband should be with us shortly. He's been at the stable attending to some terrible affair regarding two horses.' She shrugged, rolled her bottom lip and turned to take in the tapestry.

Sears, nor Biviano, missed the glint in her eye and the slightest upwards pull to her thin lips as she turned away. Both men smiled, despite the tension they now felt.

'Stowold is a resourceful and intelligent nobleman,' Biviano said, moving to stand beside, albeit a couple of paces apart, from Elsane.

'I suppose he is.' Her tone betraying her boredom. She turned, stepped closer to Biviano, eyes searching his face, intently. He too blushed. 'Bagnall tells me great things about you, Sir Biviano—'

'Sir?' Sears blurted the word whilst moving to sip his wine. The glass hovered before his beard as he looked over the top of it, to the two pairs of eyes looking back. Lowering it, he said, 'Apologies, milady,' and clenched his jaw as Elsane turned back to the tapestry whilst Biviano's look lingered on Sears; an amused look, a victory of one friend over another.

Biviano turned back, nodding. 'He has, has he? Well, I'm sure he does me far more justice than I deserve.'

'Of course I do, you rat shit.' Bagnall Stowold strode into the room, a dark green surcoat hanging long and flamboyant. He was armoured, maille and plate both, with his sword hanging from his hip and his hand atop its decorated hilt. It was the sort of thing a soldier noticed, arms and armour, combat attire; it was the sort of thing a soldier noticed almost as much as the way Elsane moved as she glided across to her husband, to place a kiss on his cheek. Biviano and Sears' eyes moved back to the Earl's as soon as they'd realised they'd strayed elsewhere.

Biviano cleared his throat and Sears drained his glass, the acidity of the wine twitching his right cheek.

Stowold made to speak, but Elsane cut him off.

'Bagnall, I'd rather you didn't wear your...' she waved her free hand around him and scrunched her nose '...fighting garb around our chambers. We're not in imminent danger, dear, so I do not see why you feel the need to strut around like a steel-clad peacock.'

Stowold's face hardened, but for a heartbeat, before he smiled and inclined his head. 'How silly of me, my love. I shall endeavour to have myself changed into something more fitting in future.'

'You've said that before,' Elsane muttered, turning to Sears and Biviano, her smile broad once more. 'Gentlemen, I shall leave you three to your, discussions, alas; it isn't often we have visitors to the Underkeep. I'm sure Bagnall has much to tell you regarding what it is you shall be doing here. I bid you farewell, for now.' She openly, brazenly, winked at Biviano, turned and glided from the room, drawing the eyes of all present as she did so.

Stowold turned back and cleared his throat, eyebrows high. Two sets of eyes snapped to him, followed by two sheepish smiles.

'Right, you shites…' Stowold wrung the hilt of his sword and strode towards them. 'Where's my fucking horses?'

Biviano couldn't believe what he and Sears were told by Stowold. The revelations sounded far-fetched, fanciful, to say the least. It wasn't until Stowold showed them evidence of what he'd told them that the two men believed it; baulking, gawking and stunned to silence, Biviano and Sears looked down through the glass of the subterranean window below the wide tapestry. They watched as Stowold pointed, the loss of his horses forgotten, for now. They listened and narrowed eyes as he pulled a thin chain.

Nothing happened, at first.

Clearly, Biviano thought, the chain rang a bell elsewhere. The silver strand hung in a corner barely touched by the lamplight that illuminated the smoky chamber. The chain was one of many, hanging like metallic vines from holes in the wooden boards above their heads. Moments of silence passed, with Biviano and Sears looking to Stowold, who smiled back, eyebrows lifting on occasion, lips puckering to sip at his own wine. Eventually, at the point where Biviano could hardly take it any longer and was about to say something, anything, to break the awkward silence, a light flickered. A light beyond the previously black window.

'What…?' Sears managed the first word, the rest lost to the sudden intake of a smoke-tainted breath.

Biviano couldn't even managed one word. But he did manage a thought, although it drifted lazily, like a wind-blown mist, as the shifting light beyond the window proceeded to drop, fall, descend into…

'It's true,' Biviano said, the yellow flare of a light they witnessed disappearing below the bottom sill of the strip of glass. Biviano looked to Stowold once more, as did Sears. Stowold grinned, winked, turned and strode towards the door he'd entered through, his armour audibly marking his path. He said nothing. He didn't have to. Biviano and Sears followed without question, without complaint. They didn't even look at one another as they passed through the door and descended yet more curling steps, following the Watcher of the Deep as they did so.

They didn't need to say or do anything, they just knew, now; they knew their service to Bagnall Stowold was far more important with regards to the protection of Wesson than any other role or mission or quest they could conjure for themselves. Part of being guardsman of Wesson's City Guard had been to escape their previous lives. The other half had been to serve the people of Wesson, to help in whatever way they could to defend them, to seek justice for them, even if the two of them did have an amoral swing on occasion, from their moral compasses; especially Biviano. But this? This... Biviano filled his cheeks and let out a slow breath as all that Stowold had told them sank in. And as they descended yet deeper into the Underkeep, lamps scarce on the stairwell, light in general scarce, Biviano's mind's eye watched that burning torch fall. He visualised it landing, eventually, to be extinguished in whatever lay below, and he knew... He knew that his lifelong friend and he were in the right place to do what was needed for the people. Not for Stowold, not for Barrison or Morton or any other noble with an agenda and a personal army. No. For Wesson; Altoln. For if what Stowold and his men were facing were to succeed and they fail, the recent plague would seem like a well-deserved reprieve in comparison to what would rise from beneath their very feet.

If they get out... Biviano thought, reaching the bottom step and moving into lamp-light once more, through a door and out into a circular chamber with... with a glass floor that caused him to stop abruptly. Sears crashed into the back of him, followed by several curses. ...*Wesson would be lost, its inhabitants too.*

'Flay me now.' Sears looked over Biviano's shoulder. 'It's bigger than I'd imagined. I don't think I can step onto it, Biv.'

Biviano shook his head as he watched Stowold walk out into the centre, where a large oak table sat, circular like the chamber itself. No chairs, no other adornments to the room bar lamps and torches on sconces, filling the room with an acrid smoke-filled atmosphere that clung to the ceiling before disappearing off up some unseen chimney.

Biviano looked back down, ignoring the three other men, knights by the look of their garb and the confident way they held themselves – one certainly, for it was indeed Sir Bryant who'd helped free Sears from the magistrates. Biviano looked through the floor, which started where his pointed boots stopped, through it into blackness. It was then that it hit him. 'Flay me too,' he cursed, lifting his hands out to the sides as if he walked a rope. 'Flay me for eternity, Sears, but we're stood above it… We're dangling above the fucking precipice!'

Chapter 59 – A new liege

'Well, what say you both?' Stowold looked from Biviano to Sears and back. They stood, all three, along with the three knights; the three veterans, for it was clear they were veterans. The three knights stood at equally spaced intervals to one another around the far side of the expansive table, whilst Sears and Biviano stood shoulder to shoulder, Stowold closer to them than any of his knights.

Biviano pressed his lips together in a line, nodding whilst staring at the textured map laid out before them. A network of tunnels, caverns and stalactite-like turrets and towers; inverted-gully-carved ramparts, crenellations and machicolations, all laid out before him in a grand, impressive to say the least, recreation of what allegedly lay below and all around them. The defences and enemy territories both, so they were told, of the Underkeep and the landscape, or subterranean-scape, it dangled into. *Dangled,* Biviano thought, *that's the right word. Dangled. Like bloody worms on a hook, awaiting the big bad to come swallow us whole.* He sighed and grunted, glanced sideways and upwards to Sears. He smirked when he saw Sears' cheeks puffing out into his red beard. He was clearly as deep in thought as Biviano about it all. *Deep.* Biviano grunted a laugh at that. Eyes turned to him. *We're certainly in deep.*

'I'm in,' Sears said, looking back to Biviano.

Biviano voiced his agreement. 'Thought you might be, big guy. I'd decided up top, in the other chamber, and thought you had too.' *Well, I sort of had, but I don't want you thinking you beat me to the decision.*

Sears nodded. 'I had too, I just didn't say so.' The red-haired giant of a man shuddered and looked down, past his feet, into the depthless-ness below. Taking a deep breath, he looked back up, met everyone's eyes one by one and finished on Stowold's. 'But I'm in, my lord. How could I not be?'

Stowold smiled, nodded his thanks and turned to Biviano. 'And you too, Biviano.' He grinned.

'Looks like it, milord.' Back to lower district accent now.

'Grand!' Stowold shouted, much louder than Biviano thought necessary.

'Grand indeed,' the one called Sir Mechel said, beaming at the two newest recruits and rounding the table, arm outstretched. He took Sears' arm first, hand to forearm, Sears doing the same. They shook and Sir Mechel moved past Sears and did the same to Biviano. The other two knights, Sir Bryant included, followed suit, less enthusiastically, but pleasantly and genuinely enough.

Stowold was the last to embrace, arm to arm, with both men, but he seemed the most pleased of all. 'I can't tell you how pleased I am to have you both with us on this,' he said, winking at Biviano as he gripped and shook his arm. 'We've lost many recently, as I told you.' He grimaced, released Biviano's arm and stood back, looking down through the floor to the blackness beyond. 'And not just in Dockside, rescuing you,' he added, without looking up. All present knew he meant Sears, but there was no accusation, no blame in his tone.

Stowold pulled his lips into a tight smile and looked up. 'They're more active of late.' The three knights, Stowold's captains, nodded, moving back to their positions around the table. 'Since the plague.' Stowold's eyes flicked between the two newcomers, whose eyes widened at the news.

'Since the arcane plague?' Biviano asked. 'The one sent here on purpose, with malice and intent, you mean?'

'Well what other one has there been, ye fool?' Sears moved away from Biviano a little, scanning the raised map as he moved.

'Alright, big man,' Biviano said, resting both hands on the table, the glass beneath their feet wracking his nerves, but less so with all else there was to think on.

Stowold sucked his teeth, drawing everyone's attention. 'I fear it is all linked.'

'The plague and the attacks in the Deep?' Sir Mechel asked. It was clear from his question, tone and the look on his and his fellow knights' faces, that they hadn't heard Stowold's theory.

'Yes, and the mark on King Barrison.'

'You think the Black Guild is in league with whomever sent the plague?' Biviano asked, accent shifting once again to upper district.

'I do,' Stowold said, 'and I think whoever manoeuvres those below us, pulling their strings, is the same *who*, or *what*, that encouraged several goblin tribes to unite and take Beresford.'

There were grunts, swallows and licks of lips as the men present looked about each other, realising it could well be the case. Stowold knew his stuff, was learned. And more than that, was a soldier, a warrior: a commander. He lead from the front when it was needed and he did enough manoeuvring of his own to know when other folk were doing the same. All present knew it. All had seen him fight and command, some far more than other, of course.

'King Barrison's Spymaster, Lady Burr, is on her way south with a group of pathfinders,' Stowold explained. 'She's been ordered to find out what is afoot in The Marches, why we are hearing nothing from Sirreta. She may even, although it was said as a last resort by Will Morton, cross into Sirreta itself.'

'You fear whoever sent the plague…' Sears said, leaning forward, hands on the table much like most of them were now doing. He looked at Stowold, eyes flicking to Biviano, but settling on Stowold all the same. '…you fear that whoever sent that black death, whoever encouraged goblins to raid and put a mark on our King, is doing similar things in Sirreta? Or,' Sears asked, before Stowold could answer the first question, 'you think it's Sirreta doing this?'

Stowold screwed his face up and crossed his steel-clad arms across his chest. Eventually, with all eyes on him, he shrugged. 'I don't know. We don't know.' He looked about them all. 'That's why Lady Burr was sent. That's why we need to know more.'

'That's why you have something specific in mind for us?' Biviano said, standing straight. 'Isn't it, my lord?'

Stowold nodded. His eyes flicked for the briefest of moments to Sir Mechel, who cleared his throat.

'We have other suspicions…' Sir Mechel said, looking between Sears and Biviano. He was the only knight the duo had seen in Stowold's service to wear colours of his own and not the dark green of the Earl. '…closer to home,' the yellow and black chequered knight confirmed. He paused to let that sink in.

Brow high, creased, Biviano nodded for Sir Mechel to go on.

Sears cut in before Sir Mechel could speak. 'You don't just guard from hairless, pale-skinned dwarves then?'

'That would be rather short-sighted, Sears,' Stowold said. 'I'm the Watcher of the Deep, man, but I'm also the Constable of Wesson and the Earl of Stowold. It's my duty to look down, up and to each side when searching for threats and suspecting treachery. The Deep is what we know, it's been our trade for decades, our ancestors'…' he pointed to Sir Mechel, '…some for centuries. No, Sears, we don't just guard Wesson from the bastards below. We guard it, or attempt to, from enemies without and within. Hence my enthusiastic storming of the Samorlian bastard Cathedral, and…' he said, pointing at Sears. 'And, good man, why I rode into Dockside with my own men to drag your hairy arse out!'

Sears swallowed and inclined his head. 'For which I'm eternally grateful, milord.'

'I'm sure you are,' Stowold said, looking between them both once more, 'but let's hear what Sir Mechel has to say, no?'

Sears nodded, followed by Biviano. They both looked to Sir Mechel.

Blind me, Biviano thought, *that was a subtle telling off from Stowold, Sears. And the plot's about to thicken, by the looks of Sir Mechel's face.*

Looking around everyone, the chequered knight continued where he'd been about to do before Sears had interrupted. It wasn't long until they all fell into silence, Sears and Biviano's wide eyes once again on Stowold's. The Constable of Wesson nodded, confirming Sir Mechel's fears; Sir Mechel's accusations of a man far above his own station. Of a man with no less power than Bagnall Stowold, in fact; more, perhaps.

'Well, stone me and throw me down this pit of yours.' Biviano glanced down and tightened his grip on the table before him. 'You seem bloody sure about this, milord?' He looked at Stowold.

'We're *not* sure but we suspect, and that's as good as being sure when deciding whether to look into someone or not; whether to investigate them or not.' He smiled. Biviano cringed.

'Hence your want of our services,' Sears stated.

'Hence my *need* of your services, Sears. Precisely so.'

Biviano sighed. 'So, we're not here to delve into the depths and fight upside down sieges and such?'

Sir Bryant actually chuckled at that, and Stowold grinned.

'Not yet, no,' Stowold said, looking to his captains and back. 'Not yet. Looking into our quarry will do for now. But know this,' his grin dropped away altogether, face darkening, the mood in the room darkening with it, and it had been dark to begin with, 'if you two get caught, by him or his men. If you two get hauled into one of his estates, castles or some such place. Well,' Stowold shook his head, 'there will be no one riding to rescue you this time. You're on your own, and you're certainly not under my employment. Understood?'

'Best not get caught, had we,' Biviano said, flashing a grin.

Sears turned to Biviano, clearly incredulous of his mirth at such an announcement.

'But if you do,' Sir Mechel said, hesitantly, 'we'll have something for you to sup. Save them the trouble of torturing you, see?' He smiled, but it was forced. A brave face for their sakes.

'Save you two the trouble of going through it, too,' Sir Bryant added, face as serious as sin.

'And save *you*,' Sears looked from Sir Bryant to Stowold, 'the trouble of being found out.'

'Well, quite!' Stowold grinned once more. 'We wouldn't want the High Lords of Altoln at each other's throats now, would we? Not during uncertain times like these, eh?'

Sears grunted a humourless laugh and looked sidelong at Biviano, who merely nodded.

In for a penny… Biviano thought, grinning back at Stowold. 'Doesn't change anything for us, my lord,' Biviano said, confident he spoke for Sears too, despite the big man's hushed curses. 'We'll do it, or die trying.'

'Marvellous!' Stowold bellowed, clapping hands together. 'This calls for a drink. Follow me.' Stowold moved for the stairs they'd descended earlier. Sir Mechel followed Biviano and Sears off the glass floor, never looking down whilst the two men he closed on did nothing but. As Biviano and Sears reached the stone of the steps and breathed a joint sigh of relief, they looked to one another and nodded once.

Biviano heard Sir Mechel grunt a laugh as Sears thumped his partner on the shoulder and ascended the stairs, Biviano close on his heels, Sir Mechel bringing up the rear whilst Sir Bryant and the unnamed knight, who'd said nothing the whole time, remained in the circular chamber.

What The Three have I got us into now? Biviano thought. He shook it away and instead focused on the wine likely waiting them at the top of the steps. *It's about time I had another drink. I've just about felt the effects of our binge wear off.*

***

Core cursed then spat as the one-armed swordsman severed the link to another of Core's toys.

'See how you like your baron back,' Core snapped, throwing down the useless blackened heart he'd been manipulating, and snatching the dead baron's head from his closest apprentice. 'Send the archer you have into the cottage,' he ordered a goblin, who sat on the far side of the tavern's taproom. The bleary-eyed whelp nodded, manipulating the shrivelled heart she held.

'Whatchya about, Core?' another goblin said, dropping down

next to the old, walnut faced necromancer.

'Hush now and watch.'

Core and his closest apprentices stared into the puddle of piss before them, their lips peeling back to reveal brown and crooked teeth.

Three villagers ran as the headless baron Core controlled charged through Hinton, sword drawn. The dark image was yellow-brown and cloudy, but there was enough firelight about the village they watched for Core to operate his mounted toy.

'So much better with a head,' Core explained. 'The brain moves toys far quicker than the dulled and pained heart.' Apprentices nodded, eyes as wide as goblin eyes could be.

One apprentice laughed as the headless baron rode down a woman who'd attempted to divert the baron's attention from a fleeing family, who ran from a small building Core had targeted for several days.

'There's the cottage.' Core jerked his chin at the puddle of piss. He bounced as he spoke and worked the brain, as if it were him and not his prize toy atop the reanimated destrier.

Approaching the open doorway of the small cottage, Core willed the hand of the baron's shield-arm to pull on the reins, slowing the horse so he could lean down, squint and stare at something in particular on the ground of the sacked village.

The puddle revealed what looked like the body of one of Core's toys, an archer, lying prone within the darkness of the cottage itself. Core looked up at a particular apprentice across the room, who looked back and shrugged before throwing the useless heart she'd been manipulating.

Core hissed and the apprentice scurried away.

Leaning in for a closer look at the puddle, Core watched on, unsurprised by now, as the one-armed swordsman moved into the street to stand before the headless baron. Defiant wasn't the word. The man near on impressed Core; if it wasn't for how much the human had frustrated and angered him.

Black eyes paled as Core worked his magic. His fingers flexed and hooked, wiggled, pointed and squelched within the baron's severed head, which sat in his gore-soaked lap; stolen linen braes ruined. 'I've had days of this annoying bastard,' Core muttered as he worked. 'But I do like a challenge...'

The baron's horse reared, front hooves lashing out in an attempt to brain the crippled man.

The one-armed swordsman deftly side-stepped the attack and fled, again, and Core shrieked with anger and frustration, throwing the baron's head across the room.

The goblin apprentices scattered.

An incredible bang was followed by an equally loud retort of stone on stone as whatever the human army had launched at Beresford struck and shook the curtain wall. Core's weak heart skipped a beat and left him clutching at his left arm, fearing the worst. The pain he feared never came, but he was drawn from his necromancy nonetheless, despite knowing it would leave his toys in Hinton vulnerable. He had no choice though, for whatever it was they'd begun hurling at his walls was likely to bring them down if there was much more of it. And that couldn't be allowed.

'The walls, the walls!' Core shrieked, voice catching as he rose from the heads lined up before him, the tops of their skulls removed, his hands and fingers wet from the contents.

A hulking hobyah pushed through the tavern door, its red armour scuffed and dented, face bloody and torn. 'Came from wall,' it said, a broken bottom tooth catching on its upper lip as it spoke, skewing its words.

'Well, back to it!' Core prodded the last of The Red Goblin's bodyguards out of the building and into the fire-lit street beyond with his stained and pitted, silver-plated staff of bone.

As the hobyah loped off, half a dozen armed but wary goblins following behind, Core rapped on the door of the building next to his tavern.

He rapped again on the wood, this time with his silver-plated staff and a little less patience.

He was about to full on hammer on it when he heard the handle squeak and saw it turn. The door opened and three gaunt goblin faces peered out, their expressions slack, eyes sunken, hollow even.

'Leave your toys and come with me. Bring everyone.' Core released a string of hacking coughs before turning and leaving for the wall. He snatched a surprisingly clean hooded mantle from one of his apprentices and pulled it over his own head, despite the relatively warm night. He heard his apprentices shuffling along behind him, heard one of them call lazily to the rest of their coven to follow, from the house he'd knocked on. He hated how the necromancy he'd taught them left them little more than drunken husks, but it was necessary to aid him in spreading fear across the north, as The Red Goblin wanted; as Dignaaln wanted.

Easily catching up to him as he ambled along, Core's acolytes fell in about him, matching the old goblin's pace as he made his way to the curtain walls of Beresford. He needed to see for himself what the newly arrived human army was using, and it was time to work out a plan to defend the town and its walls from those who would take it back.

Chapter 60 – Longsword

'Anything?' Sears said, eyeing the yellow and black chequered knight.

Sir Mechel nodded. 'Anything. Stowold's armoury is our armoury. You're of his household now, have been for two whole days, you lucky gets. You need to arm like it now though. You're not solving crimes in Park District or being chased by gangers where you two are going.' Sir Mechel eyed Biviano, who was eyeing a longsword. 'A knight's weapon that, Biviano.' Sir Mechel grinned.

Sears frowned. *What does that mean, besides the obvious fact?*

Without a word, which was also unusual, Biviano put the longsword back on the rack and picked up a simple arming sword and a rondel dagger. 'I like these,' he said, turning and looking Sir Mechel up and down, armour and all. 'The straight tri-blade of the rondel is perfect for punching through plate. Like the harness you wear, Sir Mechel.'

Sir Mechel grinned, his defence against words as solid as his armour. 'Yes, they are. I'll leave you two to it. Meet me in the map room when done. I can trust you to find your way, gentlemen?'

'You can, milord,' Sears said, before Biviano could say anything else.

Sir Mechel nodded and left the lamp-lit armoury.

Sears turned on Biviano, who was testing an arming belt around his skinny waist. 'Well?' *This better be good,* Sears left out.

'Well, what?' Biviano said, eyes on the looping of his new black belt.

'Well, what was all that about?' Sears closed on his friend, pulled him around.

Biviano looked up, frowned and shrugged. He looked back down and finished knotting his belt. 'There,' he said. 'A fine fit. Will go nicely with the new colours, coif and helm.' He sheathed his new sword and dagger and made to move away from Sears. 'I'm thinking a shield, too.'

Sears took Biviano by the maille clad shoulders and held him firm.

Sighing ridiculously, Biviano looked up from beneath the rim of his new – identical to his previous – kettle-helm.

'You were a prick to Sir Mechel. He's been nowt but nice to us.'

Biviano shrugged again. 'I can't deny that. Seems like a lovely bloke, for a knight.'

Knight...? 'That's what made you bristle.'

'Eh?'

'Knight!'

'You're making no sense, ye fat shit. Now let me go before I—'

'Fall to the ground, wailing like a child?'

Biviano folded his arms across his padded chest and looked left, and made a point of it.

'Proving my point. A child.' *And a bloody stubborn one.* 'Spit it out, Biv.'

Another sigh, less heavy; genuine. Biviano managed to shrug Sears off this time, or rather Sears let him. Sears knew Biviano well, likely better than the man knew himself... certainly better than the man knew himself. He'd spent enough years with him after all. Decades in fact.

'Well? What about him saying *longswords are for knights* got to you? You could take it if you—'

'It's not about the sword, Sears. Or any of this.' He waved his arms about the richest armoury either of them had ever seen or imagine, outside the King's own, they were sure.

Sears said nothing. He stood back and waited for the inevitable spilling of the proverbial beans.

Taking a deep breath, Biviano moved away, back to the longsword. He hefted it and swung it. He set into a series of deft movements that Sears hadn't seen the man perform before, with such a weapon, anyway. Although he wasn't surprised Biviano knew how to.

'It's coming back to you, isn't it?' Sears asked, knowingly. 'It's been a long time coming, but I've not looked forward to it.'

'How much did I forget this time, Sears?'

Sears crossed to a stool and sat, leaning back against the stone wall which he hardly felt through his new padding and maille. He stretched his thick legs out and crossed them at his booted ankles. 'It's not quite like that. You don't forget these things as such, but—'

'Remember them, from the others.' Biviano turned and met Sears' sad stare. 'How many has it been?'

It was Sears' turn to shrug. 'I'm no math mastering mage, Biv. However many it usually is across so many generations.' Sears let that sink in and wondered if it truly did, if it could. *How much does he know?* He watched his friend replace the longsword. He watched him pace, head down, eyes moving everywhere and nowhere at once, or so Sears assumed, knowing him as he did. The kettle-helm cast a black shadow across Biviano's eyes. 'Ye do know of what I speak, mate, don't ye? Ye *do* know how many generations it's been?'

Biviano looked at Sears, face screwed up, pock-marks appearing fuller, deeper than usual. He shook his head and winced all the more. 'Yes and no. It comes and goes. *He* comes and goes, or they, I'm not sure. And when they or he or whoever does come along, I know more, feel more.' He kicked an imaginary stone and paced some more. Sears let him, said nothing. 'Other times; most of the time,' Biviano continued, eyes on the racks of weapons, 'I'm just me.' He smiled. Genuine. 'And those are the best times.'

'The other times?' Sears pushed, needing to know where his friend was at. 'Are they more frequent of late?'

Biviano stopped and faced Sears, chin up. Sears could see the muscles working in his friend's jaw, his new maille coif on a table, not yet donned. Biviano nodded. 'More than ever, Sears. More than ever. And ever since that bloody plague.'

Sears swallowed hard, nodded and pursed lips beneath red beard.

'How do, gobshites?'

Sears and Biviano jumped and turned to the door, the moment shattered by the recognition of the loud voice. Sears cursed back, Biviano followed suit.

Bollingham stood in the doorway, the widest grin stretched across his face. 'Miss me?' their former comrade from the City Guard said. He adjusted his bastard-sword carrying, plated belt that hung about his knee-length surcoat of dark green. Maille shushing and plate schynbalds shining, the former guardsman strode into the room, Stowold's serpent- and tower-emblazoned badge upon his chest.

'Like fuck we did,' Biviano said, unable to hide his own grin.

'Aye, what Biv said.' Sears rose and took Bollingham's outstretched arm, looking him up and down. 'You can't be serious, Bolly?' Sears breathed the words, staring from spurs and schynbalds to vambraces and spaulders, all of which covered riveted maille from head to literal toe.

'You better believe it, you fat shit,' Bollingham said, turning to take hold of Biviano's hand. 'I'm a bastard knight!' Bollingham crowed, laughing long and hard.

Sears and Biviano simply shook their heads and gawked at Sir

368

Bollingham, who turned a full circle and, arms out wide, grinned back.

'And you two are my bitches!'

Chapter 61 – Back on the road

Glad of his new kettle-helm to shade his eyes from the sun, Biviano lifted his chin and watched Sir Bollingham – as he was insisting on being called – ride ahead of the small group.

'This is killing me,' Biviano muttered.

Sears pulled alongside and looked down from his carthorse. Their new liege lord, the Earl of Stowold, was short on horses and had apologised when Sears was handed the reins of the workhorse. Sears had merely shrugged and climbed into the saddle, accepting it as fact. What Stowold had meant, Biviano knew, was that Sears had lost Stowold two expensive horses – or so Biviano had told the Earl – and Sears was paying for it by riding cheaper mounts. Biviano had grinned at that. He grinned again as he rode along on his slender palfrey, a rope trailing off to another horse he'd been given. The rest of the group had the same, their second mounts of a slightly bigger, if not destrier-sized, build, whilst Sears had a second carthorse plodding alongside him.

'How's your carthorse?' Biviano asked, without looking at Sears; rolling with the easy pace Bollingham set them, Biviano looked to his second horse and was glad to have been given the one he'd ridden when he, Stowold, and the City Guard had stormed Wesson's Samorlian Cathedral. It was far from a big horse like Sears', nor was it a destrier like Bollingham's second mount. Leaner, calmer, but with a dangerous flair one needed in a horse one rode into a fray, Biviano's second horse was his perfect match. He felt comfortable in the saddle; on the road. He leaned forward and patted the palfrey he rode on the neck whilst regarding Sears' answer: a curse. Biviano grinned all the more. 'Least you're mounted. Last time we travelled this road, ye ginger get, it was our feet doing the walking. Remember?'

'How could I forget, mate.' Sears looked back at the three riders behind, then forward once more. 'Look at Bolly, prancing like a plated prick. An open-faced bascinet atop his ugly head and he thinks he's a bloody baron or some such. He's even made Pelse lead his destrier, as well as the man's own animal. Poor skinny git is likely to be pulled in two if they're spooked. He'll be calling him his squire next.'

Biviano was nodding before Sears finished. 'Bolly's probably wearing green pantaloons under all that maille, too.' Sears rolled his eyes and Biviano carried on regardless. 'I thought we were to act as hedge-knights, looking for paid work? I ain't ever seen no hedge-knight with as much clobber as Bolly's got on, Sears. He's about as inconspicuous as your bloody red beard.'

Biviano deftly side-stepped his horse as a fist came in and down from the carthorse to his side. Glancing up at Sears, Biviano smiled wide.

'I don't know, Biv. Some of these hired swords, knights or not, earn more money than household knights. He's middling in attire is Bolly.'

Biviano mulled that over for a bit and couldn't disagree.

They rode on in a companionable silence for a while, apart from the dust-lifting hooves on the road, the snorting of horses, buzzing of flies and cacophony of birdsong all about them. After a while enjoying the manure-tainted country air, Sears looked across and down at Biviano.

'I'm glad to be back on the road too, mate.' Sears smiled before watching Bollingham once more.

'There's nothing like it, is there?'

Sears shook his head. 'Nope. It's a shame it's not just the two of us though, like old times.'

'We can hear you!' the nearest of the three riders behind said.

Biviano shrugged. 'And?'

'You're a dick, Biviano, you really are,' said the rider.

'And you suck 'em, Jay Strawn. You suck 'em.' Biviano grinned wider than ever.

The half-dozen men continued on down the road, heading east with the sun descending towards the patchwork of ridge and furrowed fields behind them. They rode without speaking for some time, Biviano deep in thought and thankful that he didn't have to guide the palfrey for it to follow Bollingham.

Why does Stowold not send any of his usual men? Biviano wondered, turning to glance at Jay and the other two. All three of them, all six of them truth be told, were former City Guard. Biviano nudged his mount with his knees, left Sears' side and pulled up to the so-called knight in front. 'Bolly—'

'It's Sir Bollingham, Biv.'

'It's Biviano, prick!'

Bollingham laughed and Biviano couldn't help but smile. Despite his wonder at why Stowold hadn't sent Sir Mechel or Sir Bryant, or any of his long serving retainers, Biviano was pleased to be with lads he knew and trusted, although he'd not admit it. Well, as much as he could trust anyone beyond Sears. 'Why us?'

Bollingham snorted. 'Why you and Sears? 'Morl knows. I'd sooner have two decent men-at-arms at my back, rather than a runt and a red-bearded grunt.' Bollingham laughed again at his own joke.

Biviano rode along, eyes on Bollingham's face, which poked from polished steel. He gave no retort, nor did he ask again.

After several rocking steps, Bollingham answered truthfully. 'Stowold doesn't want anyone who's recognisable from his household. None of his knights, none of his men in general, many of whom have attended him at court or tourney.'

'Hence his sudden recruitment from the City Guard?'

'Hence his sudden recruitment from the men he fought alongside in the cathedral. Or Dockside,' he added, jerking his thumb back towards Sears.

Biviano barked a laugh, lifted his kettle-helm with his free hand and had a good scratch. His maille coif sat in oiled rags in one of the leather bags on his other mount. It was too warm as it was, without covering his neck in padding and heavy links. He only wore the helm to shade his head from the sun. In fact, if it weren't up to the prancing knight by his side, he'd have ridden in braes, hose and helm, and nought else.

'Sears didn't do much when we reached him,' Biviano said, talking of the constable led charge into Dockside to save Sears from the gangers, towards the end of the plague.

Bollingham was eyeing the scratching. 'Nor did you, by all accounts. You fainted from the plague. Which is why the old scratching there is a little nerve wracking, mate.'

The scratching stopped. 'Nits, I reckon.'

'Nits, lice, fleas. You get 'em all it seems.'

'Thanks.' Biviano screwed up his pock-marked face. 'What's that smell?' He looked about, nose wrinkling even more.

'Me,' Bollingham said, smirking.

'The Three take you, Bolly, ye prick. We're mounted and moving, against a breeze no less, and I got struck like a well-rotted corpse tried to hug me.'

Bollingham laughed, long and loud.

Sears and those behind cursed louder still as Bollingham's gaseous expulsion struck them.

They rode along without talking again, Bollingham's laughter falling away and Biviano falling back to Sears. Neither said anything, just breathed the fresh-again air and admired the view.

Biviano didn't tell Sears about the thoughts or memories or whatever they were that came to him as they rode along, following a knight, followed by more men-at-arms. It was all so familiar, but not to Biviano. It was all so familiar to the one who'd come first; to the one who'd started the line Biviano was heir to. To the hoary bastard who'd fought and ended a war.

Chapter 62 – Royce

Captain Mannino watched the crew guide *Sessio* into Royce's harbour. He took in the familiar red brick of the wharf, the walls and the towers. Scaffolding and pulleys and labourers swarmed the southern defences of the city like ants after the stamping of their nest. *Red ants,* Mannino thought, amused at his own musing. But not amused at what it meant. His subtle smile slipped to a not so subtle frown.

'Cap'n?' Hitchmogh appeared alongside, hands clasped behind his back.

'Master Hitchmogh,' Mannino replied, glancing down at the man. He made to speak, to ask a question, but Hitchmogh spoke before he could.

'She'll be here, Cap'n. Hud wouldn't let me down. Or you,' he added wryly.

Nodding, Mannino looked back to the bastardised city walls and towers. He scanned the evolving ramparts, wooden rooftops being constructed over the walkways and ornate crenellations of the outer walls. He looked in awe at the onager catapult placed atop the large box tower on the corner that had held a pitched roof during previous visits.

'They're preparing for war, Cap'n. That much is clear. And like Royce wasn't a tough citadel as it was. Now look at her, at what she'll be when they're done.'

'Oof, what!' Mannino practically spat his exclamation. 'The way Royce is going, she'll buckle under her own weight; bring down the very ground she sits upon.'

Hitchmogh frowned and looked up to Mannino as *Sessio* thumped against the wharf.

'Figure of speech, man,' Mannino said, 'figure of speech.'

'There we go, Cap'n.' Hitchmogh pointed, squinting as he did so. 'Royce's Reds, winged horses and all.'

Mannino raised his telescope, scanning the heads of those red knights present, and of their following squires and such. All of whom were male.

As the four knights rode closer, Mannino looked down and noticed the beads of sweat appearing on his first mate's forehead. 'Well, Master Hitchmogh?'

The man looked up to his old friend and pulled his lips into a tight smile. 'I've been known to be wrong.' Hitchmogh winced as

Mannino stowed his telescope upon his person and stormed off to his cabin, his trust and hopes and fears exposed in that instant.

'Of course Hud's not here,' Mannino muttered to himself as he walked. 'She'd have to see *me* if she was.' He slammed his door, snarled and dropped to his bunk, mind racing with what they were to do now. He didn't even pat *Sessio's* hull as he lay there, staring at the ceiling. And that was unusual indeed.

Chapter 63 – Besieging your own

The noise hit the six riders before the view. They'd taken three days and stopped often, Bollingham not wanting to push their mounts – despite having two a piece – or *his* men, as he called them all, much to Biviano's vocal annoyance. Bollingham said he didn't know what would await them when they made their destination, so wanted to make it fresh and ready. It made sense, although the three days was an utter and complete dawdle for anyone to ride such a distance on the King's roads. The new knight was right in his claimed reason for dawdling though; Sears winced at the dull thud of siege engines at work, the crash of their missiles striking stone. Beresford was besieged by the very family who owned it. It was their own weapons of war that attempted to bring down the centuries old walls their ancestors had built. And when Sears and his companions crested the hill, they saw the perrier and onager catapults at work, a larger trebuchet half built on the far side of the engine line.

A spattering of white campaign tents stretched out before them, ending with wicker fences and wooden palisades to protect the edge of the camp from incoming missiles. Teams of men worked about the perriers, yanking on ropes to project stones at Beresford's ramparts, whilst the ass-like kick of the onagers jerked and threw their buckets of stones up and over the walls, crashing into buildings and streets beyond. The teams had clearly been at it for days, their aims true and the missing chunks of wall testament to it, leaving crumbling crenellations like Pelse's broken teeth.

'They're trying to bring a section down, there.' Jay Strawn pointed down to their right, where extra defences had been erected around a black hole. Carters moved in and out of the hole, empty carts going in, earth laden ones coming out. They used the earth they were removing to increase the protective mounds either side of the tunnel. Their intent was clear to the six onlookers.

'Undermining,' Sears said, waving an annoying fly from his face. 'They're going to try and drop a whole section.'

'Pretty sure I just said that.' Jay frowned at Sears.

Sears ignored the man, eyes locked on the Earl of Beresford's efforts. Or rather his men's. 'Once that happens—'

'They'll charge the breach,' Bollingham said, 'and it'll be over.'

'Just like that?' The former guardsman between Sears and Biviano spoke, voice reedy, eyes red rimmed like he'd been sat too close to a smoking fire. They were always red rimmed.

Bollingham nodded. 'Aye, Pelse, just like that. Those goblin shites won't stand up to Earl Beresford's men, who wear superior armour, carry superior weapons and likely outnumber the depleted tribes behind those walls. And it's their home they're trying to get back.'

Pelse looked to Bollingham. 'Why so sure the goblins are depleted?'

It was Biviano who answered. 'They'll have been killing each other before the Earl and his men even got here.' More than one of the former guardsmen nodded at that.

'And his son,' Sears said, watching another volley of rocks strike the walls, the cracks and bangs of it following.

'Aye, Sears,' Biviano agreed, 'the prancing prick of a Duke himself: Rell bloody Adlestrop.'

All six nodded, faces grim as they followed Bollingham down the road and into the Beresfords' camp.

'Well?' Biviano asked Bollingham as the knight rode back to their position within the darkening camp. He'd been to seek an audience with Rell Adlestrop, but Biviano didn't miss the furious look on Bollingham's face; he carried his dust-smeared bascinet in the crook of his left arm and directed his destrier, which he'd switched to once in the camp, with his right. Pulling up before Biviano, who stood hands on hips by their tethered horses, Bollingham's destrier snorted and shook its head whilst he slid from the high-backed saddle.

'He's a prize prick indeed, is Adlestrop.' Bollingham handed the reins to a boy who'd appeared from the smoke drifting across the camp, a mongrel pup close on his heels.

A loud crash and a celebratory roar turned Biviano and Bollingham's heads. Dogs barked across the camp, the pup yapped and the boy grunted and fought, but ultimately managed to lead Bollingham's destrier over to the tethering post whilst the two men watched dust rise about a section of wall. A strip of crenellations had fallen, leaving a gap, again, like Pelse's patchwork teeth.

Bollingham filled his cheeks and forced out the air. 'That was a good hit.'

Biviano nodded. 'True that, Bolly.'

The knight made to correct Biviano, but gave up before asking, 'Where's Sears and the others?'

'Got themselves some stew at a fire; the prancing prick Adlestrop's men.'

Bollingham nodded approvingly, turned from the settling dust of the broken section of wall and looked to Biviano. 'And you thought you'd wait for me? Kind of you, mate.'

'No,' Biviano said. 'I thought I'd check on the horses, because you've been gone an age.'

A grunt and Bollingham set out, following the nearest smoke to its source. He stopped and turned when Biviano didn't follow.

'Well?' Biviano asked, arms wide.

'I'm not telling you what happened to have to repeat myself when telling the other four shites.' He set out again, and once more Biviano didn't follow. Sighing and rubbing his red, sweaty face with his free hand, helm held by the other, Bollingham turned yet again. 'I'm not in the mood, Biv.'

'Maybe not, but nor are ye going the right way, Bolly.' Biviano grinned and set out the opposite direction to Bollingham, as another series of thuds and crashes marked the re-launching of the perriers and onagers at the sunset-illuminated walls of Beresford.

'Wait up!' Bollingham chased Biviano. 'When we get to them, I'm hauling them in a tent to talk.'

'You're the knight,' Biviano said, as the sun dipped low and the camp shadows stretched out.

'Yes. Yes, I am,' Sir Bollingham agreed, grin broad by Biviano's side.

Sears pressed his knuckles into his eyes and yawned. 'That's pure bollocks,' he said, the words breathy as they followed the yawn. Several others accompanied Sears with yawns of their own.

Bollingham frowned. 'But that's what I said to him!' he protested, waving midges away from his sun-reddened face at the same time. The stinking, cheap-oiled lamp-lit tent was full of them, despite the smoke.

'I too call bollocks to that, Bolly,' Biviano said, from across the tent.

'It's Sir—'

'Bollocks,' Jay Strawn finished for the knight. All laughed, bar Bollingham, who scowled.

'Well I didn't say it to Adlestrop's bloody face, but I thought it.'

Sears grinned at Bollingham. 'You brave devil you. So, what now?'

'We go back to Wesson?'

Five heads turned to the deep voice, the deep voice they rarely heard, from a man that always rode at the back and spent his camp time cooking, eating and sleeping, but not talking.

'Flay me now,' Jay Strawn said, 'if the bass of your unexpected input didn't just cause my arse to twitch, Big Dom.'

More laughter, except, again, from the group's knight.

'No, Dom, we're not heading back,' Bollingham said, eyes fixed on the blunt face of the man who was shaving his scalp to within an inch of its life with a razor that made everyone shudder.

'What is it with razors?' Pelse's untimely question gained everyone's attention. Everyone, that was, except the man using the razor.

'Eh?' Was all Biviano could muster.

'What's that got to do with the discussion?' Sears added.

Bollingham grunted. 'Discussion, is it? I'm the bloody knight and you're all supposed to do as I say.'

'Well,' Pelse went on in his reedy voice, ignoring his superior and answering Biviano's confusion and Sears' question. 'It's just, I'm looking at Big Dom scraping one across his thick head, little nicks here and there as always, little flashes of light reflected from the lamps, and I'm thinking—'

'Too much,' Bollingham muttered.

'—that it's but a slither of steel Dom wields,' Pelse continued regardless. 'A little swish and a little scrape. Little.' He looked off into a non-existent distance, tonguing the gaps in his teeth.

'Little?' Biviano prompted.

'Aye,' Pelse said, 'little. A little blade.' He nodded towards Big Dom and his razor. 'No bearded axe or bastard-sword, both capable of crushing bones or lopping off limbs. No lance or poleaxe, crossbow or war bow—'

'We get the point,' Jay Strawn said.

Pelse laughed, his voice breaking as he did so. 'No point, either, Jay. You're right there.' Jay Strawn shook his head in disbelief as Pelse blathered on. 'Just a little razor-sharp edge—'

'Hence the name.' Bollingham, again muttering.

'—and nothing more. A swish and a nick and a scrape, rather than a stab and a slash and a chop.'

'Poetic.' Biviano nodded his head towards Pelse whilst looking at Sears, who grinned.

'So why fear it so?' Pelse looked about the tent, pausing for a

379

moment on everyone bar Dom.

'Who says any of us do?' Jay Strawn puffed his chest out whilst lying on his bunk.

Dom was across the space in a heartbeat, a flash of lamp-light on steel followed by multiple holdings of breaths. Jay Strawn swallowed, the lump on his throat touching the razor's edge. Beads of sweat appeared on his brow as he stared at the bald man staring back. There was a group pause in the tent, awkward, tense, and then Dom grinned, removed the razor and strode back to where he'd been sat, shaving.

'My point exactly,' Pelse said victoriously. 'Or razor's edge, as the case may be.'

'You fucking prick!' Jay Strawn surged to his feet, basilard in hand.

'Or razor's nick,' Pelse mused aloud, despite Jay's aggressive stance in the middle of the tent. 'And the smallest of edges is what scared the shit out of the lot of you. No one's tense now, with Jay stood there, broad-bladed dagger in hand. But Big Dom and his little razor...' He left it there. Left it and looked down to his filthy nails, which he proceeded to dig at with the knife from his belt. His eating knife.

'Well that was the most pointless point of all,' Biviano said, head shaking as he stared at Pelse. 'And I thought Sir Bollocks here was pointless.'

'The Three with you, Biviano, you cock.' Bollingham stood and left the tent, his departure through the heavy canvas flap briefly increasing the sounds of the continuing siege they were a part of, but not.

Jay sat, eyes locked on Dom, who was shaving around his small ears. Jay had sheathed his basilard and contented himself with murderous looks, chest puffed out more than ever.

'So,' Sears said, looking to Biviano who was swatting midges on his neck, 'Adlestrop turned down our offer of aid; said no to Bollingham's request to join his father's siege. What do you make of that, Biv? That *was* what we were supposed to be discussing, wasn't it? With our good knight, mind.' Sears grinned.

Biviano grinned back. 'Aye, ye big ginger get, that's the gist of it. Bollingham could've told us more if he hadn't stormed out, lavishly long surcoat between his legs.'

The two of them shared a chuckle and looked about their companions: Jay Strawn glaring at Big Dom glancing at Pelse staring into a non-existent distance whilst picking his nails.

Sears took a deep breath. 'Reckon' we're screwed this time, Biv, ye weasel. No matter what the plan is now.'

Biviano grunted a laugh and slapped and scratched the back of his head. 'Aye, Sears, I reckon we are, for we've got to glean some useful shit about what the polished prat Rell Adlestrop is doing, Earl Marshal or not, Duke or not. And at the moment, I can't think how?'

'Especially if he's turned down aid from us to take back his father's own bloody town,' Big Dom said, his bass tone once again surprising them all. 'For a man to turn down aid at a time like this, he must suspect us of something.'

Biviano nodded. 'Well let's hope it's not a suspicion of the truth, that we're here to spy on him, for if it is—'

'The Three might as well be with us after all.' Sears grimaced at his own words, and the rest shuddered at the thought.

Chapter 64 – Bangs in the night

An ear-splitting crack and the loudest of bangs woke the whole tent.

'Fuck was that?' Jay Strawn said, sitting in his cot.

Good question. Biviano's heart pounded as much as his ears.

A cheer went up, as loud as the bang had been, accompanied by barking dogs and braying and lowing beasts of burden.

'That's our lot,' Sears said of the bang and cheer, standing to remove the cowl from the lamp hanging in the tent.

'Our lot?' Pelse frowned. 'They've not accepted Sir Bollocks' offer of aid.'

'Cock,' Bollingham said to Pelse, standing and stretching as he did so.

'Against goblins, Pelse, the Beresford's *are* our lot. Contract of employment or not,' Biviano said, hauling Sears to his feet. They'd all slept in their armour, weapons close to hand. More in suspicion of Rell Adlestrop's men coming for them than any threat of goblins sallying forth from Beresford's gates.

'Fair one,' Pelse said, pulling on his maille coif – the only thing he'd removed.

Big Dom pushed through the tent opening from his watch. 'Should've seen that!' he said in his baritone voice.

Bollingham crossed to the big man, pulling on his own padded cap and coif before reaching for his helmet. 'Well we didn't, Dom,' he said, 'so out with it.'

Dom shrugged. 'There was a yellow flash before the bang. Something hit the wall hard following that.'

Biviano saw Bollingham frown in the lamplight.

'A siege engine made that noise?' Bollingham pulled on and strapped his re-polished bascinet. 'I assumed it'd been magic.'

'A cannon,' Biviano breathed, before Big Dom could.

'Aye, Biv's got the measure of it,' Dom said, nodding. He turned and headed back outside, everyone on his heels.

Biviano followed Bollingham out after a worried glance at Sears. Despite the lamp in the tent, the light from the multiple campfires and moon caused Biviano to squint, but for a heartbeat. The cheering died soon after it started, but the camp was noisy, alive with chatter and laughs and song.

'They're celebrating it,' Jay Strawn said, last out of the tent, basilard in hand.

Sears shoved the man hard. 'Put the blade away, ye prick, before ye get us all arrested.'

Jay snarled. 'Caution is my friend, Sears.'

'Aye, and my fists are mine and ye'll be—'

'Enough!' Bollingham turned and glared at the lot of them.

'Ooh...' Pelse started, but Biviano shook his head.

'Time to get serious, lads,' Biviano said, eyeing them all. 'There should be no cannons in Altoln, let alone used by Altoln. Happen this is what we were sent to find out, eh?'

Bollingham was nodding. 'I think you're right, Biv.'

'Course he is,' Sears said, pushing in alongside is friend. 'So, Sir Bollingham, what now?'

Biviano saw Bollingham start at that.

'Yes, well,' Bollingham said, all eyes now on him and in a serious capacity.

'We get to asking around,' Biviano prompted.

Bollingham licked his wine-stained lips and nodded. 'Whilst morale is high.' He met Biviano's eyes. They nodded to one another. 'Right, ye shits,' Sir Bollingham continued, confident now, as he gave his orders, 'we split up and head out into the camp. Be subtle but be joyful and loud with it.'

Pelse screwed up his face. 'Eh?'

Biviano sighed. 'Blend in. Make merry. Cheer the fucking cannon, but enquire about it at the same time.'

'Where it's come from, if there are more,' Sir Bollingham added. 'Just don't get caught asking.'

Pelse frowned again. 'Ask but don't get caught asking?'

'Good,' Biviano slapped Pelse on the back, 'ye've got it. Now let's head out, eh, Sir Bollingham?'

Sir Bollingham smiled. 'Aye, Biviano. Let's head out.'

***

A calamitous crash of stone caving in yet another rooftop nearby was followed mere heartbeats later by the now familiar boom, bang and crack of the gun firing its pathetic stone balls at the curtain walls. A cheer followed the cannon's firing and it was that sound that annoyed the goblin necromancer the most.

'Can you not let me sleep!' Core shrieked as loud as his hoarse throat would allow. 'Days of this shit,' he muttered as he scrambled painfully to his feet. 'Crash, bang,' he continued, to himself, 'thump, boom, bloody smash and trash your own town, why don't you? Bloody pink skinned pricks of limp bastard whore-pokers.'

'What?' came a muffled voice from beneath the flea infested blanket Core stood over. A swift boot and the grunted question turned into a stream of curses to rival Core's own.

'Up, turds. Up I say. The bloody lot of you are with me. Now!' he yelled the rest, throat be damned, and stormed from the building and out into the night. Cursing some more as he limped along, silver plated cane at his side and stolen hood pulled up, Core rapped and hammered on every door he passed. 'Up, you gobshites! Up, up, up and at 'em. I'm sick of the bastard noise and stones and arrows and shit. I'm sick of being woken and I'm sick to the hind teeth of you shites sleeping whilst I can't.'

The young apprentice who opened his door before it was knocked on fell back at three raps of the silver cane, which cracked from his forehead, losing him his consciousness for his eager troubles.

'Blood God's bits,' Core cursed, rolling his black eyes and limping off once more, a crowd of goblins in his wake, some eagerly, most in barely contained annoyance or rage.

Another something struck a rooftop further to the south of the gatehouse, for which the gathering goblins were heading.

A runner came loping down the detritus- and body-strewn street, the goblin messenger nearly as tall as the – now dead – hobyahs that had originally accompanied The Red Goblin when he'd taken the west bank of Beresford.

'What news?' Core demanded.

Coming to a stop, hands on knees, the panting goblin answered. 'They're… tunnelling.'

The mass of muttering, coughing and grunting goblins gathered around Core and the runner.

'Tunnelling where?'

'That way.' The runner jabbed his clawed finger south. 'Under the wall. To burn the foundations.'

Core sucked his teeth and shrugged. 'No matter,' he said, shoving the runner over and setting out once more, 'they won't have time for tunnelling when we're done with them.' There was a half-hearted cheer at that, followed by an enthusiastic roar as Core stopped and glared backward. Nodding and grinning at the response, the old necromancer limped on, cane thumping as he thought of all his kin lost over the weeks-long occupation of

Beresford. And of all the fun they'd had too. But that time was past, because he'd decided it was past. Their work was done and, at any rate, there was hardly food left to sustain them much more than a couple of days, and after that, well, knowing his kin as he did, Core knew he'd sooner stick it to the humans before what remained of the clans turned on one another.

It was time to answer the humans' noise and missiles with some surprises of his own; some of the humans' own. It was time for the wrinkled and ragged necromancer and his young coven to release the toys they'd gathered within the town, breaking the siege once and for all.

It was time to release Beresford's dead.

Chapter 65 – A bloody smile

Sears walked up to the fire, rubbing his hands. It was far from a cold night, but the darkness held a chill a good fire could warm away. 'Lads,' he greeted, crouching and holding his large hands out to the writhing flames and glowing logs.

A grinning face appeared next to his, glancing at him sidelong. 'Ye see it?' the man asked Sears. The flames danced their light across the soldier's plate arms and legs and riveted maille, and Sears couldn't help but appreciate the excellent craftsmanship of the tiny rivets through flattened links, not to mention the expensive, blued plate. The maille alone was better than any Sears wore, and that was saying something considering his had come from Stowold's armoury. The man's hauberk was well kept, too. Oiled, the sheen of it putting Sears' road dusted hauberk to shame, whilst the spaulders and rerebrace, couter and vambrace were etched with lines of what looked like Samorlian scripture. The leg pieces were decorated in similar script, but Sears looked up to the grinning face and smiled back before his gawking got him into trouble. He cursed himself for not taking note of the man's surcoat. Was he one of Adlestrop's, or his father Beresford's? Or someone else's? It was a dark livery, with no obvious devices, but the fire's light wasn't enough to notice whether the surcoat was black or a dark blue, or green, like Sears' gambeson. Sears shrugged inwardly, supposing it didn't matter.

'The cannon?' Sears asked, grasping at the fortuitous opportunity that had presented itself.

The man laughed. 'Aye, man, the bloody cannon.'

'Samorl knows I heard the thing.' Sears laughed. He grinned inwardly at using Samorl's name to the apparently religious… knight? He was certainly equipped as one.

Nodding, the knight – for Sears had decided it so – leaned in to Sears, who tensed. 'I saw it fire,' the knight said, before pulling away.

Sears frowned, slapped at a biting midge the fire's smoke failed to deter, and turned on the man. 'Bollocks!' The knight likely had seen the cannon fire, but Sears knew that to prod a boastful man to offer up information you first had to call him a liar.

'No lie,' the knight said, frowning back. 'I saw the engineers fire the thing. Saw it smash a chunk from the wall the big trebuchet they're building would struggle to do.'

Sears sniffed and nodded. 'I heard it was good, but not that good.' He slapped at another midge and cursed whilst doing so.

'Well, take it from me, friend, it's better than you heard.'

'I suppose dwarven shit usually is though, eh?' Sears bated the hook.

The knight frowned, turned his head for a second and looked straight back at Sears. 'It isn't dwarven, man. Rell Adlestrop had it made! That talk is across camp. That there cannon smashing the wall every half-day is man-made, my friend. *Man. Made.*' He said the latter slowly, accentuating the words as he locked Sears with an intensive stare, so as to strike home the incredible point of it.

This is easier than I thought. Sears learned more in that one sentence than any of them had since their arrival. It was then that Sears saw the skin on the man's belt. 'Wine?' he asked, nodding to the container. Sears wasn't a wine man, but to sidle further into the knight's trust, he thought it a good plan. The knight grinned and unhooked the skin, before offering Sears a pull.

'Don't mind if I do, friend.' Sears grinned and obliged the knight. *Sirretan red, like that shit in Stowold's keep...* He frowned. *Who is this man? Blued plate and good riveted maille, Sirretan red in a skin on a fine, plated belt... yet talks common and crouches by a fire surrounded by the rank and file?* Narrowing his blurring eyes, Sears returned the knight's wine, went to ask a question, slurred his words and collapsed into darkness.

'I've another, Sire.'

Biviano scowled at the man dragging him along. His scowl turned into a grimace as he saw Sears' unmoving form by the fire. Biviano groaned aloud as he saw two more men being lead in, iron manacles about their wrists like the ones he wore himself. Jay Strawn and Pelse gave Biviano withering looks of their own. *Well, this went well,* Biviano thought. *I wonder how Big Dom and Bolly are getting—*

'Unhand me, I'm a bloody knight, you fools!'

Biviano sighed and looked from Bollingham to the man standing on the far side of the fire, wearing nothing but boots, black hose and white braes, his chest bare. The man's belt held a glittering, gold-hilted dagger. No sword or pouch. He looked like he'd been dragged from his bed. A man stepped out of the tent beside him dressed in shining blued plate and maille. The impressively armoured man walked straight to the fire and emptied out what looked to be a skin of wine. The fire hissed. Biviano frowned at the black, heraldry-free surcoat the knight wore. He looked about their captors in general. Those of them wearing armour wore decent armour, far more plate than was normal this side of The Marches, unless you were a high lord, rich knight, or bodyguard to some Earl or the like. *And all of them wear black,* Biviano thought, his suspicion rising. It wasn't the livery of any lord Biviano knew to be present on the field. He grunted. *They're much like us.*

'And you are?' Bollingham said to the half-dressed man, who was too casual to be anything but their captain, despite the richly armoured knight stood over Sears' prone form.

'I am who I am,' Captain said, flashing a smile at Bollingham. 'And you are?'

Sir Bollingham's face hardened. 'Detained without accusation.'

Good one, Bolly. Biviano was unable to hide his amusement at that.

'And your joker?' Captain lifted his chin to Biviano. His accent was odd, like Sirretan, but not.

'A nobody,' Bollingham said flatly.

Biviano frowned.

Captain laughed. 'It is like that, is it? Very well, I shall state a plain fact and we can go on from there. None of you wear colours—'

'Nor do you or yours.' Jay Strawn spat into the fire, producing a hiss.

Captain nodded and smiled. 'Hence my suspicions, for I know my role and why I do not wear any colours, bar the black I choose for my men and I. It does force me to wonder why you and your men wear nought but green though? No badge, insignia or heraldic device. Not even a chevron or bend upon your green field. It is strange or it is simply what I suspect it is, unless you are pathfinders of the King. But I think not.'

'You wish to know who our lord is?' Biviano asked in clarification, trying to take control of the situation away from his stupid companions.

'Is this an Eatrian Parliament?' Captain said, anger flecking his tone. 'That you can all talk at once and discuss your situation? Or is your knight here,' he indicated Bollingham, 'in charge of your small band?'

'He is our lord and the captain of this company. We're

mercenaries,' Biviano said, before Bollingham could speak.

'And I am Rell Adlestrop himself,' Captain lied. His men laughed. 'You are here to spy. That bit is simple truth. I know fellow sell-swords when I see them and you are not they. What is also simple truth is that you are here to spy on my employer's cannon. But to what ends, I ask you? To take plans perhaps? And for whom? I do not yet know, but I will. Oh, by the gods below, gentlemen, I will know. For I am paid well to know such things.' Captain turned and strode into the darkness between tents.

'He means torture,' the man stood behind Biviano said, his accent Altolnan, local even. Biviano could hear the glee in the man's words.

'We gathered that,' Biviano said, as Pelse started muttering to himself in a panic, Jay Strawn cursing along similar lines.

'We're fucked,' Bollingham blurted, fear stretching his face and draining the colour.

'No...' Biviano grinned. '...the half-dressed bastard captain is, I promise you that!' He said the latter louder, to the mercenaries surrounding them.

As Bollingham frowned and the man behind Biviano punched him on a shoulder that was near on used to it, a shout went up from the direction of Beresford's gatehouse. And as confusion set in and horns and drums sounded, the half-dressed captain who'd disappeared between the tents staggered back out, a red, gushing line stretching literally from ear-to-ear across his throat. He collapsed face first into the fire, scattering logs and sparks. Black clad men cursed whilst others shouted warnings in a mixture of accents and languages. And from the darkness strode Big Dom, a wicked grin spreading across his face and a bloody razor in his ham of a fist.

Biviano saw their captors look at that razor as one. He saw them scatter, the richly armoured knight the first of them. Grunting a laugh at the irony of it all, Biviano was about to call for Big Dom to find the keys to the manacles when he saw the real reason for their captors' swift departure. He saw the new threat lurching, jerking and staggering towards them like the turfing out of a tavern in the wee hours of the morning. But these men and women weren't drunk, he saw in horror, they were dead.

No order was given by Sir Bollingham, or Biviano. It wasn't needed. Big Dom heaved an unconscious Sears onto his back with a groan, after glancing behind him and cursing, and the lot of them ran the same way their captors had, manacled to a man apart from Big Dom, and running for their lives as the dead of Beresford made chase.

Chapter 66 – Tables turned

Biviano dragged in cold, woodsmoke tainted air, chest heaving as he did so. His throat hurt and he was dying for a drink. Dying. He shuddered at the thought of what he'd be doing after death if he fell in such a place. Steel rang on steel and thwacked against leather and flesh and bone all over the camp. More horns sounded and booted feet hammered the ground, charging to and fro down the paths between tents. Screams punctuated it all, guttural, terrified, in denial and more, every kind of scream and every kind of moan and groan, dead, dying and curled up hiding.

'Clear!' Big Dom led them across a wide path where the grass was flattened from too many boots and hooves. Dogs barked, oxen lowed and horses whinnied; one screamed, too close.

'They're in with the horses,' a boy shouted, his words twisted through sobbing fear. He ran past the group, telling them the news as if they needed to know, but not stopping. He disappeared behind a white tent.

'With me!' a man shouted from somewhere in the general direction of the horses.

Another man screamed, although it could have been a woman for the pitch of it.

Biviano thought he heard the sound of crossbows twanging, but no shouts or cries of pain followed. He didn't suppose the dead would cry out though. *What hell is this?* he thought, before following Big Dom down another line of tents. They came out onto an opening, a large camp fire in the centre. A man staggered about, ablaze, silent as he tripped on a rope and fell into the offending tent. The canvas went up in the time it took the burning corpse to climb to its feet and stagger towards the group.

'I hate this, I hate this, I hate this…' Pelse continued through broken teeth, shaking his manacles and giving the burning corpse a wide birth as Big Dom waded in, the spear he'd found punching through the burning face and propelling the corpse to the ground, all with an unconscious Sears over one shoulder.

'Keep moving!' Biviano shook his manacles down the gradual slope, away from the large, fire- and moon-lit walls behind them.

The group ran on, Big Dom leading and the best armoured – Bollingham – bringing up the rear.

'In here.' Big Dom plunged into a large galley tent, the colours of its stripes lost in the darkness. As they entered, shoving in around tables and benches, the sound of several armoured men passed by outside. There came shouted orders and what seemed to be an organised assault on some named position of the camp that Bollingham's men didn't recognise.

'They're overcoming the shock of it all and re-taking the camp.' Biviano said to Bollingham.

Bollingham nodded. 'Aye and when they do...' He left it at that, let the implications sink in.

'We need to move again,' Biviano said. 'Get out whilst we can.'

'Back into the night with those things?' Pelse whined more than said, eyes wide.

Biviano shoved Pelse hard. 'Yes, ye soft sod, it's practically day with all the fires and the moon, now come on.'

Pelse scowled but nodded and followed. Biviano led this time, despite his bound hands. Leaving the tent, he ran headlong into the very man who'd manacled him. They collided together and hit the ground hard. The man let out a high-pitched shriek, his terror dribbling down his leg.

'Get him off!' Biviano shouted. He scrambled up when the weigh left him, turned and saw Sears, standing, snarling and holding the mercenary in an arm lock. The man yelped and pleaded to be released, wide eyes searching the darkness between tents.

Sears' eyes glowed like the many fires about them and the man paled, pleaded and struggled all the more.

Biviano grinned at Sears, then looked back at his previous captor. 'How quickly roles reverse, eh, ye shit?'

'Shut up, Biv, he's what we've needed,' Bollingham said, satisfied with it all. 'Now run!'

They did as Sir Bollingham bade them, prisoner yanked along with Sears, and quickly, for a group of corpses approached at speed.

Chapter 67 – On the run

Seven armoured but unarmed – apart from one razor – men ran down the moon-lit road, maille rustling and five manacles jingling. The seventh's hands were bound with a belt, a gag about his mouth. They were followed by one staggering corpse of a man, lower jaw missing, swollen tongue lolling. The corpse might have been faster, might have been able to catch the trailing prisoner of Sir Bollingham's small company, if not for the kick to the knee it'd received from Sears a quarter mile back.

'This is getting old fast.' Biviano stumbled in the dark and nearly fell behind the rest. Sears' strong grip on his painful shoulder hauled him up and on. After the grunt of it all, Biviano said, 'Someone should go… finish the thing. We can't keep running… with all this clobber on.'

'Be my guest,' Jay Strawn said, from the front, his run as uneven as the corpse at their rear, his breathing as ragged as everyone else's.

'Easier said than done… with no weapons.' Pelse's red-rimmed eyes remained as wide as they'd been at their capture, face as white as the corpse's; his heavy breathing born of fear as well as exertion, Biviano knew, for he felt the same.

Jay Strawn spat as he ran. 'I'd do it… if that shit of a mercenary's bastard mates… hadn't taken my weapons. I loved that fucking basilard… Bastards!' He shouted the latter back at the terrified, stumbling man who Sears dragged along. Jay had gone on about his stolen basilard more than anything since they'd escaped the camp.

'I know you would, Jay, but—'

'For 'morl's sake,' Big Dom cut in on Biviano whilst halting. 'I'll do it myself.'

The running company slowed to a halt, turned and gaped as Big Dom casually walked back to the running corpse, hooked it around the neck with one thick arm, spun it and proceeded to saw through its neck at great speed with his razor, all whilst snarling and shrugging off the clawing of its broken-nailed fingers and the slobbering of its thrashing tongue.

Sears winced, Biviano grunted a laugh, Jaw Strawn jogged on a little further and Pelse threw up, spattering Sir Bollingham's maille sabatons, causing the knight to curse and shove Pelse over. The prisoner gagged behind his… gag, at the sight and sound and smell of it all.

As the headless corpse fell to the ground, Big Dom raised the head and grinned, before throwing it into the bushes at the side of the road. 'Done,' he said, dropping to one knee and cleaning his blade on the corpse's clothes. 'I've never slit a throat without blood spurting before.'

Their prisoner fainted.

Sears spat. 'Great, now we're to carry him.'

Biviano's eyes widened as he took in the big man. 'Says you, ye ginger get. Poor Big Dom had to carry you—

'Piss off, Sears!' Biviano attempted to twist away from the pain of the punch he'd received to his shoulder. Sears grinned.

'I'm not carrying that prick.' Big Dom pointed his cleaned razor to the unconscious mercenary. He strode past the lot of them, except Jay, who was a way ahead down the road and, by the sounds of it, muttering about his beloved basilard.

Sears sighed and turned to see everyone walking away, except Pelse, who proceeded to wipe sick from his mouth with the unconscious man's sleeve. At least when he looked up to Sears, Pelse had the decency to shrug an apology before standing and hurrying after the others, panting as he went.

All Biviano did was grin and wink before quick-stepping away. 'We should have grabbed weapons on our way out of camp,' he said, to the groans of all as Jay began his rant once more.

A little way on down the road and Sears grunted from behind Biviano, who tensed instinctively. Nothing struck him so he glanced back. Sears carried their prisoner as Big Dom had carried him, and was grunting with the exertion of it.

'We were busy running from the dead,' Bollingham said to Biviano, 'otherwise I'd have chosen horses over weapons.'

'Good point,' Biviano conceded, putting some distance between his shoulder and Sears' fist. Despite the armoured man Sears carried – they'd not had time to strip his armour, after all – Biviano knew the big oaf could still deliver a blow if Sears felt Biviano deserved one. 'We've a long old walk back to Wesson.'

Pelse nodded and licked his lips, wincing as he did so. 'Aye, and all the while we'll be walking manacled on the King's road with a man bound and gagged over one of our party's shoulders.'

Silence followed, from the group at least, for the night offered many sounds: a barn owl in the near distance, some rustling in bushes that raised hairs on necks and painted pictures of dead men and women and children in Biviano's mind. They walked on a while without talking, the only sound from the group being their boots on the ground and the odd curse or huff or sigh.

'Did ye hear 'em get back into Beresford?' Biviano asked of them all, sick of the awkwardness the silence allowed.

'The horns and cheers?'

Biviano nodded, then voiced his agreement to Sir Bollingham.

'Aye,' Bollingham said. 'I reckon the goblins didn't get the gates shut quickly enough after… after releasing the town's dead.'

'My thinking too.' Biviano sped up a little to walk alongside Sir Bollingham. 'Ye think they took the town back by now?'

Sir Bollingham nodded. 'Reckon so, Biv, aye. Reckon as soon as the horns sounded and the cheer went up, horses and men clattered through those gates. I reckon that was when the far side sent their own across the bridge, against the barricades. I reckon Beresford is ours once more, Biv.'

Biviano looked to his friend. 'Ours, or the Beresford's?' Sir Bollingham frowned, so Biviano went on. 'We were sent against the Beresfords, Bolly. Or against the younger, Rell. A lot has happened around here so far this year and a lot more is going to happen, methinks. Sears had the right of it when he said we were with the Beresfords with regards to goblins, but if the town is Earl Beresford's once more, in full, I'm for thinking it's us and them now.'

Sir Bollingham nodded solemnly at that.

Biviano sighed. 'And I'm not sure ours and theirs and sides of this and that are as clear as these nobles make out. There's been baronial wars in the past and—'

'Hold on, Biv.' Sir Bollingham grabbed Biviano's nearest manacled wrist as they walked along, Bollingham's own manacles rattling in the process. 'Just because our liege lord wants to know what another is up to, doesn't mean baronial war.'

Shaking his friend off, Biviano shrugged. 'I know, but it doesn't mean it isn't either. One uses cannon, which none of them are supposed to have to start with, and another sends spies, us, against him. There's a fair amount of betrayal and suspicion and shit going on here, Bolly. Ye not think? And the only thing keeping it all together is King Barrison. The way I see it anyway.'

Sir Bollingham filled his cheeks and let out a long breath. He shrugged too, his spaulders creaking. 'Let's get this mercenary bastard back to Stowold and see what our next orders are, eh?'

Biviano looked sideways, caught Sir Bollingham's eye. 'And you're happy to do that, are you? Whatever those orders may be?'

'Yes.' The answer was short and sharp, as was the look Biviano received. 'It's what we do. It's what we've always done. It's for an Earl now, not a captain of the City Guard is all.'

Biviano sighed. 'I do like him,' Biviano admitted. 'He's done a lot for Sears and me.' He laughed. 'He bloody well knighted you, mate, and offered me the same.'

'Aye and Rell shitting Adlestrop and his father have done nought but...' Sir Bollingham jingled his manacles. '...clamped these on us and threatened us with torture by men who don't even wear their colours.'

As oppose to us... Biviano looked down at his plain green tabard and back to their prisoner's black, the man bouncing with Sears' loping steps. 'Aye, fills me full of reassurance.'

Sir Bollingham said nothing as they strode on, nor did Biviano, feet aching, clammy body sweating under too much padding for the lengthy run they'd endured, and iron bound wrists chafing.

Everything was so much simpler when it was Sears and me.

'I've had a thought,' Sears said.

I take that back, Biviano thought. 'Go on, big guy.'

'Pelse had a point earlier,' Sears went on, glancing to the man he mentioned.

'About?' Sir Bollingham said.

'Walking the roads in this state, with Rell Adlestrop wronged by us, as he'd see it.'

There was quiet for a while.

'We're going to trek through fields and woods and shit, aren't we?' Pelse asked.

'It'll take us an age,' Jay Strawn complained, followed by a string of curses.

'But it'll save us our necks,' Biviano said and, to his surprise, Sir Bollingham agreed and gave the order to leave the road.

'Wish I'd never fucking spoke,' Pelse muttered as they hit the fields.

'You can always start that now,' Sears said, and Biviano barked a laugh as the group headed into the night.

***

Core fell back through Beresford's streets, his guards sticking close, a mix of fear and glee in their maniacal eyes and grins. Oh how he hated his kin sometimes. Were there any goblins of intellect left in Brisance?

'With me,' he shouted, turning a corner and running as best as his heart, lungs and legs would allow, silver cane clacking alongside him as he ran. The humans had surprised him by forcing their way into Beresford as he'd tried to sally forth with his toys. That had been two days ago. Two. Already! With the sound of horns and shouts and hooves pounding the earth in the hours and days that followed. But he'd survived and evaded thus far, every street the humans took cost them dearly.

Core's fingers flexed as he stumbled along, his eyes twitching, runny nose wrinkling and gut churning; with discerning effort, a pile of corpses he past clambered, crawled and stood, to head in the direction Core ran from. Some of his dozen or so guards yelped and some squealed with excitement as the staggering corpses accelerated into loping runs, their moans joining the multitude of horrific sounds accompanying the murky dawn.

Core ran on and found his escape; unfortunate it was, for his guards, that they were not included in his survival plan.

Their guttural, terrified and agony-filled screams, from the impact of needle-tipped bodkin arrows, crossbow bolts and ash-shafted spears; polearms and whatever else spitted them or hacked into them, bore Core away on a raft of floating corpses: rotten arms paddling, legs kicking and goblin necromancer smirking as he floated down river, Beresford burning once more.

'So long, my fair kin,' Core said, watching from the misty waters as the last of the goblins fell to human steel.

Oh, how he loved war.

Chapter 68 – Bedraggled homecoming

Errolas, Amis and Salliss had all agreed with Correia. Correia
wasn't sure whether it was through actual agreement, because of
her rank as King's Spymaster, or, more than likely, because she'd
been in a foul mood when approaching them in Lord Temn's food
hall. Regardless the reason, the four of them, made five by one of
Royce's Reds who'd been ordered with them by Temn, rode and
flew from Landon Hill as soon as they were able. Provisions had
been prepared, as had the beasts, and so it was that over the
coming days, Correia was guided north by a sour faced knight of
Hud's company. Salliss clung to Correia's back, the hippogriff the
best mount to proceed with two riders. Or so Hud's knight had
said, near on spat. They flew and they rode, camped and sought
hostel in farm houses and little known hamlets where heads turned,
mouths gaped, fingers pointed and Correia spoke to cooks, often
bringing away hastily written recipes. She'd been asked, many times
and by varying members of the group, about Fal and the others,
about her plans and about the cooks and their recipes. Each time
she snarled or frowned and shrugged, depending on her mood.
None of those times did she answer. None of those times did she
feel she could. Each conversation about such subjects ended
before they'd begun and, eventually, her companions stopped
asking. More to pain Correia was the increasingly haunted look on
Errolas' face as he wondered about his friends; on Salliss' face as
she wondered about her family and friends and Queen, and nation.
All of their faces set grim, brief flares of mirth around hearths not
enough to break the tension or melancholy of the group. War was
coming. No, war was upon them and they were heading away, not
towards it. That might not have been too bad if they hadn't left
those they cared for behind, Hud's man included.

'There she is,' Errolas called across the wind, pointing with a
slender finger.

Correia squinted against distance and cold both, against
moisture and the bluster that faced them each day they took to the
sky. Only one had been spent fully on the ground, riding. A day
full of rain and heavy black clouds. Correia acknowledged her luck
that more days hadn't been like that in Altoln, despite the summer.

'Wesson?' Correia shouted back to the pegasus-riding elf. She
still couldn't get over his shorn hair. It made him look different,
which mirrored how everything felt to her.

'Wesson,' Errolas confirmed.

Heart and stomach leapt as Correia gave the order to descend. Hud's man led them down, spiralling as they had many times. She wasn't used to the beast she rode, Salliss at her back, but her confidence had risen, if not her skill. The powerful animal followed the others as the ground swirled, trees and patchwork fields rising to meet them, the walls of her home city growing on the horizon, far less smoke rising in comparison to Correia's last return to Wesson. They were to ride, not fly, through the gates. She hadn't come this far to have a windlass bolt punch her or any of the others from the saddle. Wesson was a different place after the plague and Correia had no idea how much had changed since she'd last been there. *Much, I expect. And not for the better.* She sighed and clenched her teeth and tensed as the equine-raptor touched down, a tad more gracefully than the pegasi she noted. And on they rode, Correia taking the lead towards the southern gates of Wesson and its palace. Her home.

***

'This better be good.' Stowold reined his palfrey in before a bedraggled group being held at Wesson's Eastern Gate. 'I'm not accustomed to being summoned by a gatehouse captain, especially after I appointed the blasted man but a week ago. And especially not when it's bloody well raining.' He rocked back when he took in the men held at the gate. 'You look like shit, the lot of you.'

A sodden, filthy and exhausted Sir Bollingham cleared his throat and held up his blood-crusted manacles. 'Begging your pardon, milord, but that new captain you appointed wouldn't let us pass, despite me being a knight and all, and despite three days roughing it, off the roads.'

Stowold's eyes drifted to the black clad stranger stood and held by Big Dom, belted wrists and gagged mouth drawing more attention by the surrounding guardsmen than the other men's manacles. Stowold sighed and rubbed at his wet face. 'Very well,' he said, turning his horse on the spot. 'Have them escorted to my estate, Captain.' He didn't even bother to ask why they were manacled and why they had been off the roads. He had enough on his plate as it was.

The fresh-faced captain nodded eagerly and bowed, but said nothing.

'But, milord?'

'Save it, Biviano. Save it until you're dry and cleaned up and fed and free of irons and the shit of the road… and vomit,' Stowold said, sniffing the air. 'Always with the vomit.'

Sir Bollingham made to speak and Stowold rode off, ignoring the shaking of manacles and the curses and the confused questions and protests that started at his back. He rode off and he grinned, despite the pin pricks of rain on his face. They had answers, his men, or rather it looked like they had someone who had answers. All he need do now was ride home, take the bath he'd been intending to take and await their return and report – which would be lengthy, no doubt.

Then we can work out what that little prick Rell Adlestrop is up to, Stowold thought, beaming as he rode. Beaming, that was, until he realised his unheralded spies had called for him in person, at the main gates. Beaming, that was, until he realised none of them had been in the company of a single horse, never mind the twelve he'd let them ride out with, five of which had been destriers. Not the best destriers, but expensive all the same.

Bagnall Stowold swore at length and drove spurs into his palfrey's flanks, scattering the folk in his path and riding recklessly all the way back to his estate.

Chapter 69 – Assassin

'Can't believe the bastard made us walk.' Pelse forced the words through tight lips as a servant scrubbed at his filthy face, another at his back.

'I guess after the time we took marching from Beresford—'

'And after losing more of his horses,' Sears interrupted Biviano.

'—Stowold thought nothing of letting us walk through the city,' Biviano finished, nodding and wincing his acknowledgement to Sears' words as a servant worked at removing a fat tick from his grubby ankle.

Jay Strawn merely sighed with satisfaction and leered at Big Dom's servant whilst an older woman brushed at his black fingernails.

'I've never seen so much hot water in my life,' Sir Bollingham said, eyes wide at the large, sunken bath he sat at one end of. Steam rose from the now mucky waters, as servants bent and scrubbed and tended each of them.

'And you a knight.' Biviano grinned over at Sir Bollingham, who raised two fingers, but grinned back all the same.

'I could get used to this,' Big Dom rumbled in his bass tone. The girl massaging his nicked and scarred scalp tittered.

Jay Strawn frowned. 'Why'd he get the pretty one and I get—' He took a slap from the old dear who'd been brushing his nails. She spat in the water, between his legs, and stormed off to the accompaniment of much laughter, and a curse from Jay.

'Is this what Stowold has regular like?' Pelse asked, face cleaner than it had ever been.

Biviano nodded, then cursed with pain and relief as the tick was finally removed. 'Reckon so, Pelse,' he said, studying the little beastie he'd taken from the girl as she proceeded to wash him with a gusto he reckoned a stable boy would use on a filthy pack horse.

'I could get used to this too,' Sears said.

The rest of them agreed, none of them continuing with any word of what Stowold might say once they reported their findings. Nor did they mention the mercenary who'd been taken to a cell by Sir Bryant and two wicked looking men. Biviano was glad no one mentioned that, for the thought of it sparked memories of Ellis Frane and the bowels of the Samorlian Cathedral. He was equally glad no one mentioned it for Sears' and, in turn, all their sakes.

If what I think might happen to that man, bastard or not, reaches Sears...

401

Biviano shuddered and pushed the memories of red eyes and red flames away. He pushed them away and laid back, enjoying the luxury he and his friends were receiving… *Likely before Stowold's verbal roasting of us all.* Again he shuddered at the thought and again he pushed it from his mind, one last painful thought slipping through. *If only we'd retrieved the bloody horses.*

***

Rain swept in off the sea as Correia and her group moved through the tall gatehouse and into the palace's outer bailey. The sky had darkened through cloud and dusk shortly after their landing and she'd grunted a laugh at that. It was summer in Altoln and yet in rolled the rain as if to greet her with mockery. Mounted men-at-arms of the palace escorted her party to stables, although she'd insisted it wasn't necessary. The answer the gate captain had given her struck a chill through her no rising wind or sudden downpour could best. They'd hardly stabled their winged mounts, passing reins to gawking stable hands, before bells rang throughout the palace. Bells and shouts, horns and barks – officers' orders and dogs alike.

Correia felt what little colour remained drain from her face. She hesitated, but for a heartbeat, her companions looking about in confusion. She ran, travel and emotional fatigue forgotten. She drew swords and charged full tilt across an already rain-slick courtyard, footsteps on her heels, shouts and questions and warnings ignored. One word ran through her mind: *Assassin.* One face: King Barrison. *Father.*

Soldiers massed and soldiers moved. Bells tolled and crossbows were loaded. Knights ran from towers, squires and pages carrying shields and swords and hastily arming them as they went. Figures ran across ramparts, sheets of rain blurring their outlines, hampering their views of the ground below. Correia passed men shouting for her and her companions to stop. None dared question her when she snapped who she was. Some followed, caught up in the speed of it all, the confusion and excitement.

'Where's Barrison?' Correia yelled as she rounded the base of a drum tower, familiar armour and hardened face meeting her.

'In his receiving chamber.' Sergeant Grannit lead Correia and her companions without question.

'How many?' Correia asked between breaths as they filtered

through a guard-crowded doorway. Her companions received confused and suspicious glances, glares even, but none challenged, not with Sergeant Grannit and Lady Burr at their head.

'We don't know,' Grannit admitted. He slowed to give an order to two men before speeding up again. 'Gate guards found dead—'

'Which gate?' Correia saw soldiers searching servants, faces awash with fear or determination or both.

'Kings Avenue trade,' Grannit replied, clanking up a twisting staircase, his breaths now as heavy as Correia's as they ascended. She could hear the others at her back, following quickly, wordlessly. She didn't know how many had tagged along. Didn't care.

'Hold!' shouted a baritone voice as the group left the stairs and neared a corner. Grannit slowed, but didn't stop.

'It's Grannit,' he said, now at a fast walk, hand on sheathed sword. 'I've Lady Burr with me,' he added, stopping before rounding the corner.

'Who else?'

'Her companions, now—'

'Come, slowly.'

Grannit looked to Correia and nodded. She nodded back. Grannit held arms wide and rounded the corner, Correia sheathing her swords and doing the same. She didn't have to look behind her to know Errolas and any others would match them.

Correia knew the palace well, very well, and knew the stretch of corridor they were entering. She gritted teeth as more bells pealed in the near distance, and another horn sounded, closer. Walking the corner, she saw a set of double doors and two halberdiers. She knew them both.

The two men raised their polearms and stood to attention as the group approached. Their heads faced front as ever, but their eyes searched, quested those behind Grannit and Correia in a way they normally would not. Finally before the two guards, they turned and rapped on the large door, which opened from the inside. Through went Grannit, Correia on his heels and Errolas and Salliss and Amis on hers.

'Correia!' Will Morton stepped from a window, two of his knights flanking him. All three were armed and armoured and liveried in the Duke's colours. All three kept their hands on their sheathed swords despite knowing who entered the King's outer chamber, much the same way Grannit had. 'Sergeant,' Morton added, nodding to the veteran. Grannit nodded back and peeled off to the side, to address two halberdiers and two crossbowmen stood there, bows spanned and bolts loaded.

'What's happening, Will?' Correia dropped formalities and rushed to her father's brother-in-law and friend. She heard the double doors thud behind her as they met.

Morton's eyes past her to those who'd entered behind her. He looked back, brow creased.

'They're reliable. They're with—'

'Aye, lass, but where are the others? Sergeant Falchion and company.'

Correia swallowed hard. 'There's much we need discuss, you and I, and fa— King Barrison.'

Morton grunted a laugh. 'That's an understatement at a...'

Shouts from beyond the door. Threats of violence. Tension in the room rose. Hairs stood to attention on necks and arms and anywhere a lack of armour allowed it.

'Correia, we're to the King,' Morton said. 'Sergeant Grannit and his men will hold this room. We need to move Barrison—'

'Who's with him?'

Morton grimaced.

'He's alone?' Correia said through clenched teeth.

'We move, now,' Morton said as all went quiet beyond the doors.

Grannit growled orders and Morton's knights drew their swords, nodding to Morton as they did so.

'With me,' Morton said, drawing his bastard-sword and moving to and through a small side-door, his men between him and Correia, who followed, curved swords in hands, her companions doing the same. Again, she didn't have to look back to know they were with her.

They practically ran down a tight corridor in single file before ascending yet more curling steps, up into the broad tower Barrison held as part of his private quarters.

'Do we have mages with us?' Correia asked Morton over his knights' shoulders.

'Not here,' Morton replied, 'not in his chambers. He forbade it.'

'He what?' Correia balked at what she was hearing. Where were all the soldiers that could and should be flooding these rooms and corridors?

'You know him, Correia,' Morton continued as they climbed up and along, round and across Barrison's abode. 'I've stepped up all I could around the palace. Gods, all I could around Wesson and Altoln. But here? I have no say here, Correia.'

'I know,' she shot back, as much to silence Morton as anything else. She needed to think. She needed to get her head around it all. She hadn't even known there was a mark on her father until the palace bells had tolled.

They crossed a lounge and passed through another door, up, up once more, armour clanking and boots scuffing stone steps, voices echoing.

'There's been several attempts thwarted over the past few days—'

'What?' Correia was incredulous. *Several? Who was ordering...?* Well, that wasn't hard now was it? Whoever was organising the war in Sirreta and the plague and gods knew what else was doing this. *Several attempts?*

'We had a poisoner in the kitchen. Found by a dog and its handler. Thankful I am that I pulled those two from the City Guard, much to Stowold's annoyance for he wanted them for his own household.'

Morton reached a door, stopped and took a breath. He turned back and his knights shifted so he could see Correia. 'He doesn't want to believe it, lass. Our King's confidence in our protection of him is enough to make me cry, but these assassins...' Morton swallowed, shrugged and knocked on the door without looking. 'That's why I needed you back here, Correia.'

'Enter!'

Correia recognised her father's chamberlain's voice through the door and over the shifting and panting of those before and after her in the corridor.

Morton pushed through the door. Correia and the others followed.

Chapter 70 – Arrow in the dark

'Sir Merrel, get down to Sergeant Grannit, now!'

Errolas turned and saw Morton directing his stunned knights. Stunned. Everyone was stunned, none more so than Errolas. He looked down to his shaking hands, strung and recently used bow in one, second arrow in the other. He'd drawn the second in case he missed with the first. The sound of the running assassin in the sudden, impossible darkness had been hard even for Errolas to hear, but the shock of the assassin's trick had quietened everyone, thankfully for Errolas, and the King. Errolas looked to King Barrison, who was looking in turn at the dying assassin before him, the ageing King's breaths coming quick and heavy.

'He came so close,' Amis de Valmont said, walking towards the bleeding, unconscious assassin, sword in hand. Correia moved towards the King with Amis, who plunged his sword into the assassin's back to finish him off. An accurate thrust that surely found his heart, Errolas knew.

'If I had missed with that arrow…' Errolas didn't bear the thought. He jolted as a steel-clad hand slapped his back.

'But you didn't!' Morton grinned at Errolas, wrapping the further-stunned elf in an uncomfortable hug, all edges of cold plate and riveted maille. Morton barked a deafening laugh in Errolas' sensitive ear. 'You're a hero, elf.' He pushed Errolas out to arms-length, grinning at him some more, scar pulling at his lip. 'A bloody hero!'

Correia shrieked. Errolas turned, heart missing a beat.

Morton released Errolas as Amis moved for the King, bloody sword held offensively, Correia in a heap near the dead Eatrian assassin. Confusion took the room again and it was all Errolas could do, whilst seeing the stunned look on Correia's face as she glared in horror at the yellow chevalier, to knock and draw his second arrow.

King Barrison roared as Amis came at him, raising his own sword in defence. Barrison managed to parry the first blow as Amis attacked with unbridled aggression.

Errolas loosed his arrow and, with utter disbelief from him and all present, Amis knocked the missile from its flight, his gauntlet batting it away like so many pesky flies.

Too risky to draw and loose another with Barrison so close to his target, Errolas threw the bow and drew his sword, launching into a sprint which saw him overtaking Morton's roaring charge.

I won't make it, Errolas thought, as Correia surged to her feet and lurched towards Amis, anger and fear overpowering her and allowing her hasty attack to be swatted away with as much ease as Amis had swatted arrow from flight.

Barrison attacked back, sword thrusting, but doing little to best Amis' effortless defence.

The chevalier-come-assassin turned, palm open, eyes... black. A surge of nothingness pulsed from that palm, punching Morton and Errolas back as if struck by a destrier's kick. There was no pain in the impact, only the reversal of momentum and the gut-wrenching shock of it as man and elf, Duke and Ranger, slid back across the floor.

A flare of white drew Errolas' eye before he could right himself. A flare that came from Salliss' sword. The woman surged forward, sword trailing, and Errolas knew not whether the woman he'd grown to know and care for was for or against him and his friends; for or against King Barrison.

When Errolas looked to the now shrieking Amis, a sound the elf wished never to hear again, the hatred in Amis' eyes told him all he needed to know. Salliss was not an ally to this beast, and as if to prove it, her rapid assault caused Amis to fly in defence from his attack on King Barrison. Literally fly!

Wretched wings erupted through cloth and armour both, causing a wind in the chamber as the incubus swept away from the oncoming Witchblade. Salliss jumped to intercept, her leap impossible if not for the powers Errolas knew she possessed.

Part-armoured incubus and energy-wreathed Witchblade met mid-air. They fought as they descended to the floor, before the great, stain-glass window closest to King Barrison, which glowed with the remaining yet fading light of the day.

Correia scrambled backwards, away from the ensuing violence. She rushed around the fray and took up a defensive position by the King, who stood panting behind her, then by her side.

Errolas was on his feet and rushing towards the duelling duo whilst Morton ran to his King, flanking the man along with Correia.

Salliss screamed and the purest white light bathed her and the room and those within, to a painful level. Errolas slowed and flinched away, hand raised to block the radiance.

The following agonising, demonic shriek dropped Errolas to his knees, hands now across his ears as his sword clattered on stone. More shouts of anger and fear followed. Errolas knew them to be Correia and Barrison and Morton.

Glass shattered, a crack and smash followed by a tinkling of colourful shards and lead on stone, but not many; Errolas' mind flew back to Fal's home and a fleeing witchunter, but for a heartbeat – glass falling out, not in. *Someone's left via the window?*

'Or some *thing*,' Errolas whispered, standing and seeing the scene before him through blinking eyes. Salliss knelt, blood on the hand she studied before her ashen face. And Correia hugged Barrison, who hugged her back, crying the both of them. Morton stood, hands on knees, bastard-sword forgotten to the floor as he shook his head and sucked in great, audible breaths.

Errolas staggered towards Salliss, their eyes meeting as she looked up to his approach. A smile touched her lips. Not a cocky smile, or one of mirth even, but relief, Errolas knew. Relief that it was over. Relief that she'd survived the fight and caused Amis de Valmont, the incubus, the latest in a line of assassins, to flee.

Crouching by her side, relief struck Errolas too as he saw that the blood on Salliss' hand was not her own. It turned black as they looked at it, a demonic smear of wretched blood that Salliss proceeded to wipe on her clothes as quick as she could. 'I wounded him… it,' she said, voice trembling through the shock of it all.

Pulling her into a tight embrace, chin on her head, rocking slightly, Errolas looked to the trio by the open window and smiled. Morton was stood now, fists pressed into his lower back, arching in age-related aches and pains, whilst Barrison held Correia at arms-length, bearded cheeks wet with tears; joy and thankful relief in his blue eyes as he looked at Correia.

The arrow that entered through the broken window with the rain-flecked wind was visible to Errolas for but a moment before it thudded into the side of Barrison's head, exploding with blood and skull and brain-matter from the other side. His corpse tumbled sideways to the floor like the falling of a grand oak.

Noise and time was lost to Errolas as he saw Barrison fall, the moments dragging on in horror and disbelief as the great man left the world.

Errolas' heart ran cold as Correia screamed, as he saw the flights of the assassin's tool sprouting from Barrison's head.

'No,' Errolas whispered, whilst Correia continued to cry out in

shock and pain, and Morton did the same. 'No… It can't be…'
    The black arrow was elven.

Chapter 71 – Tumultuous and bleak

'And there you have it, milord.' Sir Bollingham sipped at the red wine he'd been given and watched Stowold's latest reaction to all he'd told him; he pursed his lips and pressed both index fingers to his chin, the rest of his fingers linked. He nodded slowly.

'What's your take on it all, Biviano?' Stowold said, eyes shifting to him.

Biviano saw Sir Bollingham frown, near on snarl.

It's not my fault Stowold wants my opinion, Bolly.

'Well, milord...' Biviano hadn't been prepared for this. He'd been too busy relishing the wine and food they'd been given, and the fact that Stowold didn't seem to like folk in his attendance unless they'd been cleaned up good and proper. 'My initial worry was of a baronial war—'

'Pah!' Stowold sat forward, face lit up with mirth. 'Truly?' he managed, eyes locked on Biviano's.

Oh, now you smile, Biviano thought of Sir Bollingham. Shrugging, Biviano simply said, 'Yes.'

Shaking his head, Stowold sat back in his chair and glanced around the company. 'Well, we have news from the man you took—'

'Already?' Pelse asked, impressed. The fact he'd interrupted an Earl seemed lost on him. Until, that was, he noticed everyone else staring at him with incredulity. 'Pardon, milord, I—'

Stowold waved it away. 'Yes, Pelse, already,' Stowold confirmed. 'I set a mage I have at my command to it. Spilled as soon as the woman put on an illusionary show of some creature or other.' Stowold grinned but said nothing.

'And, milord?' Biviano dared, although his mind fell into a thankful realisation that their captive hadn't been tortured. No matter his taking of Biviano in the Beresford camp, Biviano didn't wish what he'd seen Ellis Frane endure on anyone. He glanced to Sears, who was being suspiciously quiet. *Big ginger get is embarrassed for getting drugged, I reckon.* Biviano did his best not to chuckle aloud at that. Sears offered him a minute sneer, just for Biviano to see. *Oh, how well he knows me.*

'And, Biviano...' Stowold held his empty glass out and waited, not long, for a servant to fill it. The pause pulled several forward, to the edge of their seats. 'And,' Stowold went on, 'he told me all about Rell Adlestrop's human-crafted cannon. He told me all about

410

that and he told me all about Adlestrop's planned harrying of the north.'

'Eh?' Pelse again, mouth running before his brain.

'Eh, exactly, Pelse.' Stowold smiled. The smile faded, replaced with a worried look none of the men missed. A rare look for a man with Stowold's power and confidence.

'Milord?' Sir Bollingham ventured.

Stowold sighed and sipped at his wine. 'I fear,' he said, meeting all of their eyes, one by one, 'that our little Duke of Adlestrop intends to increase his holdings in the north. More than he already has, I might add. And to do that... well, how would you think he intends to do that?'

There was a silence before Sears beat Biviano and Sir Bollingham to the punch, both men looking to him, surprised. 'By marching on Northfolk,' Sears said, a bitterness tainting his tone.

'By marching on Northfolk,' Stowold confirmed.

'Which is why he drew his southern forces to assist his father in taking Beresford back, rather than his closer levies in the north?' Biviano stated, more than asked.

'I fear so.' Stowold took more wine and rubbed at his brow. 'We've enough going on in Altoln without this,' he admitted freely. 'But for Adlestrop to bring his southern army north and leave his northern captains in place, what are we to think he will do with his well-travelled and blooded southern lot now Beresford is back in the hands of his father?'

There was hardly a pause before Biviano and Sir Bollingham both said similar.

'Ride north with them,' Biviano said.

'Take them north,' Sir Bollingham said at the same time. Both flashed a competitive glare each-others way.

Stowold nodded. 'Indeed, he will.'

'Or so we think, milord,' Big Dom rumbled.

'Or so we know,' Stowold countered. 'According to Rell's arrogant ways and according to his mercenary that you brought back with you from Beresford.'

'What does this mean?' Sir Bollingham said, wine forgotten.

'It means,' Sears said, 'that the little shite's men will be burning villages and raping women before winter comes to steel what little they have left.'

There was a hint of fire in Sears' eyes, Biviano saw. He felt near on the same as his friend at the horrific thought of it all. 'But why?'

he managed. 'Why now? Why risk a war with Northfolk when there's enough shit happening?'

'Hubris?' Stowold offered. 'He's been raised being told that everything he wants he can have. Gods below, he's an heir to the throne of Altoln, albeit a slight one what with Edward in good age and health. If someone has hinted to him that he can take Northfolk for his own, or that he can't, even, then the little shite may want to prove them right or wrong on the matter. It's not like he hasn't raided there before, either.'

'Surely he wouldn't go through all this planning for such a boast, milord?' Sir Bollingham asked.

Stowold shrugged. 'Perhaps not for such a reason, but he is going to do it, or certainly seems to be, from what we've learnt. And my fear, gentlemen…' Stowold met all of their eyes once more. 'My fear is that we will need our brittle alliance with Northfolk come long. Big things are happening. Grand, scary things and we will need every friend and their sword that we have and can find and make. Creating new or awakening old enemies now is not an option.'

Pelse frowned all the more as a thought clearly occurred to him. 'Isn't Edward Prince of Norfolk?'

'In title alone, Pelse,' Stowold confirmed. 'It's a tradition and nothing more. He holds no power there. No more than any other Altolnan royal, anyway.'

'Tell the King,' Sir Bollingham said, matter-of-factly. 'He will stop this, my lord. I'm sure of it.'

Stowold shook himself at his knight's words, then continued on in what seemed to be stoic determination, whilst some unknown decision warred behind his eyes.

'Stop his son's closest friend and ally?' Stowold shifted in his seat. 'I fear not.' He let out the longest sigh of all. 'My friends—' he took them all by surprise at that, '—I have received the gravest of news. Grave, secret news.'

Biviano's stomach churned. *Hence why the loss of arms and horses have seemingly been forgotten?* he thought, with a dread that fell across all present.

Everyone looked to one another, brows creased, throats moving as they swallowed down what was to come.

'Milord?' Biviano dared.

'King Barrison is dead.'

Several intakes of breath, a curse and a groan.

More than one made to talk, but Stowold raised his hand for silence and it was given.

'I shall discuss this with you further, but you must not... *must* not, gentlemen, discuss it again, once outside this room. Am I clear?'

Several nods.

'Am I clear?' Stowold rasped, leaning forward in his chair, eyes murderous and moving to every face before him.

'Yes, milord,' came the chorus of replies.

'Very well,' Stowold said, leaning back. 'I have only just been informed of our loss myself, this evening, but I shall explain all I know and we shall discuss your following mission.'

'Milord?' Sir Bollingham ventured once again.

'You are to openly ride north as a true company of mine, bolstered by Sir Mechel and his. You are to beat Rell Adlestrop to the Reaver families on the border and you are to ride on, into Northfolk, with a message from the King, the Lord High Constable of Altoln and I.'

'But my lord, you said the King is—'

'But nothing, Sir Bollingham. Outside this room and outside of King Barrison's own chambers, he is alive... for now. His chamberlain and immediate staff are aware and in agreement. And so it is that we continue to act as such. Do not make me regret telling you six of his tragic demise. Do not make my trusting you come back to bite me and Altoln both. The firing of cannons and the loss of my horses is nought compared to what is at stake now.'

And there it is, Biviano thought, of the horses lost, although it paled into comparison against all else.

'Your trust is safe with us, my lord,' Sears said, with a surety as he looked around the men in the room. 'It won't come back to bite you, will it lads?'

Biviano and the others met their friend's red eyes. Red eyes glistening with the threat of tears from the news that struck them all a blow, and they nodded as one.

Biviano offered his friend a tight smile and a second nod as their eyes met.

And so we head north once more, big guy. On an open mission for our new liege lord and our dead King. North. Back home.

***

413

'Well?' Morton asked, slumping in the comfortable chair Ward Strickland provided.

'Well,' Strickland said, eyeing the Lord High Constable. 'I'm surprised how often it is you seek my council of late.'

Morton scoffed and plucked the glass of wine from the table. He eyed the glass, watching how ruby light shifted as he passed the glass across his view of the chamber's window, at the top of Tyndurris.

'Exquisite workmanship, isn't it?' Strickland said, indicating the glass.

Morton grunted before gulping down the rare wine. He clunked the glass back down. Strickland flinched. 'You're the Lord High Chancellor as well as this guild's master, Lord Strickland. It is in that guise that I seek you out, to discuss matters of state, not... glass or magic.'

Strickland smiled.

Morton scowled and poured himself another glass of Sirretan red.

'I don't know, is my honest answer,' Strickland said, before sipping at his own wine.

Sighing hard, Morton rubbed his scarred face with his free hand. His wine slopped from the glass during the vigorous movement. 'I'd like to say I appreciate the honesty.'

'What can I say?' Strickland said, a laugh touching his words. 'I have no idea if Edward will replace me, or you.' Morton glared at him. 'Well, come on, my lord, that is what you wanted to know, is it not?'

Morton huffed. 'Can you not... scry it, or some such?'

'Matters of state, not magic, you said—'

'This is serious, Ward!'

Strickland sighed, his mirth falling way. 'I know it is and you know I know it is, my lord, but I cannot tell you what I do not know. Do you want me to tell you what I do know?'

There was a pause before Morton reluctantly nodded for Strickland to go on.

'I know that you have agreed to let Severun loose in Dockside again, and completely untethered this time, since you didn't consult me.' Morton made to speak, but Strickland held up his finger. 'Let me finish, my lord.' Morton nodded. 'I also know that the Black Guild is near destroyed, but for the brute who sails the seas, and his third of the guild.' Morton again went to speak and again

414

Strickland stopped him. 'And,' Strickland said, his voice low, conspiratorial, 'a little birdy—'

Morton grunted. 'Heh, probably literally.'

'—told me,' Strickland went on, despite the interruption, 'that the arrow which took our King's life was elven?'

Morton froze. He held Strickland's stare, but froze all the same. After several pounding heartbeats, he asked, 'How do you know?'

Strickland sighed, exasperated. 'Does it matter, Will?'

Morton rocked back this time, at the familiar, but conceded the point all the same. 'I suppose not,' he said, exhaustion sweeping across his every feature.

'Question is, why didn't you tell me? You made out a bloody incubus stole Barrison's life. A damned demon that travelled with Correia Burr of all people. Magic take me,' Strickland breathed. 'Why the lies?'

Morton sat forward and placed his glass on the table, carefully this time. 'Listen to me,' he said, deadly serious, exhaustion forgotten, sword across his lap as ever. 'The demon was there.' He let that sink in. 'I witnessed the fucker myself!' he added, for effect. 'The incubus travelled as a Sirretan chevalier, as you have been told, and assaulted Barrison in its true form. He reached Barrison's chamber after I bloody led him there with Correia, whilst others dealt with an Eatrian assassin. Eatri! Of all bastard places. Then...' Morton said, temper rising from the memories of the fateful day. 'And then,' he said, calming himself, 'we bested the beast, or rather the Sirretan Witchblade, Salliss de Pizan, did. Sent it crashing from the window by Barrison's side.'

Strickland frowned at that; at the change of the story he'd been told.

'And then...' Morton winced at the thought of it.

'An arrow came in through the window? In rain-filled winds... at dusk,' Strickland said, incredulous at the thought. 'Just like that?'

Morton nodded. 'Through the fucking window. Just like that.' He was red faced now, shaking with anger and sorrow both. He sat back into the chair and rubbed at his face with both hands, rubbing away the tears that threatened him. 'He was my oldest friend, Ward,' Morton said through hands. 'I loved him as a brother... I married his sister and it meant something,' he said, lowering his hands and looking to the magician. 'I loved her. Still do despite her losing my first and only son at birth. Despite her leaving me at the same time.' He grunted a bitter laugh. 'I can only thank the gods

415

that she wasn't around to live through this.'

Strickland offered a tight smile. 'They're all together now, if you believe it. Brother and sister and your son.'

'I don't know what I believe in that regards, Ward. I really don't.' Morton laughed it off and shook his head, burying it all back where he kept it. 'And now? Now we have a war brewing. We have Orismarans, and worse, marching through and besting Sirreta, by Correia's accounts. We have the shitting Beresford's smashing up their own town with cannons of all things and sending men north. North? Fuck knows what for when the little twat Rell has holdings and men up there already? But Stowold's trying to find that out, so I'll leave him to that and the shit that goes on below our feet, whilst we take on the stress of Sirreta and...' he paused. He looked to Strickland and held that look. Drew it in. 'And Crackador,' he said, with as much weight as he could put behind the ancient name.

Strickland frowned. He opened his mouth and closed it again. Frowned some more.

Morton nodded. 'Severun confirmed it. Your very own—'

'Not our own. Not now. I know what he did wasn't—'

'Shut up and listen, Ward. I beg you.'

Strickland rocked back, but nodded all the same.

'He's as if a weight's been lifted from him, your wizard. Take that from me. He's clearer than I've seen him, ever. Although to be fair, I'd never taken the time to listen to him much before the damned plague. But that... that right there, Ward; *that* was sent to us in that bloody arcane scroll, by Crackador! Severun swears it. Swears the great-dragon has returned and wants Wesson.'

'Wesson?' Strickland asked. 'Specifically?'

Morton was impressed the man had taken the return of an ancient, great black dragon so well. 'Yes,' he said. 'Wesson specifically, according to Severun. Says he had a feeling of it. From the will the beast was trying to impose on him these past months; since the scroll.'

'Why?'

Morton shrugged. 'I don't know. He doesn't know. Who bloody knows? But we have all I said to contend with, plus a fucking dragon of all things, plus—'

'What else?' Strickland balked now, at it all. He looked lost with the world, at the thought of yet more.

'What else?' Morton grunted. 'We have the return of Alden-

416

bastard-Fenn to contend with, after near on wiping out his guild – small fry compared to the dragon and his armies and demons, I admit, but a more immediate threat than the rest, I have to say. That and—'

'And?' Strickland gaped before draining his glass. He reached for the bottle of red and took a swig from that. 'And?' he repeated, whilst Morton finished his own wine and offered his glass for more. Strickland obliged.

'And, my lord Strickland,' Morton went on, 'we've got Edward the Black fucking Prince's coronation and reign to organise and survive! I've not even sent him word of his father's demise yet… Because I don't know where he is? And so I haven't sent word of it at all, to anyone! Not to Royce of all people, Keeper of the Privy Seal as he is. Not to anyone. In fact, I've taken liberties and replied to a dozen written requests for shit and bollocks in Barrison's stead, with his bloody seal; had myself appointed Regent, secretly, temporarily. And if that's not bad enough, Ward…' Morton took a deep breath before going on. '…Edward's been playing with The Three, according to a new source.' Morton let that sink in; let the news of everything sink in along with their soon-to-be King's dallying with three of the most unpredictable and dangerous beings on the continent. 'Although I know not where he sailed from there,' Morton admitted.

Strickland stared at Morton. He stared and drank his wine. Morton did the same, for what else was there for them to do when their futures, and that of Altoln, appeared tumultuous and bleak.

***

Errolas' heart quickened as footsteps entered the dungeon corridor. It quickened more so as the footsteps stopped outside his cell.

'Correia?' he dared, hoped.

'Lady Burr won't be seeing you, elf,' came the gruff voice of the palace gaoler.

And here I hope I'd be seeing her as Fal and Sav did, in Wesson's prison. How long ago that seems…

Keys tinkled and clattered and locks clunked and turned, the sounds loud to Errolas after his recent stretch of near silence in the small, cold cell. The glow of lantern light forced its way through the gap that appeared between wall and door, causing him to flinch.

'Food?' Errolas asked, again hopeful.

'Aye, food.'

The bowl slid, rolled and spilled its contents across the stone slabs. Errolas dived for the pottage, scooped and scraped the slop, tasted and winced at the slop. He managed to get at least some of it down before the lamp light escaped where he could not. The door slammed and the lock turned, the click-clunk a familiar sound to him now.

Errolas sat back in the darkness, hands cold and wet. A shudder ran through him at what he endured, what he may have to endure; what Brisance would endure with all that was to come. And he despaired.

Epilogue

'I must see him.' Dignaaln strode up to the uncoiling sentry, the moss- and lichen-padded pyramid towering above them both, framed by the collaged greens of the Orismaran jungle.

'You wouldn't want to if you saw what mood he's in.'

Dignaaln turned to the rasp of a voice behind him. He hated that he never heard the Naga warlord approach. 'Ah, Molurus. You please me with your—'

'No need for lies, Dignaaln,' Molurus hissed, sliding past and moving the sentry aside with a flick of his hand. Dignaaln followed the length of Molurus into the darkness of the temple. He followed the serpentine humanoid in and watched as he stretched out down the stone steps, kinking to control his descent, muscles rippling under his patterned scales. The temperature dropped as they descended further into the carved passageway. Dignaaln's confidence dropped to match. A shudder ran through him whilst, after hundreds of steps, the temperature rose once more. It was becoming as hot as the jungle above, hotter still. The glow of the under sanctum flared from an opening as they levelled out and turned a corner, a grinning red face greeting them as they approached an archway, lit beyond by Him.

'Good day to you, Chieftain.' Dignaaln wore his most charming smile, despite wanting to rend red skin, flesh and muscle from goblin bone.

'Long has it been, Dignaaln,' The Red Goblin said, grin unfaltering despite Dignaaln's lingering regard. 'Long indeed.'

Dignaaln merely nodded as he continued on, brushing past the sickening excuse for an ally.

All three: goblin, Naga and Dignaaln, dropped low from survival instinct alone as a rumble shook dust from the ceiling and vibrated, bounced even, stones across the floor.

Dignaaln turned to the semi-reptilian commander and The Red Goblin.

The latter shrugged. 'He lost his tether to someone important a while back. Hasn't cheered up since.'

Molurus winced as the under sanctum shook once more, his tattooed face wrinkling, scars deepening and body-come-tail curling tight about him.

And I lost my fucking horse. Woe is me, Dignaaln thought.

'Dignaaln?' The voice shook inside and outside of Dignaaln's head and he feared for his last thought's security.

'Master,' Dignaaln said in return, holding his breath thereafter. He released it after a pause where no one spoke, albeit filled with the rasping breath like a hurricane's wind through so many trees.

As Dignaaln opened his mouth, dared to attempt a prompt, his master spoke again; boomed again.

'Enter.'

Molurus offered Dignaaln a sympathetic smile before sliding away in pursuit of The Red Goblin, who'd wasted no time in leaving the scene.

With a deep breath, which he hoped would not be his last, Dignaaln did as he was bade and stepped into the gargantuan chamber to see the great-dragon within.

So ends the third book from the tales of the Black Powder Wars.

Thank you for reading:

Black Arrow
Third book from the tales of the
Black Powder Wars

Reviews are more than welcome and incredibly helpful.
Please also feel free to contact me on the following sites:
jpashman.com
Facebook
Goodreads
Instagram
Twitter: @JP_Ashman

#BlackArrow
#BlackPowderWars
#Dragonship
#FantasyHive
#FALL

Also available:

Black Martlet
First short story from the tales of the
Black Powder Wars

Dragonship
A standalone short story

FALL
A scifi short story

J P Ashman is currently working on:

Black Prince
Fourth book from the tales of the
Black Powder Wars
(Due for release 2019)

Biography

Born Lancashire, England, J P Ashman is a Northern lad through and through. His parents read to him from an early age and encouraged his imagination at every turn. His Career may be in optics, as an SMC technician, but he loves to make time for writing and reading every day. Now living back in Lancashire after five years in the Cotswolds with Wifey and their little Norse Goddess Freya, he is inspired daily by everything and anything, from history to science, his reef tank to the environment.

Writing is a huge part of his life and the medieval re-enactment background and tabletop gaming lend to it; when he's not writing the genre, he's either reading or playing it. He plans to keep writing, both within his current series, and those to come, whether short stories or epic tomes.

www.ingramcontent.com/pod-product-compliance
Lightning Source LLC
Chambersburg PA
CBHW030647120726
47905CB00001B/101